"The Road [illegible]

and

"Crooks Go Straight"

TWO CLASSIC ADVENTURES OF

by Walter B. Gibson
writing as Maxwell Grant

with a New Historical Essay
by Will Murray

Published by Sanctum Productions for
NOSTALGIA VENTURES, INC.
P.O. Box 231183; Encinitas, CA 92023-1183

This Nostalgia Ventures edition is an unabridged republication of the text and illustrations of two stories from *The Shadow Magazine,* as originally published by Street & Smith Publications, Inc., N.Y.: *The Road of Crime* from the October 1, 1933 issue, and *Crooks Go Straight* from the March 1, 1935 issue. Typographical errors have been tacitly corrected in this edition.

International Standard Book Numbers:
ISBN 1-932806-74-1 13 DIGIT 978-1-932806-74-8

First printing: September 2007

Series editor: Anthony Tollin
P.O. Box 761474
San Antonio, TX 78245-1474
sanctumotr@earthlink.net

Consulting editor: Will Murray

Copy editor: Joseph Wrzos

Cover restoration: Michael Piper

The editor gratefully acknowledges the assistance of Dwight Fuhro and Geoffrey Wynkoop.

Nostalgia Ventures, Inc.
P.O. Box 231183; Encinitas, CA 92023-1183

Visit The Shadow at www.shadowsanctum.com and www.nostalgiatown.com

The Shadow™

Volume 11

CONTENTS

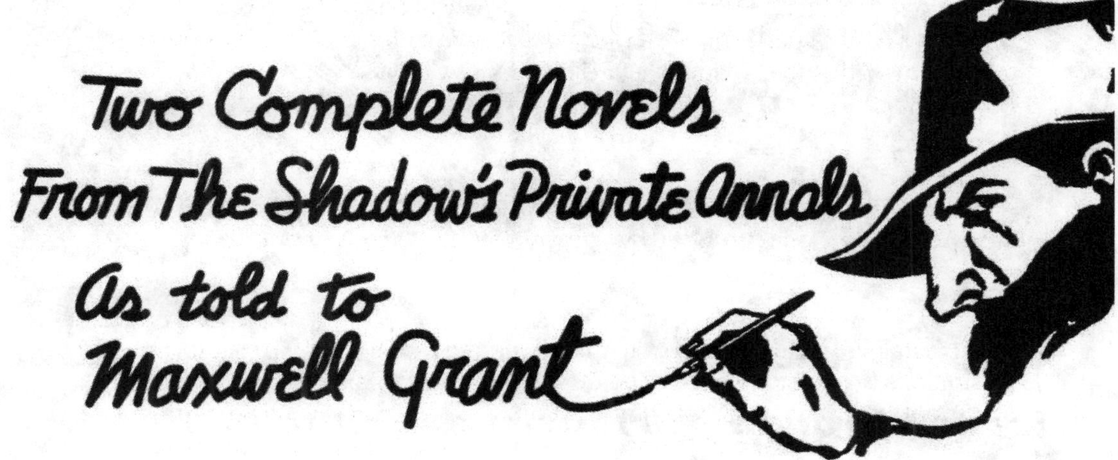
Two Complete Novels
From The Shadow's Private Annals
As told to
Maxwell Grant

Thrilling Tales and Features

Cover art by George Rozen
Interior illustrations by Tom Lovell

ROAD OF CRIME

It leads through various ways—but in the end it comes to The Shadow, creature of justice and vengeance

From the Private Annals of The Shadow as told to

Maxwell Grant

CHAPTER I
A GENTLEMAN OF CRIME

"UXTRY! Uxtry! Read about the big bank holdups!"

Graham Wellerton stopped as he heard the newsboy's cry. He proffered a few pennies and received the final edition of a New York evening newspaper. He glanced at the headlines as he walked along in the bright illumination of Forty-second Street, then thrust the sheet under his arm as he entered a subway kiosk.

While he waited on the platform for an uptown local, Graham Wellerton again surveyed the headlines. His eyes ran rapidly down the columns.

After a few short minutes of swift perusal, the man quickly learned that no new clues had been gained by the police relative to the crimes that had struck at noon that day.

Subway riders were reading their newspapers with avid interest when Graham Wellerton boarded his local and took a seat in a corner. His own newspaper tucked under his arm, Graham surveyed the composite crowd in the car and wondered what their varied reactions might be concerning the chief news of the day.

For New York sensation seekers had been treated to a contrast. The columns in the evening journals were, in themselves, food for a grim debate on crime.

Was crime profitable? One news account said no; the other said yes.

Two hordes of bank bandits had struck at noon, in different parts of Manhattan. Those who had invaded the Parkerside Trust Company had been routed in a spontaneous fray which had left half a dozen mobsters dead and wounded. But those who had entered the Terminal National Bank had gained swift success. With the aid of tear gas, they had eliminated tellers and bank patrons. The robbers had escaped unscathed with thousands of dollars in currency.

STUDYING his fellow passengers, Graham Wellerton placed them in two definite classes. One group, he felt, consisted of those who gloried in the victory over crime—who gained high satisfaction in the outcome of the fray at the Parkerside Trust.

The others, Graham decided, were those who held a secret envy for robbers who had looted the Terminal National and had made so perfect a getaway.

Idly, Graham played a game of human analysis. He noted the people who were reading about the thwarted robbery. Most of them possessed an air of stability. Those who were eagerly perusing the accounts of the successful raid, however, were curious, bitter-faced individuals who seemed to gloat in the knowledge that wrongdoers had gained a momentary triumph.

In considering those whom he thus classified, Graham Wellerton adopted an odd neutrality so far as he himself was concerned. Had he included himself, he would undoubtedly have placed himself in the select category. In dress, appearance and manner, Graham was the most distinctive occupant of the subway car.

Tall, handsome and dressed in perfectly tailored clothes, Graham had the appearance of a polished man-about-town as he sauntered from the car when the train stopped at an uptown station.

But the smile upon his face was reminiscent. Not so many hours before, Graham Wellerton, in another subway car, had represented an opposite class of society. Then he had been wearing baggy trousers, heavy sweater and checkered cap.

Graham was still smiling as he tossed his newspaper into a trash receptacle. The accounts of the bank holdups had included descriptions of just such individuals as he had been at noon this very day. Evening had brought the present transformation.

So far as the bank holdups were concerned, Graham's neutrality was one of balance. He was pleased that the attempt upon the Parkerside Trust had failed; he was glad that the Terminal National robbery had been successful. For Graham knew something that the police did not suspect: namely, that both raids had been ordered by one master of crime.

Two lieutenants had been employed, each the leader of a band of marauders. One—"Wolf" Daggert—had failed at the Parkerside Trust. His minions had been overpowered, his own escape had been a matter of luck.

The other—Graham Wellerton—had succeeded at the Terminal National. By cool strategy and swift action, he had gained his end without the loss of a single henchman.

No longer the rowdy that he had appeared to be by day, Graham Wellerton, in his gentlemanly guise, hailed a taxicab as he stepped from the subway.

Lounging in the back seat, he lighted a cigarette and, amid the puffs of smoke, emitted soft chuckles. From a position as a lesser gangster, he had risen to a lieutenancy which equaled that of Wolf Daggert. Today, he had shown his superiority over Wolf.

Graham Wellerton was anxious to hear what the big shot would have to say. That was his mission tonight—a visit to the big shot. From now on, Graham would rate above Wolf Daggert. The big shot liked smooth workers.

Yet the smile of triumph upon Graham's face was sour at the corners. Despite the proficiency which he had shown in crime, this handsome young man was not overpleased with his calling.

THE cab pulled up at a huge apartment house. Graham Wellerton, his face no longer showing traces of satisfaction, alighted and paid the driver.

Wellerton strolled into the lobby, approached the doorman and inquired if Mr. Furzman were at home. The doorman asked the visitor's name, made a short call over the apartment telephone and ushered Graham to the elevator.

The car stopped at the fourteenth floor. Graham stepped out and approached a doorway at the end of a short corridor.

The door was ajar. A stocky, iron-jawed individual opened it without a single word. Graham Wellerton entered and waited until the door was closed.

"Hello, Gouger," he said to the stocky-faced man. "Is King Furzman ready to see me now?"

Gouger nodded. He opened a door at the right of the little anteroom in which they were standing, and motioned the visitor to enter. Graham walked through the doorway; Gouger followed and closed the door behind him.

The anteroom remained silent. A small, gloomy chamber with three doors, it served only as an entry. It was the appointed spot where Gouger, bodyguard to "King" Furzman, awaited visitors who were announced.

Now that one visitor had entered, there was no occasion for Gouger to remain until another call came from the downstairs lobby. But during that interim, an unexpected visitor was due to make his appearance.

Scarcely had the door at the anteroom closed behind Gouger and Graham Wellerton before the knob of the door from the corridor began to make a slow turn. Something clicked softly in the lock. The door moved inward.

A figure entered the anteroom. The door closed behind the silent visitor. Within the range of light stood the tall form of a spectral visitant who had entered here despite the fact that the door was securely locked.

This being was completely clad in black. His principal garb was a long, flowing cloak, that gave his form a grotesque shape. The upturned collar of the cloak obscured the stranger's features.

Above the cloak, the silent visitor was wearing a broad-brimmed slouch hat which completely hid his forehead. The dull light of the anteroom showed only the eyes of the mysterious arrival. From beneath the hat brim, a pair of blazing orbs shone with sinister gleam as they peered toward the two doors that led into the apartment.

Like an apparition, this weird stranger had followed Graham Wellerton into King Furzman's abode. Merged with the darkness at the far end of the corridor, the black-cloaked phantom had been waiting for someone to arrive.

Neither Graham Wellerton nor Gouger had detected his uncanny presence; neither was aware that The Shadow, master of the night, had observed their meeting at the opened door!

THE SHADOW!

Spectral figure of darkness, he was one who sought the spots where crime was fostered. A master of mystery, his very name was terror to the underworld! A lone wolf who battled the hordes of crookdom, a supersleuth whose prowess of investigation knew no equal, The Shadow had entered here to learn facts concerning bold crime.

The gleaming eyes spied the door upon the right. A soft, whispered laugh came eerily from unseen lips. The tall form glided across the carpeted floor and reached the closed door. A black-gloved hand slowly turned the knob. The door yielded.

Peering through a narrow crevice, The Shadow spied an empty room, which was almost totally dark. The one source of illumination came from a narrow archway which was hung with heavy curtains. Beyond that was a room lighted by floor lamps—a condition which signified that someone was present there.

The Shadow entered the gloomy room and silently closed the door behind him. His tall form was totally obscured as it clung to darkness in its path toward the heavy curtains. Only the slight swish of the black cloak was audible.

The Shadow halted when he reached the curtains. His weird shape merged with a hanging drapery.

The eyes of The Shadow peered into the room beyond. They spied one man—Graham Wellerton. The visitor, his coat, hat, and cane laid aside, was seated in an easy chair, smoking a cigarette.

A handsome face, above the peaked points of a tuxedo collar—that was the visage which The Shadow saw. Graham Wellerton, tonight, was a gentleman of crime. As such, he was awaiting the arrival of the big shot—the man whom he called King Furzman.

Graham Wellerton's eyes, steady despite their idle appearance, were fixed upon a door at the opposite side of this reception room—the spot from which the young man knew King Furzman would enter.

Intent in thought, Graham Wellerton gave no attention to the draperies at the archway. He did not see the blotting patch of darkness that crept slowly inward from the other room and became an unmoving blotch upon the floor.

That single sign of The Shadow's presence was motionless as The Shadow waited. An interview was in the making—an important conference between Graham Wellerton and his superior, King Furzman.

The ears of The Shadow would listen, unsuspected, to whatever might be said; and in the meantime, the eyes of The Shadow were gazing sternly upon Graham Wellerton, the gentleman of crime!

CHAPTER II
THE BIG SHOT

THE door at the opposite side of the room opened. A stout, dark-haired man stepped into view. Graham Wellerton arose from his chair and smiled in greeting. The other man grinned broadly and gave acknowledgment with a slight wave of his hand. Graham sat down and the stout man took a chair opposite him.

Graham Wellerton, gentleman of crime, was face to face with King Furzman, racketeer and big shot, whose word was law to skulking hordes of evil mobsters.

King Furzman, like his visitor, was attired in tuxedo. But where Graham's clothes were smoothly fitting, Furzman's, despite the efforts of the big shot's tailors, were rumpled and misshapen. Furzman's stiff shirt was bulging and his fat bull neck stuck turtlelike from his upright collar.

The difference in the faces of the two men was apparent. Graham Wellerton did not have the expression of a crook. King Furzman, though he sought to maintain a frank and friendly expression, could not hide the brutal, selfish characteristics that were a latent part of his physiognomy.

This meeting was one, however, that could have but a single outcome—an expression of approval on the part of King Furzman. Confident in that knowledge, Graham Wellerton adopted an attitude of easy indifference and waited for the big shot to begin the conversation.

"Good work, Wellerton," began Furzman. "You pulled a clean job today. The best part of it was the way you slipped the swag to Gouger, where he was waiting for you. He could have walked here with it."

"Certainly," agreed Graham. "We made a perfect getaway. I could have come here with the dough myself—but you wanted me to pass it to Gouger instead, so I did."

"Well, it's tucked away here," returned Furzman, "and you'll get your cut of the dough anytime you're ready for it."

"Better hold it for me," said Graham nonchalantly. "I'm not broke—and I can collect later on."

"You've got me beat, Wellerton," admitted the big shot. "Wolf Daggert always hollered for his split right after the job was done. You don't seem to worry about it."

"Why should I?" questioned Graham. "I've got good enough security."

"How?"

"The cash that's coming in the next job," replied Graham suavely. "It will be bigger than this one."

"Say"—Furzman's growl voiced his approval— "that's the way to talk. I like to hear it because I know you mean it. Wolf never talks that way; howls for his split—that's all he does."

"But he won't howl tonight," asserted Graham.

KING FURZMAN scowled as he heard the words. His face showed disapproval of Graham Wellerton's comment. After a moment of consideration, the big shot voiced his thoughts.

"What's the idea of that crack, Wellerton?" he questioned. "The way you spoke, it sounded as though you're glad Wolf Daggert flopped on the job today. Have I got you right?"

"You have," retorted Graham, in a direct tone. "The sooner you find out that Wolf Daggert is a has-been, the better it will be for you—and therefore for me. Figure it out for yourself, King. I pulled a sweet job today—Wolf Daggert made a total failure."

"All right. What about it?"

"Wolf has his gang. I have mine. Both outfits are yours. Therefore, there is a connection. Some of my crowd may know the fellows who were killed down at the Parkerside Trust. Is that going to improve my chances of future success?"

"No," admitted King Furzman.

"You're right it's not!" declared Graham. "What's more, it's put a crimp in the whole works. Bank tellers—watchmen—cops—they'll all be chesty now. They'll talk about the way the mob was stopped at the Parkerside Trust."

King Furzman began to nod. Graham Wellerton had gained his point. Yet the big shot was not entirely satisfied.

"Wolf Daggert is an old hand," he remarked. "He pulled some good jobs on his own—and he started out well when he began to work for me. I don't like to give him the gate, just because of this flop."

"Wolf is inefficient," asserted Graham, rising to his feet. "I knew it when I worked with him. He was lucky to get by as long as he did. He counted on me to help him, but never gave me the credit that was coming to me. You found out where I stood. You gave me my own mob. You've seen what I can do.

"Listen, King. When a crowd goes in to stick up a bank, everything depends on teamwork. It's a matter of seconds. You get the jump on the people there or they get the jump on you.

"The Parkerside Trust should have been a setup today. The tough job was the Terminal National—that's why Wolf let me take it. The odds were with him—the odds were against me. I came through and Wolf didn't."

"The tear gas was a great stunt."

"Certainly. Wolf could have used it on his job, but he didn't show any brain work."

"I can't let Wolf out."

"I'm not asking you to. But I'm telling you this, King: while Wolf is working in New York, I'm not!"

The big shot surveyed his lieutenant narrowly. His fat lips took on an ugly leer.

"You're thinking of quitting, eh?" questioned Furzman. "Figuring maybe you'd better take it soft—"

"Forget that stuff," interposed Graham. "I'm not through. I'm going somewhere else—that's all. Someplace where the pickings will be as soft as in New York—someplace where Wolf Daggert can't crimp my game."

King Furzman drew a fat cigar from his pocket and bit off the end of the perfecto while he continued to stare at Graham Wellerton.

"All right," growled the big shot. "Where are you going?"

"I'll tell you tomorrow night," said Graham. "I've got a couple of cities in mind—and I'll decide after I've thought it over."

"Yeah? How do I know you'll be sticking with me?"

"Your men will be with me."

"Well—that's a point—"

"And you've tucked away your security. You owe me a split, don't you? All right; I won't ask for it until I come back with some more."

King Furzman began to nod again. Graham Wellerton's arguments had been effective. The young man watched the big shot and waited for the psychological moment to speak further. The time came.

"King," said Wellerton quietly, "you're cagey. You've got to be, in your game. You deal with an ordinary lot of crooks, like Wolf Daggert. But I'm different. I didn't choose crime as a profession. It was thrust on me.

"I like to talk man to man. I know how you're situated, even though you've never told me. You prefer rackets to crime—but the rackets were getting you in trouble. Not with the police, but with other racketeers. So you went in for crime.

"You're backing a bunch of bank robbers. You took on Wolf Daggert. I came with him. You figured I could run a crowd of my own and double up on the gravy.

"You're covering up very neatly. You don't want to quit. I don't blame you. You've treated me square enough—because it's profitable. I'm sticking because I'm in the game of crime. I'm working for you—therefore I'm thinking of your interests.

"I want a free hand outside of New York. It will be better for you because I'm at a distance. It will be better for me because I'll be clear of Wolf Daggert."

HAD an ordinary henchman talked in this manner, King Furzman would have boiled over in rage. But he sensed from Graham Wellerton's tone that the lieutenant was working for a sensible understanding.

The big shot's scowl slowly disappeared; nevertheless, he made no statement of approval. Instead, he tried questions on another tack.

"You say you didn't choose crime?" he asked. "How did you come to get into it, then?"

"I could make a long story out of that," responded Graham, with a sour smile, "but I can give it to you briefly, just as well. My father had a lot of money. I landed in a jam. I had to raise dough to hush things up. I ran into Wolf Daggert, here in New York. He tipped me off to some ways to pick up cash."

"Why didn't Wolf try them for himself?"

"I'll tell you why. He was too yellow to take on the jobs he gave me. He collected a percentage on my work. Then I left New York and went out on my own."

"How long ago?"

"About three years."

"You hit it good?"

"For a while—yes. Then I landed back in New York and needed more money. I heard what Wolf was doing and I worked for him again. I intended to blow later on; then you picked me to head my own mob. Here I am."

King Furzman pondered. He could see that Graham Wellerton was one criminal in a thousand. He knew that his lieutenant had spoken frankly. This was the first outspoken conference that Furzman had ever held with Graham.

The big shot saw that Graham had been working for a break—for the time when success would enable him to give his straight opinion regarding Wolf Daggert. Graham had chosen the right time to assert himself. King Furzman, although he did not say so, regarded this smooth-working lieutenant as a henchman far superior to Wolf.

Furthermore, there was merit in Graham's suggestions. The big shot, supposedly a racketeer who was coasting along on past profits, was anxious to avoid anything that would connect him with crime. Rivalry between two lieutenants was a bad feature.

"All right," said Furzman suddenly. "Take your mob—work on your own—but let me know where you're going. If Wolf flops again, he's through—"

A rap at the door came as an interruption. The big shot emitted a growl. The door opened and Gouger poked his head into the room.

"Wolf Daggert is downstairs," he informed. "Shall I tell him to come up?"

"Sure," responded the big shot.

Gouger disappeared. He was going to the anteroom by the other route—through the apartment. It would only be a few minutes before Wolf Daggert would arrive.

"I'm all set, then," declared Graham Wellerton.

"Yes," agreed King Furzman. "Take your mob wherever you want to go."

"We'll start out tomorrow night," said Graham quickly. "I'll have the crew ready. I'll come here and tell you my plans. They won't know where I'm taking them until we're on our way—maybe not until we get there."

"Good stuff," nodded the big shot. "You're all right, Wellerton. I've got your idea now. You know how to handle a mob. Keep them guessing."

The conversation ended. Graham Wellerton resumed his chair and lighted a cigarette. King Furzman applied a match to the cigar which he had been chewing. While neither man was observant, the long black patch upon the floor drew slowly toward the curtain at the archway. The Shadow, hidden listener to all that had been said, was retiring into a darkened corner of the next room to await the passage of another visitor—Wolf Daggert.

Whatever might be said after the third man had arrived, The Shadow would also hear. The foe of crime, this phantom of the night had come to a spot where crime was in the making.

His presence here a mystery, his knowledge veiled from those who plotted crime, The Shadow had heard the plans of Graham Wellerton. Now he would listen to the pleas of an unsuccessful crook, when Wolf Daggert faced the big shot.

The Shadow's presence was a proof that he had had a hand in thwarting crime. That presence also signified that The Shadow would have much to say ere crime again struck!

CHAPTER III
THE SHADOW'S PART

GRAHAM WELLERTON and King Furzman looked up as two men entered the room from the archway. The first arrival was Gouger. The bodyguard kept on and passed through the door at the other side of the room.

The second man stopped just within the curtains. He looked from King Furzman to Graham Wellerton; then back from lieutenant to big shot. Without a word, he tossed his hat and coat upon a table and took a chair.

Wolf Daggert was a crook whose nickname was well chosen. His face was peaked and cunning. His teeth, which showed between sordid, roughened lips, had a fanglike appearance that was bestial. The man's manner was one that made an observer expect a snarl at any moment.

With half-clenched fists and ugly, sneering grin, Wolf Daggert turned his pale face toward the other men as though he expected challenging words. His gray eyes moved restlessly and his whole manner indicated tense nervousness.

King Furzman eyed Wolf Daggert coldly. Graham Wellerton gazed at the newcomer with an air of indifference.

In this strained atmosphere, not one of the three men happened to look toward the floor. Hence the trio failed to see the streak of blackness which was again moving steadily inward from the curtains.

The dark splotch became motionless. Cold, steely eyes were peering from the curtain. The archenemy of crime was on the watch. The eyes of The Shadow were viewing the scene within King Furzman's reception room.

"Well," barked Wolf. "You goin' to say somethin'? Let's have it."

His remark was impersonal. Either Furzman or Graham could have answered him. The big shot was the one who spoke.

"There's nothing much to say, Wolf," declared Furzman. "Things seem to have gone sour—that's all. Maybe you didn't plan the job right."

"You been talkin', eh?" Wolf glowered at Graham. "Think because your job went through you've got the edge on me?"

"Lay off that, Wolf!" growled Furzman. "You're talking to me, see? You said you were coming up here to tip me off to what queered your game. Spring it."

"Sure, I told you that," agreed Wolf. "Over the phone—after the job was queered and my mob took the bump. I got plenty to tell you, too—and if this chesty guy had hit what I hit, he'd be cryin' plenty."

Wolf indicated Graham as he spoke.

"That's your way of looking at it, eh?" quizzed Furzman. "Well, Wolf, you've got to show me. The Parkerside Trust was no tougher than the Terminal National—not as tough, for that matter."

"Maybe not," admitted Wolf, "but I got double-crossed. That makes it different, don't it?"

"Double-crossed? How?"

"I don't know."

"You mean by one of your mob—"

"I don't know. All I can tell you is that some guy got wise—and the job was stacked against me."

"You mean the police—"

"No!" Wolf snarled as he leaned forward in his chair. "The cops—bah—if they'd been wise, we'd have knowed it. I'll tell you who queered the job—just one guy—The Shadow!"

WOLF'S thrust struck home. Graham Wellerton, staring straight at King Furzman, saw the big shot's lips twitch. The mere mention of The Shadow's name was enough to cause any big criminal worriment.

"I'm tellin' you straight," insisted Wolf. "If the bank was wise—if the cops was wise—there'd have been somethin' to show for it. But here's what happened.

"Right inside the bank is an old stairway that goes down to the safe deposits. They blocked it off, see, when the bank was made bigger. Nothin' but a solid wall down there now.

"The mob goes in. They start to cover the tellers. Then right out from the rail around that old stairway comes the shots. Pickin' the gang off like they was flies.

"What happens? The customers duck for cover, the tellers an' the watchman yanks out their guns. Half the mob was crippled—the rest started to scram. The bank boys had the edge. They clipped the outfit."

"The newspapers said nothing about it," interposed Furzman, as Wolf paused. "According to the accounts, the bank tellers resisted the attack."

EZRA TALBOY, uncle of Graham Wellerton, who by legal but unscrupulous methods, had ruined Graham's father. Now Talboy is a wealthy, influential citizen in his community—the community into which Graham, crook of great ability, finds himself.

"Sure," snorted Wolf. "That's what they did—after The Shadow started it. None of them bank guys knew who began the mess. They grabbed the credit when the cops got there."

"What became of The Shadow?" questioned Furzman.

"How do I know?" retorted Wolf. "He didn't show himself. He must have walked out with some of the customers. He's a smart guy—The Shadow—I found that out today."

"What do you think of this?" asked the big shot, turning to Graham Wellerton.

"It sounds to me like an alibi," returned the gentleman of crime.

"Yeah?" snarled Wolf. "You think I'm lyin'? I'll fix you—"

"Someone may have caused the trouble," interrupted Graham calmly, "but it couldn't have been The Shadow."

"Why not?" questioned Wolf.

"Because," Graham responded, looking squarely toward his questioner, "if it had been The Shadow, you wouldn't have made a getaway without a couple of bullets somewhere in your body."

"Yeah?" Wolf was again indignant. "Well, it was The Shadow right enough—you can ask Pinkey Doremas if you don't believe me. He was just inside the door when the shots began—"

"Where is Pinkey now?"

"Down in Red Mike's place. He got plugged twice—I had to shove him in the car. I've got a sawbones down there to look after him—you know, the old doc who's in wrong an' who comes around whenever we need him."

Graham Wellerton was leaning back in his chair, chuckling merrily. Wolf Daggert stopped short to stare at him. King Furzman angrily demanded the cause of Graham's merriment.

"Do you want to know why I'm laughing?" questioned Graham. "I'll tell you why, King. Wolf is yellow—up to his old tricks. He never went into that bank with the mob. He was laying outside and he helped the only man who managed to get away—Pinkey Doremas—the one nearest the door when the firing started!"

WOLF'S lips were fidgeting. The peaked face gang leader stared angrily at Graham, then glanced nervously at King Furzman. At last he spoke, in a wheedling tone.

"I ain't yellow," he pleaded. "I wasn't in the bank—but it wasn't because I'm yellow. You know the getaway counts, King. That's why I was outside—"

"Wait a minute!" Furzman's exclamation was delivered in a serious tone. "We're getting at something now. How far down the street were you, Wolf?"

"About a hundred feet," said Wolf reluctantly. "Yeah—just about a hundred feet—"

"Around the corner," added Graham calmly.

"What if I was around the corner?" blurted Wolf. "It don't matter where I was, does it? I know how to manage my mob—"

Graham was enjoying another chuckle at Wolf's expense. The yellow gang leader had admitted his cowardice. King Furzman, however, saw a more important angle to the situation. It was the big shot who ended the controversy between the lieutenants by injecting a growled interruption.

"The Shadow was in it, all right," decided Furzman. "You can't blame Wolf, Wellerton. The Shadow can queer any job when he starts out. Say—this is bad all around."

"How?" questioned Graham.

"The Shadow must have picked up the trail of Wolf's mob," declared the big shot seriously. "They say he's always snooping around to see what the gangs are doing. He cleaned up the mob today; his next step will be to get Wolf. That may lead him here—to me—to you—"

"All of which can be avoided," interrupted Graham.

"How?" quizzed the big shot.

"Let Wolf lay low," declared Graham. "Have him keep away from here—take his time about getting another mob. Then"—Graham followed the plan that he had suggested prior to Wolf's arrival—"I can slide out of town with my mob and work somewhere else. That leaves you clear, King."

The big shot nodded solemnly. Wolf Daggert, thankful that criticism had ceased, said nothing. The arrangements which Graham Wellerton proposed came as a logical solution to the all-important problem.

"That's the way we'll work it," decided King Furzman. "There's no use taking chances if The Shadow is in this game. He's dangerous—and since he crimped you, Wolf, there's a big chance that he'll be after Wellerton next.

"You're laying low from now on—get that, Wolf? As for you, Wellerton, you can make your own plans. Stop in tomorrow night and tell me where you're heading. When will you be here?"

"Nine o'clock," said Graham.

The gentleman of crime arose, picked up his hat and coat and reached for his cane. Wolf Daggert eyed him maliciously, then turned to King Furzman.

"What am I supposed to do now?" he asked. "Scram? On account of The Shadow?"

"The less you're around here, the better," returned the big shot. "You move along—and stay away until I call for you. That's all for tonight."

Gloomily, Wolf picked up his hat and coat. He prepared to follow Graham Wellerton. King Furzman arose and went to the door to summon Gouger. Graham and Wolf watched him. The long black streak began to fade away from the floor; slowly, steadily, a large silhouette dwindled into nothingness.

GOUGER appeared and led the two men to the anteroom. He ushered them out into the corridor; then returned. Gouger did not see the weird figure that moved stealthily after he had passed. He did not suspect the presence of The Shadow.

On the sidewalk in front of the apartment building, Graham Wellerton and Wolf Daggert parted. No words of farewell were exchanged between these lieutenants of King Furzman.

Graham surveyed Wolf with a parting smile; Wolf, in turn, glowered at the man who had been successful where he had failed.

GRAHAM WELLERTON, crook by necessity, who finds the mesh of crime enveloping him even more as time goes on. Then he becomes a master crook himself—big enough to tell the big shot what to do. His plans are upset by another lieutenant of the chief, so Graham finds himself back in his home town, unknown. What happens then makes this thrilling yarn the best you've ever read!

Neither noted the tall, vague form that stood within the darkness of the entry to the lobby. Neither knew that The Shadow had followed them here; that the master of darkness was watching their departure.

King Furzman had spoken facts, not mere possibilities, when he had suggested that The Shadow, after breaking up Wolf Daggert's game, might trail Wolf to learn who was the man behind the attempted bank robbery.

The Shadow had heard Wolf's telephone call to King. He had come to observe lieutenant and big shot when they met.

In so doing, The Shadow had gained another point. He had learned that the successful pillaging of the Terminal National had also been ordered by King Furzman; he had learned the identity of the big shot's other lieutenant—Graham Wellerton.

To The Shadow, a skulking rat like Wolf Daggert was one who could be watched by agents, one who could be trapped the next time he attempted crime in Manhattan. King Furzman, pretended racketeer who dealt in robbery, was one whom The Shadow could strike at will.

But in Graham Wellerton, The Shadow had discovered a crime maker of another caliber. Here was one who dealt in strategy; a man who contemplated an expedition to another city; a crook who was wise enough to slide away from Manhattan when the going became too hot.

From his hidden observation post, The Shadow had studied this young chap who had the clean-cut appearance of a gentleman, but who dealt in crime as a profession. Graham Wellerton, with a trusted mob at his heels, was planning crimes that must be stopped at the outset.

As Graham Wellerton and Wolf Daggert walked in opposite directions, The Shadow emerged from the entry. His tall form became a vague outline that moved swiftly and invisibly along the street, following the path that Graham Wellerton had taken.

The Shadow was on the trail of the gentleman who dealt in crime. Before this night was ended, the master of detection would learn more—perhaps all—concerning the affairs of Graham Wellerton, bank robber deluxe.

CHAPTER IV
THE SHADOW VISIBLE

GRAHAM WELLERTON gave no thought to possible followers as he strolled along the street to a subway station. During the ride downtown, he had no idea that anyone was on his trail.

When he emerged from the subway, he walked to the pretentious apartment building where he lived, and rode upstairs in an elevator. He entered his fourth-floor apartment, raised a living-room window to gain some cool air, and seated himself in a comfortable armchair.

Idly speculative, the gentlemanly crook gave no thought to events outside that window. The opening was on a courtyard, not far from a fire tower. While Graham sat smoking a cigarette, a silent action took place upon the intervening wall between tower and window.

Hazy in the illumination from the tower, a tall black form of human proportions stretched out along the wall. Clinging to the bricks in batlike fashion, it began a precarious passage toward the open window.

Squidgy sounds, lost in the dull murmur of basement machinery, told of The Shadow's progress. With rubber suction disks attached to hands and feet, the stealthy intruder was moving steadily along a vertical wall.

The Shadow's form was shrouded in blackness when it arrived at a spot but a few feet distant from the open window. Keen ears were listening for any sound from within Graham Wellerton's living room.

The Shadow's head moved forward. His keen eyes were about to peer upon the lighted scene, when a rap at the door of the apartment caused Wellerton to arise quickly from his chair. The Shadow eased back into darkness as Graham approached the window, lowered the sash and drew the shade.

Hardly had the gentleman crook headed toward the door before The Shadow was at work. A black-gloved hand, freed from the rubber cup, extended itself and pushed the window sash several inches upward. Speedily, blackened fingers manipulated the window shade.

All this was done while Graham was walking across the floor. By the time the young man had reached the door, The Shadow's eyes were peering through a three-inch space between the windowsill and the sash and shade above.

When Graham Wellerton opened the door, he stepped back and his face came into the light. The Shadow, keenly observant, saw a look of mingled anger and dismay upon the young man's face. This was caused by the unexpectedness of the visitor—a woman—who wore an expensive but gaudy garb.

THE woman possessed a handsome face, yet there was something about her countenance that rendered it unattractive. Perhaps it was the hardened smile upon her painted lips; possibly it was the challenging glint that came from her dark eyes.

Whatever the cause, Graham Wellerton seemed annoyed because the feminine visitor had appeared, and the woman seemed pleased at the man's dismay.

"Not so glad to see me, eh?" was her first question. The tones were harsh. "Well, it was time I looked you up. Here I am!"

"How did you find my apartment, Carma?" questioned Graham angrily.

"That's my business!" the woman snapped. "I've found you before, haven't I? All right—I'll find you again!"

"Perhaps," returned the young man, seating himself in a chair by the window. "Nevertheless, there was no reason for you to come here. I told you that I would see you tomorrow—to give you the money that you want."

"I'll take the cash now, big boy," prompted Carma. "Five grand—kick in."

"I promised you three thousand."

"I want five."

"I haven't that amount."

"No?" Carma's tone was scoffing. "Say—you must work cheap, big boy. After that Terminal National robbery, you ought to have plenty of dough."

"What makes you say that?" quizzed Graham angrily. "Where do you get the idea that I was in on the Terminal National holdup?"

"I read the newspapers," laughed Carma. "I know the kind of work you do. Come on—five grand!"

Irritably, Graham drew a roll of banknotes from his pocket and peeled off fifty bills of hundred-dollar denomination. His bundle of cash was still a stout one when he replaced it in his pocket.

"This will do for a while," volunteered Carma. "But when I want more—I'll get it. Understand?"

Graham eyed the woman as she took a chair and lighted a cigarette. The young man chewed his lips, then spoke in a concerned tone.

"Someday, Carma," he remarked, "this is all going to end. Your demands for money are becoming more and more troublesome."

"I've got the goods on you, Graham," retorted Carma harshly. "You'll keep on paying—that's all."

"Let's be reasonable," suggested the young man. "It's about time you called quits on the racket. Otherwise—"

He paused as he caught the woman's glare. Thoughtfully, Graham assumed a reminiscent tone as he changed the subject to a discussion of the past.

"A FEW years ago," he said, "you and I were married. You know very well that I was shanghaied into matrimony. I don't even remember the ceremony. You showed me the marriage license—that was all."

"Granted," replied Carma. "You made a big mistake when you went into that speakeasy where I found you goofy from bad booze. If your old man hadn't had a lot of dough, I'd have left you there. But when I found out who you were, I married you."

"And when I woke up," retorted Graham, "I knew the whole affair was a frame-up. I told you I was through. I left. Then you came around and threatened to blackmail my father."

"He had dough," said Carma. "He could have paid. It would have been quits then."

"It would have been best," admitted Graham. "I didn't see it that way at the time. So I went out to raise cash to keep you quiet. A crook spotted me"—Graham was careful not to name Wolf Daggert—"and showed me the way to easy money."

"A great fellow," declared Carma, "whoever he was. You've been in the money ever since, big boy."

"Crooked money," said Graham bitterly. "Stolen money. Once I started, I had to keep on."

"And you went at it right."

"I figured it as a temporary proposition," declared Graham. "I hoped for a break. I thought it had come when my uncle swindled my father out of all his money. My father died. You were powerless—for I was no longer heir to a large estate. So I thought. That was when I left New York."

"That was when I used my noodle," laughed Carma. "I kept on your trail, didn't I, big boy?"

"Yes," grunted Graham. "You started a new racket. You knew too much about my criminal activities. Everytime I picked up a bundle of cash, you were there to grab your share—always the big share."

"Turn on the radio," sneered Carma. "Maybe a little soft music would make you feel better."

"I came back to New York," declared Graham, "and I landed in with some big workers. More money here—until you bobbed up again. You wanted a larger share of the cash. I've had to give it to you."

"Or I'll squeal," laughed Carma. "Between that marriage license and what I know about you, you've got to pay. Plenty!"

"If I happened to be a quitter," returned Graham, "I'd give up the game. I'd take the rap—even if it meant twenty years in the pen."

"Not you, big boy," scoffed the woman. "You like your freedom too well. Maybe you'll try to ditch me again—I'm always watching for that."

"Maybe," said Graham. "But not while things are going good here in New York. Someday, though, I may find a town where I can settle down without you knowing where I am."

"What about Southwark?" suggested Carma, in a baiting tone.

Graham Wellerton leaped to his feet. His eyes were furious. His fists clenched. His words were bitter as he blurted forth condemning tones.

"Southwark!" he snarled. "Never mention the name of that place! I hate everyone who lives there, now that my father is dead. My uncle—my mother's brother—old Ezra Talboy—the meanest skinflint in the world! Worse than you, Carma—and that's saying a lot!

"I wish some calamity would hit that town! Kill everybody in it! I wouldn't trust myself in Southwark. The very name enrages me!"

"You're not a killer," said Carma, with a deprecating laugh. "You never will be. Even if you were in Southwark, you wouldn't commit murder. Ditch me again, big boy, and I'll find you. But I'll give you a tip right now—I'll never look for you in Southwark."

"I'm not a killer," admitted Graham. "That's the only reason my uncle goes on living. He pilfered my father's money; I'll never get a cent of it. Yet Ezra Talboy still lives. No—I draw the line at murder—and that's the only reason you're alive, Carma. Dozens of times I've wanted to kill you."

"But you never will," said the woman calmly, rising as she tucked the five thousand dollars in her handbag. "Well, so long, big boy. Look me up after the next big job. If you don't, I'll find you, wherever you are."

"I don't doubt it," retorted Graham. "You're a jinx right enough. I'll probably move to another apartment now that you've come here."

"Suit yourself," laughed Carma, as she walked to the door and sarcastically blew a kiss in Graham's direction. "Don't forget when my next allowance is due."

AFTER the woman had gone, Graham Wellerton paced up and down the room. He hated Carma—and he had reason. He remembered when first he had met her—Carma Urstead—a typical gangster's moll.

Graham had seen the woman only once or twice prior to the event in the speakeasy. He could remember now how he had awakened from a drunken stupor to learn that he had married Carma Urstead. He recalled how he had cursed her; how he had departed, hoping never to see her again.

Carma had trailed him everywhere. In desperation, Graham had sought Wolf Daggert, the gangster whom he had met frequently at nightclubs in Manhattan. Wolf had shown him the way to crime; Carma had necessitated Graham following the course that Wolf offered.

A smile of grim, determination appeared upon Graham Wellerton's firm face. The young man strode to a corner of the living room, picked up a telephone, dialed a number and began to speak in a low, cautious tone.

His words were not audible at the window. The Shadow, listening, softly raised the sash and shade. His tall form stepped into the living room. Graham, seated at a telephone table, heard nothing but the talk of the man at the other end.

Sash and shade were lowered. Like a phantom, The Shadow glided to the doorway of another room. There, his form obscured, The Shadow stood close enough to overhear what Graham Wellerton was saying. The gentleman of crime was talking to members of his mob.

Across the floor stretched a streak of blackness, a shade that ended in a weirdly shaped profile. The silhouette, the visible token of The Shadow, appeared upon the carpet by the table where Graham Wellerton was seated.

"All right, Frank," Graham was saying. "Put Pete on the wire... That you, Pete?... We're moving out of town tomorrow night... Have everything set... Now listen—I'll tell you where to meet me."

Graham Wellerton's eyes froze. Staring over the mouthpiece of the telephone, they spied the silhouette upon the floor. Instinctively, the young man knew that the blackened profile signified the presence of a human being. Another thought flashed through his mind—the identity of the personage who had somehow entered this room.

The Shadow!

Despite a chilling tenseness, Graham retained his composure. Pete's voice was coming over the wire, inquiring where the meeting was to take place. Graham realized that if his conjecture was correct—that if The Shadow were watching here, any statement of a meeting point would be suicidal.

"Wait a minute, Pete." Graham's voice came steadily. "I'd better wait until I've seen the big shot. I'm dropping in on him around nine o'clock. I'll call you from there... That's right... Wait around until you hear from me."

Graham Wellerton hung up the receiver. Without moving from his chair, he drew forth a cigarette and lighted it. Staring over the flicker of the match, he watched the spot upon the floor. Slowly, with progressive glide, the streak of darkness dwindled into nothingness.

THE SHADOW was here. Doubtless he had slipped into the obscurity of the adjoining room. Graham smiled. He arose from his chair, sauntered to the window, raised shade and sash and stood staring into the darkness of the courtyard, whistling softly as he flicked cigarette ashes down into the space below him.

The gentleman of crime could hear no sound, yet he seemed to sense that eyes were watching him, that a living presence was gliding through the room. He knew that he was at the mercy of The Shadow, yet he held the hunch that the master of darkness would depart without striking.

For the crux of crime would come tomorrow. Graham had heard of The Shadow's ways; how the weird specter of the night toyed with the plans of evil schemers and bided his time until their contemplated crimes were nearing the point of completion.

Two minutes passed. Graham puffed his cigarette furiously, then tossed the butt from the window. He turned back into the living room. The atmosphere seemed relieved. He was sure that The Shadow had gone.

Graham smiled.

He knew now that The Shadow must have learned Wolf Daggert's ways; that the phantom warrior had been at King Furzman's this evening. From that point, The Shadow had taken up Graham's own trail.

Tomorrow night, The Shadow would again be at King Furzman's, there to learn what Graham Wellerton intended. Graham's smile increased. He thought of the two visitors who had been in this room tonight.

Carma.

Graham had tricked her. She fully expected him to remain in New York. Once he had started for a distant city with his mob, Graham felt sure that he could successfully lose the woman who had been his Nemesis. She would not be able to find him.

The Shadow.

There was a more potent enemy. Yet Graham Wellerton felt sure that he had tricked The Shadow also. Tomorrow night, Graham would not visit King Furzman. A telephone call to the big shot would serve instead of a personal call.

With King Furzman warned, with Wolf Daggert lying low, with Graham Wellerton out of New York, The Shadow would be frustrated in any effort to break this ring of crime. Graham, now, would be the only active worker; by the time he could be traced, he would be bound to another destination.

Still smiling, the gentleman of crime stared at the spot of carpeting which now was clear of the blackened silhouette. Graham Wellerton had seen the visible sign of The Shadow. Forewarned, he was prepared to deceive the master who battled crime.

CHAPTER V
THE WARNING

ANOTHER evening had come to Manhattan. King Furzman was seated in the room where he received his visitors. The big shot was anticipating the arrival of Graham Wellerton. Tonight, Furzman was to hear his lieutenant's plans.

The big shot drew a heavy gold watch from his pocket and noted the time as half past eight. Wellerton was due to arrive at any minute. Furzman, as he chewed the end of a fat cigar, wondered just what locality the daring gentleman crook intended to invade.

Not once did Furzman glance toward the heavy curtains that hung between this room and the next. The big shot did not notice the strange, sinister blot that projected from those draperies. Less sensitive than Graham Wellerton, King Furzman failed to gain an inkling that the hidden eyes of The Shadow were upon him.

Minutes drifted by; then came a knock from the door at the other side of the room. Gouger entered in response to Furzman's growl. The bodyguard announced that Graham Wellerton was calling on the telephone.

"Tell him to come up," ordered the big shot.

"He's not downstairs," returned Gouger. "He's calling from outside somewhere—"

"Bring me the telephone," interposed Furzman brusquely.

Gouger went back into the far room, then returned with the telephone, dragging a long extension wire after him. He handed the instrument to the big shot, who took it without even moving from his chair.

"Hello, Wellerton," greeted Furzman. "Where are you?"

"I'll tell you in a minute," came the reply. "Are you alone, there in the apartment?"

"Gouger's here."

"Send him away"—Graham's voice came in a guarded tone—"and listen carefully to what I have to say. Don't repeat anything. This is very important."

"All right," returned Furzman, in a puzzled tone. "Wait a second."

The big shot made a motion with the telephone, indicating that Gouger should leave. The bodyguard went back through the far doorway.

"Gouger's gone," informed Furzman. "Go ahead. Spill what you've got to say."

"Just a minute." Graham's voice carried a warning note as it came across the wire. "Hold the phone away from your ear, King. See if my voice can be heard."

STILL puzzled, but convinced by Graham's impressive tone that the matter was important, Furzman obeyed the injunction. He noted that Graham's next words were hopelessly indistinct when heard without receiver to ear.

"Can't make outa thing," said Furzman, again speaking into the mouthpiece. "Your voice doesn't carry at all, the way you're talking. What's up, Wellerton? What's the idea—"

"Easy, King!" Graham's voice was low but distinct. "I'm putting you wise to something important. Don't say a word to give away what I'm telling you. Someone may be listening."

"Where?"

"In your apartment."

"Who?"

"The Shadow!"

King Furzman sat in momentary bewilderment. As he waited, unable to speak because of his surprise, he heard new information coming across the wire.

"I'm over in Jersey, King," declared Graham. "I'm here with the mob. We're starting out tonight for Grand Rapids, Michigan. We're going to knock off a couple of banks out there and—"

"You're coming here first?"

"Sh-h!" Graham's voice hissed across the wire. "I'm not taking any chances, King. The Shadow was covering me last night. He may be laying up at your place right now—waiting for me to show up. That's why I don't want to come there."

"I see," commented King, nervously glancing about him.

"Our first job"—Graham's voice was still cautious—"will be the Riverview Trust in Grand Rapids. Listen, King—Wolf Daggert pulled a big mistake by coming up to see you last night. The Shadow was on his trail then—now he's on mine. But I'm sliding out on him.

"Keep Wolf away. Tell him you don't want to see him. Count on me for a while. I'll get the gravy you want. Watch things until you're sure that The Shadow isn't going to bother you.

"We're heading West—in cars—and we'll be two nights on the road. We're going to hold up the Riverview the night after we get to Grand Rapids. I know all about the bank—it does a big night business, It's a setup—"

"Say, Wellerton," interrupted King Furzman, "if this stuff is on the level as—"

"It is on the level," came back Graham's quick response. "It's a tough situation, King. Don't take any chances. I've given you the lay; you know what I'm going to do. You can't be too careful."

All of King Furzman's doubts were dispelled. The big shot found himself becoming nervous. Wolf's theory that The Shadow had broken up the robbery yesterday noon; Graham's convincing statements that The Shadow was following up the victory—these were sufficient for King Furzman.

"I've got you, Wellerton," he declared, in a decisive tone. "Go ahead with the lay the way you've planned it. When will I hear from you?"

"I'll get word to you," returned Graham. "But I want you to be sure that The Shadow's not on deck before I come back to New York."

"All right," said Furzman. "Leave that part of it to me."

A click came over the wire. The big shot hung up. He mopped his forehead thoughtfully; then began a succession of nervous glances, his gaze traveling to all corners of the room.

Almost before his eyes, the black streak that indicated The Shadow performed a fadeout. The big shot did not notice the motion of darkness on the door.

"Gouger!"

The bodyguard appeared in answer to Furzman's summons. The big shot made a sweeping motion with his hand.

"Look around the place," he said. "Make sure there's no snoopers here."

"Not a chance," rejoined Gouger. "Say, King—the way I keep that outside door locked—"

"Take a look anyway," ordered the big shot.

WONDERING, Gouger walked out between the curtains. He was heading for the anteroom to begin his search. King Furzman picked up the telephone. He dialed a number.

"That you, Wolf?" he inquired. "This is King Furzman. Say, Wolf— that idea of yours about The Shadow sounds right. I got a tip-off from Wellerton. He says The Shadow was on his trail, too."

"He says what?" Wolf's reply was an incredulous tone over the wire.

"He says The Shadow is on his trail," repeated King. "That is, The Shadow was on his trail, until he managed to duck out."

"Where?" came Wolf's question.

"That's my business," snapped Furzman, remembering Graham's injunction to say nothing regarding his whereabouts. "The point is that Wellerton figures The Shadow trailed you here last night."

"So that's his game, eh?" Wolf's snarl sounded clearly in the receiver. "Tryin' to blame somethin' on me. Say, King, don't let that egg stall you. He's got somethin' up his sleeve. He's out to double-cross you, Wellerton is."

"I know where he's gone," declared the big shot harshly. "I want you to keep away from here. Lay low for a while."

"Honest, King," came Wolf's plea, "I ain't handin' you no boloney. Let me come up there tonight—I can put you wise to the kind of a bird Wellerton is. He's tryin' to slip somethin' over on you. Say—he couldn't duck The Shadow if that guy was on his trail—"

"Can the gab, Wolf," ordered Furzman. "You won't get anywhere by knocking Wellerton. You heard what I had to say. Lay low until you hear from me."

"Listen, King—"

Wolf's plea was cut short as Furzman hung up. The big shot set the telephone heavily upon a table and growled to himself as he stood staring at the wall.

His mind was at odds. Graham Wellerton's warning had been impressive; Wolf Daggert's doubts, however, began to change the matter.

King Furzman wondered.

Was Wolf right? Had Wellerton been stalling?

It was conceivable that Graham could have some game of his own; that he had followed Wolf's lead and used The Shadow as an alibi.

The big shot's face was grim. His eyes were angry. With hands thrust in his tuxedo pockets, he fumbled with the revolver that he kept there. At last he brought his hands into view and reached for the telephone again. On the point of giving Wolf Daggert another call, he laid the instrument aside.

Two lieutenants, at odds with one another. Were both on the square or were both crossing the big shot? Weighing the matter, King Furzman considered yesterday's episodes.

Wolf Daggert had failed. Graham Wellerton had succeeded. Moreover, Graham had deliberately left his share of the loot in Furzman's possession. That was the deciding point. Graham Wellerton was on the level.

A new thought came to King Furzman. Graham Wellerton was a keen worker. He had suggested that The Shadow might even now be spying on the big shot. Gouger had started out to search the apartment. How was he making out?

Turning, King Furzman looked toward the archway with its hanging draperies. He stopped suddenly. His eyes became fixed; his body rigid. In one instant he had gained positive proof that Graham Wellerton's warning was a sound one.

Standing within the range of light was a living apparition of darkness. A tall figure, clad in black, was blocking King Furzman's path. The folds of a sable-hued cloak were motionless. The face of the being who wore that garment was hidden beneath the projecting brim of a black slouch hat.

The only tokens of the hidden face were two gleaming eyes that burned with steady light. Despite the hypnotic power of those sinister optics, King Furzman could visualize the entire form of the personage before him. His startled gaze took in the muzzle of an automatic that projected from the folds of the cloak, held firmly by a black-gloved hand.

King Furzman made no motion. Like a statue, he stood gazing at the spectral figure which had so silently materialized itself. There was no mistaking the identity of this weird phantom that had seemingly emerged from nothingness.

King Furzman, erstwhile racketeer who had turned his hand to crime, was face to face with the mastermind who battled men of evil. The gasp that came from the big shot's twisted lips was proof of the recognition that was in his mind.

King Furzman was face to face with The Shadow. Graham Wellerton's warning had failed to save the big shot from this meeting with the archenemy of crime!

CHAPTER VI
THE BIG SHOT SPEAKS

KING FURZMAN, as he faced The Shadow, was a man who betrayed consternation. The big shot was a man who constantly wore an expression of cold brutality—a mask which ever hid the emotions which he felt. The mask had lifted now. Stark fear had replaced King Furzman's habitual glower.

The big shot was knowing the fear that had gripped other crime wreakers when they had encountered The Shadow. Furzman's forehead glistened with perspiration; his hands were limp; his body trembled. Through his mind was passing all that he had heard concerning the vengeance which The Shadow had delivered to those who sought to thwart his purposes and his ends.

Before the first shock of fear had passed, King Furzman gained new knowledge of The Shadow's terrifying presence. The token that came was an audible one—a whispered laugh that shuddered as it came from unseen lips. Quavering reverberations, silent shocks of impending doom, beat weirdly against Furzman's eardrums.

Then came the voice of The Shadow. It followed the persisting echoes; it carried an eerie note that resembled a sneer, yet which held a strain of bitter mockery. Each whispered word was delivered in an uncanny tone that changed King Furzman's trembling into a state of tense fixation.

"King Furzman"—The Shadow's statement sounded as a knell—"you have plotted crime. That is why you have met The Shadow. You can hope for no deliverance while I am here. You will tell me what I wish to know."

Unconsciously, the big shot found himself nodding in reply to The Shadow's words.

"You have heard from your henchman," resumed The Shadow. "Graham Wellerton has told you where he has gone. Give me that information."

Tensely, Furzman tried to resist the threat. The eyes of The Shadow glinted. The muzzle of the automatic moved forward with a subtle thrust. Furzman replied mechanically, hoping only to avoid the menace of The Shadow.

"Wellerton has gone"—the big shot's voice was no more than a gulping gasp—"to—to Grand Rapids—gone with his mob—"

"His purpose," came The Shadow's cold demand.

"Bank holdup," gasped Furzman. "The—the"—the pause was hopeless—"the Riverview Trust will be his first job."

"The time," quizzed The Shadow.

"Two nights from now," gulped Furzman. "Two nights from now—before nine o'clock—"

THE SHADOW'S laugh was one of whispered scorn. The tone provoked new terror in King Furzman's evil brain. Despite the fact that he had told the truth, the big shot knew that The Shadow was not yet through with him.

"You have money here"—The Shadow's words broke in a hideous, sneering chuckle—"money which does not belong to you. Tell me where you have hidden it."

"In the wall of this room," panted the big shot. "Behind the third panel from the door—in a safe—"

"The combination," prompted The Shadow, with his terrifying aftermath of whispered mirth.

"Three—four—one—eight—" Furzman spoke in monotonous fashion, as though his lips worked of their own accord.

"Your crime is proven," came The Shadow's sinister judgment. "You have profited by the work of others. You shall suffer of your own accord. That telephone"—the blazing orbs stared beyond the big shot—"will be the instrument that will deliver you to the law. Pick it up."

The big shot obeyed.

"Call detective headquarters," ordered The Shadow. "Ask for Detective Joe Cardona. Tell him who you are. Tell him you are waiting for him. That is all. Remember"—the tone was ominous—"one word concerning my presence here will seal your lips with the cold rigidity of permanent doom—"

Pangs of terror brought convulsive shudders to King Furzman's stout frame. The big shot's knees were quaking, his hands could scarcely lift the telephone. In a quavering voice, the man called as directed.

He could hear The Shadow's whisper coming closer; staring, he saw the black cloak swish and show its crimson lining as The Shadow moved to a point no more than a yard away.

"Your man Gouger," warned The Shadow, "has completed his search for me. He is in the other room. He does not know that I am here. He—like yourself—belongs to the police—"

A voice was clicking over the wire. The Shadow's sinister tones ended. King Furzman, fighting for his life, asked weakly for Joe Cardona. He heard the reply that Cardona himself was on the wire.

"This is King Furzman," said the big shot, pathetically. "I'm in my own apartment, Cardona. I—I want to talk to you here"—Furzman's voice broke as his eyes stared toward the glowing orbs that were The Shadow's eyes—"I—I was in on those bank robberies yesterday. The dough is here—in the wall of this room—"

Furzman's lips were twitching, his eyes were moving furtively, trying to escape the terrible gaze of The Shadow. Suddenly, they became transfixed with a gleam of wild hope as they saw beyond the shoulders of the black-clad master. With a short gasp, Furzman stepped back a little. The telephone dropped from his hands.

There was a swish as The Shadow whirled. Furzman's sudden gaze, his defensive action—both were indicative, but The Shadow's keen intuition was already working when the signal came.

Before the telephone had clattered to the floor, The Shadow was facing the draped archway where the figure of a man was looming in the darkness of the room beyond.

Gouger was there. Purely by chance, the bodyguard had come back over the trail which he had taken through the anteroom. Arriving in the darkened space between anteroom and reception room, he had heard the sound of King Furzman's voice.

THE instant that he had observed the blotting form of The Shadow, Gouger had drawn his revolver to point it toward the menacing figure in black. Swift in action, steady in aim, Gouger had acted with prompt precision; but as his finger touched the trigger, The Shadow, miraculously alert, had swung.

A mere turn would not have sufficed. The Shadow's whirl, however, was a sweeping move. As his tall form swung, it whisked to the right, just as Gouger's revolver blazed from the darkened room.

A bullet singed the left shoulder of the long black cloak. The Shadow's lips responded with a mocking cry of laughter—a weird peal that was no longer hushed.

While taunting mirth rang through the room, Gouger swung his revolver toward the enemy in black. His finger, still upon the trigger, was about to loose a second bullet when a terrific roar came from The Shadow's automatic.

The shot was perfect. Beyond the archway, Gouger tottered. The bodyguard's revolver fell from the useless hand which held it. Gouger collapsed upon the floor.

If Gouger was prompt in action, so was King Furzman. The revolver shot from the other room dispelled the power of The Shadow, so far as the big shot was concerned.

With the first spurt of flame, King Furzman's nerve came back to him. His hand sped to his pocket. His fingers yanked forth the revolver that was there. On the upswing, the big shot drew his weapon just as The Shadow's shot felled Gouger.

... as his finger touched the trigger, The Shadow, miraculously alert, had swung.

With that shot, The Shadow turned. Furzman's upward-moving revolver was racing with the automatic that came in a wide sweep as The Shadow whirled back to meet his first enemy. Both guns reached their aiming points at the same instant. Two reports sounded as one.

But another phenomenon occurred. The form of The Shadow seemed to collapse a split second before his finger pressed the trigger. King Furzman remained bolt upright.

When the guns boomed, both figures were momentarily motionless; then, as The Shadow's form became erect, King Furzman's body swayed and crumpled. His revolver slipped to the floor beside him.

The Shadow's wits had prevailed. Simultaneous shots, each delivered with quick accuracy, had gone forth from rival guns. But The Shadow had dropped away from Furzman's aim.

The big shot's bullet, aimed for The Shadow's

heart, had done no more than clip the upper edge of the black slouch hat. The Shadow's bullet, with Furzman's body as its target, had found its appointed mark.

A SARDONIC laugh came from The Shadow's lips. The tone seemed to carry a note of tragedy. Once again, The Shadow had performed swift deeds that were essential to his ceaseless war against men of crime. The fallen telephone, connected directly with detective headquarters, had recorded the shots of the unexpected fray.

Forces of the law would be on their way, to find that grim justice had been delivered; yet the part which The Shadow had played would never be known. Such was The Shadow's method.

He had offered King Furzman a chance to live; the big shot had sought to kill him in return. King Furzman, therefore, had received the reward which he deserved.

Swiftly, The Shadow went to the wall and opened the panel of which Furzman had spoken. He turned the combination of the safe and loosed its metal door. He then closed the panel so the opening would have to be discovered by the searching detectives. King Furzman had admitted to Cardona that the stolen bank funds were in the wall of this room.

The black cloak swished. Swiftly, The Shadow glided away. He passed through the anteroom and left the outer door unlocked. His tall form disappeared down a stairway at the end of the corridor.

The Shadow had gained the information that he sought. Graham Wellerton, speeding westward with his mob, would be due for a surprise. King Furzman, the big shot, had spoken. He had given out the facts which he had heard from his lieutenant.

King Furzman, alone, had known his lieutenant's plans. Now The Shadow knew them also. Knowing where crime was due to fall, The Shadow would be there to strike!

CHAPTER VII
CHANCE INTERVENES

THREE long minutes elapsed after the departure of The Shadow. The corridor outside of King Furzman's apartment was silent and undisturbed. Then came the clang of an opening door. A man stepped out from an elevator which had stopped at the fourteenth floor.

This visitor was an unexpected one. He was not an officer of the law. Mere chance had brought him here during the interim between The Shadow's departure and the arrival of the police.

The man from the elevator was Wolf Daggert!

The fang-toothed gangster looked about him in a furtive manner. He knew that he was taking liberties in paying a visit to this place against King Furzman's orders. That was why he had not announced himself in the lobby. He had sneaked past the doorman to board an elevator; the operator had not seen the action and hence had raised no objection.

Wolf approached the door of the big shot's apartment. He rapped softly, then loudly. There was no response to his knocking.

Wolf was restless. In his mistrust of Graham Wellerton, he felt it imperative to talk with King Furzman; yet he knew that the big shot would not welcome his intrusion.

After half a minute, Wolf nervously placed his hand upon the doorknob and gave it a turn. He was surprised when the barrier opened.

Stepping into the anteroom, Wolf glanced about in a puzzled manner. Where was Gouger? Why had the attendant left the door unlocked?

Wolf saw opportunity. He would walk boldly in, surprise King Furzman and inform the big shot of Gouger's negligence. This would break the ice for the interview which Wolf was so anxious to gain.

Closing the outer door behind him, Wolf took the course toward the reception room. He reached the darkened room through which he had to pass; there he stumbled upon something which was lying on the floor.

Staring, Wolf discerned the body of Gouger! Leaning down to touch the inert form, Wolf found his fingers in a pool of blood.

Startled, the gang leader stepped over Gouger's body and entered the reception room. A short gasp came from his evil lips as his eyes viewed the motionless form of King Furzman.

Springing forward, Wolf reached the big shot's body. He raised King's head and stared into the big shot's whitened face.

"King!" panted Wolf. "King! Are you alive?"

Eyelids trembled. King Furzman's glassy gaze stared directly at Wolf Daggert. The dying big shot did not seem to recognize the face before him.

"Who got you, King?" questioned Wolf anxiously. "Who got you? Not—not The Shadow?"

King Furzman's head gave a feeble nod. Anxiously, Wolf stared about him as though fearing a sinister presence which still might be within this room of death. Then, to Wolf's ears, came the gasping tones of dying words.

King Furzman was speaking; his voice was scarcely audible.

"The Shadow," he said, weakly, as his eyelids closed. "The Shadow. He got me—"

A pause; then came disjointed statements, from lips that scarcely moved:

"Wellerton—gone—Grand Rapids—his mob—Wellerton—"

The head dropped back as Wolf held it. King Furzman's body stiffened in death. Wolf stared at the gruesome countenance of this man who had been his chief. Scattered thoughts flashed through the gang leader's brain.

WOLF had come here to damage Graham Wellerton's connection with the big shot. Predominating in the evil gang leader's mind was a hatred for Wellerton, whom he had encouraged into crookery and who had outgrown his sponsor.

Wolf had been sure that The Shadow had intervened at the Parkerside Trust holdup. Wolf, therefore, felt that his own failure had been justified, and Graham Wellerton's success at the Terminal National had made the dose more bitter.

Had The Shadow traced King Furzman through Wolf? Possibly; yet Wolf, proud of his own craftiness, was looking for another explanation.

His eyes gleamed shrewdly; his lips twisted with hatred. He thought of Graham Wellerton, away on the road to Michigan.

A keen suspicion came into Wolf's mind. The gang leader arose; his fists tightened. His thoughts changed suddenly, as Wolf spied the telephone upon the floor. At that moment, the gang leader's schemes dwindled as the instinct of self-preservation took hold upon Wolf's evil brain.

Had King Furzman tried to make a call for aid before encountering The Shadow? King was dead; so was Gouger. Both had been shot in some swift fray. Wolf realized that the telephone might have served as an alarm.

Quickly, the evil-faced gang leader hurried toward the anteroom. Arriving there, he peered into the empty corridor; then skulked forth toward the elevators. He heard a clang at one of the metal doors and made a quick dive for the safety of the stairway.

HE was just in time. The door of the elevator shaft opened and out stepped a swarthy individual whom Wolf recognized as Joe Cardona, ace of New York detectives. Sneaking down the stairway, Wolf thought only of making a getaway.

As he reached a lower floor, the gang leader heard men coming up. Hastily, the gangster tried apartment doors and was fortunate enough to find one that opened.

He discovered that the apartment was empty. He found a window that was some ten feet above the roof of a low, adjoining building. Wolf scrambled through this exit. He beat his way across the roof, broke open a trapdoor and dropped down into the top floor of an old-fashioned apartment building.

From then on, escape was easy.

As Wolf hurried from the vicinity of the apartment house where King Furzman had been slain, his scheming mind again began to function. Thoughts of Graham Wellerton, free and on the road to independent crime, were infuriating to Wolf.

Entering a cigar store, Wolf made a telephone call. He spoke in an eager tone to the man who answered.

"That you, Garry?" Wolf inquired. "Yeah. This is Wolf Daggert... Say—can you get hold of a good fast wagon? Good... I got somethin' that'll work out great... Sure—I'm scrammin' from New York... No—the bulls ain't on my trail... I'll put you wise when you show up with the boat. Sure. I can meet you at the garage. Where is it?... Give me the address."

ONE hour later, Wolf Daggert and his companion, Garry, were whirling along a New Jersey highway. Wolf, his evil face wearing an ugly smile, was pouring out his story while Garry replied with understanding chuckles.

"If we get a break," Wolf was explaining, "we'll catch up with them guys before they get to Grand Rapids. They'll be goin' straight there—"

"We may pass them on the road," commented Garry doubtfully.

"Maybe," agreed Wolf, "but that ain't goin' to matter anyway. If we get into Grand Rapids ahead of them, we can make out all right. Say—wait until I get a hold of Wellerton's mob and spill what I've got to say—"

Wolf's speech ended; the gang leader stuck his head from the side window of the speeding car and looked upward to see a huge monoplane roaring overhead.

The swift metal bird, its searchlight ablaze, was winging past the automobile at tremendous speed. Wolf settled back in the seat and turned to Garry.

"Say," he commented, "that guy was hummin' along. Boy—if he was bound for Grand Rapids, he'd get there plenty quick."

The airplane's hum was fading far ahead as Wolf Daggert completed his statement. The shrewd gang leader said nothing more. His thoughts were of the chase which he had undertaken, a pursuit that would end when he and Garry had caught up with Graham Wellerton.

Chance had intervened. By a freak of fate, Wolf Daggert had learned facts from the dying lips of King Furzman. The gang leader knew where Graham Wellerton was heading; he was ready to spoil the plans of the man whom he hated.

New territory lay ahead. Graham Wellerton had planned to invade a district where The Shadow would not trouble him. Wolf Daggert now was planning a course that would enable him to profit by Graham's brains.

Yet in his calculations, Wolf Daggert never dreamed that King Furzman had squealed to The Shadow before the battle in the apartment. Little did Wolf suppose that Graham Wellerton was riding into a trap; that he, Wolf, in seeking Graham, was placing himself in the same predicament.

That swift plane that had sped far ahead! Merely as conjecture had Wolf suggested Grand Rapids in connection with it. Actually, the gang leader would have picked the Michigan city as the least likely destination to which the monoplane might be traveling.

Had Wolf known who was riding in that ship, his thoughts would have changed from eagerness to trepidation. Realization of grim danger would have made the yellow gang leader turn back toward New York.

For the pilot of the silver-winged plane was a being who rode in darkness. His destination was the city of Grand Rapids. Hurling forward through the night, The Shadow was aiming for the place where crime would later fall.

When Graham Wellerton's mob advanced upon its intended foray, The Shadow, enemy of crime, would be there to shatter the attack!

CHAPTER VIII
MOBSMEN CHOOSE

TWENTY-FOUR hours later, two sedans pulled up beside a filling station at the side of a lonely road. A man in a dark gray overcoat stepped from one automobile and approached the filling station, ordering gasoline for both cars.

The service man noted a frank, well-featured face beneath the visor of a cap. He also saw a dark sweater under the half-buttoned overcoat. He classed the stranger as an ordinary tourist in informal garb. He went out to fill the gas tanks.

The man with cap and overcoat was Graham Wellerton. His mobsmen were lounging in the cars, ready to proceed as soon as the tanks were filled. The squad of raiders, traveling in a pair of automobiles, was not many hours from its final destination.

As Graham Wellerton walked to the front of the first machine, he came into the glare of headlights that were arriving along the road. Brakes ground as a coupe swung in beside the sedans. The door of the coupe opened and a familiar figure stepped forth.

Graham stared as he recognized Wolf Daggert.

There was a malicious gleam in Wolf's eye—a token which made Graham instantly understand that something was wrong. Graham, however, quickly recovered from his surprise.

"Hello, Wolf!" he exclaimed. "How did you get here?"

"I'll tell you later, Wellerton," returned the gang leader. "Slide one of your men into my car. I want to ride along with you."

Graham motioned to a man in the front seat of the first sedan. The fellow clambered out to take Wolf's place in the coupé. Graham sat behind the wheel of the sedan; Wolf dropped into the seat beside him. The sedan started forward and the other cars followed.

"What's the gag, Wolf?" queried Graham.

"I'll tell you when we get away a bit," returned Wolf. "Pick a side road where we can stop. There's trouble back in New York. I came after you to put you wise."

GRAHAM felt ill at ease when he heard Wolf's words. He suspected malice on the part of the yellow gang leader. He could not understand why King Furzman would have dispatched Wolf in pursuit of the secret expedition.

Nevertheless, Graham could see no possible danger from Wolf's presence. In accordance with his companion's suggestion, he picked a side road and brought the sedan to a stop. The other cars came up in back.

"All right, Wolf," ordered Graham brusquely. "Let's hear what's on your mind."

The mobsters in the rear seat were leaning forward to catch Wolf's words. Other men were coming up from the sedan behind. Wolf laughed sourly, while he waited for all hands to arrive.

"Have you read the newspapers?" he queried, at last.

"No," returned Graham shortly. "We've stayed away from towns during our trip. We haven't seen any of today's news."

"Take a look at this, then," stated Wolf, pulling a folded newspaper from his pocket. "Out here—you can read it by the headlights."

Before Graham could object, Wolf was clambering from his seat and making for the front of the sedan. Graham's mobsters, eager to know what was up, were following. There was nothing to do but act in accord with Wolf's suggestion. Graham hurriedly stepped to the road.

As he reached the front of the car, Graham heard growls of astonishment coming from the men who had arrived ahead of him. Shouldering his way through the crowd, Graham seized the newspaper that was in Wolf Daggert's hands and stared at the headlines. His gaze hardened.

Graham was reading an account of King Furzman's mysterious death. The affray in the apartment was reported as an unexplained killing. Most potent of all was the discovery of stolen funds in a wall safe behind a panel of the big shot's reception room.

"What do you think of that?" queried Wolf Daggert, as he watched Graham scan the headlines. "Who do you think gave King the bump?"

"The Shadow?" questioned Graham.

"You guessed it," retorted Wolf with an evil leer. "The Shadow bumped King Furzman!"

Audible responses came from the mobsters. This piece of information was startling. All turned to Wolf for further news. The gang leader showed his ugly teeth. His lips twisted as he prepared to loose the scheme that was in his mind.

"Kind of funny, ain't it?" he quizzed. "The way you named The Shadow the minute I asked you who you thought bumped King. You seemed to know a lot about it, Wellerton."

"I warned King Furzman," retorted Graham. "I told him The Shadow had been trailing me—"

"Yeah?" queried Wolf. "Did you tell these fellows about it, too?"

"No." Graham faced his mobsmen. "I ducked The Shadow, boys. That's why I kept mum about it. I knew The Shadow would still be in New York and—"

"I'll tell you about The Shadow." Wolf's snarl was an interruption. "It was The Shadow who queered my mob when we tried to hold up the Parkerside Trust. That's news, ain't it?

"Kind of funny, wasn't it, that The Shadow picked on me? Kind of funny that Wellerton here was hitting the Terminal National, right at the same time? Well, The Shadow may be tough—but he can't be two places at the same time.

"Then Wellerton starts out for Grand Rapids. What does The Shadow do? He comes in an' bumps King Furzman. He kills the big shot, boys—an' gets the dough that Furzman has—"

"Lay off that stuff!" challenged Graham. "You're looking for trouble, Wolf. I get what you're driving at."

"It's time you got it" was the retort. "I know your game, Wellerton. Making me a sucker—making King a sucker—so The Shadow would be busy takin' care of us. I know who tipped off The Shadow—"

Graham Wellerton leaped forward. He was ready to beat Wolf Daggert to a pulp. His spring, however, stopped abruptly. Wolf had anticipated it. The leering gang leader had whipped out a revolver.

With the muzzle of a gun covering him, Graham had no chance. He subsided, but his jaw was set as he eyed Wolf Daggert firmly.

ANGRY murmurs came from the mobsmen. Trouble was in the balance. Wolf Daggert's insinuations had reached receptive ears. While Wolf held his gun, while Graham glared in return, a feeling of unrest and dissatisfaction stirred the brutal minds of the assembled mobsmen.

"King Furzman told me how to reach you," declared Wolf. "I got there while he was dying. I didn't have time to look for any dough. I scrammed just before Joe Cardona showed up with a flock of dicks—"

"And so you trailed me," interrupted Graham. "Came along to queer a good lay—to make trouble—to muscle in on my job—"

"That's it," jeered Wolf. "There's the giveaway. Your job, you say. You ain't workin' for King Furzman no more. Ditched him, didn't you—left him to The Shadow—"

"Gag that guy," growled Graham, appealing to the mobsmen, as he indicated Wolf with a nudging thumb.

Grunts of doubt were the response. Not a mobsman stirred. Wolf's accusations had already proven fruitful. Graham Wellerton had played his high card. Wolf Daggert trumped it with an evil laugh.

"Come on, gang," suggested Wolf. "Grab me—put me on the spot. You know me—like you know Wellerton here. He's your boss. Grab me—before I can tell you the rest of it."

Yellow in face of fire, Wolf Daggert was the opposite when he dealt with mobsmen. These were men of his ilk; he understood them. His sarcastic request that Graham's command be followed was a stroke of cleverness on his part.

"All right, men," interposed Graham calmly. "Take your pick—between Wolf and myself. Listen to what this yellow guy has to say—"

"I'm yellow, eh?" snarled Wolf. "You call this yellow—comin' to tip off some real guys to the game you're playin'? Think you're smart, you silk-hat gorilla. That's all you are, Wellerton. You worked for me once; you got in right with King Furzman an' he gave you a mob of your own. Then you queered my lay so you'd look good an' I'd look punk. Then you double-crossed King—"

"Double-crossed him?" queried Graham. "Say—my cut from the Terminal National job was there with the dough the cops grabbed. What do you think of that?"

"You didn't collect what was comin' to you?" Wolf's tone was a hoarse laugh. "Say—do you think we're a lot of punks? Tryin' to hand us baloney like that? Listen to him, gang. Then listen to me.

"I was goin' great until this bozo began to chisel. He's the guy that let The Shadow get wise to what I was doin'. Some of you fellows worked for me when Wellerton was takin' my orders. Was The Shadow mixin' in it then?"

As Wolf turned his head from side to side, he momentarily forgot Graham Wellerton. With a savage cry, the young man precipitated himself upon the leering gang leader. He gripped Wolf's gun wrist; the two men locked themselves in a furious struggle.

With the muzzle of a gun covering him, Graham had no chance...

"Get him!" gurgled Wolf, as Graham's hand gripped his throat. "Get the double-crosser!"

Garry, the man who had come with Wolf, was the one who ended the indecision. Mingled with Graham Wellerton's mobsmen, he echoed Wolf's cry.

"Get the double-crosser!"

Two mobsmen responded. They leaped upon Graham Wellerton and dragged their denounced leader away from Wolf Daggert. Had Graham used discretion, he might have saved his cause; instead, he furiously swung against the men who had seized him. That brought the entire mob.

In the fray, Graham's overcoat was ripped from his body. He went down under force of numbers.

Wolf Daggert was snarling imprecations. He had won over the entire squad of mobsters. Two men had pinioned Graham Wellerton's arms behind him. They were dragging the young man into the back seat of the first sedan.

"We're goin' ahead with the Grand Rapids job," Wolf decided. "But this bird's goin' to be out of it—the dirty double-crosser. Come on—move along an' we'll put him on the spot."

"How about finishin' him right here?" growled a mobsman.

"Farther along," rejoined Wolf. "Too near the main road here. We'll cut over through the country. Leave it to me—I'll give him the bump."

Men leaped back into the cars. The caravan started. Graham Wellerton, pinned by two men, was huddled in the back seat of the first sedan. Wolf Daggert, his revolver threatening, crouched on the floor directly in front of the prisoner.

As the cars rolled along, Graham began to realize his predicament. He knew that his only hope for life lay in turning the men against Wolf Daggert. With an opportunity to talk, he might be able to swing the tide the other way. But Wolf's revolver made him wary. If Graham began to argue, Wolf would shoot. That was obvious.

"Keep lookin' for a good spot," growled Wolf, to the man at the wheel. "Somewhere that'll do to dump this double-crosser after I plug him."

"Here's the place," rejoined the driver. "Right ahead."

A snarling laugh came from Wolf Daggert's lips as the gang leader peered over the front seat. The lights of the sedan showed a twisting, slanting road, an embankment on the left; a ravine on the right.

"Ease up," ordered Wolf. "Here's where he goes out."

As the driver applied the brakes, Graham Wellerton did the unexpected. The mobsman on his right was opening the side door of the sedan. With a sudden leap, Graham broke free from his captors and dived in that direction.

Hands clutched furiously as Graham hurled himself against the door. The car was traveling at less than thirty miles an hour when the barrier burst open and Graham Wellerton paused momentarily upon the brink, while the man closest to him made a wild grab to stop his escape.

Turning his body, Graham delivered a swift punch squarely in his captor's face. At the same instant, Wolf Daggert swung to aim his revolver at the maddened prisoner. Momentarily freed, Graham lost his balance. With a startled shout, he launched from the car, just as Wolf fired two rapid shots.

IT was impossible for Wolf to tell whether or not his bullets had gone home. Graham's hurtling form had struck the turf at the top of the embankment. From the car, stopped within a dozen yards, Wolf could see the flying form traveling in long bounds down the side of the rough ravine. The other cars had halted.

Mobster eyes were watching the body of Graham Wellerton as swift momentum carried it to the bottom of the gulch. The form of the ex-gang leader crashed into a thick clump of brush. As it disappeared, saplings wavered in the moonlight, indicative of the force with which the body had struck.

"Looks like you got him, Wolf," laughed a mobster.

"Yeah," agreed the gang leader. "I fired close enough, but he was on his way. Maybe one of you guys had better go down there an' make sure."

There were no volunteers. At spots, the sides of the sloping ravine were precipitous. Both descent and return would be difficult. Graham's body had ended its wild trip more than one hundred feet away.

"Car comin' this way," informed the mobster at the wheel. "See the lights?"

Wolf observed a tiny gleam from a turn in the road a quarter of a mile ahead. The approaching car went out of sight as it took another bend. Its arrival here would occur within another minute.

"Get goin'," growled Wolf.

The sedan started. The other cars followed promptly. The three automobiles passed the approaching machine. Apparently, Wolf's car was merely a vehicle that was hogging the narrow road and slowing up two cars behind it.

"Keep on," ordered Wolf. "We don't want no trouble. That guy that we just passed won't suspect nothin'. It's a sure bet that Wellerton got the works."

"That trip he took didn't do him no good," laughed one of the mobsters. "It don't matter whether you gave him any lead or not."

"I plugged him," decided Wolf, beginning to resent any doubts regarding his marksmanship. "Give him two bullets. One's enough when I use the gat."

THE cars were speeding onward. The leading driver was talking about the best way to reach a main road. Graham Wellerton was a matter of the past. Wolf Daggert was the leader now.

"We're in no hurry," declared the gang leader. "We'll go ahead with the job Wellerton planned. That bank in Grand Rapids will be our gravy—and you can bet nobody's going to interfere. Wellerton saw to that."

This was the only intimation which Wolf Daggert delivered regarding the menace of The Shadow. There was a positiveness in the gang leader's tone. He knew that The Shadow had been in New York; that King Furzman—the only man who had known Graham Wellerton's plans—was dead.

The Shadow!

Wolf chuckled in the assurance that the black-clad phantom would not be on hand to spoil the robbery that lay ahead. He, Wolf Daggert, had profited by Graham Wellerton's schemes. Not for an instant did Wolf suspect the truth.

Graham Wellerton's foray was already doomed to failure. This mob of New York bank robbers was traveling directly into a trap which would be well set when they arrived.

The Shadow was already in Grand Rapids, awaiting Graham Wellerton's mob. He would receive the enemy tomorrow night. The change of leadership would make no difference.

Wolf Daggert, by usurping the power which Graham Wellerton had possessed, was directing a crew of hardened mobsters into The Shadow's snare!

In plunging from the moving sedan, Graham Wellerton had merely chosen a present danger in lieu of one which he would have unwittingly encountered had he traveled on with a mob at his command.

The trip into the depths of the obscure ravine was a much more desirable experience than the foray on the Grand Rapids bank—although Graham Wellerton had no cognizance of the fact.

Wolf Daggert, triumphant, was in a much less desirable position than Graham Wellerton, vanquished. Wolf was gloating over his victory. His evil joy would cease tomorrow night.

The Shadow would be responsible for that! Mobsmen had chosen a new leadership. The result would be the same—a futile surge against the hidden might of The Shadow!

CHAPTER IX
A MAN FROM THE PAST

GRAHAM WELLERTON opened his eyes. He found himself staring straight upward into moonlight. He was lying on a matting of thick grass, fringed by clusters of scrubby bushes and light saplings. The gurgle of a brook was sounding in his ears.

At first, Graham had no recollection of how he had reached this spot. A medley of scattered thoughts ached through his brain: King Furzman—Wolf Daggert—Carma—these three who had played a part in his career of crime seemed somehow responsible for his present plight.

Graham tried to collect his ideas into a reasoned process, but failed in the attempt. Somehow, he realized that he was no longer working for King Furzman; he also seemed to know that Wolf Daggert had caused him trouble. These thoughts were disturbing, but through them, Graham had a vague belief that all that might have happened had at least freed him from Carma.

Unsteadily, Graham managed to rise to his feet. He experienced a sickening sensation and a pain in the back of his head. He rubbed his face; dimly, in the moonlight, he saw blood upon his hand. Moving weakly toward the brook, Graham stooped and began to bathe his face in water.

This experience was refreshing; nevertheless, Graham had difficulty in remembering recent events.

One impression stood out; that of a wild leap from a traveling automobile. Responding to the thought, Graham began to feel his arms and legs as though expecting to find some broken bones.

Revolver shots! They had come with that leap. Graham smiled weakly. He had escaped the death that was intended for him. He had fallen far; he had crashed through snapping boughs and scratching brambles; but he was still alive. There was satisfaction in the thought.

Mechanically, the young man forced his way through a mass of bushes and came to the side of the ravine. He picked his way up the steep ascent, gripping clumps of thick, dry grass, slipping and tottering at times as he made the climb. At times, he caught hold of projecting chunks of rock. His fall down the ravine had been fortunate in that he had escaped these.

Graham sank exhausted when he reached the brink beside the road. He felt many aches. The climb had been a painful one. The jarring effects of the fall were apparent. Graham had a slight limp as he regained his feet and started to walk along the road; but the trouble departed as he continued.

Actually, the young man was suffering from a slight concussion of the brain, caused by one of the jolts that he had experienced. This injury, while it curbed his mental processes, made him oblivious to the minor hurts which he had sustained.

LIMPING and bleeding from small wounds, his face bearing livid scratches, Graham Wellerton made a sad appearance as he trudged along on a meaningless quest. He was a natty gentleman of crime no longer; he looked like a battered rowdy who had emerged from a strenuous brawl.

Hazily, Graham recognized his plight. He was somewhere in a rural district, illy clad and away from the help of friends. For the first time, Graham's thoughts pertained to money, and he shoved his hand into the pocket where he had carried a roll of more than six thousand dollars. It was empty.

Startled, Graham came to a halt. He turned to head aimlessly back toward the ravine; then came a momentary burst of memory.

He recalled himself as a captive in an automobile; he remembered a captor seated beside him. That was where the money had gone. One of his former associates had frisked his pocket after Wolf Daggert had decreed his death.

Graham Wellerton did not have a dime. He laughed hoarsely and began to trudge onward. After a mile of long, winding road, he came to a crossroad and stared gloomily at the signpost. He noted names there and repeated them in a familiar tone; then, while his thoughts were still confused, he turned to the left and began to walk along.

Where was he going? Why?

Graham did not know. He knew that he was miles from the main road where Wolf Daggert had overtaken the marauding band. He could recall that event now. But he had no desire to go back to the main highway. He was following this little-used road in response to some peculiar awakening of long-forgotten memory.

Another crossing. By the moonlight, Graham Wellerton read a new sign and laughed. He resumed his progress. As he reached a fork, he instinctively took the road to the right. He seemed to recall events of long ago, when hiking had been his hobby.

Steady tramping became monotonous. Not once did Graham Wellerton desist from his steady, plodding pace as he covered weary miles. A predominating purpose was banging in the back of his head. He was going somewhere; he would not stop until he arrived. His whole condition was governed by a mental cloud.

Minutes became hours. Graham, was indifferent to the passage of time. At last he struck a macadamized road and breathed a long sigh of relief. This long tramp had been a weary experience; without knowing it, Graham had covered a distance of nearly twenty miles; but the journey seemed to be nearing a logical end.

A picket fence showed on the right. Dull moonlight revealed a grilled gateway. Graham Wellerton stopped and peered through the upright bars of the gate.

Gray tombstones, whitened by the shimmering light, showed the place to be a cemetery. Graham felt a desire to enter the graveyard—why, he did not know. The iron gate resisted his feeble efforts to open it. Desisting, Graham continued his course along the road.

This time a wooden fence stopped him. He looked upon the expanse of an old abandoned racetrack. He wanted to climb that fence; to run around the half-mile oval. Weariness, coming with increased recognition, caused him to change his mind. He resumed his roadway plodding.

He passed houses set back behind rows of evenly-planted trees. He found himself entering the main street of a town, where occasional lights shone from overhead. Then came a sound that made him stop and listen intently. A loud-chimed clock was tolling the hour of four.

EACH reverberation of the beating gong was a driving stroke in Graham Wellerton's brain. Surging recollections came in furious deluge.

Quickening his pace, the dazed man moved along the street. He began to eye buildings that seemed familiar. He turned a corner down another lighted street. He came to a building that stood apart. It looked like a large store; but its barred windows proved that it must serve some other purpose.

Graham Wellerton read a large-lettered sign above the building. The words were plain in the light from the street. An angry scowl came to Graham's face as he saw the legend:

EZRA TALBOY
STATE BANK

The irony of the present moment came clearly to Graham's mind. Clouds lifted. He understood. Until this minute, he had not realized in what part of the country he might be; he had known only that he was somewhere between New York and Grand Rapids. Now he knew that he was in the town of Southwark.

Every important incident since the ravine was suddenly explained. The first signpost had pointed to the town of Southwar; so had the next. Then

Graham had found himself upon a familiar road. He had followed the natural direction of his boyhood hikes, back to the town of Southwark.

The cemetery—that was where he had so often visited his mother's grave. The racetrack—that was where he had run races with his boyhood companions. This building had been his father's bank. The house beyond it was Graham's old home.

The name of Ezra Talboy signified the truth which Graham had learned while absent from the town of Southwark. Ezra Talboy, brother of Graham's mother, had swindled Graham's father of all he owned. Well did Graham remember his sour-faced uncle. Ezra Talboy must be an old man by this time—a mean-hearted skinflint living on ill-gained wealth.

GRAHAM WELLERTON clenched his fists as he approached the bank building. His head was no longer swimming. He had regained his normal faculties. He wanted to smash through the grated windows. He reached in his pocket to feel for his revolver. It was gone. The weapon had been stolen also.

Surging wrath, unquenchable hatred—these were the elements which ruled Graham Wellerton. He despised this town of Southwark, hated every person who lived within its limits. He had a mad desire to do damage here, coupled with a wish to leave the town as soon as possible.

While Graham hesitated between these mixed emotions, a footstep sounded behind him. Graham turned quickly to find himself facing a burly man in uniform, who held a leveled revolver.

"What you doing here?" the man demanded.

"Nothing," retorted Graham huskily. "Just looking around."

"Yeah? At four o'clock in the morning?"

"I just landed in town. Motor accident out on the road—"

"Tell that to the Judge. I'm pinching you. Come along!"

Complete weariness was having its effect. Without a word, Graham Wellerton submitted to the officer's order. He found himself marching back toward the main street, down an alleyway to the old town jail. The journey ended when Graham collapsed upon a battered cot in a barred cell.

When the officer had left, Graham rolled over wearily upon the cot. His long tramp showed its results. Forgetful of all but fatigue, Graham Wellerton fell asleep. The brightness of morning was the next waking impression that he gained.

SOMEONE was shaking the barred door. Graham looked up to see the man who had arrested him. The officer ordered him to come along. Graham obeyed. He was taken into a small courtroom where a handful of men were gathered.

Graham recognized the justice of the peace. Old Silas Schuble had been his father's friend. He noted another elderly man whom he knew: Harwin Dowser, Southwark's principal lawyer. Dowser was evidently here to take up some other case, for he did not express interest as Graham was brought up before Justice Schuble.

"Vagrancy is the charge," said the officer who had brought Graham to the courtroom. "I found this man wandering around the town at four in the morning.

"Name?" quizzed Schuble, sharply, looking at Graham.

"George Gruger," said Graham quietly.

"What defense do you offer?" quizzed the justice.

"None," returned Graham, in a dull tone. "I was just hiking through town."

Schuble eyed the young man sharply. Graham repressed a smile when he noted that the justice did not recognize him. To Graham, that was an achievement. His memory of his father had touched his pride. He did not want to be recognized while in Southwark.

"Unless you can give some account for your presence here," declared Schuble severely, "I shall be forced to sentence you for vagrancy."

"I don't mind," returned Graham.

"Thirty days in jail," decreed the justice.

As the officer led him from the courtroom, Graham noted that Harwin Dowser was eying him curiously. Graham met the lawyer's gaze with an indifferent glance. Dowser turned away. Moodily, Graham, allowed himself to be conducted back to his cell.

Much though he detested the town of Southwark, he was to be its guest for the coming month. The irony of the situation was impressive on that bright morning. Graham could not help but smile.

He had escaped the law on many occasions when he had been engaged in dangerous crime; this time, when he had been committing no offense, he had been arrested and sentenced.

Graham felt his hatred for the town of Southwark increasing beyond its former measure. He realized that he was a man from the past, a stranger no longer recognized in the town where his father once had been the most prominent citizen.

Whatever his career elsewhere might have been, Graham had never done a wrong within the bounds of Southwark. Yet this was his reward—in the one place where he had lived an honest life.

Graham Wellerton had come home after years

of wandering. Unwelcomed, unrecognized, he had been sentenced to jail on a charge of vagrancy. Graham Wellerton did not care. His mob had gone over to Wolf Daggert—that connection was ended.

As for Carma, Southwark was the last place in all the world where she would look for Graham!

CHAPTER X
THE SAMARITAN

Two dozen men were tramping along a rough road. Behind them came three others, armed with rifles. A command sounded from the rear; the gang fell out at the side of the road. One of the guards opened a huge box that was standing beside a tree. Each of the two dozen men advanced in turn to take out a pick.

Methodically, the road gang fell to work. Under the watchful eyes of the armed guards, these prisoners began their daily toil. Pick points clicked upon stone. Snatches of conversation began.

Road work in this county was no sinecure, yet it lacked the barbarity so popularly supposed to dominate all chain gangs. Two dozen short-term prisoners, under the supervision of several competent guards, were allowed reasonable privileges so long as they kept busy with their picks. Graham Wellerton, drafted to this toil, found it an annoyance rather than a hardship. He was in his fifth day of service and he had taken his temporary fate in a philosophical manner.

He paid very little attention to words uttered by the other prisoners, but today, something that he heard made him listen for further information.

"Out in Grand Rapids," one man was saying. "The paper that I seen was a coupla days old—"

A pick clicked in interruption. Then came a question that told more.

"You say the cops plugged seven of 'em?" a man was asking. "Didn't none of 'em get away?"

"It wasn't the cops," Graham heard. "That's the funny part of it. When the holdup started—"

Words were intermittent as they came to Graham's ears, but the young man caught the important details of the story as he labored away with his pick.

A squad of armed marauders had entered the Riverview Trust in Grand Rapids, a few nights ago. Before they had been able to engineer the holdup, shots had broken loose. The sight of dropping raiders was the first token of the contemplated robbery.

The shots had been delivered from the semi-darkness of the street. Mobsmen had started to flee; they had been shot down. Others had dashed into the bank to be met by watchmen and tellers. Police had arrived to find seven victims.

It seemed that mutiny must have broken out in the ranks of the raiders during the crucial moments of the attack. There was no other explanation for the startling result. The case was a baffling one.

GRAHAM WELLERTON was grim as he swung the pick. He knew the answer to this frustrated crime. The broken attack was a repetition of the Parkerside disaster in New York, where Wolf Daggert and his henchmen had been repulsed.

The Shadow!

Somehow, that master of crime detection had learned Graham's schemes. He had arrived in Grand Rapids ahead of the raiders. Had Graham still been in command of his men, he would have gone down with his mobsters.

Graham chuckled in sarcastic fashion. He realized now that Wolf Daggert had done him a good turn. By usurping the leadership, Wolf had put himself in a mess. The evil-faced gang leader had walked into the trap intended for Graham.

Seven men in the gang. Graham made a mental calculation. His own men had numbered nine. Wolf, with Garry, made two more—a total of eleven. That left four at large. Graham growled his contempt of the situation.

He was glad that three of the four had escaped; but he was positive that he knew the identity of the fourth man—Wolf Daggert himself. The cowardly gang leader had played his old trick of staying back with a few reserves while the main mob attacked.

"Around the corner," muttered Graham. "That's where he was—the yellow cur."

As Graham marveled at The Shadow's skillful cunning, he realized that Wolf had been in luck. The Shadow had been expecting a mob headed by Graham Wellerton—a leader who went with the advance. The Shadow had arranged to break up such an attack.

Instead of Graham, Wolf had appeared as leader—if he rightfully deserved such a title. Wolf's idea of leadership was to lurk until the flight began; then to lead the way. That was why Wolf had escaped The Shadow.

Nevertheless, Wolf had failed; his present predicament was as bad a one as Graham's.

Swinging his pick automatically, Graham Wellerton considered all angles of the case. He realized that when he finished his thirty-day term, he would have to choose a new course of action. A fresh start in crime—that seemed the only possibility. As he labored, Graham found himself in a dilemma.

Crime, now that he was temporarily away from it, seemed a sordid, futile existence. On the contrary, any course that would fit in with recognized ways of society was just as distasteful.

Why should he, Graham Wellerton, attempt to live a law-abiding life? Justice—as the world saw it—was not to his liking. The young man thought of his uncle, Ezra Talboy.

There, he decided, was a man as crooked as they made them—a swindler, a thief, a heartless wretch. Yet Ezra Talboy, by staying within the rules set by law, had gained full title to the wealth and prestige which he had actually stolen from Graham's father.

GRAHAM'S own plight soured him further. Here, with the road gang, he was paying a penalty demanded by so-called justice. He was serving a short term for vagrancy—his only crime having been the instinct of self-preservation.

He had come to Southwark in a dazed condition, a fit subject for human kindness. He had been seized by an officer anxious to make an arrest. He had been committed to jail in a cold-hearted fashion.

"Hey, there, Gruger!"

The repeated call from one of the guards caused Graham to suddenly realize that the shout was for him. He stopped his work and turned around.

"Don't you know your own name?" questioned the guard.

"I'd sort of forgotten it," responded Graham with a sheepish smile.

"Fall out with the rest of the gang," ordered the guard.

Graham saw that the prisoners had quit their work and were enjoying temporary respite as they sat along a grassy embankment beside the road. Graham joined his companions. While two guards, rifles ready, were on watch, the third was talking with a stranger who had alighted from an automobile.

"That's Ralph Delkin," one of the prisoners was saying, in a low tone. "Big manufacturer down in Southwark."

"What's he doin' here?" asked another prisoner.

"He's on some county committee," came the explanation. "Supposed to check up on the road gangs."

"To see that we keep grindin', huh?"

"No. They say Delkin's a good egg. Won't stand for no rough stuff. You notice they gave us a layoff when he showed up? That guy won't stand for no meanness."

"Say—who's the Jane with him—the kid comin' over from the car?"

"His daughter, I guess."

Graham Wellerton was looking in the direction indicated. He remembered Ralph Delkin from years ago. He noted that time had not greatly changed the man.

In appearance, Delkin was stern and square-jawed; in action, brusque and businesslike. There was an air about him that symbolized the real type of man.

Delkin, Graham estimated, must now be about forty-five years of age. The girl who was approaching him was certainly his daughter. Graham remembered her as a child—Eunice Delkin. She was now in her early twenties and Graham, as he watched her, was impressed with her beauty.

Ralph Delkin was looking along the row of prisoners. His practiced eye was studying each face. His purpose was apparent; he was here to pick out any who might have cause for protest at harsh treatment which had been received.

GRAHAM noticed that Eunice followed her father's gaze. There was a frankness in her expression that made each toughened prisoner feel sheepish. Until she came to Graham, Eunice met only wavering glances; but as she looked at the former gentleman of crime, something in Graham's cold stare caused her to steadily return the gaze.

Graham Wellerton smiled disdainfully. Eunice Delkin was beautiful; her light hair, her frank eyes—these were the features which most impressed him. But Graham could not help but compare her lot with his own.

His father—like hers—had been a prominent citizen of Southwark. But he, Graham Wellerton, was an outcast, sentenced to the road gang by so-called justice, while she, protected by her father's high standing in the community, had never been forced to experience the harsher side of life.

Ralph Delkin was turning away. He spoke to his daughter. Still glancing at Graham Wellerton, Eunice plucked her father's sleeve and spoke. Delkin turned and looked at Graham. His eyes became puzzled. He spoke to the guard. The man replied; then looked toward Graham and beckoned.

Rising, Graham slouched forward, still wearing his challenging smile. As he neared the little group, Delkin advanced and spoke to him in a low tone.

"You're Graham Wellerton, aren't you?" asked Delkin.

"My name is Gruger," retorted Graham, loud enough for Eunice and the guard to hear. "George Gruger."

Ralph Delkin looked at this daughter as though there must be some mistake.

The girl shook her head emphatically. She looked squarely at Graham.

"He didn't know his name was Gruger a few minutes ago," said the guard. "I had to holler at him three times."

"This man," said Eunice quietly, "is Graham Wellerton. There is no question about it. I remember him."

The even modulation of the girl's tone was convincing. Her voice was kindly; her attitude was friendly. Graham was forced to assume a gruff indifference in order to meet this positive statement of his identity.

"What of it?" he questioned. "Suppose I am Graham Wellerton? What's that to anyone around here?"

Ralph Delkin extended his hand. Graham turned quickly to pretend that he did not see the gesture. His eyes were toward the other prisoners as he heard Ralph Delkin speak.

"Your father," said Delkin, "was my friend. I am your friend, Graham."

With a shrug of his shoulders, Graham stalked away toward the other prisoners. He did not want Delkin's friendship. Nevertheless, he could not stand and face a man who offered him a handshake; nor could he look into the frank eyes of a girl who had picked him out as his father's son from among two dozen criminals.

When Graham Wellerton reached the embankment and finally turned about, Ralph Delkin and his daughter were walking back to the automobile. Graham laughed roughly. He felt that he had forestalled this one advance of friendship.

At the noon hour, however, when a car arrived with lunch for the prisoners, Graham was informed that he was to go back to Southwark. Figuring that his term on the road gang was ended, he boarded the automobile and sat in the back seat with a hard-faced man who never said a word.

Graham knew this fellow. Ellis Taussig was his name; he had been county sheriff ever since Graham's boyhood. Southwark was the county seat; and Taussig had evidently come up from there.

The car reached the town and pulled up beside the courthouse. Taussig ordered Graham to alight.

Instead of leading the young man toward the jail, he took him into the courthouse. They walked through a corridor and reached a small room. As Graham entered, he was quick to recognize the people there.

JUSTICE SCHUBLE—Harwin Dowser, the lawyer—these were the first two whom Graham Wellerton noticed. Then he saw another pair: Ralph Delkin and his daughter, Eunice. Graham hesitated; Sheriff Taussig pushed him forward.

Justice Schuble spoke. His tone was an inquiry as he looked at the young man before him.

"You are Graham Wellerton?" he questioned.

"Yes," admitted Graham, with a defiant glance.

"Since I have been informed correctly," declared Schuble, "I shall immediately arrange your release. I sentenced you for vagrancy purely because you refused to give a reason for your presence in the town of Southwark. As a former member of this community, you are entitled to your freedom here."

"You are making a mistake," retorted Graham coldly. "I have no business in Southwark. Much though I detest the town, I was unjustly forced to be its guest for a period of thirty days. I have no money; I have nowhere to live. Therefore you will be forced to arrest me again for vagrancy.

"After the thirty days—or as many more as you choose to give me—have ended, I intend to leave this contemptible district where thieves are honored and rogues hold office—"

Graham broke into a sneering laugh as he saw the furious expression on Justice Schuble's face. Harwin Dowser, evidently here in Graham's behalf, sprang forward to make a plea that the young man's contempt be overlooked. Sheriff Taussig and Ralph Delkin did not know what to say. It was Eunice who solved the problem.

Stepping forward, the girl looked squarely into Graham's eyes. Her expression of disapproval was one that caused Graham to end his condemning statements. Then, turning to the justice, Eunice made the winning plea.

"Please forget this outburst," the girl said. "Graham does not realize what he is saying. He will not be a vagrant while he is here in Southwark. My father and I are inviting him to live at our home. He should have been informed of that before his release was mentioned."

"Very well," decided Schuble. "I shall overlook the contempt which has been expressed. I am releasing Graham Wellerton in the custody of Ralph Delkin."

It was Eunice, again, who ended all objections. Before her father could step forward, she had extended her hand to Graham. The young man was too stupefied to exhibit the discourtesy which he had shown to Ralph Delkin that morning. Mechanically, he shook hands with Eunice; then received the clasp which Ralph Delkin extended.

THE Delkins took Graham in their automobile. When they arrived at the house, Delkin remarked that he would make arrangements for new apparel and whatever else Graham might require. He added that there would be a job for Graham in the plant. It was then that Graham regained his challenging air.

"You're going to a lot of useless trouble, both of you," he asserted. "I don't want your friendship. I hate Southwark, and I have no regard for anyone who lives here. If you think that you are doing me a kind turn, you are wrong. If you insist upon my remaining here, I can tell you in advance that you will be sorry."

"Don't talk that way, Graham," responded Delkin, in a kindly tone. "My friendship toward you is a real one—"

"Graham will learn that, father," interposed Eunice. "He will appreciate our sentiment. He will learn to like it here."

Graham Wellerton made no remark. He was prepared to resist any display of friendship that came from Ralph Delkin, but he could not force himself into an argument with the girl who had persuaded her father to do him this kind turn.

Graham's silence indicated that he was willing to remain. Without further discussion, Ralph Delkin conducted his resentful guest to the room which had been provided for him. Thus did Graham Wellerton begin a new term of residence in the town where he had spent his boyhood.

Ralph Delkin, at Eunice's behest, had played the part of good Samaritan. He had accepted Graham Wellerton in memory of the young man's father. Little did he suspect that he was sheltering a man who had but recently been the leader of a band of desperate crooks.

To Graham Wellerton, a short stay at Delkin's home would prove acceptable purely as a period of recuperation. In his heart, the man who had returned to Southwark was planning a new career of crime.

For the present, only, he was accepting the conditions imposed upon him. In his heart, he carried no thanks toward the people who had shown him friendship.

Soon he would go his way again. With a new start, he would take up crime with a spirit of vindictiveness. Alone, Graham Wellerton smiled grimly as he thought of the past. Wolf Daggert would be out of his life; Carma would never find him.

There was only one person whom Graham Wellerton considered as a menace. That one was the strange, unknown being called The Shadow.

What did The Shadow matter? Graham was sure that he could travel beyond the reach of the master of crime.

In that surmise, Graham Wellerton was wrong. The Shadow, weird and mysterious, was to play an unexpected part in events which were already shaping Graham Wellerton's destiny.

CHAPTER XI
THE SHADOW SUSPECTS

DAYS had passed since Graham Wellerton's arrival in Southwark. Days had drifted into weeks. Freed from the necessity of crime, Graham Wellerton had entered a period of restful recuperation. He had, through misfortune, gained security which he would not have known had he met The Shadow face to face.

Had Graham Wellerton been leader of the band which The Shadow had encountered in Grand Rapids, the depredations of the holdup gangs would have been ended. The Shadow, after his forced elimination of King Furzman, had dealt a terrific stroke against the foes of the law.

Yet crime had known only a brief interlude. New events had arisen in the Middle West, to inform the warring master that his final stroke had not been one of complete elimination. Facts, in the form of newspaper clippings, were proof that work still lay ahead.

In a high floor of a New York office building, a chubby-faced, lethargic man was sitting at a desk, studying newspapers that lay before him. This quiet individual, Rutledge Mann by name, was known to his friends as an investment broker. Actually, however, Mann served as contact agent for The Shadow and one of his duties was the assembling of printed crime news.

Clipping as he perused the out-of-town newspapers, Mann had assembled a small heap of items pertaining to successful raids made by bank robbers in small towns of the Middle West. As he put the clippings into an envelope, Mann leaned back in his chair and stared idly from the window.

The towers of Manhattan did not attract Mann's eye. The investment broker was lost in thought. He was speculating on affairs which concerned The Shadow. This was a relaxation in which Mann seldom indulged; but recent events had caused him to wonder just what lay behind the present chain of circumstances.

By his constant reading of the newspapers, Mann had learned to detect the hidden presence of The Shadow in many instances. Of The Shadow himself, Rutledge Mann knew very little. The investment broker merely supplied information and handled detail work for his unknown master. But whenever Mann discovered the unusual in the news, he could sense that The Shadow had loosed his hand against those opposed to the law.

There had been bank robberies in New York. One raid had been shattered on the same day that another had succeeded. Then such raids had ceased in the East.

The next occurrence had been an attempted

holdup in Grand Rapids—one which had been mysteriously foiled.

Mann, reading between the lines, decided that The Shadow had accomplished that deed and had terminated the outrages of successful robbers who had headed West from New York.

So far—good. But what of the intermittent robberies in small towns—the work of a few men—that had been occurring since?

Mann again picked out a reason. A few of the last gang must still be at large, committing depredations on a small and stealthy scale.

Shortly after sending the first notices of such robberies to The Shadow, Mann had received word to communicate with Harry Vincent, one of The Shadow's active agents. Mann had given Harry a sealed envelope which had come by mail from The Shadow. Mann knew only that Harry

... Harwin Dowser sprang forward to make a plea ...

was to go to a town called Southwark, to make certain investigations.

What did Southwark have to do with the bank robberies? Most of them were in the vicinity of that town—in fact, today's clippings told of raiders breaking into a bank not more than fifty miles from the town where Harry Vincent was stationed.

But why had The Shadow singled out Southwark as a headquarters for his agent? That problem completely perplexed Rutledge Mann.

The investment broker sealed his envelope of clippings. He walked into an outer office. There, the stenographer handed him a letter which had just arrived in the mail. It bore the postmark of Southwark. Mann ripped open the envelope and found another envelope within. A special report from Harry Vincent.

Leaving his office, Mann went to the street and took a taxicab to Twenty-third Street. He entered a dilapidated building, ascended an old stairway and approached a battered door on a floor above the street.

This door had a grimy glass panel; on it was inscribed the name of "Jonas."

Rutledge Mann poked the envelope of clippings through the mail chute; he followed it with Harry Vincent's envelope. With a last glance at the cobwebbed glass panel, the investment broker departed.

This unusual office served as The Shadow's letter box. Apparently, it had been vacant for some years. Mann, in all his visits, had never observed signs of occupancy. All letters which Mann placed there, however, eventually reached their desired recipient—The Shadow.

A FEW hours after Mann had made his visit to the office on Twenty-third Street, a click sounded in a pitch-black room. Light replaced darkness. The illumination came from a weird blue lamp that hung, shaded, above the polished surface of a table.

The rays of light seemed to fade as they encountered the thick darkness beyond that limited area. One luminous circle was all that pervaded this room. Heavy, gloomy atmosphere cast a dominating awe.

Out of darkness came two white, creeping objects. They were hands—human hands, lithe and long-fingered—that moved like detached creatures of life. They rested within the circle of light. Alike in formation, they differed in one point only.

From the third finger of the left hand gleamed a flaming jewel. Like a living coal of fire, it flashed glimmering sparkles upward from mysterious depths.

Somber maroon in its original color, the stone turned to a brilliant purple; then faded to a pale azure that sent forth leaping sparks of brilliant, uncanny light.

This gem was the token of The Shadow. It was a priceless girasol, a rare jewel unmatched in all the world. Its weird hues symbolized the mysterious personality of the amazing being who wore it. Moreover, the gem gained strange effects from the ghoulish light that shone from above.

As the color-changing girasol told the identity of its wearer, so did the bluish light from the lamp reveal the place where the master of mystery now was stationed.

The Shadow was in his sanctum—an unknown abode somewhere in Manhattan—a mysterious room of blackness where no other than himself had ever been!

One hand moved away. It returned and dropped envelopes upon the table. Some had been opened previously.

From them now came clippings—accumulated references supplied by Rutledge Mann. Two sealed envelopes were torn open by the strong but slender fingers. These were the envelopes which Rutledge Mann had so recently placed in the mail chute of the office on Twenty-third Street.

The eyes of The Shadow—eyes hidden in darkness beyond the lamp—studied the clippings. The hands added them to the former items.

Then came Harry Vincent's report sheet. It was a concise message, written in code. The Shadow read the inked words as rapidly as if they had been in ordinary writing.

Hardly had the invisible eyes completed their perusal before the written words began to fade one by one.

This was an expected phenomenon. In all communications to and from The Shadow, the agents used a special type of ink which vanished shortly after being exposed to the air. Through its agency, all messages were automatically destroyed. Any that fell into wrong hands would be gone before they could be deciphered.

A low laugh sounded from the gloom. The Shadow was considering the message from his agent. Harry Vincent had done well in Southwark. Yet his findings had produced a problem which even The Shadow had not anticipated!

THE SHADOW, in his trip to Grand Rapids, had struck a powerful blow against a band of raiders supposedly led by Graham Wellerton. The Shadow knew that the leader—and a few men with him—had managed to escape purely by staying in the background while the main body invaded.

Summoned back to New York by important errands there, The Shadow had been awaiting developments, knowing that the missing crooks would bob up somewhere. Minor bank raids had come of evidence of their activity this side of Grand Rapids.

The Shadow had ordered Harry Vincent to the territory, to glean preliminary information. Not long ago, The Shadow had heard Graham Wellerton tell Carma that he would never go back to the town of Southwark. That had been when Graham was on the crest of successful crime. Now, with circumstances altered, Graham might deliberately have changed his former decision. Southwark, of all places, might best serve as a temporary refuge.

Here was the report from Harry Vincent. The Shadow's agent had discovered Graham Wellerton in Southwark. But in his careful inquiry—Harry was an ace when it came to getting information in strange towns—he had learned that Graham had arrived there the night before the Michigan bank raid had been foiled by The Shadow!

This was the reason for The Shadow's laugh. Weird mockery seemed to hover within that black-walled room. Ghoulish echoes persisted even after hidden lips had ceased their mirthful utterance.

The Shadow had corroborated a suspicion which had been lurking in his intuitive brain—namely that Graham Wellerton had not been with the bank robbers at Grand Rapids!

What was Graham Wellerton's purpose? How and why had the gentleman of crime parted from his men? Why was he no longer engaged in robbery?

These were questions which The Shadow was resolved to answer.

Hands reached across the table. Earphones came into view. A tiny bulb lighted, showing that The Shadow had formed a connection. His weird voice spoke in a whisper. Across the wire came a quiet reply:

"Burbank speaking."

Burbank was The Shadow's hidden contact man—the one who kept in touch with agents when they were at work. He was always accessible by telephone, to relay messages through to The Shadow.

"Report from Marsland," ordered The Shadow.

Burbank gave a brief reply. Cliff Marsland, The Shadow's agent who played the part of an underworld mobsman, had gained no trace of Wolf Daggert. He had been unable to find any clue to a hideout where the skulking gang leader might be staying.

"Report from Burke," demanded The Shadow.

Another reply. Burbank had heard from Clyde Burke, the newspaper reporter on the New York *Classic* who was in The Shadow's service.

Burke had been deputed to keep track of Carma Wellerton. He learned that she was living under the name of Carma Urstead, and that she was still in New York.

Communication ended with his contact agent, The Shadow performed a new action. His hands produced a large map and spread it on the table. The fingers placed tiny pins upon towns marked there—the places where small bank robberies had been attempted.

PROMINENT on the map was the town of Southwark. The trail was closing near that point. This one town would be a likely spot for another raid, if the robbers were still in that vicinity.

Was this of Graham Wellerton's making; or was the former leader free from crime—with chance bringing his henchmen to that district?

Whatever the case might be, The Shadow could see a trail as plainly as if it had been marked on the map. A hundred miles away from Grand Rapids, it formed a zigzag eastward. Southwark might well be in its path. Defeated marauders, beating their course back toward New York, were trying to glean profits by minor depredations.

The pins were drawn away. The map was folded by the hands. The bluish light went out with a resounding click. Through the pitch-black room came the sinister tones of a hollow laugh. Sneering tones of mirth broke into a jibing peal that changed to shuddering whispers.

Back came the eerie mirth in ghostly echoes from the walls. Again and again the reverberations answered, as though a goblin horde had cried to its master from the depths of unseen corridors.

When the last sibilant jeers had faded away, deep, heavy silence was all-pervading. The sanctum was empty. The Shadow had departed. The master of the night had left upon his errand to stamp out the last vestiges of broken crime.

CHAPTER XII
DELKIN CONFIDES

THAT same evening, Graham Wellerton was seated alone in the living room of Ralph Delkin's Southwark home. The former gentleman of crime was now a gentleman of leisure. Sprawled in a large chair, his feet stretched out on a comfortable stool, Graham Wellerton was reading a newspaper which he had selected from a stack beside him.

During his sojourn at Ralph Delkin's home, Graham had not turned his hand to a single bit of work. He had shown no inclination to do anything but loaf. Attired in new clothes which his benefactor had bought him, well-fed with sumptuous fare, he was living at ease and showing a constant indifference toward those who had befriended him.

Reading the newspaper, Graham found passing interest in the account of a small and rather unprofitable bank robbery which had been committed in a town not many miles from Southwark. Graham smiled. Wolf Daggert and his defeated minions were trying their luck on a small scale.

Graham wondered if Wolf were afraid to return to New York. Probably, Graham decided. After cracking a few more cribs, the skulking gang leader would probably head for a more profitable territory, but he would not be likely to show up in Manhattan for some time to come.

Graham could figure the system that Wolf was using. With three men at his command, the leader was making short, quick raids; then lying low, probably in some obscure section of the countryside. Graham wondered if, by any chance, Wolf and his men would visit Southwark.

This town would be a logical spot. The State bank, owned by Graham's uncle, Ezra Talboy, was a profit-making institution. The region surrounding Southwark was hilly and it possessed some isolated and abandoned strips of farmland. Hiding out—an art in which Wolf Daggert excelled—would be easy hereabouts.

Graham pondered. Much though he disliked the thought, it seemed wise to remain in Southwark for some time to come. It was the part of sanity to continue this life of leisure.

Graham realized that his own status was none too good in his hometown. While he lived quietly here at Delkin's, he was free from suspicion; but should he make a sudden departure, others might wonder.

What irony it would be if he should go away just prior to a chance raid by Wolf Daggert and his men. He, Graham Wellerton, might be suspected of criminal activity. Should Wolf Daggert be captured and questioned, a mere mention of Graham's name would cause the yellow gang leader to squeal.

With a past to protect, Graham decided that it would be best to lie low and wait until Wolf Daggert had departed from this district—or until something had happened to the skulking gang leader who had already caused Graham trouble.

Later, opportunity would arrive to leave. Graham had been looking forward to the time when he could safely leave Southwark. Yet, as he considered the matter now, that day seemed strangely remote. Growling to himself, Graham wondered if he were becoming soft—if the thought of future crime might be actually distasteful.

FLINGING the newspaper to the floor, Graham lighted a cigarette and stared upward at the ceiling. Analyzing himself, he was forced to the realization that he was not a crook at heart. For the first time in many months, necessity for crime was no longer existent, so far as Graham was concerned. The young man found himself regretful of his past.

Why? Graham angrily asked himself the reason. What influence had prevailed, here in Southwark, to bring Graham to such a realization?

Various reasons were possible. One by one, the young man rejected them. While Graham was in this state of mind, the real answer appeared. Eunice Delkin entered the room.

Graham stared moodily and gave no greeting as the girl sat down in a chair a short distance away. Despite the sullenness in his gaze, Graham found himself admitting that Eunice was more than merely attractive. She was beautiful; and the quiet smile which she gave Graham had an immediate effect.

The young man realized that he admired Eunice Delkin beyond all persons whom he had ever met before. The reason for his mental conflict regarding crime was now apparent.

In his heart, Graham was in love with Eunice Delkin. At the same time, he realized that insurmountable barriers made it impossible for him to express the sentiment which he felt.

His past—with its crime—that was bad enough. Had his career been the only obstacle, Graham might have seen a possibility toward future happiness. It would be possible, under proper circumstances, to make amends for deeds of crime. Graham had no money; there was no way of establishing himself, except through taking advantage of Ralph Delkin's friendship. Even that might lead to happiness; but a final barrier remained. Graham was thinking of Carma.

That marriage into which he had been tricked! It was the factor that made happiness impossible. Graham had never thought of Carma as his wife. To him she was still Carma Urstead, a gangster's moll who had worked deceit and profited thereby.

As he studied Eunice Delkin, Graham Wellerton admired her frank, understanding countenance. He thought of Carma Urstead, whose overpainted face always bore traces of a mean, selfish nature. If the past few years could only be obliterated! That was Graham's single thought.

Although Eunice Delkin did not know the thoughts that were passing in Graham's mind, she realized that something was troubling the young man. She smiled sympathetically. Graham, to cover his thoughts, mumbled in grouchy fashion as he puffed his cigarette.

"Are you worrying about anything, Graham?" questioned Eunice in a kindly tone.

"No," growled the young man. "What difference would it make, anyway?"

"A great deal," rejoined Eunice. "I should like to see you happy—to see you enjoying life here."

"Not much chance of that," retorted Graham. "I hate this town. Maybe you think I'm ungrateful toward you and your father. Maybe he wonders why I won't take a job in his factory, even after he showed me the plant and made me an offer. But I don't care. Think what you want about me."

"Would you like to know what I think about you?"

"Yes." Graham's tone was challenging. "Go ahead. Criticize me. Speak out."

"I think," declared Eunice gently, "that you have suffered greatly in the past. Your mind is overburdened by misfortune. You need friendship; and it must be given patiently, with no thought of a response on your part.

"The longer that you resist the kindness which my father and I are seeking to show you, the longer will I, at least, be patient with you. Life has treated you badly. It may take many months for old wounds to heal. I am determined, however, that you will some day appreciate our friendship and come to remember it as the real brightness in your life."

Graham Wellerton had no reply. One word of criticism might have brought an outburst; but he realized that it was impossible to argue with one so fair-minded as Eunice Delkin. The young man sat in silence. Feelings of hatred surged through his brain; but they were all directed toward himself.

DURING this long pause, while Graham Wellerton was coming to stern realization of his past mistakes, Ralph Delkin entered the living room. Eunice arose to greet her father. Delkin kissed his daughter; then spoke in a serious tone.

"I should like to talk to Graham," he said. "Alone. You do not mind leaving—"

"What is the trouble, daddy?" questioned Eunice, in a tone of apprehension.

"I can tell you later, darling," responded Delkin. "For the present"—the man's tone was worried—"I would rather talk with Graham."

Nodding, the girl left the living room. The door closed behind her.

Ralph Delkin turned to Graham Wellerton. The young man was perplexed. He wondered if something had occurred to give his protector an inkling of his past. Delkin's first words, however, dispelled that idea.

"I'm in trouble, Graham," declared Delkin. "Something very unforeseen has arisen. I have to talk to someone."

"Thanks," returned Graham dryly.

Delkin did not note the sarcasm in the young man's tone. Pacing back and forth, the Southwark manufacturer wore a worried, doubtful air. Finally he turned and spoke again.

"Your uncle," he said to Graham, "is deliberately set to swindle me. Yet his means are fair—within the law."

"As Ezra Talboy's ways always are," interposed Graham.

"You mean your father's case," nodded Delkin. "Graham, that's why I'm talking to you. Ezra Talboy swindled your father. I have detested the man ever since. I have only done business with him under pressure. Now I have come to a point of regret.

"I needed money not long ago. Fifty thousand dollars. I wanted it to keep my plant open—to pay deserving men and let them work during a poor business period. I wanted to avert unemployment in Southwark.

"Ezra Talboy loaned me the money for three months, with a promise of renewal for another ninety days. I gave him the best security possible—my plant and its equipment, valued at more than a quarter of a million.

"I exhausted nearly all of the fifty thousand. I saw my business through the difficult period. The plant is now showing a slight profit. One month from now, it will be wiping out all deficits."

"But in the meantime," reminded Graham.

"That's it," admitted Delkin. "My notes are due within a few days. I dropped in to see Ezra Tallboy—to remind him of the extension. He has refused to give it."

"Which means?"

"That my entire plant passes into his control. I lose everything—all for fifty thousand dollars."

"Money which you do not have."

"Money which I paid to my faithful employees."

Graham Wellerton leaned back in his chair and emitted a raucous laugh. Ralph Delkin stood in amazement as he heard the young man's merriment.

"That's what comes from your folly, Delkin," jeered Graham. "You dealt with that old skinflint—although it was against good judgment. Why? To help out a lot of employees who should have been laid off. Your workmen have been living along at your expense. Now you are going to pay the piper.

"Gratitude! Where is it? What does it amount to? You brought me here—you insisted upon treating me well. I took your favors; and I warned you that I did not want them—that I would give you no return.

"If you expect advice from me, I have none to give. If you want sympathy or encouragement,

HARWIN DOWSER, wealthy and clever lawyer, who acts an important part as advisor to those implicated in this plot of crime and wealth.

those are lacking also. You deserve what you are getting—and it's coming from the chap that's most capable of giving it—Ezra Talboy."

RALPH DELKIN was frantic. Graham Wellerton's jeers had a double effect; they made the manufacturer angry and they also drove him to a state of pitiable hopelessness. Between these mingled emotions, Delkin paced across the room and half staggered from the door. Graham could hear his footsteps pounding up the stairs. The young man chuckled with evil glee.

Graham looked up to see Eunice Delkin standing beside him. The girl had entered the room silently. As her eyes met Graham's, Eunice put a question:

"What is the trouble with father?"

"Business," sneered Graham. "Misplaced trust. He is going to lose everything, because he was bighearted and believed what other people told him. I rubbed it in—I told him he was a fool. How do you like that? You've found cause to criticize me now, haven't you?"

"None at all," replied Eunice patiently. "I am sorry for you, Graham. Sorrier for you than I am for father. He and I can stand poverty. My only regret is that you will suffer also if we can give you a home no longer."

Quietly, the girl left the living room. Graham could hear her going upstairs to talk to her father. The young man found himself recalling the sincere words that Eunice had uttered. He began to fume—to curse himself for his own meanness. Rising from his chair, Graham walked about the room. His eyes fell upon the newspaper which he had dropped on the floor.

A determined sparkle came in Graham Wellerton's eye.

Crime!

He had abandoned that profession. He realized now that he would never be a crook again. But with a consummate desire to go straight came a willingness to once more participate in criminal activity.

Stealthily, Graham Wellerton donned hat and coat. He strolled out through the front door and stepped into darkness. The chill wind of the night was invigorating. It gave him a new impetus.

Once again—for the last time in his life, he decided—Graham Wellerton would play the part of a gentleman of crime.

CHAPTER XIII
THE ROBBERY

HEAVY winds were sweeping the deserted Southwark street as Graham Wellerton made stealthy progress away from Ralph Delkin's home. Storm clouds had gathered overhead; these added to the blackness of the faintly lighted byway chosen by Graham.

During his stay at Delkin's, Graham had left the house only on rare occasions, but his few excursions had been sufficient to refresh his memory regarding the streets of Southwark. Sidling through the night, Graham reached a road which led him toward Ralph Delkin's factory; a short distance farther on, he took a lane to the right.

Through the black night loomed a ghostly mass of gray. Graham had reached the cliffs of an old quarry—a spot which he had long remembered. They had been blasting at the quarry during the past week. Graham felt sure that he would find what he had come to seek.

The young man drew forth a flashlight which he had picked up in Delkin's home. Using it discreetly, he found a huge red box which bore two words in white:

DANGER
DYNAMITE

The box was fastened with a large padlock.

Graham picked up two large stones. He let the padlock dangle upon the piece of rock which he held in his left hand. He used the other stone to deliver a series of sharp blows.

The padlock broke. Graham opened the box, played the flashlight within and removed a stick of dynamite from the mass within.

Closing the box, he retraced his steps. He turned this time toward Delkin's factory which lay farther down the side road. Graham used his flashlight intermittently and soon arrived in the vicinity of the plant.

A few lights from factory windows enabled the stealthy man to approach with ease.

Graham had been here with Ralph Delkin. He had made mental notes of the place. He knew that a watchman was on duty, but he did not expect to encounter the guardian. Delkin's plant turned out metal castings and it offered no spoils of value for prowlers. The watchman's duties were no more than mere routine.

Graham forced a basement window and entered the lower portion of the factory. He found an unlocked storeroom. He went in and turned on a light. The room was windowless. Moreover, it contained the very supplies which Graham required.

The young man crumpled his dynamite into a small pail. He found some cakes of soap and began a mixture. All the ingredients that he needed were here. The room contained all sorts of odd equipment, even to a pair of small electric stoves.

Cautious at times, Graham paused to listen. He heard nothing of the watchman. Probably the man did not intend to visit this obscure portion of the factory. Graham applied himself to the task before him. He was mixing "soup"—the compound used by safecrackers.

When the job was done, Graham took his supply of explosive and left the storeroom. He made his way through the window and started back along the road. He had fuses in his pocket—he had obtained these from the dynamite box. Everything was ready for tonight's work.

WHISTLING winds and heavy clouds were broken by distant flashes and occasional rumbles. A thunderstorm was approaching. It was not the season for such a disturbance, but that did not trouble Graham Wellerton. The storm was to his liking—provided it did not break too soon.

A roar sounded from overhead. Graham paused to look up from the lonely road. An airplane was passing, its lights low. Graham did not envy the pilot. He decided that the ship must be making for the airport on the other side of Southwark, to avoid the approaching thunderstorm.

"WOLF" DAGGERT, gangster, who led Graham Wellerton into the ways of crime and nursed him along —only to find his pupil becoming more apt than himself, usurping his position as chief aide to the big chief. But Wolf's own ambitions are not so readily thwarted. The crook has other cards to play before the deals in this complex plot are concluded.

Graham thought no more of the airplane. He was too much concerned with his own problems. He was moving carefully along the road, yet he was anxious to make good time. Preliminary raindrops came as a warning that the storm might break.

Graham passed directly by Ralph Delkin's home. He noticed upstairs lights. He hid his soup behind a hedge and strolled into the house. He could hear Eunice talking with her father.

Whistling as he strolled about the hall, Graham knew that his absence had not been noticed. He was making sure that he would be heard from above, so that Ralph and Eunice Delkin would believe that he had been in the house throughout the evening.

A muffled thunderclap reminded Graham that it was time to proceed. He slipped from the door, regained his hidden explosive and started along the street. He slipped out of sight behind a tree as a coupé turned a corner and came into view. The car rolled by without stopping.

Graham congratulated himself that he had not been observed. In that belief, he was wrong. Peering eyes had noticed him; even as he watched the departing coupé, a strange, invisible figure dropped from the moving car some fifty yards beyond the spot where Graham was standing.

Graham kept on his way. He was nearing the business section of Southwark. He turned into a narrow side street and drew up beside his uncle's bank.

Laying his soup aside, he drew forth tools that he had taken from the factory storeroom. He deliberately set to work to open one of the barred windows at the side of the old bank.

The task proved amazingly simple. Graham chuckled. His uncle, the old miser, had been too cheap to install burglar-proof devices. Getting into the bank was almost as easy a task as breaking into Delkin's factory.

Graham clambered through the open window. The storm was breaking outside. People would be indoors. This was the time for the job. Graham stared out into blackness; then hurried away from the window, realizing that it would be unwise to show himself in case a flash of lightning might suddenly occur.

Such a flash did come a few moments later. Graham was not at the window to see it. Hence he did not observe a chilling sight—a spectral phenomenon that human eyes would have considered unbelievable.

In the sudden brilliance of a vivid flash, total darkness was transformed into day. In the midst of the street scene remained one touch of blackness. A human form—a spectral figure in inky cloak and hat—was revealed just outside the open window of Ezra Talboy's bank.

Tall, sinister, and silent, this being stood like a visitor from another world. The Shadow, weird master of darkness, had come to Southwark. Riding in a coupé piloted by Harry Vincent, the agent who had met him, The Shadow had spied Graham Wellerton. The Shadow, wizard of gloom, was trailing the gentleman of crime!

GRAHAM WELLERTON, within the bank, was not thinking of The Shadow. With his flashlight sending intermittent flickers, he was choosing between the large vault and a small safe which stood in Ezra Talboy's office. With a grin, Graham chose the safe.

The young man began his task. He worked his explosive mixture about the safe in preparation for a blast. He was pleased with the soup that he had made.

"Slam broth," chuckled Graham, using his favorite term for the explosive soup. "Wait until this wakes old Uncle Ezra. He'll pop out of bed when he hears this."

Graham arranged his fuse. He applied a match. He backed from the office, across the outer room and waited by the window. The results were startling.

The charge went off just as a terrific flare of lightning burst outside. The soup exploded with a roar amid a tremendous thunderclap. The mighty outburst of the heavens outdid the explosion both in flash and sound.

A strange occurrence! But Graham Wellerton, as he faced the office, failed to see the most amazing phase of it all.

Standing within ten feet of him was a tall personage in black—a creature who might well have materialized with the thunderbolt, so uncanny was his bearing.

Graham fancied that the rumble of the elements had drowned the roar of his explosion. He was wrong. The flash and its dull reverberation had been witnessed by another than himself—The Shadow!

Graham had intended that the explosion be heard. He believed, with reason, that it had not. Nevertheless, the occurrence did not change his necessary action.

Hurrying to the broken safe, Graham began to go through the papers that he found there. His flashlight glimmered upon three documents held together by a paper clip. He read them eagerly. There were notes, to the sum of fifty thousand dollars, signed by Ralph Delkin.

A chuckle of elation came from Graham's lips. So intent was Graham that he did not realize a presence which had moved to a few feet behind him. He did not suspect that other eyes were staring over his shoulder; that the burning optics of The Shadow were also reading those documents.

The Shadow faded like a living phantom as Graham Wellerton arose. Carrying only those stolen notes, Graham hurried to the window and dropped out into the street. He headed back along the way that led to Ralph Delkin's factory.

The rain was slight; the storm seemed to be passing around the town of Southwark. Graham Wellerton, no longer burdened with his soup, made quick progress by means of the occasional lightning flashes. Not once did the young man look behind him, so sure was he that he had eluded detection.

Thus he did not see the phantom shape that followed in his wake, always maintaining an even distance behind him. That figure duplicated all that Graham Wellerton did, as the young man reached the factory, went through the open window and found his way to an office on the ground floor.

Here The Shadow watched while Graham, his flashlight again in use, approached a small safe and fingered the dial. Graham had seen Ralph Delkin unlock that safe. The manufacturer had made no effort to hide the combination. The safe contained nothing more valuable than business accounts which Delkin kept here to avoid possible destruction in case of fire.

Graham Wellerton placed the three notes in the safe. He closed the door and locked it. The Shadow merged with darkness at the side of the room. He watched Graham depart; then followed.

Graham closed the basement window and made for the road. The Shadow softly raised the window, slipped through and closed it behind him. He followed Graham along the lonely road until the young man reached Ralph Delkin's home.

When Graham Wellerton disappeared into the house, The Shadow still lingered. From his hidden lips came a sighing laugh, that blended with the whistling wind that still marked the presence of the passing storm.

THE SHADOW had come to Southwark to forestall crime. He had seen crime in the making. He had made no effort to prevent it. For The Shadow had seen a purpose other than evil in Graham Wellerton's actions. The keen brain of The Shadow had divined that the former crook had not been working for his own gain tonight, but for someone else.

Until The Shadow learned all the contributory factors to this case, The Shadow would restrain aggressive action. One test remained. If Graham Wellerton had planned further robbery, the temptation of the broken window in Ezra Talboy's bank would still remain.

That was why The Shadow waited, watching silently from darkness. He was lingering to learn if Graham Wellerton intended to venture forth again tonight.

CHAPTER XIV
BIRDS OF A FEATHER

WHEN Graham Wellerton had regained his accustomed seat in Ralph Delkin's living room, he felt a peculiar sense of satisfaction. He realized that he was through with crime forever. Tonight's experience had been an odd one. He had acted as a criminal, but he felt that he had served the cause of true justice.

Graham had not seen his uncle, Ezra Talboy. Yet he felt a great contempt for the man. So far as crookedness was concerned, Ezra Talboy won the grand prize. The old man's dealings with Ralph Delkin had been nothing more than legalized crime, in Graham Wellerton's opinion.

All crime seemed sordid to Graham, yet the young man was pleased that he had committed tonight's robbery. He realized that he had not done it from a sense of gratitude to Ralph Delkin. He had performed the deed because he admired the grand courage which Eunice Delkin had displayed in the face of approaching adversity.

Graham intended to turn in. He felt sure that his actions of tonight would never be traced. He knew that his uncle would never dare accuse so fine a character as Ralph Delkin of entering a bank and robbing a safe to take away notes that bore his name. Graham realized, however, that it would be wise for him to establish an alibi through Delkin. Hence he was pleased when the manufacturer suddenly appeared in the living room.

Evidently Delkin, in his talk with Eunice, had gained some of the girl's courage, for the man showed no more signs of nervousness. He spoke in a friendly tone to Graham and seemed to take it for granted that the young man had been in the living room for the last two hours.

"I'm going to stay up for a while," announced Delkin, in a cordial manner. "I'm going over my accounts, to see how badly off I am."

"Think I'll turn in," returned Graham in a sleepy tone.

As he left the living room, Graham had a sudden thought. He realized that normally, the robbery of Ezra Talboy's safe would have been discovered by this time. Roaring thunder, however, had drowned the sound of the explosion. If the broken safe were not discovered until morning, people would not know at what time the bank had been entered.

This would certainly have an effect upon any alibi. Graham saw but one way out. The storm had abated. He must go back to the bank, cause enough disturbance to arouse Ezra Talboy from his home adjoining the old building and make a quick getaway here to Delkin's.

Graham saw an easy way to do this. He went upstairs to his room, opened the window and stepped out on the roof of a low back porch. He dropped to the ground and circled to the front of the house.

THE setup seemed perfect. Graham thought of all possibilities as he hurried along the street. If there were people at the bank, it would mean that the blown safe had been discovered. A quick return to Ralph Delkin's would suffice.

If no one was in sight, it would be easy to alarm Ezra Talboy, then hurry back to Delkin's. Up by the porch roof, then downstairs to chat with Delkin for a while. That would make a perfect alibi, for Ezra Talboy would set the time of the entry into the bank as the time of the alarm.

Absent from Delkin's sight for no longer than fifteen minutes, Graham could easily prove that he would not have had time to enter a window and blow a safe. Graham chuckled thoughtfully. He was sure that he would avoid all suspicion, so why worry about such consequences?

Once again, Graham Wellerton was followed. The Shadow, taking up the trail, was moving silently and invisibly. He was there to witness the former crook's next deeds.

As Graham reached the side street that led by the bank, The Shadow paused. The street was silent and deserted—a reentry through the side window would be easy. Yet Graham Wellerton was not going in that direction. He was heading through a space behind the bank—toward the house which adjoined the building—toward Ezra Talboy's home.

A soft, whispered laugh came from The Shadow's lips. The black-garbed phantom moved slowly on the trail. Well did The Shadow divine Graham's purpose. He knew that the young man intended to give an alarm.

At the back door of Ezra Talboy's home, Graham Wellerton paused. This had once been his father's home. Graham knew that there was an inside passage between the bank and the house. It was better, however, to make some noise here than go back into the bank. Graham tried the knob of the door.

To his surprise, the door opened!

Cautiously, Graham crept forward. He heard the sound of growling voices. He saw light trickling from a door that was ajar. Realizing that something must be wrong, Graham approached and drew the door open inch by inch.

He peered into a little room—its only window a small opening in a tiny court between the house and the bank building. At the other side was the door that connected, by a passage, to the bank. The occupants of the room, however, were of most interest to Graham.

There were three men in the room. One was Ezra Talboy, sprawled in a great chair, attired in pajamas. The others were men who carried revolvers. They were threatening the old man.

"So you didn't like it when we began to work, huh?" one intruder was growling. "It ain't so nice, gettin' your feet singed with matches? Well—that ain't nothin' to what'll happen if you've given us the wrong combination to your vault. Savvy?"

Graham Wellerton had recognized the men. The speaker was Garry, Wolf Daggert's pal. The other man was Pete—one of Graham's own men. As Graham stared, the door opened, and another man stepped into view.

"Say," greeted the newcomer, "the old mug has given us a phony steer. We can't get into the vault nohow."

Graham knew the speaker as another of his old underlings—a fellow called "Greaser." These were the three who had avoided The Shadow in Grand Rapids, along with Wolf Daggert. At this very minute, Wolf Daggert must be in the bank building, working at the vault, trying a combination which had been forced, by torture, from Ezra Talboy's lips.

"So you bluffed us, eh?" snarled Garry. "Tryin' to stall? Well, you'll pay for it!"

Before Ezra Talboy could utter a scream, Garry had clapped his big hand over the old man's mouth. Greaser launched himself upon the old man's form to prevent a struggle. Pete, with calm indifference, lighted a match and began to apply the flame to Talboy's toes. Graham could see his uncle writhe pitifully.

GRAHAM WELLERTON was unarmed. Nevertheless, he was a man of courage, and he knew the failings of these fellows who had served under him and Wolf Daggert. There was no time to treat with them; the moment was here for action.

With a furious leap, Graham sprang through the door and fell upon Pete, the nearest one to him. With a powerful swing, he sent the ruffian sprawling on the floor.

Greaser leaped up and drew his gun; before he could level the weapon, Graham clipped him on the jaw and sent him down in a heap. Garry, the last of the trio, sprang away from Ezra Talboy and jerked a gun into view, aiming it at Graham.

This was a wise move. Garry was away before Graham could overwhelm him. With a quick dive, Graham plucked up the revolver which Greaser had dropped in his fall and turned to meet Garry's attack.

The man fired first. His shot was wide. The bullet whipped through the edge of Graham's coat. Quickly, Graham responded with a shot. Garry snarled as the bullet nicked his left shoulder.

Fiercely, Graham turned to meet Pete, who he knew was coming up. He fired one wide shot. Pete leveled his revolver in return. Graham's second shot was wide; then came the burst of Pete's revolver.

Graham heard a scream behind him. Then he felt a stinging sensation in his own right shoulder.

As he staggered away, Graham half turned and saw Ezra Talboy kneeling on the floor in back of him. Intuitively, Graham knew what had happened.

His uncle had leaped up from the chair. Scurrying for safety, the old man had crossed in back of Graham just as Pete had fired. The bullet, passing through Graham's arm, had ended its swift course by lodging in Ezra Talboy's body.

Graham's right fingers were numb. The young man managed to clutch his slipping revolver with his left hand. He realized, dazedly, that he was on the spot.

Pete was aiming for a second shot; Garry was leveling his revolver. Graham saw Greaser rising to his feet, pulling another revolver into view.

Then came a cannonlike roar from the door through which Graham had entered the room. With a snarl, Pete collapsed. Graham, seeing Garry and Greaser turn their aim toward the door, also stared in that direction.

For an instant, he thought he detected the outline of a tall, human form. Then, as gangster revolvers barked, fierce tongues of flame shot from the muzzles of automatics, and terrific reverberations seemed to shake the room.

Greaser and Garry tumbled to the floor. Graham fancied that he caught a whispered tone of mockery from the door. He wondered who had been there—the space was empty now. Still dazed, Graham turned to see Greaser, wounded, aiming in his direction. Before the crippled gangster could control his wavering hand, Graham leveled his own gun and fired two bullets into the man's body.

Staring at the forms that were lying on the floor, Graham had one new thought—Wolf Daggert. Clutching his revolver firmly in his left hand, Graham pushed his way through the passage to the bank. He found a light switch and clicked it with the barrel of his revolver. The big banking room was illuminated instantly. Graham saw that the place was empty.

He knew the answer. Wolf Daggert, cowardly as ever, had fled for safety when he heard the roar of guns. The yellow gang leader had evidently dived through the broken window and made a quick escape, leaving his companions to win or lose.

Weakly, Graham moved back into the house. He came to the room where the bodies lay. He knew that some rescuer had saved him from death—but why had the stranger departed, leaving him alone?

Four men—three crooks and Graham's uncle—all seemed dead. Birds of a feather, thought Graham. He felt singularly apart from all of them. Sickened from loss of blood, Graham stared at the forms on the floor. He looked closely at Ezra Talboy's face. He saw his uncle's eyelids flicker. The old man was still alive!

GRAHAM felt no pity toward his uncle. Yet the new turn of mind which he had gained tonight had given Graham a softer feeling toward life, had purged him of the brutality which had never been more than an assumed phase of his character.

A telephone was in view. Graham dropped his revolver and lifted the receiver. He spoke as he heard an operator's voice.

"Call Sheriff Taussig," ordered Graham. "Tell him to come at once to Ezra Talboy's home. Call for a physician—at the hospital—"

The young man dropped the receiver. He sprawled into a chair and clutched his wounded arm. Then, as the throbbing dulled, Graham stared toward his uncle. Ezra Talboy, with an effort, had propped himself against the side of the great chair in which he had been tortured. He was surveying Graham with curious, steady gaze.

Coldly, Graham Wellerton stared in return. For the first time in many years, he was face to face with his uncle, the man whom he detested most in all the world. The two were alone, in a room with three dead crooks lying on the floor.

As they gazed with challenging eyes, neither Graham Wellerton nor Ezra Talboy knew that another presence was close at hand; that The Shadow, the stern fighter who had eliminated their common enemies, was watching them from the gloom beyond the doorway!

CHAPTER XV
A FAMILY REUNION

"WHO are you?"

As Ezra Talboy put the question to his nephew, Graham Wellerton was astonished to observe the old man's recuperative powers. He knew that his uncle was severely wounded; nevertheless, Ezra Talboy seemed to evidence no concern about himself. He was more interested in learning the identity of this stranger who had come to rescue him.

Graham Wellerton eyed his uncle coldly. He could see the avaricious gleam upon the old man's face. He could see the scheming expression which he had always remembered Ezra Talboy to possess. With a grim smile, Graham gave a direct reply.

"I am your nephew," he declared. "I am Graham Wellerton, your sister's son."

"I thought so." Ezra Talboy chuckled weakly. "My nephew—come back to play the part of a good Samaritan. I suppose you feel that you have done a noble deed—to rescue me from those who were torturing me."

"Some may feel that I deserve a bit of credit."

"Some may," snorted Ezra Talboy, "and some may not.

"I have no thanks to offer. I had no use for your father, with his foolish pride that he called 'honor.' I have no use for you, now that I observe you to possess his ridiculous characteristics."

Graham Wellerton stared in amazement. Of all the despicable wretches he had ever known, Ezra Talboy was the worst. But for his own wounded plight, Graham would have yielded to the impulse of throttling the old scoundrel.

"I give you no thanks," repeated Ezra Talboy. "I heard you were in town, and I was waiting for the time when you would come to greet me. You have chosen an excellent opportunity. I suppose you were passing by, wondering if it was too late to drop in and see your old uncle. You noticed that something was wrong, and came in to aid me.

"Do you know what this means? You are an intruder—like these dead men on the floor—so far as the law is concerned. You will be questioned when the sheriff arrives. I shall not say a word to save you."

As the old man chortled gleefully, Graham Wellerton stared in amazement. He had classed Ezra Talboy as a black-hearted wretch; he did not believe such ingratitude was possible. He began to realize that his own meanness toward Ralph Delkin must have been a hereditary weakness. Ezra Talboy's calloused attitude was the most incredible human quality that any man could possibly possess.

"I detest you," declared Ezra Talboy. "I detest you because you remind me of your father. His honor—bah! I ended that folly when I deprived him of all he possessed. He was always proud of his son, always hypocritically sad because I had no children to be my heirs. He died penniless—your father—and now you return to reap a new harvest of my hatred!"

Ezra Talboy spat the final words, and his eyes glittered as he watched for their effect upon Graham Wellerton. The nephew, however, had caught the evil spirit of his uncle's tone. With sudden inspiration, Graham determined to beat the old man at his game.

"You old fossil!" ejaculated Graham contemptuously. "Do you think I came here to save your useless hide? Do you think I have been living in Southwark in hopes of making friends with you? Do you think I threw myself into a battle with these bank robbers only on your account?

"You never were so wrong in all your life. Let me tell you a little about myself. I am a bank robber—and a capable one. These men who came here tonight were my underlings. They had double-crossed me. Their new leader—the only one who escaped—had tried to kill me.

"I suspected that they would come to Southwark. I was waiting for them. I knew they would attack your bank. I have been watching; and when they entered here tonight, I followed. You see the result. Three of the four are dead. One has escaped. He is a fugitive.

"You and I are alike, Uncle Ezra. We both are crooks. You work legitimately; I by stealth. You speak of revenge. What is your picayune grudge against me—my father's son—compared to the score I had to settle with these yellow rats who now lie dead?

"You do not know the joy of vengeance. Nor do you know the joy of evil. You compared me with my father; the comparison is false. The qualities that I have inherited are yours—and I have done more with them in a few years than you have accomplished in a lifetime.

"I am no hero. I am a crook. I could kill you now; but I do not intend to do so. I am quite capable of handling any situation which may arise. When the sheriff arrives, I can convince him that I came here purely by chance. As a liar, I am as competent as you, Uncle Ezra."

The sarcasm of Graham's statement had its effect. By taking a negative treatment of everything that the old man had said, Graham had gained Ezra Talboy's admiration. Graham's story, true enough to be convincing, caused Talboy to stare in utter amazement at his nephew.

At last, the old man's feelings became apparent. Vainly trying to arise from his resting place, Ezra Talboy extended his hand. He had recognized in his nephew a man as crooked as himself. Never in his life had Ezra Talboy paid tribute to anyone who was good of nature. His own soul was evil. He appreciated viciousness.

"So"—a coughing spell interrupted Ezra Talboy's statement—"so—you take after your uncle. Good—good boy. I am very well satisfied. You are—a crook—"

The tones ended in a hoarse chuckle. Again, Ezra Talboy coughed. His eyelids closed. Graham Wellerton, contempt showing on his face, knew that he had tricked the man he hated. He had found Ezra Talboy's weakness—an inherent love of evil.

All the while, burning eyes were studying this strange scene. Graham Wellerton did not see the observer who lurked beyond the door. His own gaze was upon Ezra Talboy's huddled form. The watching optics disappeared as the throb of a motor sounded from somewhere outside.

To Graham Wellerton, that vague noise signified the arrival of the law. Calmly, despite his aching wound, Graham waited, with real confidence that all would go well. He was sure that his words had had effect. Soon he would know. The test was coming.

Two long minutes passed. Footsteps were stamping in the hallway. Three men burst into the

With a furious leap, Graham sprang through the door...

room. With Sheriff Ellis Taussig at their head, the summoned rescuers stopped in awe as they observed two men living with three dead bodies close beside them.

Ezra Talboy opened his eyes. Before his uncle could speak, Graham Wellerton boldly forced the issue. Half rising from his chair, he spoke to Ellis Taussig.

"I came to see my uncle," he asserted. "He was being tortured by these men. I saved him. This is the result."

Ezra Talboy, evil admiration glowing in his eyes, spoke the words that Graham had hoped to hear.

"What my nephew says"—a cough came from Talboy's blood-flecked lips—"is true. He—he came here at an opportune moment. He—he saved me from torture—and saved my life—for the present.

"Whatever he may tell you is correct. He worked to help me. He and I are in accord. We"—the old man's lips formed a strange smile—"were having a family reunion. A reunion—after many years—many years—"

More men were coming into the room. One, evidently a physician, was leaning over Ezra Talboy's form. He snapped quick orders. Two others picked up the old man and carried him from the room. Graham knew that they were taking Ezra Talboy to the hospital.

"Look after this fellow," said Sheriff Taussig in a kindly tone, as he indicated Graham. "He looks done up."

Graham smiled weakly as the doctor began to examine his wounded arm. It was not the fact that aid had come which caused his smile. It was the knowledge that a frank admission of his past, with no confession of his present change of heart, had served him well.

He was to be the hero, after all. Ezra Talboy would never tell the facts which Graham had admitted. The old man had explained the whole affair. He had called it a family reunion, in which his nephew had saved him from murderous death.

Yet through Graham's brain throbbed a new thought—an idea which related to matters unexplained. Graham, alone, knew that he was not the one who had effected this rescue. Some unknown hand had brought about this present state of affairs.

Who had fired those shots from the doorway? Graham did not know. The possibility of The Shadow being here did not once occur to him. Graham knew only that some weird and hidden presence had intervened—that without its help, this odd reunion between himself and his uncle would never have been completed!

CHAPTER XVI
GRAHAM STATES FACTS

THREE days had elapsed since the affray at Ezra Talboy's home. Graham Wellerton, recuperated from his wound, was seated in Ralph Delkin's living room. The young man was alone, idly passing the early afternoon in a leisurely fashion.

Eunice Delkin entered. The girl's eyes were sympathetic, as they turned toward Graham. The young man seemed moody; Eunice thought that she knew the trouble.

"It is too bad, Graham," she said. "Too bad to think that after your brave effort, your uncle died. We feared that he would not recover, but no one expected that he would pass away last night. Father hesitated to break the news to you this morning—that was why he did not tell you until he was leaving for the factory—"

"Don't worry about me," interrupted Graham. "I am not sorry because my uncle died. There was no good will between us."

"But your uncle said that you had saved him!" exclaimed the girl. "It seemed so wonderful to think that you had gone to his home to make a friendly visit!"

"You are mistaken, Eunice," declared Graham cryptically. "I had a different purpose in visiting my uncle's home. When he told his story, I offered no objection—that is all."

"Another purpose?" echoed Eunice. "What other reason could you have had?"

"You may learn that later," said Graham. "After I have gone from Southwark."

"You are leaving us?"

"Yes. Today."

As Graham arose, Eunice stared in bewilderment. This decision was an unexpected one. The girl seemed wistful. She placed a restraining hand upon Graham's arm, and urged the young man to remain.

"You can't leave here now!" Eunice exclaimed. "You have found yourself, Graham! You have been so different since the night you saved your uncle's life—so friendly—so patient—"

"I did not intend to leave Southwark," interposed Graham, "until my uncle died—as I expected he would. Now that he is dead, there is nothing to keep me here."

"Nothing?" questioned Eunice sadly. "I thought—we thought, father and I, that you would learn to like us, to appreciate the friendship and the hospitality that we offered. You are free to leave here, Graham, but there is every reason why you should stay."

"There is every reason why I should leave," responded Graham. "I have been a cad. I came to the realization that I was wrong. I have tried to make amends—to reward you and your father for the kindness that you have shown me."

"You can do that best by remaining."

"Not now, Eunice. I have only one more favor to ask—one that I believe your father will grant. That is sufficient money to enable me to leave town and go somewhere else."

"But Graham! You must explain your reasons!"

Graham Wellerton shook his head. A heavy feeling gripped his heart. He was sick of crime—through with it forever, and it hurt him to realize that the only way he could have found to reward Eunice and her father had been through theft.

RALPH DELKIN had not yet found the notes which Graham had placed in his safe. Graham had done that job with elation; he had since experienced the reaction. For the first time in his career of lawlessness, he had thought of other persons while committing a deed of crime. The paradox—the belief that the end justified the means—had produced chaos in his mind.

He had recalled all his previous crimes—actions impelled by thought of selfish gain. He realized that Eunice Delkin was so far above him that comparisons were futile. The thought that he had stooped to crime to insure this girl's happiness made him feel that he was a creature unworthy even of contempt.

What would Eunice think if she knew him to be a crook? All Graham's usual indifference faded at the thought. He wanted to leave Southwark before this beautiful girl would know that he had dealt in crime.

Let Ralph Delkin find the notes; the manufacturer would understand. He would destroy those paper obligations, without, Graham hoped, mentioning the subject to his daughter.

Graham Wellerton walked toward the door. He was going upstairs to pack some luggage. Then to the factory, to borrow money from Delkin, and after that a departure to begin a new and honest career.

It grieved Graham to realize that he was forced to leave behind him the one person who had ever shown understanding. Graham liked Ralph Delkin, but he knew in his heart that the manufacturer had tolerated his idle term of residence only because of Eunice's persuasion.

The girl was not willing to see Graham depart without further discussion. Eunice stopped the young man at the door, and quietly demanded a reconsideration of his decision. This increased Graham's misery; it did not, however, change his notion. Firmly, Graham repeated that he was leaving Southwark.

The front door opened while Graham was still insisting that nothing could change his mind. Ralph Delkin appeared. At sight of her father, Eunice decided that she had found an ally. She turned to Delkin and blurted forth the news.

"Graham wants to leave, father!" exclaimed the girl. "He says that he can no longer remain in Southwark. He will not tell me why."

"I know the reason," returned Delkin calmly. "Graham—I should like to talk with you for a few minutes—in here—"

Delkin indicated the living room.

GRAHAM turned from the steps. He knew that Delkin had discovered the notes in his safe. Eunice followed the two men into the living room. Ralph Delkin turned to bid his daughter to leave. Graham Wellerton shook his head in resignation.

"Let Eunice remain," he asserted. "She may as well know the truth—now that you have learned it."

Ralph Delkin nodded. He was serious as he noted the resignation in Graham's tone. Reluctantly, the manufacturer drew the clipped papers from his pocket and held them out for Graham to see.

"You placed these in my safe?" he questioned.

Graham nodded.

"How did you get them?" quizzed Delkin.

"I broke into my uncle's bank," declared Graham. "I blew open his safe. I found the notes and took them. I knew the combination of your safe, and opened it to place the notes there."

"I thought that the burglars blew the safe," said Delkin in a puzzled tone. "That was Sheriff Taussig's decision—a most logical one. The sheriff said that they must have lacked sufficient explosive to blow the vault. How could you have blown the safe? You were wounded—"

"I went there early in the evening," explained Graham, in a dull tone. "I came back afterward to see if an alarm had been given. That was when I discovered burglars torturing my uncle."

Ralph Delkin began to understand.

He nodded as he looked at the notes in his hand. He seemed at a loss. At last, he spoke in a sincere tone.

"You did wrong, Graham," he said. "Nevertheless, your motive was excusable. Still, these notes do not belong to me. If your uncle were still alive, I would be forced to return them to him. Now that he is dead, I must declare them to his estate."

"I thought so," returned Graham. "That is why I decided that I would leave town—one reason why, at least. I knew that you would not want to incriminate me—so I felt that it would be best to leave you free to act as you desired."

Regretful in tone, Graham unconsciously turned toward Eunice. The girl approached and laid her hand upon his arm. There was no reproach in her voice.

"Graham," she said, "you did wrong. Father and I could not accept a favor of this sort. But we can find a way to arrange matters without your leaving Southwark. No one will know of this but father and myself. We shall remember only the intention—not the deed."

The girl's gentle persuasion was almost irresistible. Graham Wellerton felt the mad desire to say nothing more—to accept these terms without a comment. Then came a wave of remorse; the knowledge that Eunice knew nothing of his past. What right had he, a despicable crook, to further prey upon the sincere friendship of this girl and her father?

There was only one way out—a complete confession. With surging thoughts, Graham Wellerton broke forth with a complete denunciation of his evil past.

"I'LL tell you why I'm leaving Southwark," he declared bitterly. "I'm leaving because I'm a crook. I've been a bank robber. Those men who were torturing my uncle were once members of my mob. I belong in prison—not in the home of respectable people.

"I'm not going to jail. That would be futile. Nor am I staying here; that would be unfair. There are only two people living who could prove my past guilt"—Graham's face hardened as he thought of Wolf Daggert and Carma Urstead—"and if I can dodge them, I can go straight.

"That's why I'm leaving here, so that I can try to live right. But I'd never impose upon such fine people as you. I know you think I'm scum"—Graham was observing the expression of disapproval on Ralph Delkin's face—"and that's why I'm glad I've told you everything. I don't deserve your friendship. That's all."

Graham could see that his words had had full effect upon Delkin. The honest manufacturer had drawn away, apparently alarmed by Graham's presence. If that was the way Delkin felt, Graham decided, how much more disdainful would Eunice be! With that thought, Graham turned toward the girl. He stood dumfounded, as he gazed into her eyes.

Eunice was pale, but her face had lost none of its kindliness. With a forgiving smile, the girl looked directly into Graham's eyes and gave her answer to his self-accusation.

"The past does not matter, Graham," she said. "This is the present and the future lies ahead. You are honest. You have told the truth. You desire to live a straightforward life; begin it here, in Southwark, with friends who understand."

His daughter's confidence caused Ralph Delkin to change his attitude. He seemed to lose his temporary aloofness. Although he did not speak, Delkin nodded, to show that he would second his daughter's invitation.

"I appreciate this, Eunice," gulped Graham. "I'll never forget this friendship. But I had better go—away—on my own. I need a little money—that's all—"

Ralph Delkin pulled a roll of bills from his pocket and proffered the cash. Eunice began an objection as Graham took the money.

"Graham must not leave us, father!" she exclaimed. "It is not right—he needs us more now than ever."

"I'm leaving," announced Graham quietly.

Ralph Delkin found himself in the position of mediator. Abashed at his own lack of confidence, the manufacturer was ready to add his pleas to those of his daughter. Graham, his heart burning, broke forth in a new effort to make himself appear worthless.

"There are people who know what I have done," he asserted. "Two people—one a crook—the other a woman—my wife. Yes—my wife. She is living in New York, under her maiden name, Carma Urstead. She will cause trouble if she knows I am here. She has always caused me trouble."

A gleam of understanding flashed in Eunice Delkin's eyes. The girl's intuition prompted her to put a pointed question.

"This woman who has caused you trouble," queried Eunice. "Was she the person who forced you into crime?"

GRAHAM did not reply. Looking at his face, however, Eunice knew that she had struck the truth. Graham saw that further words would only prompt Eunice to again urge her father to make Graham stay in Southwark. Quickly, the young man turned to Ralph Delkin.

"You can understand," said Graham. "You see why I must leave. All I ask is that my confidence be kept."

"Yes," agreed Delkin. "You had better go."

Swinging, Graham walked past Eunice. The girl turned to call to him. Her father stopped her. Graham hurried upstairs and packed. When he came down, he found Eunice, pale and worried, standing beside her father.

"I shall drive you to the station," declared Delkin. "Eunice has consented to your departure."

Graham could see that the girl had been

reluctant. Only her confidence in her father's judgment could possibly have made her come to this agreement.

As Graham walked toward the door, Eunice extended her hand. As Graham received it, he could see true sympathy and lasting friendship in the tear-dimmed eyes that looked toward him.

"We must start," declared Delkin.

Eunice was standing at the door when Graham looked back from the departing car. Graham Wellerton caught one last glance, and his heart filled with admiration for the wonderful spirit of the girl who had been his true friend.

Graham did not speak to Delkin as they rode along. There was nothing to be said. The pair arrived at the station. Graham alighted and took his bag. Silently he extended his hand in farewell. He noticed that Ralph Delkin was looking beyond him. Graham turned.

Coming from a car which had swung up to the station was Sheriff Ellis Taussig. The official was making directly for Graham Wellerton. Taussig's gruff voice blurted forth before Graham could speak.

"Where you going, young fellow?"

"Just leaving town," responded Graham quietly.

"Not yet," chuckled Taussig. "You're coming up to Harwin Dowser's office, along with me."

"What for?"

"You'll find out," responded the sheriff. "Say, Delkin—have you got time to drive us up there? You're a friend of Wellerton's—"

Graham saw Ralph Delkin nod. At the sheriff's urge, Graham entered the car. As they rode along the street, he wondered what had happened. Had Wolf Daggert been caught? Had the yellow gangster lingered long enough to catch a glimpse of Graham and denounce him as a crook?

Graham worried; then, with calm indifference, he waited the outcome of this unexpected event which had interrupted his much-desired departure from the town of Southwark.

CHAPTER XVII
MISGAINED MILLIONS

HARWIN DOWSER'S office was located in a building near the Southwark courthouse. As Graham Wellerton and his companions climbed the stairs to the lawyer's headquarters, the reformed crook felt more than ever that he was about to encounter the unexpected.

Of all the men whom he had met in Southwark, Dowser had impressed Graham as the most sanguine. The lawyer, a political figure in this county, possessed unusual qualifications. Where Ezra Talboy had accumulated wealth by usurious practices, where Ralph Delkin had gained much by straightforward business dealings, Harwin Dowser had reached a state of importance by practically monopolizing legal affairs in this vicinity.

The adviser of every person of prominence, a man whose influence had direct effect even upon old Justice Schuble's decisions, Dowser was one whose friendship could be powerful, and whose enmity could be a tremendous obstacle. Even now, it seemed as though Sheriff Taussig was no more than Dowser's errand boy.

In fact, the sheriff's presence and behavior were most unusual. If the man had come to arrest Graham, why had he not done so? If nothing but a private conference between Graham and Dowser was the matter at stake, why had the sheriff been deputed as the lawyer's messenger?

Considering these questions, Graham entered the office and found himself face to face with Harwin Dowser. The elderly lawyer, sharp-featured and keen-eyed, arose to receive the young man with an air of gravity. Solemn as a British barrister, Dowser waved Graham and the other visitors to chairs.

"Graham Wellerton," announced the attorney, "you are the nephew of Ezra Talboy, deceased. As legal representative for your late uncle, I have important matters to discuss with you. The presence of these other witnesses is not material. My words will be brief, and there is no reason why others should not hear them."

GRAHAM sensed at once that Ezra Talboy, before he died, must have held a conference with Harwin Dowser. He realized that the lawyer was about to make a revelation. The presence of the sheriff became ominous.

If Dowser intended to brand Graham Wellerton as a crook, Ellis Taussig, the bluff representative of the county law, would lose no time in leaping to action.

"Ezra Talboy," announced Dowser, "was a peculiar man. I state that as a simple fact. His will, which he made many years ago, was a most unusual document, in that it made no provisions for any person who bore a relationship to Ezra Talboy, nor did it include any philanthropic clauses."

Graham Wellerton smiled sourly. This reference gave a plain analysis of his uncle's mean and avaricious tendencies. Graham could picture Ezra Talboy, alive in the past, worrying over the disposal of his ill-gotten gains.

"Before his death," continued Dowser, "Ezra Talboy called for me. At his request, I brought his will. At his order, I destroyed the document. In its place, I prepared a new and simple will which states all of Ezra Talboy's final bequeathment in a single clause.

"Ezra Talboy's entire estate, freed from any other provisions, is left to his nephew, Graham Wellerton. Young man"—Dowser extended his hand—"I congratulate you as the recipient of a fortune which may be conservatively estimated at ten million dollars!"

Graham Wellerton was staggered. This unexpected turn came to him with the suddenness of a blow. He stared at the other men in the room, observed the solemnity of their faces, and wondered if he were in a trance. Then, as his senses became composed, a horrible doubt swept over him.

Ten million dollars.

How had Ezra Talboy accumulated that sum? There was but one answer. The old skinflint had wrenched his wealth from suffering men. Among those millions was Graham Wellerton's own patrimony—money that should have come to him from his father—but with it were other sums that rightfully belonged to other persons. Forgotten men, who could never now be located, were the real owners of those usurped millions!

Graham looked toward Ralph Delkin. He caught a cold expression upon the manufacturer's face. He knew what Delkin was thinking. Had Ezra Talboy had his way, Delkin's factory would be part of those ill-gotten assets. Graham realized that in his own pocket he had money that he owed to Delkin. He recalled the discussion at Delkin's home, when he, Graham Wellerton, had announced his intention of going straight.

Would it be straight to take these millions? No. He had branded his own uncle as a crook worse than himself. A man who took money gained by evil measures was lower than a thief. As Graham looked at Ralph Delkin, he thought of Eunice.

What would she think of this turn in Graham's fortunes? Graham knew. He realized that if he profited by his uncle's death, the girl would at last have cause to regard him with contempt.

Then came a flare of hatred—a survival of the past. Graham understood why his uncle had left him this money. It was not through gratitude for Graham's attempt to save his life. It was because Ezra Talboy had gained fiendish delight in the fact that he had found his nephew to be a crook.

With Ezra Talboy, possession of wealth had been an outlet for evil. Dying, the old man had gained a wicked joy to know that he could place his entire fortunes in the hands of a nephew whom he considered as evil as himself.

That burning thought, together with Graham's regard for Eunice Delkin, caused the young man to make an astounding decision.

"Ten million dollars," pondered Graham aloud. "A great deal of money, gentlemen. The amount, however, is quite immaterial. My uncle had the privilege of leaving his money to me. I, in turn, have the privilege of refusing it. Since he bequeathed it without proviso, I shall reject it in the same spirit."

GASPS of amazement came from the other men. Even Ralph Delkin seemed astonished. Graham Wellerton smiled wearily and glanced at his watch as he turned to Sheriff Taussig.

"I thank you for your trouble, sheriff," he said. "Unfortunately, you have caused me to miss my train. That involves the necessity of my remaining in Southwark a few hours longer."

"One moment, Wellerton," insisted Harwin Dowser sharply, as Graham was turning toward the door. "Are you serious about this matter?"

"Why should I be otherwise?" retorted Graham.

"Because," declared Dowser, "this plan—if you go through with it—will cause many complications. As administrator of the estate, I shall have many problems with which to deal."

"You can't force the money on me, can you?"

"I cannot do anything else with it."

"How does that concern me?"

"In various ways," decided Dowser. "For instance—are you married?"

The abruptness of the question startled Graham. He was on the point of giving an affirmative reply; then, as Dowser eyed him keenly, he took an evasive course.

"Suppose I did happen to be married," he said thoughtfully. "Would my wife have the right to a share in my estate?"

"She would have cause for objection," stated Dowser, "if you refused the bequest. Moreover, if the money should be held in trust, or administered in your behalf, she would be entitled to a share, at least, in the event of your death."

"Hm-m-m," responded Wellerton. "Marriage is an odd thing, isn't it? I've often considered matrimony. It's a problem. You see, gentlemen"—he paused to look at Delkin and Taussig—"the thought of possessing great wealth annoys me. I had intended to tramp around a bit—perhaps as a vagrant."

Graham smiled as he made this subtle reference to his homecoming in the town of Southwark.

"However," added Graham, "the problem of marriage brings me to a dilemma. What would you do"—Graham was looking directly at Delkin as he spoke—"if you were in my circumstances?"

THE question was an excellent one, in consideration of the facts which Delkin knew about Graham, as told today. Indeed, Graham's mention of Carma had placed Delkin in full knowledge of the most important fact. Graham waited patiently for the manufacturer's answer. It came.

"I should accept the legacy," announced Delkin.

Sheriff Taussig muttered an agreement.

It was Delkin's decision alone that decided Graham. The manufacturer would tell the entire story to his daughter, Graham felt sure. Eunice would know how Graham had deliberately refused to accept tainted millions; then had changed his decision due to circumstances which involved the woman who had forced him into crime. Moreover, Delkin would mention that Graham had left the question up to him.

Graham Wellerton turned to Harwin Dowser and stared squarely into the old lawyer's shrewd face. Graham's mind was thinking quickly. The young man realized that, with wealth, he could do good to balance the evil committed by his uncle.

"I accept," decided Graham.

"Good," returned Dowser, smiling.

Graham Wellerton sat down and lighted a cigarette. He realized that great work lay ahead. Simultaneously, he could undo Ezra Talboy's evil work by turning misgained millions into funds spent for philanthropic purposes.

With the same joy, Graham knew that he could frustrate Carma's claims for wealth. The woman did not know he was in Southwark. By the time she had located him—if that time should ever come—the wealth could be diminished by Graham's own efforts.

THUS did Graham Wellerton begin his new career. Instead of becoming a wanderer, he had gained tremendous wealth. Only two persons of the past could block him. One, Wolf Daggert, was a fugitive; the other, Carma Urstead, did not know what had become of Graham Wellerton.

There were two others who knew the truth regarding Graham Wellerton. The young man thought of them as he sat alone with Harwin Dowser. Those two were Ralph Delkin and his daughter Eunice. They would never reveal what he had told them, Graham felt sure.

Strange that Graham Wellerton forgot one other! Oddly, his mind failed to consider The Shadow. Dazed by thoughts of wealth, Graham's brain no longer dwelt upon the unseen stranger who had saved his life the night that Ezra Talboy had been mortally wounded.

Potentially, Graham Wellerton was a crook with millions at his disposal. Although he planned to use his wealth for good, it might reasonably be judged that he would spend the hoarded coin for evil—by any who knew his past.

The Shadow knew Graham Wellerton's past. The master of darkness had seen the young man's present, here in Southwark. The Shadow, bound on other errands, had left this vicinity, but his agent, Harry Vincent, still remained, a temporary resident in the town.

An amazing future lay ahead of Graham Wellerton—a career now on the balance point, ready to swing toward evil or good as Graham himself might decide. That fact would not escape the watchfulness of The Shadow!

For The Shadow, master of justice, was one who remained ever vigilant. His hand was one that aided those who strove for right; his same hand was one that struck down all who favored evil.

Well would it be for Graham Wellerton if he persisted in his determination to devote another's misgained millions to affairs of restitution. Woe to him should he weaken in his mission.

The Shadow knew the past; The Shadow would know the future!

The Shadow always knows!

CHAPTER XVIII
THE PAST RISES

THE next month proved an amazing one to the town of Southwark. First came the announcement of Ezra Talboy's great wealth—a sum that far exceeded the most extravagant beliefs of those who had tried to estimate the size of the old miser's hoard. Coupled with that was the remarkable news that Graham Wellerton had inherited the entire estate left by his uncle.

These facts were the beginning of a new era. Even while the estate was still undergoing settlement, Graham Wellerton launched forth a campaign that was bewildering because of its Utopian qualities.

Every worthy representative of charity that called upon Southwark's new multimillionaire was granted a reception that was more than welcome. Every local institution found itself the recipient of a handsome gift, the greatest being a promise of half a million dollars to the County Hospital.

More than that, the affairs of the Southwark State Bank took a strange turn. Extensions were granted to those who had received loans. Farmers whose mortgages would have been foreclosed were accorded fair treatment. In all his business dealings, Graham Wellerton showed a fairness that surpassed all belief.

Human beings are difficult creatures to convince. Hence Graham's open methods brought a curious medley of reactions. To many citizens of

Southwark and the surrounding territory, Graham Wellerton was regarded as an idol. This was particularly true of those who had dealings—direct or indirect—with the man himself.

There were some who openly expressed the sentiment that Graham Wellerton was a fool. This group included those who were cautious and accumulative by nature, particularly those who profited least by Graham Wellerton's benefactions.

Finally, there was a shrewd class which looked for a game behind it all—sophisticated individuals who saw in Graham's prodigal philanthropy the making of a scheme which would someday have a startling development.

Among those who admired Graham Wellerton was Sheriff Ellis Taussig. One who regarded the young man as a fool was old Justice Schuble. An individual in the group who looked for the catch was Harwin Dowser.

None of these three expressed their thoughts. Taussig, hard-boiled and taciturn, showed his admiration by listening to the praises voiced by others. Schuble, solemn in his position as justice of the peace, said nothing. Dowser, as Graham's attorney, did not discuss his client's affairs.

As weeks went by, however, Graham noticed the effect which his actions were having upon Dowser. The old lawyer had become a wise owl. Often Graham wondered what was passing in the attorney's brain. He did not care, for he felt sure that Dowser, a man who handled the affairs of every class of society, was keeping all his thoughts to himself.

GRAHAM saw but little of Ralph Delkin. He met the manufacturer once, in a business way. Delkin appeared at the bank, bringing the three hated notes. Graham told him to tear them up. Delkin refused. He did, however, ask for an extension.

Graham granted it—on his own terms. He told Delkin that if he would not destroy the notes, he could keep them. Delkin promised to do this for a term of three months. Graham let it go at that.

However, the young man kept a careful watch on Delkin's business transactions and saw that the manufacturer was having trouble. The prosperous era for which Delkin had hoped had been delayed. Graham fancied that there would be another request for an extension at the end of the ninety days. In fact, he would not have been surprised had Delkin asked for another loan.

Several times, Graham was on the point of offering money to the manufacturer. On each occasion he desisted. He feared that he might injure Delkin's pride should he broach the subject of his own accord.

It was partly the thought of Delkin that made Graham use discretion in his philanthropic transactions. He did not wish to exhaust his funds; there might be a future time when he could put money to emergency use. Moreover, Graham had reserved a large amount for a specific purpose—to restore to certain banks the funds which he had robbed.

This, of course, Graham intended to do by proxy. In summing up the total of his depredations, Graham found that they amounted to no more than a quarter of a million dollars. Cash gained at the points of guns had often proven very disappointing in its sum.

Graham was also conscious of the impressions which he was creating. Those people who believed him foolish and those who suspected him of hidden purposes were ones whom he intended to spike. This caused him to ease his release of cash.

His most wary policy, however, was that of keeping all his dealings within a limited territory. Southwark was far from New York. Graham was not anxious to have reports of his wealth reach Carma Urstead, who he knew was there, nor Wolf Daggert, who might, by this time, be back in Manhattan.

GRAHAM was living in his uncle's old home. Among the friends whom he had made in Southwark was a young man named Harry Vincent. This chap was interested in real-estate development. He had but recently settled down in Southwark. A native of Michigan, Vincent had, however, spent much time in New York. He became a frequent visitor to Wellerton's new home.

Despite his wealth, despite his willingness to make amends for his past, Graham Wellerton felt that a great barrier lay between himself and Eunice Delkin. He met the girl occasionally on the street and always paused to chat with her for a few minutes. Both, however, tactfully avoided all mention of the past.

It was bitter to be living here in Southwark and yet be forced, in justice, to avoid a girl whom he admired so greatly as he did Eunice Delkin. That was Graham Wellerton's one sorrow. Time and again, he felt a surge of resentment toward Carma Urstead, the adventuress who had tricked him into marriage. Graham felt that he could wipe out his criminal past; but he could never be free to seek a woman's love while Carma still remained.

In the periods of righteous exuberance which dominated his new life, Graham was so taken up with many affairs that he had little time to study individuals. In the midst of his mad whirl of monetary restitution, he could think only of new ways to help the community. Hence his career became a matter of easy routine, with no forebodings of approaching disaster.

The end of the first month found Graham Wellerton completely oblivious to any thoughts of hostility on the part of other persons. His only worry concerned Ralph Delkin. Graham knew that adversity could produce strange changes in individuals; and with his knowledge that Delkin's affairs were troublous, Graham tried in vain to think of some way that he might approach the manufacturer with an offer of financial aid.

Hence when trouble did strike, it came with the effect of a bombshell. In one brief episode, Graham Wellerton found himself in a terrible situation which he had lulled himself into believing would be impossible.

IT happened on an evening when Graham was at home. Harry Vincent had dropped in for a chat. The two young men were indulging in reminiscences; and both, by natural coincidence, were using discretion in their talk.

Graham Wellerton, jocular and sophisticated, was taking great care not to mention anything that would give an inkling to his old career of crime.

Harry Vincent, pleasant and frank in manner, was carefully avoiding any statement that might reveal him as The Shadow's agent. Harry was just lighting his pipe when the doorbell rang.

"Sit still, Vincent," urged Graham. "Probably someone to see me for only a few minutes."

"Think I'll be running along," responded Harry, donning his hat and coat to accompany his host to the door.

No one was in sight as Graham opened the door. Harry stepped out upon the porch. Graham saw him tip his hat as a figure moved in from the side. Harry kept on; Graham stepped back as a woman entered.

Had Graham Wellerton looked beyond this visitor, he would have seen Harry Vincent step to the side of the path and wait. But Graham had no thought of what might be happening outside. Harry Vincent had passed completely from his mind. Totally dazed, Graham was closing the door and was staring in consternation at the face of the feminine visitor who had come to see him.

All the misery of the past seemed suddenly hoisted upon Graham Wellerton's shoulders.

The woman who had entered his home was Carma!

CHAPTER XIX
THE DEMAND

To Graham Wellerton's dazed eyes, Carma's painted face was a sneering mask. The young man stood stock-still as the woman strolled past him, entered the living room and settled herself in a comfortable chair. Despairingly, Graham followed. Carma greeted him with a coarse laugh.

"Not glad to see your long-lost wife, eh?" the woman jeered. "Thought you'd double-crossed me, big boy?"

"When it comes to double-crossing," returned Graham huskily, "you are the real artist."

Carma took the words as a compliment. She tilted back her head and laughed. She lighted a cigarette, then eyed Graham with a cold glare of malice.

"You're worth a lot of dough, aren't you?" questioned the woman.

"That's my affair," retorted Graham.

"Spending it pretty free, I hear," was Carma's remark. "Doing nice things around this place. Gone goody-goody, haven't you?"

Graham made no reply.

"Well"—Carma's tone became scoffing—"you can spend it the way you want—provided I get my share. I'm giving you a break. Pay me off and we're quits."

Graham maintained his silence.

"Fifty-fifty," Carma kept talking. "That's on the original amount. Get the idea, big boy?"

"Your demands are moderate, aren't they?" quizzed Graham, in a sarcastic tone.

"They are," agreed Carma. "That's not all gravy—by a long shot. I'm not the only one who is coming in for a big profit."

"You mean—"

"That this may be a hick town, but there's people here who know their onions. Get that? Flatter yourself, old bean—you fooled me right enough. I'd never have looked for you here, but someone sent for me."

"Someone in Southwark?"

"Someone in Southwark," sneered Carma. "Laugh that off. A small-town bozo with big-town ideas."

"Whom do you mean?"

"Guess for yourself."

"You mean—someone who learned that I was crooked? How could anyone here have landed that fact?"

"I'm not telling all I know," Carma laughed. "You muffed things a bit—that's all—around the time your uncle took the bump. Thought you had good friends in this burg—people who wouldn't get envious when they saw you throwing your cash away, like the sap you are.

"Well, someone got ideas—and I'm not telling you how or why. The finish of the big idea was to bring me here. Little Carma has a way of getting dough—so far as you're concerned. You've heard my terms. I want five million dollars."

"How soon?" questioned Graham sharply.

"Pretty quick," taunted Carma. "You'd, better start thinking about it pronto. Fix it up tomorrow. Then you can go down to see your lawyer the day after. I'm staying at the Southwark House. Carma Urstead is my name—Carma Wellerton to you."

"When are you coming back here?"

"Tomorrow night."

"And you expect me to have all the arrangements prepared?"

"Yes. Settle the way you'll divide. When I show up, give me the figures. If it's on the level, we'll make a legal settlement the next day. You and I and the lawyer. If you don't come through, I'll cook you."

Carma rose defiantly. She strode toward the door of the room. Graham followed her. At the front door, he put a short, abrupt question:

"Who told you I was here in Southwark?" demanded Graham. "Who looked you up in New York?"

"Wouldn't you like to know?" returned the woman. "You've got a noodle. Use it. The more you think, the more you'll know it's pay up. It won't do you any good to argue with the man who brought me here. He has you tied up—and he knows everything. It's curtains, big boy."

Carma turned and opened the door. As she walked defiantly from the porch, Graham Wellerton slammed the door. He paced back and forth, fuming. Malice dominated his thoughts. All his past resentment toward the world surged violently through his brain.

As he pondered over Carma's words, Graham became enraged. He noted that it was not quite eleven o'clock. Seizing his hat and coat, he stormed from the front door, rounded the bank building and strode in the direction of Ralph Delkin's home.

In his fury, Graham, did not notice a coupé parked near his house. The car rolled silently along the street after Graham had disappeared from view. When the young man neared Delkin's home, the car was on that street, its lights extinguished. Harry Vincent was watching from a distance.

Lights were showing in Delkin's living-room windows. Graham rapped at the door. Eunice opened it. Staring beyond the girl, Graham, saw Ralph Delkin.

Without a word to Eunice, the young man strode forward to encounter the manufacturer. Delkin arose from his chair and stood in surprise as he faced the intruder.

"What is the matter, Graham?" he questioned.

"The matter!" Graham looked at Delkin, then at Eunice, who had entered the room. "I've been double-crossed—that's all. Misplaced confidence."

"What has happened?"

There was a peevishness in Delkin's tone. The man seemed worried and Graham took it as a sign of guilt. In cold, scoffing terms, he broke loose with an outpour of indignation.

"My wife is in town," he asserted. "She has come here to demand money. She told me how she discovered where I was. Someone in Southwark sent for her."

"Someone in Southwark!" echoed Delkin feebly.

"Someone who has learned about my past," declared Graham. "Someone who has seen a way to make me pay out millions. It's blackmail, of the meanest kind."

"This is most unfortunate," observed Delkin.

"For me, yes," sneered Graham. "But not for the man who is to profit by his treachery. Someone has squealed—and there's only one man in Southwark who knows the facts about me—only one to whom I have revealed my past life."

"You are accusing me?" queried Delkin harshly.

"No," scoffed Graham. "You are accusing yourself. I was right when I was crooked. I trusted no one then. I refused your friendship because I suspected everyone who ever pretended to be my friend. You're no worse than a lot of others, Delkin, but you're no better. Carma put me wise without realizing it. You're the one who framed this game!"

"Get out of my house!" ordered Delkin indignantly. "Get out, before I call the police!"

"You won't call anyone," retorted Graham. "You're playing too big a game—"

"Graham!" It was Eunice who interrupted. "You know well that my father would not betray you. You must not talk this way!"

Graham paid no attention to the girl's words. Face to face with Ralph Delkin, he poured out his contempt of the man whom he had branded as a traitor.

"I told you to destroy those notes," declared Graham. "You refused. Why? I'll tell you. Because they were made out to my uncle; because they bore dates that will stand as proof of the robbery I committed. Where are the notes now?"

"At the factory," asserted Delkin.

"I want them," said Graham. "At once."

"You will not get them by demand," returned Delkin. "Wait until you have come to your senses. This is outrageous—"

"So you're keeping them, eh?" jeered Graham. "Well—go ahead. They don't matter. Carma is your trump card. She's here—to make me pay. I know your financial situation, Delkin. I've been ready to offer you aid should you request it.

"Instead of coming to me fairly, you turned crook yourself. Thought you could lie undercover and pick up a lot of easy cash. Didn't trust me, because I told you that I'd been a crook. Well, the damage is done. I hope you're satisfied. I warn you, though, that I'm going to fight this game to the end."

TURNING, Graham thrust himself past Eunice and reached the door. He swung to deliver a last tirade before departing. His face bore the sordid venom that had characterized it during his career of crime. The words that spat from Graham's lips were filled with malice.

"I warned you when you first offered me your friendship," Graham reminded. "I warned you that you would be sorry—both of you. I softened; but I'm toughened again. I'm warning you now—to look out!

"You'll hear from me, Ralph Delkin—and you'll never forget the revenge that will be mine. You've joined in a blackmail plot, and if I don't come through, you'll tell the world that I was mixed in crime.

"You won't have to tell the world"—Graham's tone was bitter—"because I'll attend to that myself. You'll learn just how tough I can be. When I strike, you will feel it."

As Graham glowered, Eunice Delkin stepped forward. She advanced straight to the young man and looked steadily into his eyes. Graham stared coldly. He expected to see antagonism in Eunice's glance; instead, he observed nothing more than sorrowful disapproval.

"Graham," said Eunice quietly, "you cannot mean these things that you have said. You know that there is no revenge in your heart. You know that father and I are your friends."

Graham Wellerton could not face this mild criticism. His tight fists loosened, his heart seemed to sink. Bitterness began to fade. Graham knew that the girl was right. Yet the last vestiges of resentment came in a final surge, and with that emotion, Graham Wellerton turned on his heel and stalked out into the night.

The tense scene was at an end. Graham Wellerton had capitulated, although he had managed not to show it. Rebuked at heart, he turned his footsteps homeward, fighting hard to balance his regard for Eunice with his resentment toward Ralph Delkin. In that effort, Graham was failing. Right feeling was triumphing over malice, despite the ordeal which Graham had undergone.

RALPH DELKIN, standing in his living room, was pale and troubled when Eunice approached her father; the man spoke in a tone of worriment.

"Graham Wellerton intends to do us harm," asserted Delkin. "I am worried, Eunice—worried—"

"There is nothing to worry about, father," interposed the girl quietly. "Graham will come to his senses. Reason will tell him that you are his real friend—that you would not betray him."

"I must have advice," declared Delkin. "If I should call Harwin Dowser now—"

"Never!" exclaimed Eunice in alarm.

"Dowser is Graham's attorney," admitted Delkin. "Nevertheless, I know him well. His services can be mine for the asking."

"It is not that, father," decided Eunice firmly. "Remember our promise to Graham; that we would tell no one of his past. Graham has accused you of betraying him—surely, you would not do so now, even though you might speak in confidence to a lawyer."

Ralph Delkin nodded thoughtfully. He slumped into a chair. His gaze seemed faraway. Eunice wondered what was passing in her father's mind.

"Promise me," said the girl, "that you will say nothing unless Graham makes some attempt to follow his foolish threat. Will you promise, father?"

Delkin gave a slow nod. He was staring toward the door; Eunice was watching him. Neither knew that other eyes were upon them; that an intruder was spying through the half-opened window. This stormy scene with Graham Wellerton had been observed by an outsider who had more than a passing interest in the affair!

When Eunice left her father alone, Ralph Delkin still seemed in a dazed state. The girl knew that he was pondering over the vague threat which Graham Wellerton had made. She felt sure, however, that all would be well.

There was one, however, in Southwark, who understood that some great calamity was threatening. Harry Vincent, agent of The Shadow, was that man. At midnight, Harry stopped in the telegraph office to send a telegram to Rutledge Mann, in New York.

There was nothing in the telegram to indicate it as other than an ordinary message pertaining to some minor business. Actually, however, the wording of the wire had a special significance. That telegram was an emergency message to The Shadow—a prompt report to tell the master of darkness that grim events were in the making.

Harry Vincent knew that The Shadow would respond. Whatever might occur in Southwark, The Shadow's might would be here to play a vital part!

CHAPTER XX
THE ANSWER

THE next day was Saturday. Graham Wellerton attended to the affairs of the short business day. As evening approached, he dropped in to see Harwin Dowser.

Graham had no intention of telling the old lawyer what had happened—at least not for the present. He knew, however, that he might have to make use of legal advice at any time. He wanted to be sure that Dowser would be in town.

In response to Graham's casual questioning, Dowser stated that he intended to spend the week-end at his home. Dowser lived in a large house about two miles out of Southwark, hence he would be accessible should Graham need him.

"What is the trouble, Wellerton?" quizzed the lawyer. "You are not worried about business affairs?"

"Nothing special," responded Graham. "I have various matters to consider and I intend to stay at home tomorrow on that account. It just occurred to me that I might find some questions that would require your answer."

Harwin Dowser eyed the young man shrewdly. The old lawyer, experienced in his study of human nature, could sense that his client was troubled. Dowser shook his head knowingly after Graham had departed.

Back in his old house, Graham dined alone and dismissed the servant for the evening. He quietly awaited the arrival of Carma, for he felt sure that the woman would come to learn the answer to her demands. Thinking of Carma brought up the subject of Ralph Delkin.

Graham lighted a cigarette and went out on the front porch to smoke. He was convinced, beyond all doubt, that Delkin had sent for Carma. He felt a strong resentment toward the man, but as he considered the matter, Graham could not regain the indignation of the previous evening.

After all, Graham had been a crook. Why should he criticize Delkin for turning crooked? The manufacturer was desperate. He had discovered a perfect opportunity to bleed a man who had much wealth.

What hurt Graham was the fact that he would gladly have offered funds to Delkin. Carma was the reason why Graham hated this whole turn of events. He was determined to balk the woman's game no matter what the penalty might be.

The night was cloudy. A thrumming announced that an airplane was passing overhead. The coupled circumstances made Graham remember that night when he had robbed his uncle's safe in an effort to aid Ralph Delkin. What strange consequences had come from that! In one short month, Graham's fortunes had risen and fallen. Tonight, another crisis was at hand.

Graham went back into the house. He sat at a desk and began to write with pen and ink. After several attempts at careful wording, which involved the destruction of unfinished effort, Graham completed his task.

AN hour had passed. There was a ring at the door. Graham went to answer it. He found Carma waiting there. The young man stared coldly, then invited the woman to enter.

Once again, Graham's eyes did not notice the space beyond the porch. Someone was there—but even had Graham stared coldly, he could not have detected the phantom figure which lingered. That weird shape was almost part of the night itself!

Graham conducted Carma into the living room. They were out of sight of the front door, hence neither saw that barrier open softly. No eyes observed the tall being clad in black that moved with spectral tread as it came to the door of the room itself.

The Shadow had arrived in Southwark. Lost in the gloom of Graham Wellerton's dimly lighted hallway, this master who battled crime was a silent observer of the interview which was now to take place!

"Well, big boy," began Carma, "here I am. What have you got to say?"

"Regarding the money that you want?"

"You guessed it."

"I have made my decision," declared Graham. "I intend to give you all my money."

"What!" exclaimed Carma. "The whole amount?"

"Exactly," returned Graham, "but not at present. That is the only qualification."

"So that's it, eh?" jeered Carma. "Trying to stall me?"

"Not at all," said Graham. "Here is the paper which I have prepared. It is my will."

"Your will?"

"Yes. A bequeathment—to you—of all the money which I may have when I die."

"Where do you get that stuff!" sneered Carma. "When you die! How does that help me?"

"I gained the money through my uncle's death," declared Graham. "You, in turn, will gain it through mine. My uncle accumulated his wealth through evil practices. He left it to me because he felt that I would use it to further crime.

"Instead, I have been using the cash for good. In respect of my uncle's feelings—no matter how unfair they may have been—I shall cease my philanthropies. I intend to live upon the interest, keeping the principal.

"Should I survive you, I shall be free to use the money as I wish. Should you survive me, the entire capital will be yours. That is a fair arrangement—a sporting chance for both of us."

"Yeah?" questioned Carma, in a malicious tone. "Well, it doesn't suit me, big boy. How do you like that? Come across on a fifty-fifty basis, or I squeal."

"Good," decided Graham. "If you do that, I shall destroy this will and leave all my money to charity."

"You will go to prison."

"For twenty years at the most. Perhaps less. I have already arranged to make restitution of funds that I have stolen. I do not relish a term in the penitentiary, but when I am free, I shall still have the bulk of my uncle's millions.

"Then, if you survive me, you will gain nothing. Even your claim for a widow's share will be nullified—in all probability. You have your choice—all when I die or nothing."

"And how does that help me now?"

"I must mention that, Carma. So long as you live, I shall provide you with a comfortable income, provided that you remain away from Southwark and keep silent. If you fail in either of these terms, I shall cut off the money that I am giving you; and I shall be willing to take the consequences."

"You think I won't squeal?" scoffed Carma.

"I think you will," rejoined Graham calmly. "Nevertheless, I am willing to face the music."

"All right, big boy," threatened Carma. "Get ready for a lot of trouble."

"Better think it over, Carma," suggested Graham. "I shall have this will witnessed tonight. I am calling my lawyer, Harwin Dowser, to tell him that I have prepared the document. On Monday, I shall deliver it to him, unless I should happen to see him before then.

"Dowser does not know that I am married. When he learns that fact, he will not be surprised to learn that I have left my estate to my wife. This will does not incriminate me in any way. So there is your opportunity, Carma. Wait—in hopes of gaining all, and live while you wait; or squeal and get nothing."

"I'll think it over," snarled Carma, rising. "You'll hear from me soon enough. Go ahead—get the will witnessed. I'm in no hurry, now that I've had your answer."

THE woman arose. She walked to the door. Graham did not accompany her. Carma went directly past the spot where The Shadow was standing. She did not see the tall being in black, nor did Graham.

Still in the living room, Graham heard the door slam. He did not hear it reopen softly as The Shadow, too, departed.

Graham went to the telephone to call some friends in Southwark. His purpose was to arrange an appointment for the witnessing of the will. Graham was resigned to whatever might occur. He would wait here until he heard from Carma.

Meanwhile, Carma was going back to the Southwark House. Arrived at the hotel, the woman entered a phone booth in the drugstore which adjoined it. As she telephoned, Carma did not notice the tall, silently moving individual who took the next booth. She did not realize that every word she said could be heard.

One call completed, Carma hung up the receiver and waited a few minutes. Then she stepped from the booth and consulted the telephone directory. Eyes were watching as Carma found the name she wanted—that of Ralph Delkin. The number was Southwark 68.

Returning to the booth, Carma called six eight. A sneering curl showed on the woman's ruddy lips as a voice answered at the other end. In smooth, easy tones, Carma began to speak. As she talked, The Shadow listened!

Carma, tonight, had received her answer. She knew that Graham Wellerton would persist in his intention. Now, Carma was plotting to turn the answer into a fortune greater than the one she had demanded!

CHAPTER XXI
THE PLOT BREAKS

GRAHAM WELLERTON spent a quiet Sunday in his home. The cloudy day seemed to hold the gloom of an approaching storm. Southwark was a dreary town on such a day as this. Graham saw no reason to venture forth.

Evening came. Graham, seated in his living room, heard a ring at the door. He decided that Carma must be here. He went to the door and opened it. He was surprised to find Sheriff Ellis Taussig.

"Hello, sheriff," greeted Graham. "What's up?"

"Nothing special," responded Taussig. "I just came in from Dowser's. He thought maybe you would ride out and see him."

"Why didn't he phone me?" asked Graham.

"The line's out of order," returned Taussig. "Dowser may be going out of town early tomorrow. He wants to see you, because he says you have some paper to give him."

"I have," said Graham. "But I am also expecting a visitor."

"Leave a note on the door," suggested Taussig. "We can get back here in a little while. An hour, say."

His keenness aroused, Graham suspected some special purpose in the sheriff's visit. Taussig was tactful. Graham half believed that if he refused to accompany the man, trouble might result. If anything had started, it would be best to learn about it now. Graham penned a brief note and stuck it to the door. He pocketed his witnessed will and went out to the sheriff's car.

Taussig said but little during the ride to Dowser's. They swung in through a gate, up a long lane among thick trees and stopped at the lawyer's home. The sheriff kept very close to his companion as the pair entered the house.

GRAHAM'S first surprise came when he entered Dowser's living room. Standing with the old lawyer was Ralph Delkin.

What was the manufacturer doing here? Graham wondered. There was tenseness during the handshakes. As the men sat down, Graham drew his will from his pocket and passed it to Harwin Dowser. The lawyer glanced at the document, then read it carefully. He made no comment regarding its contents.

"I shall place this in my safe, Wellerton" was Dowser's only remark.

Graham unconsciously glanced to a door across the room. That door, he knew, led to the lawyer's study. Did Dowser mean the safe in there—or the safe in his own office? It did not matter; but there was something else that did.

Graham noted that the door was very slightly ajar. Through the crevice, he caught a momentary gleam that disappeared the moment he observed it. He sensed that eyes had been watching him. He shuddered as a long forgotten thought came to his mind.

The Shadow!

Once Graham Wellerton had felt the presence of that mysterious being. Did he sense it now? The thought was incredible, yet it persisted. With his criminal past disturbing his mind, Graham was ill at ease. Carma in league with Ralph Delkin—that was a situation bad enough. If The Shadow had suddenly entered the scene, Graham could see naught but doom.

The Shadow warred with criminals. Graham, despite the reform which he had chosen, could not forget that he had been a crook. He feared The Shadow, and his only solace was the effort which he made to laugh off what might be nothing more than pure imagination.

"I can stay only one hour," remarked Graham cordially. "I may have callers at home—I really should be back there."

"One hour will be long enough."

Graham turned in surprise. It was Ralph Delkin who had spoken. The manufacturer's face had become determined. Graham stared, then looked at Taussig and Dowser. Both seemed stern and solemn. Graham knew that trouble was due to break.

"What is the matter, Delkin?" challenged Graham. "It appears that you have some purpose in being here tonight."

"I have," declared Delkin, rising. "You threatened me two nights ago. You told me that trouble would come upon me. It has arrived and I demand the answer."

"Concerning what?"

"The disappearance of my daughter!"

Graham was on his feet, staring at Delkin in consternation. Turning to Dowser and Taussig, Graham showed the amazement that he felt.

"Eunice Delkin!" he exclaimed. "Has something happened to her? To Eunice?"

"She disappeared last night," asserted Dowser calmly. "It looks like abduction. Delkin came to me and accused you. I told him to remain here. That is why I asked the sheriff to bring you here."

"This is horrible!" exclaimed Graham. "I know nothing about it! You may rely upon me to use every effort to aid in finding Eunice!"

"You threatened me," denounced Ralph Delkin coldly. "That is why I have told the truth about you. Dowser knows all; so does Taussig. You are a crook—the kind of a man who would stoop to kidnapping."

"You lie!" retorted Graham.

"One moment." Harwin Dowser spoke gravely as he arose from his chair. "I have represented you, Wellerton, purely as the administrator of your uncle's estate. I have no sympathy for you now that I have learned that you are a crook by nature. You are trapped, young man. You cannot escape us."

Graham glanced quickly toward Sheriff Taussig. The officer did not have a gun in readiness. Graham looked toward the door of the study. He knew that the room had another outlet. A wild desire to escape came over him.

WHILE Graham instinctively moved toward the study, trying to resist the action which would certainly incriminate him, Harwin Dowser issued a loud command. Instantly four masked men leaped into view at the wide archway which led from living room to hall. The men were holding revolvers; they covered Graham Wellerton.

"Who are these men?" demanded Sheriff Taussig, leaping to his feet.

"Vigilantes," responded Harwin Dowser sternly. "I summoned them here after you left to get Wellerton."

"Why?" questioned Taussig sharply.

"It was necessary," explained Dowser. "Delkin talked a bit about his daughter's disappearance. People called me on the telephone. They were going to seize Wellerton."

"You did not inform me of that."

"No; but new calls came just after you went out. I told the vigilantes to come here; that you were bringing Wellerton. Do not worry, sheriff. These men are on the side of the law. They will obey you. Perhaps their presence will make Wellerton confess more readily."

"Confess to what?" demanded Graham.

"To the abduction of my daughter!" cried Delkin.

Graham looked toward the door. The crowd of vigilantes had increased to eight. He decided that there must be more men outside. With nerves tingling, the young man planned to meet the situation.

"I do not know what has become of Eunice," he declared. "I have not seen her since I visited Delkin's home; Ralph Delkin says that I am a crook. He offers no proof. That settles the matter. Sheriff"—Graham faced Taussig squarely—"I expect you to accompany me back to my own home, where you found me."

As Taussig deliberated, Harwin Dowser intervened. The old lawyer held up a hand to signify that no one should move. He walked toward the hallway; the vigilantes parted. Dowser beckoned. Carma appeared in view!

"Do you know this woman?" demanded the lawyer.

"She claims to be my wife," retorted Graham.

"I am your wife," sneered Carma. "You are a crook—and I can tell the truth about you."

With sudden decision, Graham came forth with a denial. He faced the woman and hurled back a challenge to her.

"You are talking of the past," he declared. "Let me see you prove the past. Prove that I engaged in crime. Prove that you are married to me. This woman holds a grudge against me"—Graham turned to Taussig as he spoke—"and her word is insufficient to incriminate me."

Harwin Dowser, standing near the vigilantes, uttered a chuckle. His tone became a laugh. He glared at Graham Wellerton with contempt.

"You want more proof?" he questioned. "You want corroborating testimony? You shall have it. Set a thief to catch a thief. Here you are!"

The masked vigilantes parted. Another man stepped into view. This time, Graham Wellerton stared in dumbfoundment. The new witness whom Harwin Dowser had summoned was Wolf Daggert. Leering, the yellow gangster was face to face with Graham Wellerton.

Eyes were peering from the study door; eyes that even Graham Wellerton did not observe. The Shadow was a silent witness to this amazing scene!

CHAPTER XXII
THE SHADOW'S DEED

THE door of Harwin Dowser's study closed completely. A tiny flashlight glimmered in the darkened room. A disk of illumination, no larger than a silver dollar, formed a spot upon the door of the old-fashioned safe that stood in the corner.

A black hand grasped the dial. Fingers, working a combination that was evidently known to the brain which guided them, completed the work. The door of the safe opened; The Shadow's keen eyes perceived a long envelope which lay close at hand.

The envelope disappeared into the darkness. Several seconds elapsed before it was returned. A soft laugh was caught within the close-walled room. The light went out; The Shadow moved away.

The course of his stealthy tread took him through a side door of the study. From the rear of the hallway, The Shadow could glimpse the armed men in the archway at the opening of the living room.

Unseen, The Shadow turned through a narrow opening. His flashlight glimmered upon the knob of a door. Silently, The Shadow opened the barrier and descended a flight of stairs. His light was no longer at work, his steps were noiseless, even when they reached the stone flooring of the basement.

In a remote portion of the large cellar, The Shadow stopped as he reached an opening in the wall. Before him lay a stone compartment; beyond it was a sheet-metal door that bore a huge padlock. Two men were in view, seated upon overturned boxes. Both were roughly clad; both were watchful in the gloomy light that came from a single electric bulb.

One of the men arose. Strolling back and forth, he neared the fringe of darkness by the opening where The Shadow stood. The other man was not observing his companion.

A long streak of blackness crept along the floor. The standing man saw it; he turned toward the opening. Two long arms shot out and caught the fellow by the throat. Like a rat between a terrier's teeth, the ruffian was whisked into darkness.

The seated man lighted a cigarette. Holding out the package, he looked for his companion. He wondered where the other had gone. Listening, he fancied that he heard a noise. He arose and drew forth a flashlight. As he neared the opening in the wall, he turned on the torch.

The glare revealed a tall approaching figure. Sparkling eyes reflected the flashlight's glare. Before the startled man could realize what the phenomenon meant, a phantom shape shot forward and materialized itself into a dynamic fighting force. The second ruffian went down beneath The Shadow's onslaught. He, too, was dragged into the darkness beyond.

The quickness of these events had been incredible. The Shadow reappeared and swept across the lighted compartment. A tiny instrument of steel appeared in his black-gloved hand. At the first attempt, The Shadow picked the padlock on the door.

The barrier swung wide. As the light flickered into the room beyond, The Shadow moved swiftly back by the path which had brought him here. Lost in the darkness beyond the opening in the wall, he paused to deliver a whispered utterance—a strange, uncanny summons that carried a note of command.

The black cloak swished as The Shadow retraced his steps toward the stairs that led upward. The two men whom he had overcome, now lying bound beside the cellar wall, heard the faint echoes of a mysterious whispered laugh.

IN the upstairs living room, Graham Wellerton was facing the sneering glares of Carma Urstead and Wolf Daggert. The woman had told her story. Wolf was corroborating the tale.

"Sure," the yellow gangster was declaring, "this guy is phony. He worked for King Furzman—the big shot back in New York. His mob throwed him out—they were the bozos who were tryin' to rob old Talboy when he butted in."

"Hear him, sheriff," suggested Graham. "This man is incriminating himself."

"I ain't talkin' about myself," snarled Wolf. "I'm talkin' about this guy—Wellerton—the bank robber."

"Let me explain the matter," suggested Dowser, turning to Sheriff Taussig. "Shortly after Wellerton came into his uncle's estate, this man Daggert appeared here at my home. He stated that Wellerton was a bank robber; that the men whom he killed at Ezra Talboy's home were his old cronies.

"Daggert admitted that he had been connected with the group. He said that he had remained in hiding at a farmhouse several miles outside of Southwark—the old deserted place on the Surreyville road. It was through Daggert that I learned of Wellerton's wife Carma, who was living in New York.

"In order to learn the truth, I sent for the woman. She has been in town for several days. She is here to accuse Graham Wellerton of having deserted her."

Graham Wellerton stared. He knew now whom Carma had meant when she had said that a man in Southwark had sent for her. He knew now that she was in league with Wolf Daggert, and that the skulking gang leader expected a share of the spoils.

How had Wolf learned of Carma? Graham had never mentioned her name to Wolf.

"You are listening to a conspiracy," declared Graham, turning to the sheriff. "No proof is offered—merely a concerted attempt to ruin my reputation. Mr. Dowser has been deluded by these scoundrels. These statements are given by persons who admit their own unreliability."

"One moment," asserted Dowser. "I take it, Wellerton, that you think there is no proof. I do not care for your opinion. It is Sheriff Taussig whom I intend to convince. Come this way—to my study. There you shall see evidence."

The vigilantes followed, covering Graham with their revolvers. Dowser, Taussig, and Delkin drew Graham along with them into the study, where the lawyer turned on the lights. Carma and Wolf followed. The masked guardians grouped themselves within the door.

Harwin Dowser opened the safe. From it, he drew an envelope. He pulled back the flap and produced a folded paper. His sharp eyes were gleaming as he handed the document to Sheriff Taussig.

"There," declared Dowser emphatically, "you will find the proof of the first statement made. That is the marriage license, dated March the third, 1928, which pronounces Carma Urstead to be the wife of Graham Wellerton. That is the document which caused me to accept the woman's story. This will in my pocket"—Dowser handed the new paper to Taussig—"goes with it, naming the woman as heiress to Graham Wellerton's entire estate."

SHERIFF TAUSSIG opened the marriage license. He stared at it in perplexity. He raised his head and looked wonderingly about the group. His face became firm—and challenging.

Harwin Dowser looked over the sheriff's shoulder; Graham Wellerton, on the other side, did the same. A cry of amazement came from Graham's lips. In one brief instant, complete understanding of a long-continued plot came to his mind.

The marriage license which Sheriff Taussig was reading was not dated March 3, 1928. It was two years older than that, bearing the date of April 9, 1926. But that was not the astounding feature of the document. The names upon it were startling points.

Carma Urstead was named, but Graham Wellerton was not. The man whose name was given in the marriage license was Willis Daggert—Wolf Daggert!

With a cry of triumph, Graham Wellerton turned to throw his counter accusation against these two whose conspiring brains had thrust him into a life of crime.

CHAPTER XXIII
A NEW ALLY

COMPLETE confidence ruled Graham Wellerton now. He felt that he had gained the point he needed—a startling piece of information that would enable him to place his past faults squarely upon those who were responsible.

Ralph Delkin knew of Graham's career of crime. To Delkin, Graham had stated facts concerning Carma Urstead. Now that the woman was proven as the wife of another man, Graham's case was established so far as Delkin was concerned.

Through Delkin, Graham felt that he could swing Sheriff Taussig; as for Harwin Dowser, the old lawyer would have to capitulate, now that his pet theories had been disturbed. Graham realized that Carma, actually the wife of Wolf Daggert, had married him by trickery. Then, conspiring with Wolf, she had forced Graham into crime to meet her demands for money.

Evidently the woman had kept both marriage licenses: the bona fide one, which named her as the wife of Wolf Daggert; and the false, illegal document which named Graham Wellerton as her husband. Graham decided that there must have been a mistake; that Carma had inadvertently placed the first license in Dowser's keeping.

Carma was staring at the paper. The words she blurted forth merely served to prove the genuineness of the license which Sheriff Taussig was holding.

"That's the old one," cried Carma. "My old license—which I left in New York! Someone must have stolen it and brought it here. It has been put in the safe instead of the one I gave to Mr. Dowser!"

Sheriff Taussig was quick to catch the woman's statement. He stared at Carma as he waved the paper which he held in his hand.

"You mean you were married before you met Wellerton?" quizzed Taussig. "I see—married to this crook"—Taussig nudged his head at Wolf—"and working with him to put young Wellerton in bad. Well, I'm going to pinch both of you—and it will be lucky for you, woman, if that other license don't show up."

The sheriff turned to the masked men at the door. With an air of authority, he addressed the vigilantes.

"We don't need you fellows," asserted Taussig. "I'll grab these two crooks. I'll see that Wellerton sticks around until this whole matter is thrashed out."

"Hold on, sheriff!" announced Harwin Dowser. "We're not through with Wellerton yet. You forget why we brought him here. Delkin's daughter is missing. Wellerton threatened Delkin. Just because you've spotted two crooks is no proof of Wellerton's innocence. He is as bad as the others. We've got to find that girl!"

Threatening tones came from the vigilantes at the door. Two men were advancing with drawn guns. Taussig stood stock-still. His revolver was in his pocket.

"We've waited long enough," growled one of the masked men. "We're going to grab Wellerton and make him talk. He kidnapped the girl sure enough. He's going to tell us where she is."

"Stay where you are!" ordered Taussig.

"Nothing doing," growled the vigilante. "We're handling Wellerton from now on. If he don't tell us what he's done with the girl, we'll string him up to a tree."

Graham Wellerton realized his helplessness. These vigilantes, like every group that dealt in lynch law, were probably men who did not care to waste time in listening to reason. The issue had been diverted. Sheriff Taussig intended to arrest Carma and Wolf. But that would not help Graham's situation.

Taussig was helpless; Delkin was horrified. There was only one man who might be able to appease the wrath of these masked vigilantes. That one was Dowser. Graham turned to the old lawyer in appeal.

"This is your house," he said. "You may have some authority over those who have come here. If these men will wait—"

DOWSER'S warning hand seemed to hold back the vigilantes. They did not relax their tenseness. Four men in this room; four in the room beyond; all were ready with their revolvers. Dowser's decision was all that they awaited.

"Tell what you know, Wellerton," suggested the old attorney. "If you can lead these men to Eunice Delkin, they will not harm you. Where is the girl?"

"I don't know," blurted Graham.

"You must tell," insisted Dowser. "If Eunice Delkin is alive and well, your life will be spared. There is no one else in Southwark who would have had cause to steal her—no one but yourself. Where is she?"

"I don't know," repeated Graham.

"You've killed her, eh?" came the suggestion from the leading vigilante. "That's why you're keeping mum? Well—if that's the case, we'll string you up in a hurry!"

Harwin Dowser shook his head sadly. Ralph Delkin, his face pale, was pleading with the masked men to use discretion. Ellis Taussig placed his hand upon his pocket.

"If you grab Wellerton," thundered the sheriff, "I'll draw—"

"Don't!" warned Dowser. "These men would kill you, Taussig! If Wellerton will only speak and tell the truth, there is a chance for him."

"Help us out, Wellerton!" exclaimed the sheriff. "Do you know where the girl is? Can you give us any clue? We want to save your life. If only we could find a trace of Eunice Delkin and—"

The sheriff's tones ended. Taussig, his face registering astonishment, was staring toward the side door of the study. Someone was entering there, and as the figure came into the light, others, beside the sheriff, uttered cries of amazement.

Coming into this room where death threatened, brought to this place just in time to avert a crisis, was Eunice Delkin!

Pale, the girl was advancing, her eyes filled with horror. She did not notice her father. She could see only Graham Wellerton, threatened by a group of armed masked men. With a sob, the girl sprang forward and threw her arms around Graham Wellerton. Dazedly, the young man realized that deliverance had arrived; then came a thought of gladness that brightened above all his worries.

His past was cleared. Eunice Delkin had commended him for leaving paths of crime. He loved this girl; now that his marriage to Carma Urstead had been proven nonexistent, he would be free to tell Eunice of his love.

The vigilantes would release him. Perhaps the penalties of past crimes could be avoided. Yet even a jail sentence seemed trivial in the knowledge which Graham Wellerton had gained. He knew now that Eunice Delkin loved him as he loved her.

With the happy girl still sobbing in his arms, Graham turned to Harwin Dowser, confident that now the old lawyer could dismiss the threatening vigilantes. When he saw the expression in the attorney's eyes, Graham Wellerton's blood turned cold.

Harwin Dowser had become a glaring fiend. His kindly mask had vanished. In one quick instant, Graham Wellerton realized that all this evil business had been of the old man's making!

CHAPTER XXIV
GUNS SPEAK

WHILE Graham Wellerton still stared at Harwin Dowser, Eunice Delkin realized that something was amiss. Drawing away from the man whose life she had saved, the girl saw her father and turned to him. As she told her story, she pointed an accusing finger at persons whom she named.

"Harwin Dowser is responsible for my abduction!" exclaimed the girl. "He and these two!" Eunice indicated Wolf and Carma. "Last night, this woman called me on the telephone. She said that she was Graham Wellerton's wife; that she would like to talk to me. I met her outside our house. The man was driving the car. They brought me here and imprisoned me.

"Until tonight, I had no opportunity for escape. The door was locked; two men were on guard outside. Then I was mysteriously released. Harwin Dowser was the one who kept me prisoner, so he could blame Graham Wellerton!"

Harwin Dowser broke into an evil chuckle.

"What Eunice says is true," he asserted coldly. "What difference does it make? Now that facts are known, I can stifle them. The outcome will be the same—since Graham Wellerton has made his will!"

There was evil triumph in the old man's tone. Graham sensed a tremendous menace. He listened tensely while Dowser continued.

"Originally," stated the lawyer, "I planned blackmail. Then came a better opportunity. I was working with Wolf Daggert. Carma Urstead played her part. Graham Wellerton made his will. It became easier to kill him than blackmail him.

"These masked men are not vigilantes. They are mobsters, brought here through Daggert. Their job is to slay Graham Wellerton. They will do so. Unfortunately, we will have to dispose of Sheriff Taussig also—now that he has learned too much. He will die protecting Wellerton from the vigilantes.

"I was going to let Delkin out of it. He will have to die also. His daughter also stands in our way. She will die. The two will be found murdered in their home, apparently victims of Graham Wellerton's wrath."

Still persistently malicious, Harwin Dowser stared at those who were to be the victims of his evil vengeance. He pointed to the documents in Sheriff Taussig's hand.

"That old marriage license," asserted Dowser, "arrived here by some mysterious mistake. We will discover the one we want—wherever it has been placed. The old license will be destroyed and forgotten. The will, however, will remain. Through it, I and my friends will gain Graham Wellerton's entire estate."

The old man paused. His evil nature was to the fore. The four who were doomed knew well that there was no escape. With great wealth awaiting him, Harwin Dowser, now turned fiend, would certainly show no mercy.

TENSE silence. No one moved. Dowser turned to the pretended vigilantes. He raised his hand as in a signal. It was the token that murder should be done.

As Dowser acted, Sheriff Taussig overcame all hesitation. Thrusting his hand in his pocket, he reached for his revolver in an effort to make a last attempt for life.

Graham Wellerton was madly trying to shield Eunice Delkin. The girl's father saw that he could not aid. Carma Urstead was scurrying toward the side of the room. Wolf Daggert and Harwin Dowser were calmly drawing revolvers.

All these actions, performed by those of both factions, apparently meant nothing as the vigilantes leveled their guns to shoot. But before a single revolver shot broke forth, an interruption came with amazing suddenness. From the side door of the room, a pair of automatics burst loose with unexpected results.

No one had seen the presence of The Shadow as the master of darkness had arrived to watch this drama. Those who stared now saw only long tongues of flame that came with the startling cannonade. Masked mobsmen fell as bullets struck them.

Those behind turned to meet the attack. Quick shots were fired toward the spot where The Shadow stood.

Well had The Shadow calculated.

The only bullets that came in his direction were those dispatched without accurate aim. Before his enemies could fire deadly shots, The Shadow dropped them with his unerring marksmanship.

The first four vigilantes went down; as the second squad leaped to the fray, distant shots sounded beyond the front door. The Shadow's agents: Harry Vincent and Cliff Marsland, the latter brought from New York, were opening fire upon the outside watchers!

The reserve mobsmen wavered. Shots from the unexpected quarter made them hesitate. That was all The Shadow needed. His mammoth automatics continued their rapid fire. Two mobsmen, one wounded, the other unscathed, staggered through the big room toward the hall. The others lay as victims of the fray.

To Sheriff Taussig, whose gun was in his hand, The Shadow left Harwin Dowser and Wolf Daggert for the moment. The automatics were barking through the hallway, to stop the gangsters who were fleeing, and to halt those who were tumbling in from outside.

Taussig had Wolf Daggert covered; had the sheriff acted as The Shadow had expected, he could have dropped the gang leader and covered Harwin Dowser.

Taussig, however, paused; and while he held Wolf at bay, Dowser performed the action. The lawyer fired. Taussig staggered with a bullet in his shoulder.

Graham Wellerton fell upon Wolf Daggert and wrestled with the gang leader. Wolf's gun barked as Graham yanked it from him. Wounded in the left hand, Graham staggered back and fired point-blank as Wolf leaped upon him. The gangster fell victim to a bullet from his own revolver.

Ralph Delkin was grappling with Harwin Dowser. The lawyer broke free and aimed at Sheriff Taussig, who was lying on the floor. Graham Wellerton, his wounded hand pressed to his body, aimed his revolver at the old lawyer. Graham's action was too late to prevent the shot that was planned to kill Ellis Taussig, but another hand acted while the young man faltered.

A roar from the door. The Shadow had delivered another bullet from the automatic. Harwin Dowser screamed as the revolver fell from his shattered hand. Graham Wellerton, already pressing the trigger of his revolver, could not stop. His bullet entered Dowser's body. The fiend collapsed upon the floor.

Weakened by his wound, Graham Wellerton leaned upon a chair. It was then that a new factor entered the fray.

Carma Urstead was creeping toward the doorway to the living room. Suddenly the woman arose. Her face was evil as her hand leveled a mobsman's revolver toward Graham Wellerton's body.

EUNICE DELKIN saw. With a call of warning, the brave girl leaped forward and placed herself between Graham and the leveled gun. Carma Urstead sneered. Coldly, she aimed to slay Eunice Delkin. The girl never wavered.

As Carma looked toward the object of her aim, she saw a form beyond. Looming within the doorway at the side of the room was the tall figure of The Shadow. Cold eyes—a steady automatic—both were turned toward Carma.

The woman stood petrified, with finger upon the trigger of the revolver. She was afraid to fire. She knew that she was in the power of The Shadow! Slowly, she began to retreat; the glare of those steady eyes made her falter.

The Shadow warred with men. Evil though Carma Urstead was, the master fighter had no intent to slay her. He knew that the very terror of his presence would prevail; that Carma would weaken before his inflexible gaze. The gun was already wavering in the woman's grasp.

But Sheriff Taussig, prone in a corner of the room saw only Carma and Eunice. He did not know why Carma hesitated. He observed the evil glare in the woman's eyes; he fancied that she was withholding vengeance merely to enjoy it more fully. The Shadow was beyond Taussig's range of vision.

Raising his revolver, Sheriff Taussig propped himself on his right elbow, and pressed the trigger of his weapon. With that shot, Carma Urstead staggered. The revolver fell from her hand as she collapsed. Like the others, the woman had paid the penalty of crime.

A strange, creepy laugh shuddered through the room. Startled eyes turned toward the doorway. They saw nothing—these persons whom The Shadow had rescued. The master fighter, with a quick swish of his sable-hued cloak, had merged with the gloom beyond the door.

The Shadow's work was done. Justice had prevailed over insidious crime. Only a trailing laugh remained, an eerie sound which died with mystic echoes after the weird visitant had departed.

Graham Wellerton alone understood the meaning of that sinister cry. To him, the uncanny mirth meant more than The Shadow's triumph. It signified that this master fighter who knew all the circumstances had left him—Graham Wellerton—free to pursue his future along the path of right.

CHAPTER XXV
THE STRAIGHT ROAD

THE consequences of the fierce fight at Harwin Dowser's were amazing to Graham Wellerton. Villains had brought doom upon themselves, and when reason had formed from chaos, Graham found himself freed from the threatening dangers of his past.

Sheriff Ellis Taussig, recognized instrument of the law in Southwark, was the man who took control of the entire situation. To Taussig, the crimes of Harwin Dowser and his associates were evident, while the charges made against Graham Wellerton were doubtful.

The facts were plainly told. Harwin Dowser had coveted Graham Wellerton's millions. The attorney had joined forces with two schemers of criminal tendencies: Wolf Daggert, New York gang leader, and Carma Urstead, adventuress, who claimed to be Graham Wellerton's wife.

Blackmail failing, Graham had been tricked into making a will in the woman's favor. The villains had plotted murder; and to cover it by making Graham's death seem justifiable, had kidnapped Eunice Delkin. They had also called in New York mobsmen, and disguised them as local vigilantes.

With these evil deeds uncovered, Graham Wellerton stood forth as a man who deserved sympathy. The only charges made against him were those which had been advanced by scoundrels.

Moreover, an important document—one which had in some mysterious fashion replaced a false one—acted further in Graham's behalf. This paper was the marriage license that proved Carma Urstead to be the legal wife of Wolf Daggert.

Eunice Delkin's testimony showed that she had been used as a pretext for the murder of Graham Wellerton. Ralph Delkin, his daughter restored and the truth known, was profuse in his admiration for Wellerton's courage.

The past was blotted. Graham's two enemies, Wolf Daggert and Carma Urstead, were dead. Harwin Dowser no longer lived. The only persons who knew the truth were those who had heard it from Graham's own lips: Ralph Delkin and Eunice.

Two mobsters, discovered bound in Dowser's cellar, proved useful witnesses. They identified the false vigilantes as their pals. They were glad to have escaped the slaughter that had come to their evil companions.

The captured pair of gangsters said that they and their fellows had been paid to come to Southwark and follow orders. They knew Wolf Daggert as a smart Manhattan crook. They knew nothing of Graham Wellerton.

THERE was an element of shrouded mystery that perplexed those who had taken part in the affair. Some unseen personage had fought for the right that night. Graham Wellerton was convinced that he knew the identity of the hidden being.

The Shadow had obtained Carma Urstead's real marriage license. He had brought it to Southwark, to substitute it for the false document which Carma had given to Harwin Dowser.

The Shadow, Graham was sure, was the one who had trapped the two gangsters in the cellar. His hand had released Eunice Delkin; the same hand had been ready for the final fray.

Snarling mobsters had fallen before The Shadow's might. The master fighter had driven back the false vigilantes, and they had gone down in battle vainly trying to overcome his attack.

To Graham Wellerton, the presence of The Shadow seemed miraculous. Considering it, the young man realized that The Shadow had granted him powerful aid because Graham had chosen the straight road in preference to the path of crime which he had left.

EVENTS in Southwark had their sequel in Manhattan. On a certain night, some weeks after the struggle at Dowser's, a click sounded in a darkened room. Weird bluish light threw wavering rays upon the surface of a polished table. Into the realm of illumination crept two uncanny hands; living creatures that came from darkness.

The resplendent girasol caught the flickering rays from the light, and threw them back with sparkling iridescence. The glorious jewel told the identity of the man who wore it; the eerie light named the place.

The Shadow was in his sanctum.

From an envelope, long fingers drew forth

clippings and dropped them on the table. Unseen eyes studied the printed lines. These items were of varied import. The first ones which The Shadow read told of restitutions.

Bankers in New York and other cities had been the recipients of funds from unknown sources. Anonymous notes had told them that these moneys were replacements for cash and securities which had been stolen.

A single clipping spoke of another matter. It had been cut from the little Southwark daily, and it told of an important event in the Midwestern town. Eunice Delkin had become the bride of Graham Wellerton.

The light clicked out. A soft laugh shuddered through the darkened room.

The Shadow had departed from his sanctum. He had voiced his satisfaction over the final events that marked the real beginning of Graham Wellerton's new career.

The gentleman of crime had rejected the road of evil to take the path of right. His way was clear; opened by The Shadow. The secret of Graham Wellerton's past would never be known.

For the facts of the young man's forgotten past were recorded only in the secret archives of The Shadow—those massive tomes which, like The Shadow's identity itself, would never be discovered!

THE END

THE MAN WHO CAST THE SHADOW

Walter B. Gibson (1897-1985) was born in Germantown, Pennsylvania. His first published feature, a puzzle titled "Enigma," appeared in *St. Nicholas Magazine* when Walter was only eight years old. In 1912, Gibson's second published piece won a literary prize, presented by former President Howard Taft who expressed the hope that this would be the beginning of a great literary career. Building upon a lifelong fascination with magic and sleight of hand, Gibson became a frequent contributor to magic magazines and worked briefly as a carnival magician. He joined the reporting staff of the *Philadelphia North American* after graduating from Colgate University in 1920, moved over to the *Philadelphia Public Ledger* the following year and was soon producing a huge volume of syndicated features for NEA and the Ledger Syndicate, while also ghosting books for magicians Houdini, Thurston, Blackstone and Dunninger.

A 1930 visit to Street & Smith's offices led to his being hired to write novels featuring The Shadow, the mysterious host of CBS' *Detective Story Program*. Originally intended as a quarterly, *The Shadow Magazine* was promoted to monthly publication when the first two issues sold out and, a year later, began the twice-a-month frequency it would enjoy for the next decade. He eventually wrote 283 Shadow novels totalling some 15 million words.

Gibson scripted the lead features for *Shadow Comics* and *Super-Magician Comics,* and organized a Philadelphia-based comic art shop utilizing former *Evening Ledger* artists. He also found time for radio, plotting and co-scripting *The Return of Nick Carter, Chick Carter, The Avenger*, *Frank Merriwell* and *Blackstone the Magic Detective*. He wrote hundreds of true crime articles for magazines and scripted numerous commercial, industrial and political comic books, pioneering the use of comics as an educational tool. In his book *Man of Magic and Mystery: a Guide to the Work of Walter B. Gibson,* bibliographer J. Randolph Cox documents more than 30 million words published in 150 books, some 500 magazine stories and articles, more than 3000 syndicated newspaper features and hundreds of radio and comic scripts.

Walter also hosted ABC's *Strange* and wrote scores of books on magic and psychic phenomena, many co-authored with his wife, Litzka Raymond Gibson. He also wrote five *Biff Brewster* juvenile adventure novels for Grosset and Dunlap (as "Andy Adams"), a *Vicki Barr, Air Stewardess* book and a *Cherry Ames, Nurse* story (as "Helen Wells"), *The Twilight Zone* and such publishing staples as *Hoyle's Simplified Guide to the Popular Card Games* and *Fell's Official Guide to Knots and How to Tie Them*.

No one was happier than Walter when The Shadow staged a revival in the sixties and seventies. Walter wrote *Return of The Shadow* in 1963 and three years later selected three vintage stories to appear in a hardcover anthology entitled *The Weird Adventures of The Shadow*. Several series of paperback and hardcover reprints followed and Gibson wrote two new *Shadow* short stories, "The Riddle of the Rangoon Ruby" and "Blackmail Bay." A frequent guest at nostalgia, mystery, and comic conventions, Gibson attended the annual Pulpcon and Friends of Old-Time Radio conventions on a regular basis, always delighted to perform a few magic tricks and sign autographs as both Gibson and Grant, using his distinctive double-X signature. His last completed work of fiction, "The Batman Encounters—Gray Face," appeared as a text feature in the 500th issue of *Detective Comics*.

Walter Gibson died on December 6, 1985, a recently-begun Shadow novel sitting unfinished in his typewriter. "I always enjoyed writing the *Shadow* stories," he remarked to me a few years earlier. "There was never a time when I wasn't enjoying the story I was writing or looking forward to beginning the next one." Walter paused and then added, a touch of sadness in his voice, "I wish I was still writing the *Shadow* stories."

So do I, old friend. So do I.

—Anthony Tollin

INTERLUDE by Will Murray

The Shadow entered the world at the beginning of one of the darkest years of the 20th century: 1931.

The Stock Market Crash of October, 1929 signaled a sudden end to the Roaring 20s, a period of unbridled prosperity and lawlessness never before seen. The full impact did not hit until 1931. Only then did a tide of joblessness begin to overwhelm the nation. The first stark year of the Great Depression had commenced.

That epochal year started as one of the most forbidding in New York in many a memory. The national mood was grim, and this was reflected in the popular culture. In February, Bela Lugosi's portrayal of Count Dracula arrested the nation's attention on the Silver Screen. Within weeks, the American public was to meet another strange figure in black, who previously had only been a shivery voice heard over the radio airwaves. The first issue of Street & Smith's *Shadow Magazine* appeared on March 6th, the same day that Sax Rohmer's classic novel *Daughter of Fu Manchu* hit bookstores. No one suspected a legend had been born.

A mocking figure of vengeance, The Shadow was created in answer to an overwhelming tide of lawlessness created by the criminal consequences of Prohibition. During the Roaring '20s, Americans, denied the social pleasures of alcohol, flocked to speakeasies and shady basement taverns to imbibe banned liquor. Paid-off police departments often looked the other way. Most of these nocturnal establishments were by necessity run by gangsters.

The mob bootlegger rose up to become an American celebrity, hailed as a modern Robin Hood who stole from no one, but provided the average person with something the government had unjustly forbidden him.

By the late 1920s, this new type of folk hero had grown so popular that pulp magazine publishers risked civic condemnation to offer up the likes of *Gangster Stories, Racketeer Stories* and even *Underworld Love Tales*. Banned in many cities and towns, these semi-illicit periodicals sold like bathtub gin. The public loved them.

The gangster seemed invincible. The Depression changed all that. First, gangdom violently overreached itself. Bloody turf wars took a brutal toll on the romantic rumrunner myth as some of America's greatest city streets ran red with blood—much of it innocent.

As the economy collapsed, America seemed to sober up. Citizens turned against the criminal culture that now threatened their very safety. Cries for law and order swelled.

The pulp fiction editors took instant notice. The same month that saw the debut of *The Shadow Magazine* witnessed a rival house abruptly changing their *Dragnet Magazine* to *Detective-Dragnet,* announcing: "The showdown for the submachine gun terror has arrived—for fiction readers. The gangster story is on the wane. No longer does the swaggering mobster with his threat of 'the spot' hold sway with American readers.... people have long tired of that worn-out prototype of he who now languishes in a federal penitentiary. The baffling, sinister mystery drama now rules the roost."

Enter The Shadow. No coddler of crooks and rumrunners, he met the challenge of organized crime with cold laughter and hot lead. Operating outside the law, he had no compunctions about acting as judge, jury and executioner in swirling black robes. If he felt justified, The Shadow could and did offer a confronted criminal the opportunity to take his own life.

Initially, some thought the Dark Avenger merely a new species of supercriminal who preyed on lesser crooks for murky reasons of his own. But gradually, the truth became clear. The Shadow's remorseless approach to smashing illicit activity left no doubt about which side of justice he served: the law.

Those who saw him as only a calculating crime-crusher and preternatural punisher of evil never imagined that in the deeper shadows in which he dwelled, The Shadow was dedicated to unorthodox solutions to the criminal problem. His motives were obscure. Like Sherlock Holmes, whom he physically resembled, the Master of Darkness seemed in it for the sheer sake of the hunt. His was a passionless mind playing a grim game of four-dimensional chess with the police and the underworld, both of whom he manipulated like some omniscient grandmaster.

And like Dracula, he struck terror into any who challenged him. Nocturnal, hypnotic, seemingly unkillable, The Shadow was an implacable force of nature with only one prey: criminals of all breeds.

As for the company that birthed him, Street & Smith had been a fiction factory going back to the dime novel days of master detective Nick Carter. It refused to stoop to publishing a magazine celebrating the criminal element. S&S specialized in heroes. But it would take more than a detective to combat the type of big-city criminal that arose in the wake of World War I. Proficient with Tommy-guns and hand grenades, ruthless beyond humane appeal, the organized-crime gangster was rapidly dominating America's major metropolises through crime, cash and corruption.

No ordinary hero could crush such a menace. America needed an avenger.

Beyond the law, yet not above it. A seeker of justice, but a stern dispenser of vengeance when necessary. Operating in secrecy, The Shadow manipulated the machinery of justice at a time when ordinary law enforcement was believed to be broken. Turning criminals against one another, he mocked and decimated the survivors. Yet this new figure of urban folklore also acted as a burning-eyed agent of rescue where victims of evil had no other recourse. He was equally a protector and a punisher.

"When The Shadow stories began in 1931, mob crimes were rampant," Walter Gibson recalled. "New Number One Enemies were popping up as fast as the newly activated FBI could shoot them down. Prosperity was giving way to the Depression and the New Deal was still unknown. So it was only logical that The Shadow should be doing his part to bring order out of chaos."

Part of Gibson's plan for the evolving character was to cast The Shadow as a force for crime prevention. Our two novels for this volume were selected to spotlight that little-seen side of the Master Avenger.

In *Road of Crime,* The Shadow operates largely in the background, a tactic he favored in the early mysterioso phase of his long career. It's a human interest tale of temptation and redemption unlike any other Shadow story ever told.

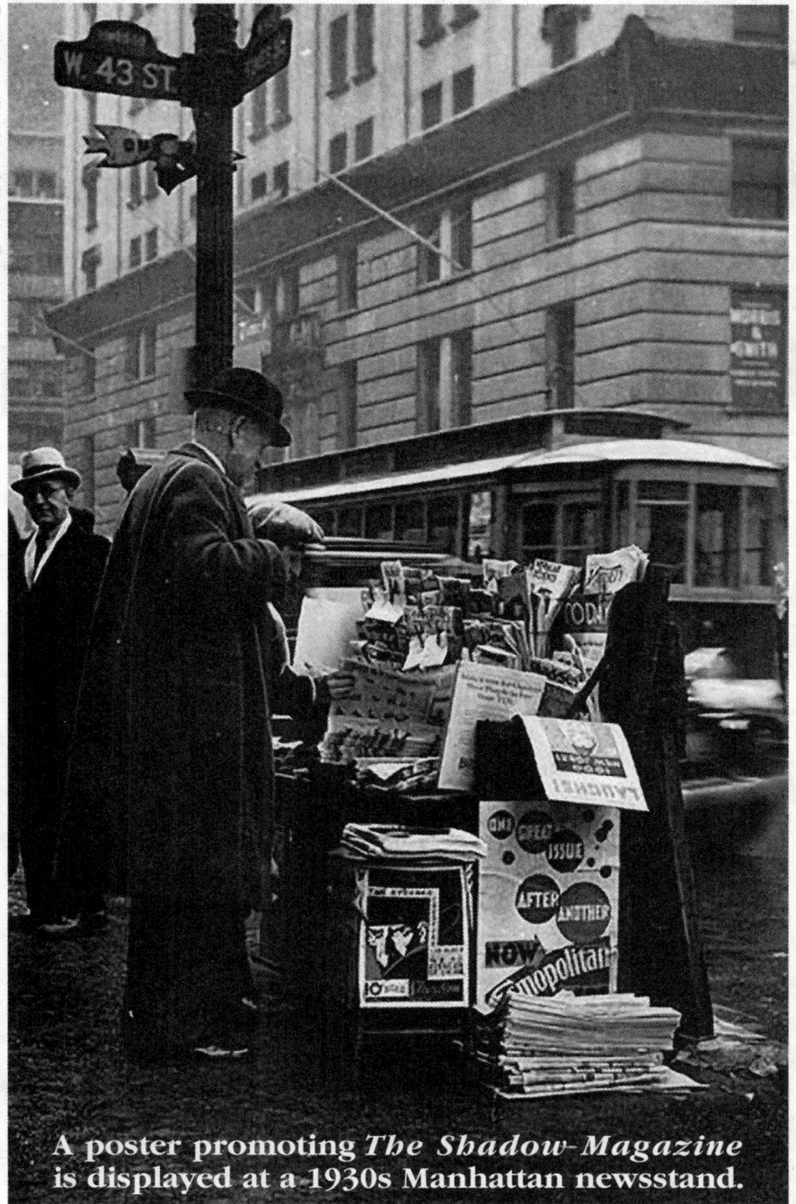

From the collection of Dwight Fuhro

A poster promoting *The Shadow-Magazine* is displayed at a 1930s Manhattan newsstand.

Gibson loved to employ a storytelling device he called the "proxy hero." That was a sympathetic character in whose destiny The Shadow took a hand. Many of his agents, like Harry Vincent, started off as proxy heroes.

Gibson explained his concept of the proxy hero this way: "He is the person, along with others like him, who is matched against the villains of the piece, in a theme which is really the personal saga of that all-important lead character, who is developed through his influence and action toward the lesser figures."

Road of Crime is one Gibson's most elaborate proxy hero stories.

Crooks Go Straight plunges The Shadow into the middle of a tangled tale of two convicted criminals trying to stay on the straight and narrow. Here, he dominates the action throughout. The contrast between these dramatically different accounts of reformed crooks reminds readers that while The Shadow may be best known for taking on super-criminals the police could not catch, it was to battle ordinary street crime that he first took up his cloak and matched .45s. •

What happens when

Crooks Go Straight

A Complete Book-length Novel from the Private Annals of The Shadow, as told to

Maxwell Grant

CHAPTER I
ABOARD THE LIMITED

THE Eastern Limited was driving through the night. To scattered passengers, seated in the lounge of the observation car, the whistle of the locomotive came as a distant blare from far ahead. The train, though long and heavy, was maintaining its fast schedule.

Two men were chatting over newspapers. Strangers who had met aboard the train, they were discussing subjects of common interest. One news story seemed to have impressed them both.

"Well," one passenger was saying, "I can't criticize the governor of this state for pardoning those two convicts. He must have studied their cases mighty closely."

"Both men were lifers," objected the second passenger. "It seems a bit radical to put them back into circulation. They were chronic offenders—"

"Wait a moment," put in the first man. He tapped the newspaper. "The facts are right here.

These chaps only went up for short terms to begin with. Steve Zurk was in for a bank robbery"—the speaker paused and referred to a column—"and Jack Targon was a swindler."

"They broke jail together, didn't they?"

"Yes. That was the rub. They took to robbing more banks. Zurk was caught; he went back into the jug. Then the law landed Targon—"

"I know the details. The pair of them made another break. More crimes. They've been in now for three years and the governor has pardoned them, despite their accumulated sentences."

"Accumulated sentences. You've hit it, friend. That's the point that won the governor over. If those fellows hadn't made their first break, they'd have finished their original terms a couple of years ago."

"I didn't realize that."

"Here, read the details."

The first passenger shoved his newspaper to the second. The latter studied the columns, then began to nod slowly as he laid the journal aside.

"That makes it different," he admitted. "They were hunted men. Crime was their only course."

"Self-preservation," agreed the other passenger. "Man's first instinct."

"I guess the governor deserves credit. Those fellows will have a chance to go straight. I'm glad that they're out. I wonder where they've gone?"

"The newspapers don't know. Leastwise, they're not saying. Zurk and Targon were whisked away in an automobile after the gates of the penitentiary clanged behind them. That's all the report that's given."

Grinding brakes up ahead. The observation car jolted slightly. The limited was heading to a stop. A distant blare of the locomotive whistle.

THE chatting passengers forgot their former subject.

"Wonder what this is?" questioned one. "Sounds like a station stop. But there's none on the schedule. We're supposed to make a nonstop ninety-minute run—"

"There's a stop, though," broke in the second passenger. He was referring to a timetable. "Place called Dupaw. Timetable says to refer to note M. Here it is: 'Will stop Saturdays and Sundays only to receive through passengers for New York.' That must be it. Somebody getting on at this jerkwater station."

"Hope there's more than one," chuckled the first speaker. "It says 'passengers'—not 'passenger.' Well, this is a Sunday, so it makes passengers eligible."

The train was almost to a stop. Peering from the window, the passengers saw the dingy lights of the station. Then the limited reached a full halt. A dozen seconds passed. Then came the muffled, heavy chugging of the locomotive.

"Dupaw, all right," observed the man with the timetable, as the observation car rolled slowly past the little waiting room of the station. "See? There's the sign."

His acquaintance nodded. The two reverted to their newspapers and began a comment on the sporting news. Like the subject of the pardoned convicts, the stop at Dupaw was forgotten.

DIRECTLY across the aisle from the conversing men was another passenger. A tall, calm-faced individual, he had been seated quietly, smoking a cigarette between thin, smileless lips. His immobile countenance possessed a peculiarly hawkish expression, due to the presence of a high, aquiline nose.

Added to the stranger's appearance of dignity was the keenness of his eyes. Though placid, they carried a sharp glint that signified a powerful brain behind them.

It was evident that this listener had heard all that had passed between the other passengers, regarding the convicts and the chance stop at Dupaw. But his expression showed no interest in the conversation that he had overheard.

It was not until the hawk-faced passenger had finished his cigarette that a change came over his expression. Even then, his flicker of countenance was scarcely noticeable. A thin smile appeared upon his steady lips. The tall passenger arose and strolled from the lounge.

His smile remained fixed as he went forward from the observation car. Through clattering vestibules, through sleeping cars where aisles were walled by the green curtains of Pullman berths, the stroller kept steadily onward. He passed through a dining car where waiters were dozing at clothless tables.

He came to a Pullman that bore the name, *Callao;* also cards that marked it as Car G 3.

The tall passenger stopped in the smoking compartment. The porter was seated there, shining shoes. He did not observe the passenger's arrival until the tall personage spoke in a quiet tone. The porter started and looked up.

"Is my compartment made up?" came the quiet question.

"Yes, sah," returned the porter, with a nod. "I figured you were back in the obsahvation cah. All made up, sah. Sorry the conductah couldn't give you the drawing room. I didn't know that it was reserved until he told me."

"That's quite all right. When I learned that the compartment was unoccupied, I decided that it would be preferable to the drawing room."

"That's what I said, sah, when I came in to move your baggage. Compahtment's better than the drawing room. Plenty big enough for one person, sah, and it costs less money."

The porter was chuckling when the tall passenger left. He recalled how this gentleman had come aboard the train and taken the drawing room of Car G 3. Then the porter had learned from the conductor that two other passengers had reserved the drawing room—passengers due to come aboard the train at Dupaw.

So the tall passenger had moved to the compartment that adjoined the drawing room. He had been offered drawing room accommodations in another car; but after viewing the compartment, he had agreed with the porter that it would be suitable.

All along the trip the porter had been wondering about those passengers from Dupaw. It was the first time in his experience on this run that the limited had made that stop. It was odd the drawing room passengers should come aboard at Dupaw; odd, at least to the porter's way of thinking.

MEANWHILE, the tall passenger had reached his compartment. Entering, he found the lower berth made up. He turned to a suitcase that was lying on the compartment chair. Still wearing his slight smile, he unlocked the bag.

From it, he produced earphones. A length of wire projected from them. Leaning into the berth, the passenger ran his fingers along the window ledge. He found the end of another wire, drew it inward and connected it with the wire from the earphones.

It was obvious that this mysterious passenger had made unusual use of his brief occupancy of the drawing room and his later removal to the compartment. He had managed to open the window of the drawing room and let out a tiny wire, which he had later fished in from the window of the compartment.

This wire formed the vital portion of a dictograph connection.

Turning out the light in the compartment, donning the earphones in the darkness, the tall passenger was listening in on conversation that was taking place within the drawing room.

A soft laugh in the darkness of the compartment. A scarcely audible whisper; yet that strange, suppressed mirth pronounced the identity of the scientific eavesdropper.

This personage who had taken interest in the affairs of the passengers from Dupaw was none other than The Shadow. Master hunter who investigated crime, The Shadow was aboard the Eastern Limited, seeking new knowledge that might aid him in his ceaseless quests.

CHAPTER II
BACK TO LIFE

WITHIN the drawing room of Car G 3, two men were engaged in conversation. These men had been muffled with overcoats when they had come aboard the limited. At present they were in shirtsleeves. One was perched upon the edge of the lower berth; the other was seated on the benchlike couch.

The man on the edge of the berth was a smiling, light-complexioned chap about thirty years of age. His face was friendly, but flexible. Behind the smile lay a touch of natural shrewdness. His eyes carried a convincing sparkle.

The man on the couch was older. Forty would have been a good estimate of his age. He was dark-complexioned and his eyes showed a brooding look. His countenance, moreover, was dour—at moments, almost sullen.

Circumstances had brought these two together; those same circumstances had maintained their companionship. The younger, smiling man was Jack Targon, erstwhile swindler de luxe. The older, dour chap was Steve Zurk, former bank robber.

Pardoned by the governor, the two were riding, unwatched and unattended, toward New York. For the first time since they had met within prison walls, they were unharried by the law. Two convicts had come back to life, with the prospect of a crimeless future straight ahead.

"Buck up, Steve," Targon was chuckling. "Can't you get it through your noodle? We're in the clear. Out of the big house. The world is ours!"

"Yours, maybe," growled Zurk. "But maybe it won't be mine. That's why I'm worrying."

"Why worry, Steve? You always said that you'd go straight if you had the chance. You've got it now. Say—that governor is a prince, the way he treated us."

"He's a square-shooter, all right."

"And this fellow Delhugh, that we're going to in New York. He must be another regular. Going to stake us, fix us up with good connections. What more do you want, Steve?"

"It's not the future that worries me, Jack. It's the past. That's what you can't see."

"Nobody's going to toss it up at us."

Steve shifted uneasily and grunted from his couch. Jack watched him with troubled eyes. At last the older man leaned back. Propping himself to suit the motion of the train, he began a troubled explanation.

"You played a lone hand, Jack," he declared. "Con games, phony checks, all that smooth sort of stuff. It was in your line."

"No longer, Steve."

"I understand that, Jack. You'll go straight. It's in you. A man can chuck anything that he has a mind to."

"Which makes it easy for you, like me."

"Not quite as easy. I was a tough mug, Steve. There are a lot of my sort who traveled with me."

"Like Beak Latzo?"

"Yeah."

There was a dejected growl in Steve's tone at the mention of Latzo's name. Jack eyed his companion closely. He saw a sharp look in Steve's gaze. Then Steve closed his eyes.

"FELLOWS like Beak Latzo," he remarked, "can never get it through their domes that a man can decide to go straight. They're always looking for word from pals who get out of stir."

"So Beak will be looking for word from you?"

"Maybe. I hope not."

Another pause. Steve opened his eyes and looked squarely at Jack. He spoke in a steady, mechanical tone.

"The bulls never knew about the team-up, Jack," said Steve. "They knew I had pals; but they didn't need to find out who they were. They never picked out Beak Latzo."

"Well, if nobody knows anything about him—"

"You know about him, Jack. You know that Beak worked with me."

"Sure I do." Targon spoke as steadily as Zurk. "You told me a lot about Beak Latzo when we were dodging posses together. But I'm mum. I've forgotten it."

"That's good, Jack. Keep it forgotten. Because it's going to be a tough trip for me. If Beak doesn't hear from me, I'll hear from him."

"He won't hear from you, will he?"

"Not by a long shot. But if I hear from him, it may look like he heard from me."

"I'm beginning to get it, Steve. That is tough. But if the bulls never knew about you and Beak—"

"I told you why they didn't know, Jack. Because they never troubled to find out. But if they started digging up the past, they would uncover it. Once they suspect a connection between me and Beak, things would be bad."

A pause, broken only by the scratch of a match as Jack Targon lighted a cigarette. He offered a smoke to Steve Zurk, who shook his head. The older man was still solemn. A blast of the engine's whistle stimulated his thoughts to words.

"The others don't count, Jack," Steve told his companion. "Beak Latzo is the only guy that's really tough. It won't be easy if he tries to needle me. But I'll handle him—in my own way.

"That's why I'm mentioning it to you. Because you know what I'm up against. If Beak Latzo begins to make things sour, I'll count on you to help me out."

"Which I will, Steve. Provided—"

"Provided what?"

"Provided that you keep on the level."

An angry growl from Steve. Jack silenced it with a prompt remark, as he reached over and clapped his hand on his pal's shoulder.

"You could say the same to me, Steve," came Jack Targon's statement. "I'm all for you if you play straight. I want you to feel the same about me. We're going back into life; we've each got the chance we want. But it's up to each of us to be on the level."

"All right, Jack," grunted Steve. "But you know I've always been a square-shooter. There was no reason to suggest that I might be going to pull something phony."

"You've been square with me, Steve. But that was when both of us had to buck the world. Now we've got the world with us. It's a different slant—that's all."

"I've figured that. I'm all for it. I told the governor so and I meant it. No more stickups and bank jobs for me. I'm out of that line, Jack."

"And I'm through with my old business. I wouldn't sell a guy a gold brick if he asked for it, Steve. Shakedowns, bum checks—all that stuff is forgotten. When I sign any name from now on, it will be my own."

JACK TARGON reached up, grabbed the edge of the upper berth and hoisted himself to the shelflike bed. Propped on one elbow, he grinned down at Steve Zurk.

"Better than the night we rode this line behind baggage," he commented. "Eh, Steve? Remember the storm that night? And the shack we found to sleep in after we dropped off the limited?"

Steve nodded.

"We're in prime luck right now, Steve," went on Jack. He was propped up against the pillows, finishing his cigarette. "We both have brains enough to make the most of it. This is a great situation. The two of us clear for the first time since we met.

"I couldn't chin with you, Steve, while those deputies were bringing us over to Dupaw. I was looking forward to this chat. You've spoiled it a bit, though, acting glum the way you are. You didn't worry about Beak Latzo when we were palling around after those jailbreaks."

"No need to worry about him then," snorted Steve. "I could have used him if he'd been around. But now I don't want him on my neck. Nor any of the others."

Released from jail, this man tries to go straight by joining an advertising agency.

JACK TARGON

"Forget Beak Latzo. Forget all of them. Look here, Steve: I was worrying—so were you—when we left the big house today. Worrying for fear people would be looking at us. Following us, watching us.

"But it was all fixed in our favor. The car was there ready for a thirty-mile drive to Dupaw. The governor had this swell drawing room all reserved so we could step out of sight. Not a person on this train knows who we are.

"We'll step off in New York just like the rest of the passengers. We'll report to this chap Perry Delhugh just as we would go into a business office. The warden told us to forget the past. We're going to do it."

"I hope I can," commented Steve, dryly. "What's more, I will. Unless Beak Latzo tries to block me. He'll be expecting word from me, that rat will."

"Maybe Beak isn't in New York, Steve."

"If he isn't there, he can be reached at the same old place. He knows I know that."

"Forget it."

Jack Targon reached from the upper berth and tossed his cigarette into an ash stand. Steve Zurk arose from the couch and entered the lower berth.

"Well," he growled, "there's something in what you say, Jack. The governor gave us a break; this fellow Delhugh is going to do the same. Even the warden helped us out by letting us come into New York on this train."

"Traveling incognito," chuckled Jack. "Unannoyed by gentlemen of the press."

"That's right, Jack." Steve spoke as though he had made a discovery. "None of the newshounds got on our trail. What did the warden do? Bluff them?"

"HE talked to them," returned Jack. "So one of the deputies said. After the reporters interviewed us last night, the warden told them how and where we were going and made them agree to lay off."

"Like as not they'll be at the station when we hit New York."

"I don't think so. That fellow Burke was the only New York reporter there. We gave him all the interview he wanted. He won't be likely to hound us."

"That's a help. If we can dive out of sight, Jack, it's going to make it easier."

"No need to dive, Steve. We'll be real men again. With a chance ahead of us. Lost in the shuffle of New York, like all the other citizens."

A pause. Then Steve remarked from the lower berth:

"This guy Delhugh must have a lot of coin."

"I guess he does, Steve. He's a philanthropist."

"Hands out a pile of dough to charities?"

"Yes. Runs welfare committees. Gets contributions to worthy causes."

"An old bloke, I guess."

"Sounds that way. But he's only going to place us. All that newspaper talk interested him, and he made an arrangement with the governor. Going to give us a lift."

"Well, I'd rather be in New York than out in this state. New scenery—big city—well, it makes me feel better."

"Forgetting about Beak Latzo?"

"You can't forget that egg, Jack. But I'm not worrying about him. Just remember what I said. Keep mum about him. I'll be on the level."

"Good boy, Steve. That's the way to talk."

Lights went out. The drawing room was in darkness as the limited roared eastward. No sound came from the upper berth. Jack Targon had gone to sleep. Steve Zurk, still awake, kept mumbling for a while; then became silent.

IN the adjoining compartment, a slight *click* sounded as The Shadow removed his earphones. Fingers, invisible in the darkness, detached the connection of the dictograph wire.

Through Clyde Burke, one of his secret agents, The Shadow had learned that the ex-convicts would be aboard this train. Clyde, a reporter for the New York *Classic,* had forwarded his chief the number of the car in which Zurk and Targon were to be located.

Knowing that the train trip would give the former outlaws their first opportunity to discuss their new life, The Shadow had boarded the Eastern Limited for the purpose of hearing them talk. He wanted to gain first-hand knowledge of their opinions.

The Shadow had gained an impression of sincerity from the discourse of both the pardoned men. Though his usual task was to harry men of crime, The Shadow had more than once aided ex-crooks to go straight.

He was ready to do that for Steve Zurk and Jack Targon. That was another reason why he had listened in on their gabfest. A soft laugh told that The Shadow was pleased with his findings. For he had learned of a menace to society with whom he well might deal.

"Beak" Latzo. The Shadow knew of the man. A dangerous mobleader, at present absent from New York. One who was apt to return to Manhattan, now that Steve Zurk was free.

Steve Zurk saw trouble ahead from Beak Latzo. At least, Steve Zurk had expressed that idea to his pal, Jack Targon. The Shadow could see a way to eliminate such trouble.

That way would be to uncover Beak Latzo.

Again a soft laugh whispered in the blackness of the compartment. The Shadow had gained a quest. To find and deal with the menacing mobleader, Beak Latzo.

CHAPTER III
THE NEW WAY OPENS

ON the following morning, a taxicab pulled up in front of a secluded Manhattan residence. The building was a large brownstone mansion, a heritage of the later years of the last century. Yet its well-kept front gave it a modern appearance.

Two men alighted from the cab: Steve Zurk and Jack Targon. Carrying suitcases, they ascended the brownstone steps and rang the doorbell. They were admitted by a dry-faced servant, who nodded as he heard their names.

The menial took the bags and laid them aside. With a bow, he motioned toward a flight of broad marble stairs.

The pardoned men went up the steps, treading upon thick carpeting. They looked about as they went; at the top they stared at each other in partial bewilderment.

Perry Delhugh's home was a place of magnificence. Marble statuary vied with rich velvet drapings. The walls were covered with thick tapestries. The rugs underfoot were of marvelous Oriental design. The former convicts had stepped into a scene of wealth.

Pausing at the top, Zurk and Targon waited for the approach of a frail, stoop-shouldered young man who was coming to meet them. The new arrival stopped in the hallway and surveyed the ex-convicts through a pair of tortoiseshell spectacles.

"Good morning," he greeted, in a weak-toned voice. "Which is Mr. Zurk; and which is Mr. Targon?"

This man, also a released prisoner, attempts a comeback with an importing firm.

STEVE ZURK

Steve and Jack introduced themselves. The young man shook hands with each, wincing slightly at the powerful grips of the visitors.

"My name is Benzig," he informed. "I am Mr. Delhugh's secretary. If you will come this way, gentlemen, I shall take you to his study. He will meet you there."

Benzig led the way along a hall. They passed the door of a room that looked like an office, in which the walls were lined with huge filing cabinets. They passed through a small, thick-carpeted anteroom; then came into Delhugh's study.

This room was furnished in quiet but expensive taste. A huge mahogany desk occupied the center; the chairs were of the same wood. Marble statuettes and jade vases stood upon tables about the room. The door of a wall safe showed beyond the desk.

The walls themselves were paneled with thick tapestry material set in mahogany framework.

Impressed by this setting of affluence, Steve and Jack looked about from spot to spot. When they turned to stare at Benzig, the bespectacled secretary had gone.

"Whew!" uttered Jack Targon. "What a place! There's been money spent here, Steve."

"Yeah," growled Steve Zurk, "and I'll bet that Delhugh is a worn-out old guy who can't appreciate it."

"Probably a dyspeptic."

"What's that?"

"A guy who lives on pills."

"And forks over dough to croakers."

"Probably. When the medicos find a rich bird that's sick, they help him get rid of his cash."

"Well, if old Delhugh is as weary looking as his secretary, I'll—"

Steve broke off. The door of the anteroom was

opening. Jack turned about as he saw Steve stare toward the entrance.

Both men were surprised at sight of the person who entered. They knew that he must be Perry Delhugh; but he was entirely different from the man that they had pictured.

PERRY DELHUGH was under fifty. Well built, of middle height, he showed no signs of the portliness that so frequently comes to a man of leisure. Though heavy, he was muscular, not stout.

His face was square. His expression was dynamic. His black hair, slightly thinned, bore only slight streaks of gray. There was a firmness in Delhugh's gaze as he studied the men before him.

Jack Targon's smile sobered as his eyes met Delhugh's. Steve Zurk, half slouching, straightened up; then shifted uneasily as he came under keen inspection. Both of the ex-convicts knew that they had met a man who could command them.

"Targon?" Delhugh spoke the name as he looked at Jack.

"Yes," responded Jack, with a nod.

Delhugh shook hands with crushing grasp. He turned to Steve; called him by name; then gave another powerful clasp. He waved the two men to chairs, then went behind his desk. There he noted the door of the wall safe, showing through the paneling.

Indifferently, Delhugh pressed a panel and a covering front slid over the safe door. Then Delhugh took his place behind the desk, pulled a box of cigars from the drawer and laid the perfectos where his visitors could help themselves.

Both Steve and Jack were impressed as they took cigars and lighted them. They knew that Delhugh had expected their visit, yet he had left the front of his safe visible, where they might take note of its existence. A small touch, but one that indicated that Delhugh trusted them.

Settling back in their chairs, the pardoned criminals waited for the philanthropist to speak.

"Gentlemen," stated Delhugh, in a deliberate fashion, "your futures have been entrusted to me. Sometime ago, the governor of the state wherein you were imprisoned decided to pardon you. He wanted to give you a fresh start in the world. An excellent purpose; one, however, that offered hazard."

The pardoned convicts shifted a bit. Jack Targon managed a smile; Steve Zurk remained solemn, with a countenance that had become a poker face.

"Some men," resumed Delhugh, "are criminals by nature. Others are criminals only by environment. The governor believes that you are of the latter class. I am inclined to accept his opinion."

Jack's smile became less forced. Steve settled back in his chair, but retained his solemnity.

"I have gained wealth," declared Delhugh. "Enough to permit my retirement from business at a comparatively early age. I have occupied my time—since retirement—with philanthropic pursuits. My contributions to worthy causes have been considerable. But I have done more than merely give away money.

"I have identified myself with various organizations that deal in welfare. I have kept records of those activities; I have managed committees and I have solicited huge sums from wealthy persons, for charitable purposes.

"In brief, my work has carried a personal angle. That is why I became interested when I learned that the governor intended to pardon you two men."

A KINDLY smile changed the inflexibility of Delhugh's countenance. The wealthy man reached into a desk drawer and produced a stack of papers that he separated into two sheaves.

"Here are facts concerning each of you," he declared. "I looked into your pasts. Not so that I could check upon you but in order that I might understand you. The records show that you have been victims of circumstance.

"I have learned more about you than either of you can realize. You, Zurk, are a man with a real business sense. One who can judge values. You showed that"—Delhugh's smile ended—"by your choice of banks that you robbed."

While Steve remained solemn. Delhugh produced an envelope and pushed it across the desk. He indicated that Steve should take it. Steve did so.

"There is a start for you," stated Delhugh. "A bank account of one thousand dollars—a loan to be repaid within one year. A letter to the manager of the Sourlain Hotel, arranging for your credit there.

"Also a personal letter to Joseph Daylin, head of the Daylin Importing Company. I have talked with Daylin. He has a job for you in his importing house. It will mean advancement."

Steve, a bit bewildered, nodded thanks. Delhugh smiled; then turned to Jack. He produced a second envelope.

"The same amount for you, Targon," he declared. "You will live at the Hotel Cliquot. Your letter of business recommendation is to Galen Flix, president of the New Century Advertising Agency. You are a man who must have sales ability. This will be your opportunity to prove it."

"This is great of you, Mr. Delhugh," said Jack, taking the envelope. "I'm out to make good; and I can say the same for Steve—"

"It is unnecessary," interposed Delhugh. "I have taken that fact for granted. I have merely arranged to further your opportunities. There is only one proviso that I require."

"What is that?" asked Jack.

"I expect frequent reports from each of you," stated Delhugh. "These will be confidential interviews that will prove of benefit. You have been pardoned; hence there is no element of parole in my request.

"I merely wish to see how the experiment is progressing. I want to know if either of you encounters difficulties or pitfalls. I shall be ready—with money as well as friendship—if either of you should require assistance."

"That's swell!" began Jack. "Say, Mr. Delhugh—"

"I have not finished." Delhugh's steady interruption stopped Jack short. "These visits that I have mentioned must be frequent at first. I would suggest that they be on alternate nights to begin with. Zurk can come here Monday, Wednesday and Friday; Targon—Tuesday, Thursday and Saturday. Around dinner time, so that brief chats will not disturb your evening plans."

"You want us to come separately?" questioned Jack, a bit surprised.

"Absolutely," affirmed Delhugh. Then, seriously: "You are to follow separate courses. Forget the forced friendship that brought you together. Become new men; then meet again on a fresh basis."

"Today is Monday." This statement came from Steve. "You want me to come here tonight, Mr. Delhugh?"

"No," replied the philanthropist. "That will be unnecessary. I shall begin with Targon's visit, tomorrow evening. Your visits, Zurk, will commence with Wednesday."

"Very well, sir," agreed Steve.

He arose solemnly and extended his hand to Jack Targon. The younger pal received the unexpected clasp.

"So long, old-timer," commented Steve. "Mr. Delhugh has served it to us straight. We're splitting; and when we get together again we'll have something to talk about instead of the big house."

"Commendable, Zurk," declared Delhugh from behind his desk. "You have accepted my plan in excellent fashion. That is the way to begin. Follow through in the same manner."

DELHUGH was pressing a desk button as he spoke. Benzig appeared from the anteroom. Delhugh stepped from behind his desk and shook hands with Steve Zurk. Then he turned to the secretary.

"Call a cab for Mr. Zurk," ordered Delhugh. "Then summon one for Mr. Targon."

Steve followed the secretary as he departed. Delhugh turned and shook hands with Jack. The young man grinned.

"You're right about Steve," he declared. "He knows his business. He grabbed the idea while I was still muffing it. But I'm not quite so dumb as I acted. I've got it now. It's a swell plan for both of us."

"The only plan, Targon," returned Delhugh, quietly. "You will find that new associations are necessary to your success. I have convinced Zurk that I can influence his future. I hope that I have convinced you in the same manner."

"You have," stated Jack. "You and Steve. The way he took it helped."

Delhugh was smiling as he picked up the stacks of papers from the desk. Jack noted scrawled letters among Steve's documents. In his own pile, he observed slips of paper that looked very much like bad checks that he had passed, years before.

The young man smiled sheepishly at sight of this evidence of abandoned crime. Delhugh did not notice the expression. He was putting the papers back into the drawer. Jack Targon turned his eyes away as Delhugh stepped from behind the desk. Then Benzig arrived to announce that Targon's cab was at the door.

Delhugh clapped a friendly hand upon Jack's shoulder. The young man grinned, no longer sheepish. Then, strolling after Benzig, he went from Delhugh's study, faring forth, like Steve, upon a new career.

Perry Delhugh resumed his seat behind his desk. His square face wore a meditative smile as he recalled his observations of these men to whom he had given aid. They had been as he had expected them to be, fitting perfectly to the descriptions that he had gained of them.

Delhugh's smile remained as the philanthropist lighted a fresh cigar. In all his work of welfare, this keen, dynamic man had never before encountered cases that afforded such unusual contrast and such rich promise of future results.

CHAPTER IV
OUT OF THE PAST

IT was evening in Manhattan. Times Square, with its galaxy of lights; broad avenues with lesser, yet brilliant illumination—these were the channels that attracted the pleasure-seeking throngs of the great metropolis.

In contrast were the side streets, where lights dwindled as one left the brilliance of the avenues. Here shaded seclusion dwelt amid the teeming city. Nervous pedestrians, as they passed certain spots, could sense impressions of lurking danger.

Not far from Times Square stood a dark-fronted building that seemed pinched between taller structures on each side. The first floor, a full six feet above the street level, was occupied by a Chinese restaurant. Above the eating place were blackened windows that signified unoccupied rooms.

A man from the side street came up the steps that led to the Chinese restaurant. He entered a hallway at the top of the steps; but instead of passing through the curtained doorway to the restaurant, he kept straight ahead along a poorly lighted hall and took to a stairway at the end.

He followed the steps to the second floor. There, by a single gas light, he noted the second door on the right, toward the rear of the building. A dim light shone through the glass-paneled front; but the door bore no name. The arrival opened it and entered.

"BEAK" LATZO

BEHIND a dilapidated counter stood a wizened, droop-faced man who eyed the newcomer with an almost startled gaze. There was reason for his semblance of fright—for the intruder was a square-set, hard-faced ruffian whose features carried a malicious leer.

"Your name's Dangler?" inquired the intruder, closing the door behind him.

"Yes," replied the wizened man with a nod. Then, in a whining voice: "Are you sure you have the right office? I am a dealer in postage stamps. My name is not yet on the door; but—"

"Cut it," snorted the hard-faced man. "I'm not a dick. You're running this biz on the up and up, ain't you?"

Dangler nodded.

"Then don't spill a line like that," growled the intruder. "It sounds fishy. Like you was a guy with a record. Nobody's got nothing on you, Dangler, even though you was in the green-goods game. Don't be scared of no bulls—nor Feds, neither."

An expression of enlightenment dawned on Dangler's face. The wizened man managed a grin.

"Are you Mr. Ortz?" he questioned.

"That's me," chuckled the hard-faced rogue. "I'm Lucky Ortz. The guy you've been expecting from Beak Latzo. I was over to your old joint; I found the card there saying that you'd moved."

"The rent was cheaper here," explained Dangler, "and the place is more secluded. I've been expecting you to stop in almost any time, since Beak told me that you would call for him. But that was three months ago."

"Beak's been out of town," growled "Lucky." "He wasn't expecting nothing while he was away. But he figured maybe you might've got a letter for him lately—"

"I have." Dangler was emphatic in his interruption. He dived beneath the counter and brought out an old, disused postage stamp album. Fishing through the pages, he produced an envelope. "This came in yesterday. Wednesday."

"Good!" Lucky took the envelope, noted the scrawled address. It had been forwarded from Dangler's former office. "I'll take it along to Beak. So long, Dangler. Paint your moniker on that door and give the bulls the haha if they bother you."

A grin on his hard face, Lucky stumped from Dangler's office. There was something contemptuous in Lucky's leer. To this man, lieutenant of Beak Latzo, fear of the law was something to ridicule.

Leaving the building that housed Dangler's office, Lucky strode eastward and then turned along an avenue. He came to the steps of an elevated station. He ascended to the platform, took a southbound train and rode for several stations.

When he again reached the street, Lucky had arrived in a most dilapidated neighborhood. He was in a district that fringed the underworld, where patrolmen were frequent, their wary eyes on the lookout for dubious characters.

Lucky passed several policemen; his gait, neither shuffling nor hurried, attracted no attention. Turning into a secluded alleyway, Lucky unlocked the door of a dilapidated house. He stepped into a darkened hall, blundered up a flight of stairs and gave five short knocks at a door that he discovered in the blackness.

A key turned. The door opened inward. Lucky stepped into a gas-lighted room with drawn shades. He was face to face with a man who looked tougher than himself. This was Beak Latzo.

THE mobleader's sobriquet was a good one.

Long, rangy and fierce-faced, Beak Latzo possessed a nose that was definitely prominent. It was a large nose, that might once have been beaklike. At present, however, it bore a flattened look—an indication that its wearer had suffered from punches dealt in fistic combat.

In fact, Beak Latzo's nose was a target at which a battler would logically aim. Moreover, it was an item of physiognomy that would unquestionably identify its owner. That accounted for the fact that Beak Latzo was at present occupying a hideout; the only course by which he could keep his presence in New York unknown.

"Well?" Beak's question came in a raspy tone. "Did you find the goof? Dangler?"

"Yeah," returned Lucky. "Not at his old place, though. He's moved to a dumpy office up over a chop suey joint."

"That's all right. Just so long as you found him. Anything there for me?"

"This is all."

Lucky produced the envelope. Beak Latzo blinked with beady eyes as he noted the scrawled address. Then he ripped open the envelope, spread out the letter that was within and began to read with eagerness.

"Is it from Steve Zurk?" questioned Lucky, noting his chief's enthusiasm.

"You bet it is!" chortled Beak. "Take a squint at it, Lucky."

"Say, it's a scrawl, ain't it?" snorted Lucky, trying to read the letter after Beak handed it to him. "All I can make out is the beginning—and 'Steve' at the end of it."

"He writes lousy," admitted Beak. "I knew his scrawl the minute I saw the envelope. It's easy to read when you're used to it, though. No trouble for me, even though I haven't heard from Steve since the last time he broke out of the big house. Here—give it to me. I'll tell you what it's about."

Beak took the letter, referred to a paragraph and then began to paraphrase a translation of Steve Zurk's poor penmanship.

"Steve figures he's in the money," explained Beak. "He's here in New York—got a job with an importer—all fixed for him by some ritzy guy named Perry Delhugh. But he's got to make it look like he's gone straight. Savvy?"

"Sure," acknowledged Lucky, in a laconic tone. "With the governor pardoning him, he's got to put up a front."

"There's only one mug wise to me knowing Steve," continued Beak. "That's a bird named Jack Targon—the one that the governor pardoned along with Steve. But Steve and Jack have split. And this guy Targon won't squawk so long as he thinks Steve is staying on the level."

"You mean Targon is really going straight?"

"That's it. But he was a pal of Steve's. So there's no trouble there so long as we stay undercover. That is, keep Steve in the clear. Savvy?"

"I get it."

BEAK LATZO folded the letter and thrust it into his pocket. He crossed the room, seated himself upon a rumpled bed and lighted a cigarette. A knowing smile appeared upon his thick, coarse lips.

"Steve thinks he can pick some nifty lays," declared Beak. "He ought to, being close to that moneybag guy, Delhugh. I'm to sit tight and wait for tips. They'll come through Dangler. Like this letter."

"You won't see Steve, then?"

"Not unless he says to. That would queer the racket. What's more, I've got to keep my own mug undercover. If the bulls spot me, they might think of Steve."

"They never hooked you up together, did they?"

"They may have. No telling about that. Not likely, but it would be too bad if they had. That won't worry me, though, about being in on the jobs."

"Why not?"

"Because Steve Zurk is a fox. When he picks a job it's good. Like clockwork. He figures everything—the setup, the blow-off, the getaway. It's a cinch working with him."

"And a double cinch this way, Beak."

"You said it, Lucky."

Another pause. Beak puffed at his cigarette, then rasped an ugly laugh.

"Nobody knows you're working with me, Lucky," he declared. "Not even the gorillas that you've lined up. This hideout's a pip; and there's others just as good, in case I've got to dive out of here.

"What's more, you're sitting pretty. The bulls have nothing on you. Even the stoolies aren't watching you for a hot tip. Besides that, they didn't lie when they called you 'Lucky.' You know how to grab the breaks."

Lucky grinned. His square shoulders hunched back as his chest swelled at Beak's commendation. The mobleader had spoken a known fact. Lucky Ortz was one character of the badlands who always managed to ease out of trouble's toils.

"Don't say much to the gorillas," warned Beak. "Just keep them ready. We'll want them on tap; because Steve moves fast when he sees a chance. It's up to you to keep going in and out of Dangler's new place. We don't want any message of Steve's to lie around until it's cold."

"Dangler's all right?" questioned Lucky. "He looks like a scary sort of guy to me."

"That don't matter," retorted Beak. "That's the way he ought to be. Scary. He was in with a green-goods outfit—I told you about it—and we chopped down the crew. He was out when we got the others; he never knew who got them.

"I went to see him, friendly like, and made him think I was a pal of the goofs that got rubbed out. Told him to lay low and keep mum. That's what he did. Knowing how scary he was, I used him for a mailing address, figuring he'd be safe.

"Just dumb enough to be useful. That's Dangler. He knows nothing, so he can't spill anything that will hurt. Steve used him before he sent me messages. It's a sure bet, particularly with you doing the collecting."

With a satisfied leer, Beak Latzo lighted another cigarette, then nudged his thumb toward the door.

"So long, Lucky," he suggested. "It don't do any good hanging around here. Check up on the mob; we're going to need them. And keep an eye on Dangler."

Lucky nodded. Donning his hat, he strolled from the hideout and closed the door behind him.

Beak Latzo turned the key in the lock. With an evil chuckle, the mobleader dropped back in his big chair.

There was reason for Beak's satisfaction. To his way of thinking, prosperous days were due. For Beak Latzo had confidence in the cunning of Steve Zurk. To Beak, the letter that had come through Dangler was a prophecy of profitable crime.

CHAPTER V
FRIDAY NIGHT

"WHAT is it, Benzig?"

Perry Delhugh put the question as the bespectacled secretary entered the study. The millionaire was seated behind his mahogany desk, busily engaged with papers.

"Those letters, sir," returned Benzig. "Regarding the funds for the Talleyrand Hospital. You told me to remind you of them."

"Ah, yes." Delhugh glanced at the clock on the desk. "Well, there are a few minutes before dinner. Do you have the file with you?"

Benzig produced a portfolio from beneath his arm. Delhugh nodded, and the secretary took out a sheaf of letters which he handed to the millionaire.

Delhugh went through the first letters rapidly. Then he stopped and read one carefully. He placed the others aside and raised the one that he had selected.

"This is the most important, Benzig," he declared. "The one from Theobald Luftus. He is willing to make a contribution of twenty thousand dollars. Think of that, Benzig! Twenty thousand dollars!"

"Quite generous of him, sir."

"Is that remark meant as sarcasm, Benzig?"

"No, no, sir! I would not have been sarcastic—"

"You should have been. Twenty thousand dollars from a millionaire like Luftus? He should have offered us fifty thousand, at least."

"But perhaps, sir, he does not have funds that he can spare."

"Read the letter, Benzig," said Delhugh, wearily. "Read it carefully. Note the comments that Luftus made." Benzig took the letter and studied it. His face remained perplexed at first; then, gradually, the secretary began to nod.

"I see, sir," he declared. "Mr. Luftus states that if the committee will visit him on Tuesday night, he will deliver them selected securities to the value of twenty thousand dollars."

"Yes," stated Delhugh. "Selected securities. That sounds well; but its meaning is obvious. Can't you see Luftus selecting those securities? Picking over a miserly hoard, seeing how little he can spare?

"That man has great wealth, Benzig"—Delhugh gave an emphatic pound to the desk—"yet his charitable donations have been almost *nihil.* I suppose, though"—the philanthropist's expression became meditative and kindly—"that we should rejoice because Theobald Luftus has relaxed to this extent. Perhaps the joy of giving once will induce him to repeat what this time must certainly be a painful duty."

"He adds, sir," put in Benzig, still studying the letter, "that he will confer with his broker on Monday, regarding the choice of securities. So that the hospital may be assured of a well-selected gift."

"A bit of dust, Benzig," informed Delhugh, with a smile. "Can you picture Theobald Luftus having any securities that would not be gilt-edged? He wants a conference with his broker. Certainly. So that he can pick out the least desirable of his stocks and bonds.

"It is saddening, Benzig"—Delhugh shook his head seriously—"really saddening, to encounter men like Luftus. They give only because public sentiment compels the strong to aid the weak. They gain no pleasure from the process; yet they are the first to claim that they are philanthropists.

"Well, let us forget those fine points. Write a letter to Luftus, Benzig. Ask him to telephone Justin Galway, chairman of the Talleyrand Fund, on Tuesday, to arrange the exact time of the call."

The chime of a dinner gong floated faintly through the open door of the study. Delhugh arose and walked toward the door.

"Type the letter before you come down to dinner," he told Benzig. "It will take you only a few minutes. Leave it on my desk with the correspondence. I shall sign it after dinner; and also dictate other communications."

BENZIG typed a brief letter after Delhugh had left. He placed it carefully upon the desk; then, without replacing the loose letters, he put his portfolio on a table in the corner. He left the study and went downstairs.

He joined Delhugh at the dinner table, in the dining room at the rear of the ground floor.

The doorbell rang while Delhugh and Benzig were dining. A servant answered it; then returned to announce that Mr. Zurk was calling. Delhugh looked up from his salad.

"Go speak to him, Benzig," the millionaire told the secretary. "Usher him up to the study. Tell him that I shall join him within fifteen minutes."

"But, Mr. Delhugh," began the secretary, "don't you think that it would be better—"

"I told you to take Mr. Zurk to the study," interposed Delhugh. "Go, now, Benzig. Do as I have ordered."

"Very well, sir."

Benzig left. He returned in less than five minutes. He and Delhugh finished their dinner in silence. Then the millionaire left the dining room and went upstairs. Arriving in the study, he found Steve Zurk seated there, awaiting him.

Delhugh shook hands with the ex-convict. He noted Steve's attire and observed that the man was wearing a new suit—one that was well-fitted and conservative. Delhugh nodded in approval. He took his chair behind the desk and offered Steve a cigar.

"Well, Zurk," he questioned, "how is the importing business?"

"Good," replied Steve in a sober tone. "I like it. I think I'll make good on the job, Mr. Delhugh."

"Any comments from the people there?"

"Only from Mr. Daykin. He is pleased."

"Excellent! Let's see; you were here Wednesday. But that was too soon for you to have opinions regarding the suitability of your new occupation. You are sure you like it?"

"Absolutely! It's a new life for me, Mr. Delhugh. A new life. Lot's different from a month ago"—Steve shook his head in reminiscence—"when I thought I was going to be in stir until I croaked."

"That's right," nodded Delhugh. "Your accumulated terms amounted to about sixty years, didn't they?"

"Sixty-five," replied Steve, with a wry smile. "I figured it the same as a life sentence. That's what I was—a lifer—"

"Let us change the subject," interposed Delhugh. "We must remember, Zurk, that your past is forgotten. I am glad to learn that your present satisfies you. As for the future, that remains with you."

He arose to indicate that the interview was ended. He clasped Steve's hand; then reminded the ex-convict that his next appointment was for Monday night.

Benzig came at Delhugh's ring and ushered Steve downstairs.

DELHUGH was at his desk, studying the other letters referring to the Talleyrand Hospital Fund when Benzig returned to the study. Seeing that his employer was busy, Benzig picked up his portfolio from the chair where he had placed it. Papers slid out as Benzig lifted the portfolio. The secretary turned to the philanthropist.

"Pardon me, Mr. Delhugh," said Benzig. "Did you take any other letters from this portfolio?"

"No," replied Delhugh, looking up from his letters. "Why?"

"The clasp was not securely fastened," stated the secretary. "Yet I am sure that I closed it tightly before I came down to dinner."

"Are the letters all there?"

"Yes, sir. But—"

"But what?" quizzed Delhugh, as Benzig paused.

"I—I was wondering about Zurk," stammered Benzig. "He was here while we were at dinner. Perhaps—perhaps he—"

"Perhaps he opened the portfolio?" Delhugh's inquiry was cold.

"Yes, sir," nodded Benzig.

"I begin to understand," said Delhugh, his face firm. "That was why you objected, at dinner, to ushering Zurk up here. You don't trust the man, do you?"

"I—I was thinking of your letters," protested Benzig. "I didn't want anyone rummaging through them. It—it was on your account, Mr. Delhugh. It wasn't exactly that I didn't trust Zurk. If anyone had come up here, I would have been disturbed."

"I see." Delhugh's voice was grave. "Well, Benzig, you and others like you constitute the menace that such men as Zurk and Targon face. Free from prison, trying to face the world, they meet with the mistrust of small-minded persons. Do you realize, Benzig, that you are helping to destroy the very work that I am attempting to do?"

"I am sorry, sir. Real sorry."

"That means nothing, if Zurk noticed your mistrust. He regards this house as one place where he is free from suspicion; where he meets with friends who believe in his honesty."

"I said nothing to Zurk, sir."

"I am glad that you did not. See to it that your actions do not disturb him in the future. These letters"—Delhugh shuffled the ones that he held—"would be of no consequence to Zurk."

"But the portfolio—"

"Contains no correspondence of consequence. You probably failed to fasten it securely. Your suspicious nature caused you to imagine that Zurk had opened it."

"I suppose that you are right, sir."

"I am right. Moreover, I am annoyed by your attitude, Benzig. This has been shabbiness on your part. Let me see no more of it."

"Very well, sir."

DELHUGH ordered Benzig to take dictation. The secretary did so, his hand shaky as he recalled the reprimand that he had just received. When Delhugh had finished giving letters, he arose, nodded a good night and went out, leaving Benzig alone to complete his typing.

His employer gone, the secretary picked up the portfolio. He examined the catch; then shook his head. Though he had been impressed by his employer's words, Benzig could not shake the one idea from his mind.

The secretary was positive that Steve Zurk had made use of his time when alone in this study. He was sure that the ex-convict had examined the letter to Theobald Luftus that lay on Delhugh's desk; and that, following that procedure, he had gone through the contents of the portfolio.

Yet Benzig, timid and fearful of his employer's wrath, had resolved to keep that opinion to himself. From now on, the secretary would have a secret duty of his own—one that he would not mention to Delhugh.

Benzig was determined to watch the actions of both Steve Zurk and Jack Targon whenever they paid visits to this house.

CHAPTER VI
THE SHADOW'S SEARCH

ONE week had elapsed since Steve Zurk and Jack Targon had arrived in New York. It was again a Monday; and evening had brought a sullen, misty blackness to Manhattan. In brilliant areas, gleaming lights cleaved the shroud of darkness; but in more isolated sections of the city, street lamps were pitiful with their feeble rays.

Pacing patrolmen were vigilant this night. This was the type of evening made for crime, when lurking footpads and bold yeggs could venture forth beneath a blanketing protection. Every byway in the underworld was a potential lingering spot for desperadoes.

Beneath the grimy, dew-dripping surface of an elevated structure, a hunched-up man was shambling along in inconspicuous fashion. At times, this fellow paused to light a cigarette. The gleam of the match—on such occasions—revealed a crafty, drawn face with sharp eyes that gleamed with shrewd glance.

Each time he lighted a match, this wayfarer kept the flame shielded by his hands. Thus the move enabled him to remain unobserved; but gave him the opportunity to look about for persons who might be watching him.

Satisfied at last that he had escaped all notice, the little man drifted off through an alleyway. Blackness swallowed him.

This prowler through the underworld was not unique. Two blocks away, a man of a different type was also looking for an opportunity to duck out of sight. Strolling along a side street, this second wayfarer came beneath the gleam of a lamp. The glow showed a steady, chiseled face that topped a stalwart frame.

Pausing at the entrance to an alleyway, this man glanced sharply along the course that he had followed. Then he stepped into the blackness between the space of buildings. He continued his pacing in methodical fashion until he had gone half a block.

The flicker of a match caught his eye. The stalwart man slowed his pace. He stepped into the shelter of an unused doorway.

The man with the match, catching the click of the other's footsteps, sidled over to the same spot.

"That you, Cliff?" came the little man's whisper.

"Yes." The response was a low one. "Anything new, Hawkeye?"

"Goofy Ketch just ducked out of the Pink Rat," informed the little man. "He's been palling around with Hunk Robo. Is Hunk down at the Black Ship?"

"Haven't seen him there."

"Think he's over at Red Mike's?"

"Clyde Burke's covering there. Reporters get by at Red Mike's. Burke's looking for Hunk, like I am. No word from him."

"There's only one place they might meet up, then. That new joint in back of Sooky's hockshop. Let's ankle over there, Cliff."

THE two men set out together, silently picking their course through alleyways. Their course showed familiarity with the underworld. Their actions indicated that their quest had been a constant one.

Unlike in appearance, these two were working for a common cause. The little man was known as "Hawkeye," a familiar prowler through the badlands. The stalwart man was Cliff Marsland, a reputed killer. Both were masking their true characters. Hawkeye and Cliff were agents of The Shadow.

With Clyde Burke, *Classic* reporter, also on the job, Hawkeye and Cliff had been scouring the underworld in search for some trace of Beak Latzo. So far, they had gained no inkling of the mobleader's whereabouts. Night after night had brought failure in the quest.

On certain evenings, another searcher had also been on the job: The Shadow, himself. Both Cliff and Hawkeye had contacted at times with their chief. Yet no trace had yet been gained. Beak Latzo, if in Manhattan, was well buried.

Lately, The Shadow's agents had altered their mode of search. They had begun to watch gorillas. This was in accordance with The Shadow's orders and it showed the craftiness of that mysterious chieftain. For The Shadow knew that if Beak Latzo should become dangerous he would require the services of mobsters. The best way, therefore, to balk Beak in crime was to look for thugs who might be members of a crew that Beak was forming.

"Hunk" Robo had been picked as a suspicious-looking gorilla. He was one who kept popping in and out; a hard man to follow.

Hawkeye had left the search for Hunk to Cliff and Clyde. He had concentrated upon "Goofy" Ketch, Hunk's pal. Tonight he had spotted Goofy, but the man had given him the slip.

The Shadow's agents had neared Sooky's pawnshop. Here their courses separated. Hawkeye sidled across a street and ducked into the cover of stacked ash cans. Cliff picked the alleyway on which the new dive was located. He strolled along, descended a flight of steps and thrust open a door.

Cliff stepped immediately into a small, stone-walled room. Grog-drinking ruffians, seated about at tables, looked up through the smoke-filled atmosphere to survey the intruder. Faces were challenging; then came recognition. Patrons of the new joint waved in greeting to Cliff Marsland.

The Shadow's agent strolled over and sat down at a table. He began to chat with mobsters who had recognized him. Meanwhile, he glanced about curiously; as one would when viewing a place for the first time.

Undercover of that natural action Cliff spied the men he wanted. Goofy Ketch and Hunk Robo, brawny, rough-garbed gorillas, were slouched in a corner, chatting as they leaned across a table.

No need to inform Hawkeye. As minutes passed, Cliff knew that the little spotter would be ready. For Cliff, if he had failed to see the men he wanted, would have made only a short stay in the dive. The longer that Cliff lingered within, the surer would Hawkeye be that the quarry had been spied.

Fifteen minutes went by. Goofy looked at a watch; then growled to Hunk. The two mobsters arose and slouched from the dive.

Cliff paid no attention to their departure. But he prepared to leave as soon as convenient. He was merely allowing time so that no one would suspect him of having interest in the activities of Goofy and Hunk.

OUTSIDE, Hawkeye saw the two mobsters appear. The little man gave them leeway. He made no move until both Goofy and Hunk had looked about to satisfy themselves that they were not being watched.

Then, as the pair strolled down an alleyway, Hawkeye sneaked out from behind the ash cans and took up the trail. Stealthy, at times almost furtive, the little man made amends for his slipup earlier tonight. Not once did he lose track of his quarry.

Five minutes after Goofy and Hunk had left, Cliff Marsland strolled from the dive that he had visited. He walked two blocks, found a cigar store that had a pay telephone and entered to make a call. A response came after Cliff had dialed, a quiet voice over the wire:

"Burbank speaking."

Cliff reported. Hawkeye had gained a trail. His report would soon be forthcoming. In his report, Cliff gave the location of the dive from which Hawkeye had begun the trail. His call finished, Cliff left the cigar store.

SOMEWHERE in Manhattan white hands were busy beneath the flickering glare of a bluish lamp. The Shadow was in his sanctum, that hidden abode wherein he made his plans. A tiny bulb blinked from the opposite wall. The hands reached for earphones.

"Burbank speaking," came a voice.

"Report," whispered The Shadow.

The report came. Word from Cliff; none as yet from Hawkeye. The Shadow hissed instructions. The earphones clattered; the little bulb went out. Then the blue light clicked. The sanctum was in darkness. A swish announced The Shadow's departure.

Fifteen minutes later, a blackened shape glided beneath the glow of a street lamp in the vicinity of Sooky's pawnshop. That was a momentary manifestation of The Shadow's mist-enshrouded presence.

Later, the same figure appeared weirdly at the entrance of an alleyway. It vanished into darkness. One minute passed; then a slight hiss came through gloom. A match flickered: Hawkeye's signal.

The trailing agent had reported to Burbank. He had been instructed to contact with The Shadow at this point. As his match glimmered out, Hawkeye sensed a swish closed by. He heard a whispered voice:

"Report."

"Trailed them to the first alley past the old Midway Garage," informed Hawkeye, cautiously. "Last house on the right. Guys there waiting for them. They went inside; the other birds moved off."

"Destination?"

"A touring car. Half a block away. Didn't recognize none of them. But it looks like some guy—maybe Beak Latzo—was crawling from his hideout."

"Report to Burbank," ordered The Shadow. "Contact with Marsland. Vincent to be ready with coupé. Cover with Marsland. Join Vincent in emergency."

A *swish.* Hawkeye blinked in the darkness. The Shadow was gone. No further sound marked the direction of his departure.

It was eerie, even to Hawkeye. Then, recovering from his momentary amazement, the little agent scurried off through the darkness to follow The Shadow's orders.

FIVE minutes passed. Then came motion in an alleyway. It was the same narrow thoroughfare that Lucky Ortz had taken on his visit some nights ago, to Beak Latzo's hideout. It was The Shadow's turn to visit that secluded spot.

Invisible in the thick gloom, The Shadow reached the locked door. A probing pick came into his gloved hand. The Shadow inserted the tool in the lock and began a silent twisting. Gradually the lock yielded.

Opening the door by inches, The Shadow shifted his unseen form into the darkened hall.

He closed the door behind him and locked it. So far, his work had been amazingly silent. Moving through darkness, The Shadow found the stairway. He ascended. A stealthy, noiseless figure, he arrived in the upper hall.

A short way off, The Shadow discerned two slight traces of light. They came from the cracks of door frames, one on each side of the hall. Moving forward, The Shadow listened at one door. He could hear the slight murmur of guarded voices.

The Shadow chose the other door. It was locked. He probed it; the barrier yielded and opened as he turned the knob. Light glimmered into the hall; then The Shadow blocked the illumination with his body. He stepped into the room and eased the door shut behind him.

The Shadow was in Beak Latzo's hideout.

Tall and spectral, the master investigator loomed like a being from some fantastic world. Close by the door, he used his pick to lock the barrier. It was a timely action. For, as The Shadow lingered, he heard a door open on the other side of the hall. Someone came across and tried Beak's door; then went back again.

Goofy and Hunk were on guard, their job to see that no one entered. They had been stationed in the room opposite. They had not heard The Shadow enter; but they had gone through the routine of trying Beak's door to make sure that it had not been disturbed.

THE Shadow looked about Beak's hideout. He opened drawers in a lopsided bureau; there he found nothing but odd items of clothing. Softly, he opened the door of a closet. A dressing gown was hanging there; also a new suit of clothes.

The Shadow reached into pockets. His hand encountered crinkly wads of paper. The Shadow drew them out and spread each in turn. He looked at the first sheet. It was the note that Lucky Ortz had brought from Dangler's.

The second letter was more recent. It, too, was from Steve Zurk. The scrawl was brief but pointed. The Shadow read it quickly:

> Beak:
> First lay: Theobald Luftus, Monday night. Penthouse, Swithin Apartments. Grab everything. Hold off until nine bells. Go the limit. Steve.

The Shadow thrust the first note back into the pocket of Beak's discarded suit. He took the new note—the one just read—to a table. There he found a sheet of paper. He produced a pen and began to duplicate the message.

Though his procedure was rapid, The Shadow produced a remarkable imitation of the scrawl. The ink dried; The Shadow placed the original sheet beneath his cloak. He crumpled his duplicated message and went to the closet, where he placed it in Beak's pocket.

The Shadow had gauged the time. He had arrived here at quarter past eight. It was not yet eight-thirty. He still had opportunity to reach the penthouse at the Swithin Apartments.

Leaving everything apparently as he had found it. The Shadow went to the door and unlocked it.

Stepping into the hall, he closed the door behind him and carefully relocked it. Cautiously, he began to draw the pick from the keyhole. It was at that moment that a warning came: the opening of a door across the hall.

Light flooded the hallway as The Shadow wheeled backward from Beak Latzo's door. A sharp oath sounded as a tough-faced man yanked a glimmering revolver from his coat pocket. The fellow who spat the challenge was Hunk Robo.

At the very moment of his stealthy departure, luck had tricked The Shadow. Ready to fare forth on a mission against crime, he was confronted by the watchers who had remained to guard Beak Latzo's hideout.

CHAPTER VII
THE BADLANDS RISE

HUNK ROBO had gained a remarkable opportunity. Stepping from the room across the hall, he had spotted The Shadow at a most timely moment. For The Shadow, cautious in action, was fully occupied in removing his pick from Beak Latzo's door.

Coming up with his rod, Hunk fired for the spinning form in black. But in his aim, Hunk calculated that The Shadow would whirl to face him. He failed to gather that The Shadow would also perform a fading movement.

Quick in his twist. The Shadow had dropped away from the door. He did not dive in the direction of the stairs, as Hunk might have figured. Instead, he made his sidling movement toward the front of the hall.

Hunk's shot, a quick one, splintered the face of the door where The Shadow had been. But the bullet was inches wide. Glimpsing the direction of The Shadow's fadeaway, Hunk aimed again. This time he was too late.

The Shadow had neither dropped nor put away the pick that he still gripped in his right hand. Instead, he used his left to whisk an automatic from beneath his cloak. Hunk beat him to the first shot; but The Shadow gained the bulge on the second.

The automatic roared its answer to Hunk's first thrust. The mobster paused, finger on trigger, then gave a sickly snarl. He slumped straight to the floor, a victim of The Shadow's deadly aim.

Behind Hunk was Goofy Ketch. This gorilla was quick with a gat. He had come up with Hunk's first shot. He was aiming as his pal collapsed. But Goofy gained no chance to fire. The Shadow did not wait until Hunk's body was clear away. He fired a second shot while Hunk was on his way to the floor.

The bullet clipped Goofy. The mobster dropped his gun and staggered backward. Doubled, he blundered against the edge of the door; then, just as The Shadow expected him to sprawl, Goofy gave the door a slam.

A moment later came the sound of a turning key. Hunk lay dead in the hall; Goofy, wounded, was in the room beyond the barrier. The Shadow's laugh sounded sinister in the new darkness that had come to the hallway.

No time to deal with Goofy. The Shadow had other work. Confident that his enemy was severely wounded, he headed for the stairs and made a quick descent. As he reached the ground floor, he heard pounding at the outer portal.

There was reason for The Shadow's swift departure. This building lay on the fringe of the badlands. Thugs were abroad tonight. Others, apparently, had been stationed close to the empty hideout.

One inkling that The Shadow was engaged in combat would mean the hue and cry of hordes. The Shadow did not fear such opposition; but he did not want to entail the delay that new fights might produce.

Turning, The Shadow headed for the rear of the building. He reached a closed door. His gloved fingers found a bolt. He drew the fastening and yanked the door open. Air whiffed into the hallway from an outer court.

Then came blinding light. Someone, stationed outside, had spotted the opening door.

As The Shadow stood revealed by the glare of a powerful flashlight, hoarse cries of recognition came from a pair of outer watchers. Revolvers barked as The Shadow dropped back from view. Vengeful forms leaped forward.

THE SHADOW'S retreat ended with abruptness. Automatics thundered out from the hallway as the cloaked fighter pumped lead into the advancers. The flashlight went clicking upon stone.

At that instant, the front door snapped. Another light shot down the hall. The Shadow wheeled to meet its glare. He fired simultaneously with a revolver shot from the front.

A bullet whistled through the swaying sleeve of The Shadow's cloak. The revolver shot was wide. But The Shadow's aim was true. Again a flashlight went clattering; its owner sprawled upon the front steps.

Shots from the outer darkness. There were others in the alley. Then, like echoes, came further shots from beyond. The fire from the front door ceased as wild oaths snarled from vicious lips. The Shadow knew the answer.

Hawkeye and Cliff had covered. Those echoes were their automatics. They were starting conflict with the invaders who had come from the front. The clear path was through the rear.

The Shadow spun through the opened door. He spied a passageway that led to the next street. He headed in that direction.

A lamplight glared straight ahead. It made his path a bad one—a course that The Shadow would have avoided under ordinary circumstances. But tonight, The Shadow had reason to get clear in a hurry. He was hazarding the chance that he would reach a deserted street.

Abandoning caution, he swept out into the open. A space between houses on the opposite side—such was The Shadow's new objective. But luck again tricked The Shadow in his purpose. A cry came from down the street:

"The Shadow!"

Revolver shots. The Shadow whirled to deal with distant skulkers who were bounding into view. One enemy spun about. The others dived for cover. Then came a shot from the other direction. Wheeling, The Shadow saw new foemen.

Chance mobsters, cruising in a battered sedan, had come into this street. They, too, had spied The Shadow. Had they held their fire, luck might have favored them. But one man had been too quick on the trigger. His wild, long-range shot had been The Shadow's cue.

Automatics belched. The Shadow's blasts were withering. Aimed for the front of the sedan, one bullet clipped a leaning mobster who was about to aim. Another shot found the windshield, shattered it and wounded the driver. The car went hurtling to the curb.

Wheeling, The Shadow took to the passage between the buildings. But now his course had taken on the semblance of a flight. This district, it seemed, was teeming with toughened crooks. The cry was passing along:

"The Shadow!"

Distant shots from far behind. They told The Shadow that his agents were still engaged in combat. Boldly, he headed back toward the street that he had left. Springing from the blackened wall of a building, he came face to face with a pair of pursuing thugs.

Action was swift. The Shadow's long arms swung. Aiming thugs staggered as automatics thudded against their skulls. Springing away from the spot, The Shadow headed down the street while cries arose from behind him. Men of the badlands were taking up his trail.

The new maneuver had its effect two blocks away. Cliff and Hawkeye, ambuscaded behind stone steps, were putting up a fight against attackers. Suddenly they saw their enemies turn and head for the direction of the shouts.

About to follow, Cliff sprang to his feet. Hawkeye grabbed his companion's arm and pointed down the street. Blue-coated patrolmen were coming up from a new direction. The siren of a patrol car whined in the distance.

No chance to aid The Shadow. Instinctively, the agents knew that he had drawn off the attackers. He had chosen a course of his own. Their duty was to follow instructions.

Diving through an alleyway that offered them retreat, Cliff and Hawkeye scudded toward the spot where Harry Vincent, a waiting agent, was posted with his coupé.

CHAOS had swept this neighborhood. The bluecoats spied by Cliff and Hawkeye were but the vanguard of the law. Police were converging toward spots where shots were heard; but the maelstrom of the district was ever on the move.

For The Shadow, following a devious trail, was burrowing deeper toward the underworld, reversing the very course that underworld hordes expected him to follow. He had dropped from sight, leaving bewildered ruffians wondering where he had gone.

Oddly, the spot where the fighting had begun was no longer a center of excitement. Wounded mobsters had stumbled away before the arrival of the police. Those who remained in the actual vicinity of Beak Latzo's hideout were dead—with one exception.

That was Goofy Ketch. The lone gorilla was still in the locked room where he had ducked to avoid The Shadow. He had rested gasping on the floor; now, as he heard firing fade, the wounded mobster managed to rise.

Unlocking his door, Goofy stumbled over Hunk's body. Catching himself, he blundered across the hall; there he produced a key and laboriously unlocked the door of Beak's room. With one hand clasped tightly to his body, Goofy looked about.

He saw no sign that the room had been entered. He opened the closet door. There he saw an open suitcase beneath the hanging garments. With one hand, the gorilla snatched down suit and dressing gown. He stowed them in the bag.

Moving to the bureau, he managed to open the drawers and pluck out the rest of Beak's clothing. He dropped these items into the suitcase, bent to clasp the bag shut; then staggered from the room, carrying the suitcase with him.

Goofy stumbled badly as he descended the stairway to the lower hall. Again he caught himself and managed to make the outer door. Fresh air revived him. Though his pace was faltering, the gorilla made steady progress as he traveled on to the deserted street.

MEANWHILE, police were spreading out through an area that began two blocks away. They had picked up wounded mobsters; they had gathered in a few hiding prisoners. But the law had moved no further into the underworld. Silence proclaimed that the fighting was ended. The police were waiting for reserves.

Within the police lines, mobsters and other riffraff still roamed at large. Had the police spread out, these ruffians would have returned to the region that they had left. As it was, they were lurking, sullen, awaiting a new opportunity to search for The Shadow.

At one spot, two mobsters were talking in gruff voices. They were close beside an old brick house, where broken windows gave gaping reflections to a street lamp. They were discussing the fact that fully two-score denizens of the badlands were out to get The Shadow.

One mobster turned to look down the street. When he swung about to speak to his companion, the fellow was gone. Instead of his companion, the mobster faced a being in black.

Burning eyes surveyed him from beneath a slouch hat. The mobster was staring into the mouth of an automatic.

"The Shadow!"

With that hoarse outcry, the thug hurled himself forward blindly.

Up came a gloved fist. Hand, weighted with automatic, caught the crook's chin. The mobster went spinning to the sidewalk.

Up the street was the front of a darkened store, with a narrow open space at the side. Wheeling, The Shadow headed there, crossing the street as he did so. Then came a cry from a corner just beyond the store. Half a dozen lurkers sprang into view. Revolvers tongued flame.

The Shadow stopped short. Then he became a weaving, swaying shape that blasted long decisive flashes from the muzzles of unlimbered automatics. Bullets sizzled toward the foemen. Slugs ricocheted from sidewalks.

Mobsters wavered before the withering cannonade. One sagged; another staggered; the rest went yelping, diving for safety past the corner. The Shadow had given these rats a taste of metal. They dared not face his swift barrage.

As the street cleared of scummy foe, The Shadow wheeled again. His tall form merged swiftly with the darkness beside the closed store. The place was nothing but an old furniture shop, one that needed little protection against burglary.

The Shadow found a grated window. He used an automatic as a lever to pry the grating loose on its hinge. He pried at the window; it came open. The Shadow entered, closing grating and sash behind him.

New mobsters had come into the street. They saw no signs of The Shadow. They thought that he had performed another swift departure. They passed the blackened store, without attempt to enter it.

INSIDE, The Shadow had discovered a little windowless office. He pressed the light switch; his cloaked figure made an ominous shape as The Shadow bent above a telephone. He was putting in a call to Burbank.

A ticking clock showed three minutes before nine. No time remained for The Shadow to reach the Swithin Apartments before that hour. He could not count upon his agents; they might still be loose, unable to report.

One chance alone remained: A tipoff to the police. The Shadow whispered instructions as Burbank answered. The contact man acknowledged the orders. Burbank was to make a prompt call to headquarters, keeping his identity unknown.

The Shadow hung up the receiver. He rested a short while, then made his way back through the store and out the window. He reached the street to find that mobsters had departed. Police had not yet arrived.

With a low, weird laugh, The Shadow began a new course from this district. Luckless would be the mobsters who might meet him now. For The Shadow, though heading toward the Swithin Apartments, was too late to beat Beak Latzo there.

Should he encounter underworld denizens, he would no longer avoid them now that his set task was thwarted. He was ready for any fray, prepared to deal fury like that which he had loosed when he saw the opportune store from which a phone call could be made.

The way had cleared, however. Mobsters had scattered to search elsewhere and to escape the advent of the police. Yet The Shadow, though steady in his gait, showed no haste.

He had left the matter of Theobald Luftus in the hands of the law. Delayed through misadventure, he had been forced to trust the mission of rescue to others.

CHAPTER VIII
CROOKS MOVE

A CLOCK was chiming nine from the mantelpiece of an oddly furnished room. A sour-faced old man was seated in a Morris chair, reading a newspaper. This was Theobald Luftus, in his penthouse atop the Swithin Apartments.

Though it was evening, Luftus was still engaged in perusing a morning journal. He was behind time so far as the day was concerned; his establishment showed that he was years backward in his environment.

For the furnishings of this penthouse were old pieces that Luftus had brought from an antiquated house. They were evidences—even to the soiled, dingy curtains—that Theobald Luftus preferred not to spend money whenever expense could be avoided.

Beyond an old sideboard stood a battered safe, another relic of the past. As a strong box, that steel container was no more than a piece of junk. Yet Luftus apparently considered it good enough to protect his belongings. For the old man's face registered full signs of security.

Someone knocked at the door of this piecemeal living room. Luftus croaked an order to enter. His bald head shone in the light as he looked upward through his glasses. Then an expression of alarm came upon his withered countenance. Luftus had expected a servant to enter through the door. Instead, two masked men stepped into view.

"What—what is the meaning of this?" blurted Luftus. "Who—who are you? What have you done with Barry?"

"You mean the flunky?" came a growl. The voice was Beak Latzo's. "Don't worry about him. We're bringing him along. Here he is."

As Beak and his companion stepped aside, two more masked men entered. Between them they had a haggard prisoner. The fellow was the servant who had admitted them. The one whom Luftus had called Barry.

Rough hands sent Barry spinning into a corner. The servant, a corpulent, middle-aged man, cringed as he stared hopelessly toward his master.

Theobald Luftus, quivering with indignation, tried to speak. Beak flourished a revolver under the old man's chin. Luftus backed against the wall.

"What's the combination to that box?" growled Beak, nudging a thumb toward the safe.

"I won't give it," challenged Luftus, in a quavering tone.

"You won't?" began Beak. "Well, we'll see—"

"Hold it!" The interruption came from another raider. This masked man was Lucky Ortz. "I can crack that piece of junk with a hammer and a cold chisel. Watch me."

He produced the tools and stepped to the corner. The first strokes indicated that he could make good his boast. Chunks chipped from the edge of the door as Lucky began his efficient work.

"Like cutting cheese," scoffed Lucky. "All I need is a start; then I'll jimmy the box. Let the old dub hang on to his secret. This is a laugh."

Luftus, his hands half raised, was clenching his fists excitedly. He recognized that the task was an easy one for Lucky. He began to blab half incoherently. Beak caught his words and snorted.

"Lay off, Lucky," ordered Beak. "The old boy don't want his trick box ruined. Saving it to amuse his grandchildren. Here—let me at it; he's spilled the combo."

LUFTUS gasped in horror-stricken fashion. Almost unwittingly, the old man had passed this news. He watched Beak step up and turn the dial, while Lucky stood by with hammer and chisel. The door of the safe came open.

Inside were stacks of envelopes, bound with rubber bands. Most of them appeared to contain documents of importance; but with the bundles were loosely arranged sheaves of correspondence.

Beak produced a soft cloth bag. Without ceremony, he and Lucky began to dump the stacks into the bag.

A hoarse cry from Luftus. The old man faltered forward, his eyes ablaze with fury. One of the gorillas blocked him, shoving a revolver muzzle against the old man's chin. Luftus subsided, backing close to Barry.

"Ropes," ordered Beak, as he and Lucky completed the rifling of the safe.

"We're going to tie those two geezers and let them cool a while—"

He stopped short and held up a hand as he was interrupted by the ringing of a phone bell. He pointed to the table where the telephone was resting.

"You'd better answer it, Lucky," he said, cautiously. "It might be one of these gorillas you left down at the hideout."

"Chances are it ain't," protested Lucky. "Let 'em ring. They'll think the old mug here is out."

"Yeah? They'll figure something's wrong. This bird Luftus looks like he never goes out. Answer it."

"But what about my voice?"

"Fake it. Tell them you're Barry."

Lucky nodded. He picked up the telephone and spoke in a tone that was a thin disguise for the servant's. He heard a gasping tone across the wire. His own voice changed. Lucky spoke in his usual tone.

"Yes," he said, quickly. "This is Lucky... Yes... What? He got Hunk? Whew..."

Lucky turned quickly to Beak.

"It's Goofy," he informed. "He's in his own hangout. Had to scram. The Shadow blew in on your hideout."

"And he got Hunk?" demanded Beak.

Lucky nodded.

Fiercely, Luftus broke loose. Springing forward, he hurled his clawlike hands at Beak's throat.

"Find out where he went from there," ordered Beak, in a tense growl.

Lucky talked over the wire. This time he had trouble in getting Goofy's reply. His tone was troubled when he turned to Beak a second time.

"He may be on his way here," explained Lucky. "So Goofy says. He figures The Shadow could be anywhere."

"Did he get into my room?" demanded Beak.

"No," returned Lucky. "That's one break. Hunk and Goofy spotted him outside the door."

"Then we're all right," assured Beak. "If he didn't get those letters that were in my pockets. But if Goofy blew the place, The Shadow might go back there."

"Goofy brought your duds with him," stated Lucky. "I'll tell him to look in the pockets."

LUCKY spoke over the wire. At first he did not receive a response. Then Goofy's voice clicked on the line. Lucky spoke. A pause; again Goofy's voice clicked. Lucky turned to Beak and nodded.

"He's got the letters," assured Lucky.

"Great," acknowledged Beak. "Tell him to burn them—in a hurry—right now—"

Lucky nodded. He gave the order to Goofy, adding comments of his own. There came another pause—a full three quarters of a minute. Then Lucky began to listen intently. He had one hand over the mouthpiece of the telephone while he reported Goofy's words to Beak.

"Goofy's read the letters," he assured. "They're both from Steve... He's burned them. Ashes out the window... Wait a minute, I can't get what he's saying... Something I can't get..."

Lucky suddenly dropped the receiver on the hook. He turned his masked face toward Beak. An oath came from Lucky's lips.

"Goofy's croaked!" was Lucky's added exclamation. "He was telling me he was wounded—I could hear him coughing! Then he gasped and I could hear him clatter to the floor, the telephone along with him. The Shadow must have got him!"

"Come on!" snarled Beak. "We're moving!"

GORILLAS seemed eager to go. They grabbed hold of Luftus and began to wind a rope about his wrists. The old man uttered a defiant protest.

"Shut up, you old fool!" snarled Beak. "You want a thump from the butt of my rod?"

"You can't silence me," crackled Luftus. "Never! I'll tell what I've heard!" He was fighting free from the mobsters. "I'll tell about Steve—about this man here—the one you called Lucky—"

Fiercely, Luftus broke loose. Springing forward, he hurled his clawlike hands at Beak's throat. The attack was effective because of its unexpectedness. Beak went staggering back, trying to bring his gun into action. Luftus yanked at his mask while the gorillas fell upon the old man from behind.

Then came a sharp cry from Barry. The servant came leaping forward from the wall, to fling himself upon Lucky. Barry had seen that ruffian about to perform a murderous act. The servant wanted to prevent it; but his thrust came too late.

Lucky's gat spoke straight for Luftus. The old man collapsed as the gorillas seized him. His body writhed upon the floor. Then Lucky went jouncing sidewise as a furious form landed on him. Ripping like a demon, Barry was clawing at this killer who had slain his master.

Lucky lost his gun as he sprawled on the floor. Barry, furious, seized it and tried to aim in vengeance. Another gun spoke. This time it was Beak's rod. Barry gasped; sidled to the floor and lay there groaning.

Beak ripped off his mask and hurled it into the open bag. He motioned the others to do the same. They complied. Hoisting the bundle, Beak tucked it under his arm. He snapped an order.

"Out by the service elevator," he ordered. "The way we came in. Get going before they come up to find out about those shots."

"I had to let the old duke have it, Beak," declared Lucky. "He was on you—and he was going to squawk—"

"You don't hear me crabbing do you," broke in Beak. "Didn't I give it to the flunky when he was on your neck? Couldn't he blab, too? They had it coming—both of them."

Four raiders hastened through the door. Silence followed their departure. Theobald Luftus was dead. Barry's groan had subsided. Death held sway in this antiquated room.

Murder had fallen despite The Shadow's efforts to prevent it. Though rescue was already on the way, Theobald Luftus and his servant had succumbed. Had Luftus used discretion, he and Barry could have remained alive, waiting the arrival of the police.

But Luftus had used wild judgment. Murder had followed robbery. The track which The Shadow must from now on follow would be a trail of blood.

CHAPTER IX
THE ONLY CLUE

SIX minutes after the departure of Beak Latzo and Lucky Ortz, an elevator arrived at the penthouse level. From it stepped a swarthy, stocky man, who was followed by three others.

The leading arrival was Detective Joe Cardona, ace of the Manhattan force. The other men constituted a squad that Joe had brought with him.

The detectives went through the apartment. They arrived at the living room. A brief glance told them that they had come too late. They saw the bodies of Luftus and Barry; beyond the crumpled men the yawning front of the rifled safe.

Joe bent over each body in turn. He saw at once that Theobald Luftus was dead. But Barry's form seemed feebly alive. Joe raised the servant's head. The semblance of a groan came from Barry's lips.

Glassy eyes stared at Joe Cardona. It was plain that Barry's wound was mortal. Yet there was a chance that the servant could speak.

Joe's gruff voice came in urging terms. Barry's lips moved.

Slow, gasping words. Yet Cardona heard them as the faithful servant tried his utmost to explain what had occurred. The statement came with breaks.

"The—the funds," gasped Barry. "Thousands of dollars—gone. Murson—Murson—the broker—he was here. He brought them—brought them all with him—"

A hideous cough. Blood showed on Barry's lips. The servant sank in Cardona's grasp.

Joe lowered the body to the floor. He came to his feet, drew out a pad and pencil and wrote down the words that he had heard.

Detectives were prowling about. They saw no sign of the departed raiders. One sleuth, out in a side hall of the penthouse, passed by the door of the service elevator, thinking it was the entrance of a locked closet.

By the time that Joe Cardona had called his squad together, their consensus was that the killers had made a deliberate getaway down through the regular elevator.

Joe went out to quiz the white-faced operator who was standing in the car, aghast at the news of murder.

"How long have you been on duty?" questioned Joe.

"Only half an hour," answered the lad. "I have the night shift. Supposed to be on at nine o'clock—I came early tonight—"

"Any other cars running?"

"Only this one."

"Your name?"

The operator gave it.

"And the fellow you relieved?"

The operator gave that name also.

"Where did he go?" asked Joe.

"To a movie, I think," said the operator. "I don't know which one. He had a date."

"Did he say anything about bringing people up and down from this penthouse?"

"Not a word."

THOUGH the shooting of Luftus and Barry had unquestionably been recent, Joe Cardona had no proof that it had occurred within the last half hour. In view of the operator's testimony, he was inclined to believe that it had happened during the previous shift.

With this false start, the ace detective turned to routine. Unaware that there was a service elevator to the penthouse, he put in a call to headquarters. While waiting for the arrival of a police surgeon, Joe began an inspection of the death room. The other detectives watched him as he examined the safe.

Out in the hallway of the penthouse, a slight tremble occurred at the doors of the service elevator. Peering eyes gazed through a crack; then the doors opened. A figure came into view. Tall, cloaked and sinister, The Shadow had arrived to find this mode of entry to the penthouse.

Hearing the sound of voices, the weird intruder moved toward the living room. Standing just outside the door, he took in the entire scene.

Cardona had stepped back from the door of the safe. He was eyeing the interior of the strong box while his squad watched him.

The bodies were fully visible upon the floor. The Shadow, from his lookout post, was able to visualize the entire setting. He remained there, listening to gruff comments that came from Cardona.

The telephone rang. Cardona gestured to a detective. The Shadow faded as the man turned in his direction. Joe's aide did not see the figure vanishing from the open door. The sleuth picked up the telephone. He growled a hello, listened, then turned to Cardona.

"A newshound downstairs," he informed. "Burke of the *Classic.* Wants to come up."

"Tell him to wait for the police surgeon," stated Joe. "You'd better go down, Cassidy. Stay in the lobby. Send Burke up with the doc."

The Shadow was sweeping along the hallway before Cassidy reached the door. He disappeared beyond the turn to the service elevator. After he heard the clang of Cassidy's departure, The Shadow stepped aboard his own elevator and closed the doors behind him. He began a descent.

It chanced that one of the other dicks came out into the hall just after The Shadow's departure. This sleuth heard the dull noise of the service elevator. But it was mingled with the sound of the regular lift, in which Cassidy was descending. Hence the incident of The Shadow's departure passed unnoticed.

The Shadow had seen the spot of crime. He knew that he had arrived too late to save Theobald Luftus. The news that Clyde Burke was coming was all that The Shadow needed.

Evidently the reporter had put in a routine call to Burbank. The contact man, always alert in The Shadow's service, had told Clyde to call headquarters. Phoning there, Clyde had learned of murder at the Swithin Apartments. He had beaten the police surgeon to the place where Cardona was.

FIVE minutes after The Shadow's exit, Clyde Burke came up with the police surgeon. The two formed an odd pair as they entered the penthouse living room. Clyde was a frail but wiry chap who looked underfed. The police surgeon, heavy-jowled and overweight, looked as though he had been summoned while in the midst of a late dinner, which, as a matter of fact, he had.

"Outside, Burke," ordered Cardona brusquely, as he spied the reporter. "Wait until after the examination."

Clyde strolled along the hall. He turned the corner; there he stopped short and noted the doors of the service elevator. He strolled back to the entrance of the living room. Lingering beyond the portal, he heard a discussion between Cardona and the police surgeon.

"It can't have happened after nine o'clock, doc!" Joe was exclaiming. "There's nobody been up or down since the operator came on his shift. These victims must have been shot before that."

"Your own statement supports my finding," returned the surgeon. "I tell you that this one man"—he pointed to Barry—"could not have lived for more than a dozen minutes, if that long. Yet you talked to him."

"Then how did those killers get away?" demanded Cardona, savagely. "I can't figure it." He turned toward the door and noted Clyde. "Why the snooping, Burke? I told you to stay out."

"Just found something, Joe," reported Clyde, in a friendly tone. "A service elevator around the corner of the hall. Thought maybe you'd passed it up—"

Clyde broke off as Cardona came hurriedly forward. The detective thrust past, followed the direction that Clyde had indicated and pulled up in front of the telltale doors. He swung about to the two detectives who had followed him.

"Didn't you spot this, Morey?" he questioned, as he indicated one dick. "You looked around out here—"

"Thought it was a closet door," interposed Morey. "Looked like it was locked. The guys we wanted were gone—"

"Are you dumb!" fumed Cardona. "Well, they're gone, all right. With plenty of time for a good getaway. This is the way they blew. Where's that regular elevator operator—"

"Went down again," broke in Morey.

"Then ring for him," snapped Joe. "Get busy. Here—come along; I'll ring myself. You might muff it."

WITH that sarcastic thrust, Cardona headed for the main elevators. The telephone was ringing in the living room; he turned in that direction, gesturing for Clyde Burke to press the elevator button. Even before Clyde did so, the sound of mechanism issued from the shaft. The elevator was coming up.

Clyde pressed the button anyhow. He heard Cardona coming back from the living room. The detective's face was sour.

"Worse and more of it," informed Joe. "You know who's on his way up? The police commissioner. Cassidy just called me. Listen, Burke; stroll around the corner and stay there until I send for you. The commissioner might be sore if he knew a reporter got here ahead of him."

Clyde grinned and nodded. He turned about and drifted down the hall, making the turn just before he heard the sound of the arriving elevator.

Glancing back, he caught a glimpse of a stalwart man of military appearance, stepping from the elevator. A momentary flash of a determined face, with short, pointed mustache. Cassidy's call had been correct. The arrival was Police Commissioner Ralph Weston.

Clyde paced the hall. Weston and Cardona had gone into the living room. The reporter knew that the two were in conference. He wanted to learn their subject of discussion; but he could only wait in hope that he would be admitted later.

Morey appeared to announce that other reporters were downstairs, according to a call from Cassidy. Weston had said to keep them there. Clyde took this news glumly. Five minutes passed, then Morey reappeared.

"Slide in," said the detective. "Cardona's fixed it for you. The commissioner is going to make a statement for the newspapers. You're on the inside track, Burke."

Clyde nodded.

"But make out like you just came up," added Morey. "Cardona told me to go down and get you. Guess he doesn't want the commissioner to know he had you up here."

Another nod from Clyde. The reporter strolled about for a minute, then sauntered into the living room.

Weston observed his entrance and gave Clyde a short nod.

"Explain it, Cardona," ordered Weston.

"IT'S this way, Burke," stated Cardona. "We landed one clue to these murders. Just one. The servant here, talked for a few seconds before he died. Mentioned the name of Murson, old Luftus' broker. Said that Murson had been here. This is the servant's statement."

Clyde noted the paper that Cardona held out. Nodding, he copied it word for word.

"Murson's first name is Adolph," resumed Cardona. "We called his home from here. Then we got his secretary on the telephone. Murson is out of town. Supposed to have gone to Washington."

"A stall?" questioned Clyde.

"We're going to find out," returned Cardona. "They're bringing us his picture and we're going to watch all the railroad stations to see if the fellow leaves New York—"

"Omit that, Burke," snapped Weston, by way of interruption, as the reporter began to make a note. "The statement to the newspapers is this: Adolph Murson is wanted in connection with the murders of Theobald Luftus and his servant. From the servant's statement, it appears that Murson brought killers with him here tonight.

"Presumably the only man who could have known the value of securities in this rifled safe was Murson. His announcement—this afternoon—to the effect that he was leaving town is an indication of premeditated crime.

"We believe that he is still in New York. Not in Washington, as he said he would be. That sounds like an attempt at an alibi. He had an eleven o'clock appointment for tomorrow morning. He changed it to one-thirty, stating that he would not be back until then. One-thirty tomorrow afternoon."

"I can use all this?" questioned Clyde.

"All except the fact that we are watching the depots," returned Weston. "You may state that the police have begun an intensive search for Adolph Murson."

"That Murson is still here in New York—"

"Yes, and that we have acted with a promptness that will prevent his departure from the city."

"That indicates that railroad stations, bridges, and the Holland Tunnel will be watched, Commissioner."

"Perhaps so. But I am depending upon you to minimize the fact; and to have other reporters do the same."

"All right, Commissioner, I think we can soft-pedal it. Particularly if we get Murson's picture."

"You will have it."

TWENTY minutes later, Clyde Burke and other reporters left the Swithin Apartments carrying photographs of Adolph Murson, brought by the broker's secretary. The other newshawks headed for their offices. But Clyde made a stop-over on his trip.

With plenty of time to make the edition, The Shadow's agent had a preliminary duty to perform. He stopped at a drugstore and made a telephone call to Burbank. He gave the contact man full details, with a verbatim report of Barry's dying words.

Clyde considered the case as he rode by subway to the *Classic* office. In his opinion, it looked bad for Adolph Murson. Yet Clyde, knowing of The Shadow's search for Beak Latzo, could see cross purposes beneath the surface of crime.

Of one thing, Clyde felt sure. The Shadow, like the police, would look for the missing stock broker. And Clyde was willing to bet his bottom nickel that his mysterious chief would precede the law in its intensive search.

CHAPTER X
NEXT NOON

AT twelve o'clock the next noon, Jack Targon was seated at a desk in the office of the New Century Advertising Agency. The ex-convict was busy rewriting advertising copy—a task that had been assigned him in order that he might gain experience.

A friendly hand dropped on Jack's shoulder. Jack looked up to recognize the austere face of Galen Flix, his new employer. Flix returned Jack's frank smile.

"You're going out to lunch with me, Targon," informed the advertising man. "We have an appointment with a friend of mine. Joseph Daykin."

"The importer?" questioned Jack, as he arose to get hat and coat. "The chap who hired Steve Zurk?"

"The same," said Flix with a nod. "And Zurk will be there also. Let us drop the subject until we meet for lunch."

Flix and Jack went from the office. They descended to the street and entered a hotel half a block away. In a quiet corner of the grillroom they found Daykin, a portly, tired-faced man, waiting with Steve.

Handshakes were exchanged. The four men ordered from the menu. Then, as they began their leisurely meal, Galen Flix looked from Jack Targon to Steve Zurk. Solemnly, the ad man came to the subject that had brought this meeting.

"I presume," he stated, "that both of you have read today's newspapers?"

Nods from Jack and Steve.

"Then," added Flix, "you have read of the murders that took place in the Swithin Apartment. The killing of Theobald Luftus and his servant, Barry."

New nods.

"Luftus was a retired manufacturer," explained Flix. "His company places all its advertising through my agency. Moreover, it imports certain raw materials through the Daykin Importing Company.

"Therefore, Mr. Daykin and I are greatly concerned over the death of Theobald Luftus. We are anxious to see his murderer brought to justice. It occurred to us that you two men"—he looked from Jack to Steve—"might have opinions regarding that terrible crime. If so, we should be glad to hear them."

Jack Targon smiled slightly. Steve Zurk maintained a poker-faced countenance. It was Jack who spoke.

"I THINK the police are all wet," he declared. "They haven't got anything on this broker, Murson. It looks to me like a bunch of crude workers decided to bust in on Luftus, figuring the old gentleman had dough.

"The coppers muffed it. To cover up their dumbness, they're following this Murson steer. There's my opinion, Mr. Flix. But it's not much of a one."

"Why not?" questioned Flix.

"Well," replied Jack, soberly, "I'm trying to forget my past; but I'll talk about it for the time being. My specialty, when I was crooked, was confidence work. Swindles mostly; sometimes forgery. I stayed away from thugs.

"They're crude, those fellows are. I always figured that if they were really smart, they'd be in some other racket. But I don't know as much about them as I might. Steve here is the chap who can give you the expert opinion on that sort of crime."

Flix looked toward Steve. The dark-faced man gave a slow, reminiscent nod.

"What about it, Zurk?" questioned Flix, in an urging tone.

"Jack is part right about it," replied Steve. "And he's part wrong. That's my opinion, Mr. Flix."

"Can you specify?" questioned the ad man.

"Yes," nodded Steve. "It's a case of even chances. Maybe those killers just blundered into Luftus's place. Maybe they were wise to go there."

"Assuming that they had a planned purpose," urged Flix, "do you think that Murson was behind it?"

"Yes," declared Steve. "And I'll tell you why. If there was real swag in that box at Luftus's, Murson would have known it."

"That's the theory held by the police."

"Yes. And it may be right. Wrong, you understand, if the raid was just hit or miss. Right, though, if there was any brains behind it."

"Do you think that Murson was with the killers?"

"It looks that way."

Jack Targon shook his head as Steve paused. The opinion did not agree with his.

"Murson would have stayed out of it," he assured. "You're getting into my field of experience, Steve. Murson, if he hired killers, would have acted smooth—"

"You never bought up a crew of gorillas, did you?" quizzed Steve.

"No," admitted Jack. "I wouldn't have been fool enough to deal with murderers."

"Why not?"

"Because I was smooth enough to handle my own jobs—"

"That's enough. You've hit it." Steve turned to Flix. "You hear what Jack says? He was smooth enough to lay off of mobs. He didn't need them."

"But you think that Murson—"

"Wasn't smooth enough. That's the answer, Mr. Flix. Here. Let me reason it out for you. I've seen enough dirty business to know how it works."

Toying with a spoon and a saltcellar, Steve began to unfold his idea. He used the articles to indicate persons concerned.

"HERE'S Murson," explained Steve, setting down the saltcellar with a thump. "A business man. A broker. He sees a chance to grab a lot of swag. He's scared though. Needs somebody to do his dirty work for him. So he finds some bum mobsters."

Steve set the spoon away from the saltcellar, to indicate the crooks approached by Murson. He lifted a half-filled glass of water and placed it at a new spot.

"Take Luftus," he decided, looking steadily at the glass of water. "He's the guy that has the stuff they want. A cinch for these gorillas, anytime they want to go after it"—he was pushing the spoon toward the glass—"but Murson over here"—he tapped the saltcellar—"is on pins and needles."

"Why?" questioned Flix.

"For fear the mob will bungle the job," replied Steve. "And for another reason. He's worried that they'll beat it with the swag. Double-cross him. So he decides he'd better travel with them"—spoon joined saltcellar—"and take no chances either way."

"Logical," nodded Flix.

"That's the way it works," said Steve. "Well, Murson, to begin with, throws a bluff that he's leaving for Washington. Then he goes up there with the outfit. They turn berserk and Murson does the same. It's curtains for Luftus and his servant.

"The bulls get there. Barry tries to squawk. Who's the first person he mentions? Murson. He says: 'Murson brought'—and then he croaks. What did Murson bring? The Mob. That's simple, isn't it?"

Flix and Daykin were nodding. But Jack Targon's eyes were steadily fixed upon Steve Zurk's face. A grim smile began to form on Jack's lips. The former confidence man became narrow in his gaze. Then, suddenly, Jack changed his expression. He lighted a cigarette and puffed in meditative fashion, as though disinterested in the case under discussion.

"I'm no dick," asserted Steve, suddenly. He pushed spoon, saltcellar and glass aside. "Maybe Murson didn't go up with that outfit; but if he didn't, he probably stuck around outside and was ready to meet them when they came out. At least, that's the way a guy like him would have worked it.

"One way or the other. With the mob or waiting for them. What Barry said makes it look like he was with them. It's possible that he brought the fellows up to the penthouse; then went out, leaving them to do the dirty work. Barry's statement would cover that.

"But the law has pinned it on Murson and I think they've got the goods. They've hit a tough snag, though. I was looking at the evening newspapers, just before lunch. None of the elevator operators at the apartment knew Murson, although they said they'd seen a guy like his picture come in there yesterday afternoon."

"Do you think it was Murson?" inquired Flix.

"Sure," said Steve. "He probably went up to look over the lay. Make sure the swag was there. But when he hit with his helpers, he used the service elevator."

A pause. A waiter brought dessert. As the four men began to eat. Galen Flix made final comment.

"THE police are watching all outgoing trains," he stated. "They are also on watch at tubes, ferries and bridges. The evening papers commented on that fact—something that the morning journals did not mention.

"Unquestionably, Murson will be apprehended. My worry was that he might not be the right man. But from what you have told us, Zurk, the law appears to be on the proper trail. What do you think of Zurk's opinion, Targon?"

"Steve knows his stuff," commented Jack, in a casual tone. "He's the one to give the opinion. Not me. Anyway, I hope they grab this bird Murson."

"So do I," declared Flix—while Daykin nodded. Then, in an affable tone, the advertising man added: "Both Mr. Daykin and myself must apologize for bringing up this discussion. We know that crime is a subject that you two gentlemen find distasteful.

"But, under the circumstances, we felt a meeting desirable. Because Luftus was our mutual friend you understand. Let us forget the matter. How is our friend Perry Delhugh? Have either of you seen him lately?"

"I dropped in on him last night," declared Steve. "Along about seven o'clock. No—it was later than that. After eight, I guess. I stayed there about an hour—maybe longer."

"I expect to call on him this evening," declared Jack. His eyes were narrowing on Steve as he spoke. "Just for a short chat."

Conversation turned to business. Flix and Daykin talked while their companions listened. All the while, Steve's eyes were steady on either Flix or Daykin. He seemed to be avoiding Jack Targon's gaze.

That was a fact that Jack alone noted. But Jack made no comment. At times, his lips pursed in knowing fashion. For Jack, despite his silence, had gained a definite opinion of his own.

His expression showed that he saw bluff behind the comments that Steve had made; that he believed the dark-faced man had concentrated on the theory of Murson's guilt in order to avoid too much discussion.

For Jack Targon knew Steve Zurk. He understood the secrets of Steve's past. He realized that he could easily have dropped remarks that might have worried his former pal. But Jack's silence was expressive. It showed that for the present, at least, he had decided to keep his real opinions to himself.

CHAPTER XI
THE HUNTED MAN

AT the time when four men were concluding their lunch in a Manhattan hotel, a fast train was speeding eastward toward the Jersey City terminal of the Central Railroad of New Jersey.

This was a Baltimore and Ohio limited that had left Washington about five hours earlier. Its eastern terminal was the depot of the Jersey Central; and passengers in the dining car were finishing their lunch in anticipation of a prompt arrival in Jersey City.

Among those in the dining car was a long-faced, dark-haired man with bushy brows and heavy mustache. Glancing from the window, he saw that the limited was nearing the long bridge that crossed Newark Bay. The man arose and went back to the club car.

Under his arm this individual carried a book that he had been reading. That accounted in part for the fact that he had not perused the morning newspapers in the club car. There was another angle, also, to his choice of reading.

Among the newspapers on the train, this traveler had not spied any of the New York dailies. He had passed up Washington, Baltimore and Philadelphia newspapers with a mere glance; then had reverted to his book instead.

In the club car, the long-faced man sat down beside a table. He looked up momentarily as another person arrived from the dining car. He observed a quiet-faced young chap who sat down and looked from the window.

Realizing that they were nearly to the end of the run, the long-faced man put aside his book. Then, on the table beside him, he chanced to spy a New York newspaper.

Someone must have brought the journal aboard. It was a morning newspaper that might have been purchased by a passenger who boarded the train at Philadelphia. The long-faced man picked up the newspaper. A suppressed exclamation came from the lips beneath his mustache.

Staring at the front page of the newspaper, the long-faced traveler had recognized his own photograph. Above it was the caption: "Wanted on Murder Charge." Below it was his own name in small capital letters:

ADOLPH MURSON

A shudder came to Murson's shoulders. Wild-eyed, the broker looked about. No one had apparently noticed the tremor that had quaked his frame. Avidly, Murson began to read the column that appeared beside his name. It was an account of murder in the penthouse of Theobald Luftus.

"Jersey City!" came the porter's announcement. "Last stop—"

MURSON rose unsteadily. His bags had gone out to the vestibule. Clutching the telltale newspaper, the broker jammed it into his overcoat pocket. He moved to the door as the train coasted into the terminal.

Stepping from the club car, Murson saw the line of heavy busses that meet all incoming trains of the B. & O. From his pocket he pulled a cardboard ticket that bore a large figure 1. He recalled that he had arranged to go uptown by bus.

His bag had already gone aboard the rear of the bus when Murson arrived and handed the ticket to the driver. Entering the bus, the broker slumped into a deep leather seat and muffled the collar of his overcoat about his chin.

He was a hunted man. Wanted for a part in robbery and murder. Face quivering, Murson tried to cover up his identity. He drew the newspaper from his pocket, glanced at the picture and tried to steady himself.

A poor photograph. An old one that had not reproduced well. It gave Murson an idea. He drew a small case from his pocket and extracted a pair of pince-nez spectacles that he seldom used. Adjusting the glasses to his nose, Murson felt that they might help him as a temporary disguise.

Drawing the newspaper from his pocket the broker held it in front of him and tried to read. He noted that the police were searching for him—according to the account; that he had presumably left for Washington the day before.

Dimly, Murson recalled an incident this morning: police at the Union Station in Washington, watching people going through a train gate. But they had been watching southern-bound passengers. Murson realized why. No one would have suspected that he, Adolph Murson, would be coming back to New York.

Murson realized something else. In Washington, he had not stopped at a hotel. Instead, he had stayed overnight with a friend in Arlington. He had left by taxicab to catch his train. Had his friend read the newspapers and informed the police that he had left for New York? Murson hoped not.

The bus had started; passing through the terminal, it rolled aboard a ferryboat. Murson continued his reading. He was nervous. He expected that police would be on the other side. He was tempted to leave the bus; but the presence of the other passengers deterred him.

Across the aisle was the young man whom Murson had seen in the club car of the train. This chap was reading a magazine, not a newspaper. Murson felt at ease on that score. Here, at least, was one who would not recognize him.

The ferry reached the Manhattan slip. Big wheels spun; chains clattered; gates were opened. The bus moved forward through a tunnellike passage. It stopped as it reached the street.

Murson groaned. He saw a policeman coming over toward the bus.

Then came a break. Another bus, one bringing passengers to the depot, rolled up from the opposite direction. The policeman turned and began to look through the windows of the arriving vehicle. He was interested more in people who were leaving New York, rather than those coming into town.

MURSON'S bus rolled northward. As it sped along a broad avenue, Murson felt a sickening sensation. He had intended to ride to the bus depot on Forty-second Street, opposite the Grand Central Terminal. He realized that there would be officers at that spot.

Fumbling for a timetable, Murson read the names of places where the bus stopped en route.

A weak smile came to his lips. He clenched and unclenched his hands, rustling the newspaper with the action. Then, as the bus crossed a broad street, he arose and stepped forward to the driver.

"I want the Zenith Hotel," he said. "You stop near there, don't you?"

"Next stop," informed the driver.

Murson held to the handle of a seat, staring through the front window. The bus rolled along another block; then, swerved and pulled up beside the entrance of a hotel. Murson stepped out when the driver opened the door. An attendant put his bag off at the back.

Not waiting for the hotel porter to pick up the bag, Murson headed through the revolving door and reached the lobby of the Zenith Hotel. He had seen a patrolman strolling down the street. In his haste to avoid the officer, he did not learn that another passenger had followed him from the bus.

It was the young man with the magazine. He arrived at the desk in the lobby while Murson was registering under the name of John Dyler, giving his home city as Baltimore.

The young man heard the clerk give Murson Room 912. Then, as Murson turned about, the young man strolled away toward a magazine stand, unnoticed by the broker.

Murson entered an elevator, a bellhop carrying his bag. The young man went directly to a telephone booth and dialed a number. A quiet voice responded:

"Burbank speaking."

"Vincent calling," acknowledged the young man.

"Report," came Burbank's order.

The young man spoke in detail. He told of Adolph Murson's trip from the ferry. He gave the broker's false name and room number.

The call completed, the young man strolled from the booth and left the hotel. Harry Vincent, active agent of The Shadow, had reported to the contact man, Burbank.

UP in Room 912, Murson was fumbling with a phone book The bell boy had gone. Finding a number, Murson put in a call. He asked for Mr. Dobbs. He was informed that Mr. Dobbs was out. Murson hung up and paced the room.

Ten minutes later, he repeated the call—with the same result. Mr. Dobbs was still out. The girl at the other end of the wire wanted Murson's name. Murson stammered incoherently; then hung up.

The broker's back was to the door. Hence Murson did not see a motion of the barrier. Though he had locked it, the door was opening inward.

Murson swung about. A cry came from his lips.

Standing in the room was a personage dressed in a dark, well-fitted suit. The intruder's face was a calm one, a molded visage that seemed almost masklike. There was something hawkish in his countenance; and his eyes were burning orbs that gleamed upon the hapless broker.

Murson sank gasping into a chair. He babbled weakly, incoherently; then buried his head in his hand.

The tall intruder's thin lips formed a smile; from them came the faint whisper of a mirthless laugh.

The arrival was The Shadow. Guised as a chance visitor, he had come here to find Adolph Murson. Within a half hour after Murson's arrival in New York, The Shadow had uncovered the hunted man for whom the police were searching everywhere in vain.

CHAPTER XII
THE SHADOW ADVISES

"You—you are a detective?" The gasped question came from Murson, as the hunted man looked up. "You have come—come to arrest me?"

"I am a friend," spoke The Shadow in a steady, even tone. "I have come to talk to you."

Murson looked bewildered. He had never seen this person before. He could not understand.

"You were calling an attorney." The Shadow's statement was a monotone. "But you learned that he was out."

"I was calling Egbert Dobbs," acknowledged Adolph Murson. "He is my lawyer—"

"Mr. Dobbs is keeping an appointment," informed The Shadow. "One that was arranged on your account. So that you would not talk to him."

"Why—why shouldn't I talk to Dobbs?"

"Because he would advise you to give yourself up to the police."

Murson groaned.

"A proper course for an innocent man," added The Shadow. "But one that brings great difficulties. I should not advise it for the present."

Hope gleamed in Murson's eyes. He realized that this amazing stranger was actually a friend. Finding relief, he blurted:

"How did you discover me here?"

"Quite simply," stated The Shadow, a slight smile on his lips. "Knowing that you were innocent, I believed that you had gone to Washington as you stated. Something that the police doubted."

"But—but my coming here—"

"You had an appointment for this morning. At your office. But you changed it to one-thirty this afternoon."

"Yes. I intended to keep it—"

"By coming in on a train that would reach New York about one o'clock. There are two such trains from Washington. On different railroads."

Murson nodded.

"I might have come by Pennsylvania," he admitted. "But I decided to take the Baltimore and Ohio."

"Two persons went to Philadelphia this morning," stated The Shadow. He was referring to Cliff Marsland and Harry Vincent. "One boarded the Pennsylvania train; the other took the Baltimore and Ohio. Both were looking for you."

"And they had seen my printed picture—"

"Yes. One man spied you. He came here in the bus that you took."

Murson began to remember the young man with the magazine. He nodded. Then his thoughts went back to his plight. His face registered a troubled look.

"Your spectacles are excellent," remarked The Shadow, maintaining his inflexible smile. "By shaving your mustache and clipping those bushy eyebrows, you can easily pose as John Dyler. Particularly if you remain here. The police are convinced that you are anxious to get out of town. Soon they will believe that you have departed."

"That's right!" exclaimed Murson. "And if I don't call Dobbs, I can sit tight!"

"For a few days," stated The Shadow.

"For a few days!" gasped Murson. "But—but what about after that?"

"You can visit the police yourself. By that time, the actual perpetrators of the crime will be apprehended."

THERE was a solemnity in The Shadow's tone that carried conviction. Murson believed the firm words of his amazing visitor. More at ease, he shifted in his chair; then delivered a question that was in his mind.

"Why are you helping me?" he asked. "Why does saving me from arrest have to do with the criminals?"

The Shadow did not give an immediate reply. Instead, he seated himself in a chair opposite Murson and brought a gold cigarette case from his pocket. He offered the broker a smoke. Murson accepted. The Shadow lighted a cigarette of his own.

"Dangerous men have come from under cover," he explained. "Successful in murder, they have dived beneath the surface. They are elated because you are wanted for their crime. Your arrest would make them cautious, because you are innocent.

"But so long as you appear to be the one the police want, the crooks will feel themselves free to move again. They will believe that you are hiding out through fear. They will act as quickly as possible, before you are uncovered.

"Our purpose"—The Shadow's tone was steady and impersonal—"is to lull them. That will be accomplished through your cooperation. I have shown you how to remain undiscovered. I shall tell you how and where to reach me in case of emergency. In the meantime, you can assist by telling me all you know regarding the affairs of Theobald Luftus."

Murson nodded; then stared speculatively toward the smoke that was rising from his cigarette.

"Those rogues made a big haul," he stated. "Pretty close to half a million, I should gauge. I can describe a few of the securities that Murson held."

"Later."

"All right. I guess you want to know when I last saw Luftus. That was yesterday afternoon. He asked me to come up and look over a lot of his stocks and bonds. I went there."

"At what hour?"

"About three o'clock. I wasn't going to Washington until about five. A visit to a friend down there. Business regarding investments. Well, sir, Luftus showed me stack after stack of gilt-edged stuff! The man was an absolute miser in his way."

"And his purpose—"

"Was to get my opinion regarding a gift of twenty thousand dollars. He didn't say who it was to. Just picked out batches of securities and asked me which he could give easiest without hurting himself.

"He said some people were coming to get the twenty thousand. He referred to a letter and mentioned that he'd have to call the people up."

"And the letter—"

"Went back into his safe along with the securities.

"YOU know"—Murson narrowed his thick eyebrows—"I think that servant, Barry, was trying to tell the whole thing from the start.

"He wanted to tell the police that I could give them information. That I was there, and that I brought old Luftus a special account book in which he could list all of his securities. Luftus was making such a list when I left."

"Would he have placed the book in his safe?"

"Yes. He kept all of his papers there. Well, sir, when I saw the New York newspaper on the train, I went into a funk. It looked bad for me. I guess I did just what you expected I'd do.

"I got out of sight. I didn't want to be arrested

and have to give my flimsy story. That's why I came here. And I'm going to stay here, like you've told me."

The Shadow arose from his chair.

"Do exactly as I have ordered," he said in his modulated tone. "Play your part as John Dyler. Answer telephone calls without alarm. You will hear further from me. Your testimony has its value. Rest assured that the real criminals will be uncovered."

The Shadow extended his hand. Murson received it. Then the tall visitor turned and departed, leaving the broker sighing in relief.

Standing by the elevators on the ninth floor, The Shadow indulged in a soft, almost inaudible laugh. He had accomplished his mission with Adolph Murson. New knowledge had been acquired.

Through his contact with the hunted broker, The Shadow had gained another step in the swift pace that he was taking toward the climax that he wanted.

With the parts played by Steve Zurk and Beak Latzo already clearing in his mind, The Shadow was prepared to deal with men of crime.

CHAPTER XIII
DELHUGH'S VISITOR

JACK TARGON had mentioned at lunch that he was scheduled for an evening appointment with Perry Delhugh. At seven o'clock, after an early dinner, Jack went to the philanthropist's home. Delhugh had finished his evening meal. Benzig conducted Jack to the philanthropist's study.

Another visitor arrived half an hour later. Benzig, going upstairs, rapped at the door of the study and entered at Delhugh's call. He handed a card to the philanthropist. An exclamation of interest came from Delhugh.

"Lamont Cranston!" he stated. "I have heard of him. A millionaire, famed for his travels. He wishes to see me, Benzig?"

"Yes, sir."

Delhugh turned to Jack.

"I think we have chatted long enough," he remarked. "Your interest in the advertising business is encouraging, Targon. You can tell me more about it on your next visit."

"You want me here Thursday night?" inquired Jack.

"Yes," acquiesced Delhugh. "Stop in for a few minutes, at least."

Jack Targon left, followed by Benzig, who went with Delhugh's order to usher Mr. Cranston upstairs.

In the lower hallway, Jack came face to face with the visitor. He noted that Cranston was a person of distinctive appearance. In fact, Jack carried a sharp recollection of the face that he observed.

A firm well-molded countenance, with an expression that rendered it inflexible and masklike. Such was the impression that Jack Targon gained. For the ex-convict had come face to face with the same person who had visited Adolph Murson that very afternoon.

UP in his study, Perry Delhugh arose to greet his unexpected visitor. The philanthropist, like Jack Targon, was impressed by the appearance of Lamont Cranston. Handshakes were followed by cigars.

While Delhugh took his place behind the desk, Lamont Cranston seated himself in an easy chair and came promptly to the purpose of his visit.

"It is a pleasure to meet you, Mr. Delhugh," stated the visitor, in his steady even tone. "I have heard much of your philanthropies. I admire the spirit of them."

Delhugh bowed in acknowledgment.

"Particularly," resumed The Shadow, perfect in his role of Cranston, "your ideas in regard to individual betterment. I have heard that you recently befriended two pardoned convicts; that you gave them a new start in life."

"One of the men just went downstairs," replied Delhugh. "Perhaps you saw him as he went out."

"I saw an intelligent-looking chap going—"

"That was Jack Targon. Former swindler. Now a coming advertising man."

"Remarkable! Let me congratulate you, Mr. Delhugh. You have chosen an excellent type of welfare work."

"It was a new idea of mine, Mr. Cranston. Somehow"—he paused speculatively—"somehow I have tired of ordinary charities. They are too impersonal. Such as this Talleyrand Hospital Fund. A meritorious undertaking; but a cut-and-dried affair."

"How so?"

"We ask for funds. We get them. We deliver them. The recipients have no contact with their benefactors."

"You are chairman of the fund?"

"No. I am the secretary. It is only one of my many philanthropic connections. That reminds me"—Delhugh looked glum—"the fund is going to be short twenty thousand dollars. Well"—he shrugged his shoulders and smiled—"I can make up for that with a contribution of my own."

"Twenty thousand dollars short?" came The Shadow's inquiry, in Cranston's easy inflection.

Delhugh nodded.

"You read of the death of Theobald Luftus?" he questioned. "The murder in the penthouse?"

A nod from The Shadow.

"Luftus had promised us twenty thousand dollars. We were to hear from him today. Unfortunately, Theobald Luftus is no longer with us."

"He was robbed of the funds intended for you?"

"Yes. And possibly of a great deal more. Luftus wrote me a letter saying that he would give us some securities of his own selection. So I fancy that he had other funds on hand."

"Did you inform the police of this?"

"No. I thought of doing so but after reading tonight's newspapers, I decided that it would be unnecessary. The police commissioner has stated"—Delhugh referred to a journal on his desk—"that the criminals who rifled the dead man's safe must have gained at least a hundred thousand dollars."

"So you would be telling the police something that they already know."

"Precisely! Moreover"—Delhugh shook his head seriously—"it would be a great mistake to make public the fact that some of those funds were being held for a gift. Many contributors to worthy causes are persons who have hoarded wealth.

"The death of Luftus, as reported, is apt to make hoarders decide to loose their miserly stores. You would be astonished, Mr. Cranston, to learn how often timid people—misers by nature—became philanthropic after they hear of robberies."

"Quite a logical phenomenon."

"It is. That is why mention of the hospital funds would have an adverse psychological effect. As far as I see it, nothing can be accomplished in the Luftus case until the police apprehend the missing broker, Adolph Murson."

"He probably knows the extent of the dead man's resources."

"Very probably. And evidence points to Murson as the perpetrator of the crime."

There was a pause while Delhugh and his visitor puffed at their cigars. Then The Shadow, in leisurely Cranston fashion, came back to the subject of his visit.

"IT occurred to me," he stated, "that I might try some individual philanthropies of my own. That is why I have come to you. I assume that you must have lists of persons who are deserving of aid."

"I have lists and records," smiled Delhugh. "A whole room lined with filing cabinets. Names by thousands, with details pertaining to their histories and circumstances."

"Could you give me access to those lists?"

"Yes. But the task of going through them would be tremendous. You would find it most burdensome. My secretary, Benzig, could begin on it. But his time is almost completely occupied."

"Suppose I turned it over to a secretary of my own?"

"You have a man available?"

"Yes. A young chap named Vincent. He has a job at present; but he would be glad of the opportunity to do evening work. Would it be possible for him to come here?"

"Certainly. There is a desk in the filing room. He could make his headquarters there. Benzig could show him the best lists. How soon would he begin?"

"At once. Say tomorrow night."

"Very good. Just what kind of cases will he search for?"

A smile showed on Cranston's lips.

"Deserving cases," stated The Shadow. "I shall have Vincent pick those which he thinks are best. Say two hundred names. From those—with their records—I shall select the ten that most appeal to me."

"And make them gifts?"

"Yes. Five thousand dollars to each of the ten persons. Anonymous gifts, dropping from the sky."

"Like manna to the hungry."

"Or rain to the thirsty."

Delhugh nodded his approval. He arose from the desk, noting that his visitor seemed ready to leave.

"Commendable, Mr. Cranston," declared the philanthropist, extending his hand to The Shadow. "This is the type of giving that I approve. Donations that bring dividends in happiness. To the donor as well as to the recipient.

"Ordinary welfare funds are necessary. Charitable enterprises must be supported. But many who contribute to them do so to gain public acclaim. Or to satisfy their consciences because they have, in the past, been grasping.

"This plan of yours is different, however. I shall be pleased to see how it works out. Just as I am looking forward to the fruits of my own experiments. Have your man Vincent come here tomorrow night. Benzig will start him on his task."

Delhugh rang for his secretary. Benzig appeared and ushered the visitor downstairs. He saw Cranston's tall form step aboard a limousine. An order to the chauffeur; the car pulled away.

IN the rear seat of the limousine, encased by soundproof glass, the being who posed as Lamont Cranston indulged in a soft, prophetic laugh.

Another step had been made toward balking men of crime.

Here, at the home of Perry Delhugh, lay new opportunity to thwart coming evil. Jack Targon had been here tonight; that was proof that Steve Zurk would also be a visitor. From now on, Harry Vincent, agent of The Shadow, would be implanted at a spot that was strategically important.

For The Shadow, following Murson's tip, had divined that the leak might have come from Delhugh's. The Shadow had learned from Delhugh's own statement, that the philanthropist had held correspondence with Theobald Luftus.

One chance for crime had been snapped from that source. New opportunities would be in the making. Crooks would gain them; The Shadow, through Harry Vincent, would learn of the opportunities that might come to men of crime.

He, too, would use the knowledge that lay at Delhugh's. With it, The Shadow would see chances to thwart the thrusts of murderous fiends.

CHAPTER XIV
WEDNESDAY NIGHT

TWENTY-FOUR hours had passed since The Shadow's visit to Delhugh's home. Manhattan's East Side lay beneath the blanket of night. A strolling man, erect of shoulder and steady in gait, went past a patrolman who was pacing near the steps of an elevated station.

The stroller kept on, unchallenged. A disdainful snort came from his lips. This fellow had no fear of cops. To Lucky Ortz, a policeman was a dumb flatfoot. For this strolling man was Lucky himself, en route to Beak Latzo's new hideout.

On a secluded street, Lucky took a darkened doorway to the left of a shoemaker's shop. He unlocked the door, entered and went upstairs. He rapped five times at a door that stood in darkness.

The barrier opened. Lucky entered to greet Beak Latzo.

"Anything new from Dangler?" came Beak's query.

"Sure," chuckled Lucky. "This. Another note from Steve."

Beak ripped open the envelope. He read Steve's scrawl; then applied a match to note and envelope and dropped them, flaming, in a metal wastebasket.

"What's doing?" quizzed Lucky.

"Nothing yet," replied Beak. "Steve says to lay low and wait."

"He said that in his last note," reminded Lucky. "The one where he told us to stick the swag in that package box in the subway, with the key hid on top where he could get it."

"He got the swag," said Beak. "He mentioned that in the note I just burned. Says to do the same with anymore we get. Unless we're in a jam; then we're to wait for new word."

"Did he say anything else?"

"Yeah." Beak nodded emphatically. "He says something I wanted to hear him say. Something I was worried about. He says he's wise that The Shadow got into the picture."

"Well, he ought to be wise. All that hullabaloo around your old hideout got into the newspapers. The bulls found the joint."

"With nothing in it."

"Thanks to Goofy. That was smart of him, dragging out your stuff, taking it to his own place. And I was wise to get it away from there. They found Goofy's body this afternoon."

"The wise part was burning those letters. That was my idea, Lucky."

"You should have burned 'em in the first place."

Beak ignored his lieutenant's remark. He began to rub his rough chin. At last he spoke.

"We need new gorillas, Lucky," stated Beak. "There's a new job coming and it'll be quick. If I know Steve, he won't let grass grow."

"On account of this mug Murson, that's still missing?"

"Yeah. That's one reason. The other's that Steve is a live wire. He's in soft and he'll use his chances. Listen, now. I've managed to lay low. Nobody knows that you're with me."

"Nobody except a couple of the gorillas. And they're in their own hideout."

"Well, get going and pick up a new mob. Steve's going to want it."

"Said that, too, did he?"

"No. But he figures we've got the mob anyway. He don't know how many gorillas we lost; I've got an idea that Steve'll pick up some dope tonight. Savvy?"

Lucky nodded.

"Well?" Beak scowled. "What're you waiting around for? I said start to build a mob!"

"O. K., Beak."

Lucky chuckled as he walked from the room. He closed the door behind him.

Beak stepped over and locked it. Then the big-nosed mobleader settled back to read the latest newspaper—one that Lucky had brought with him from his excursion to Dangler's.

AT the home of Perry Delhugh, events were taking place that fitted with Beak Latzo's prediction regarding chances for new crime. Perry Delhugh was in his study, dictating a letter to Benzig.

The letter, addressed to a lawyer named

Richard Dokeby, pertained to funds that were in the attorney's possession. It was in answer to communication from Dokeby himself; the original letter lay on Delhugh's desk.

A gong sounded, announcing dinner. Benzig went to the typewriter as Delhugh left the study. Rapidly, the secretary completed his transcript of the letter. He laid it, with Dokeby's communication, upon Delhugh's desk.

The secretary joined Delhugh in the dining room.

They were sipping coffee at the end of the evening meal when a servant arrived to announce that Mr. Vincent had arrived. Delhugh turned to Benzig.

"Cranston's man," stated the millionaire. "Take him up to the filing room and get him started."

"Very well, sir."

Benzig departed. Delhugh ordered another cup of coffee. Again the doorbell rang. The servant announced Mr. Zurk.

"Take him up to the study, Chilton," Delhugh told the butler. "Tell him that I shall join him there in a few minutes—"

Delhugh finished his coffee. Then he went upstairs. The door of the filing room was closed. He kept on into the study, where he found Steve Zurk awaiting him.

"Hello, Zurk," greeted Delhugh. "How do you find the importing business?"

"I like it, Mr. Delhugh," returned Steve.

"So I understand," smiled Delhugh. He brought a sheaf of letters from a desk drawer, ran through a few and discarded them, then passed the rest of the stack to Steve, so that the man could read the uppermost letter. It was from Joseph Daykin, head of the importing company.

A smile appeared upon Steve's lips. It was one of genuine pleasure. Daykin's letter, addressed to Delhugh, stated that his new employee had already displayed remarkable ability.

"You see what Daykin thinks of you," commended Delhugh. "Keep up the good work, Zurk. Any comments of your own?"

"None, sir." Steve spoke as he returned the letters. "Only that I'm getting the best break I ever had in my life. Thanks to you, Mr. Delhugh."

Delhugh clapped Steve on the shoulder. The visitor arose; he and the philanthropist strolled from the study. At the filing room, Delhugh paused and opened the door.

"Bring Mr. Vincent into the study, Benzig," he ordered. "I shall see you there."

Delhugh went downstairs with Steve. Benzig and Harry went into the study. It was five minutes before Delhugh returned. He shook hands with Harry Vincent.

"HOW do you like my filing room?" inquired Delhugh. "Do you think it will serve Mr. Cranston's purpose?"

"Absolutely," returned Harry. "But it will take at least a week to go through all those records."

"A long job," nodded Delhugh, "but one which you appear capable of handling. Well, Mr. Vincent, I suppose you are anxious to proceed with your work. Benzig, you can go back to the filing room with Mr. Vincent."

"Just a moment, sir." Benzig was at the desk, blinking through his heavy-rimmed spectacles. "I saw Mr. Zurk with you in the hall. Did he come up here while you were still dining?"

"Yes," returned Delhugh. "Why do you ask?"

"Because, sir, these letters—this stack—they were in your drawer—"

"I took them out myself, Benzig."

"But these other two letters." Benzig was a little nervous. "The one from Dokeby; and the reply I typed. Did you move them?"

"I may have. Look here, Benzig. Are you still suspicious of Zurk?"

"Not exactly, sir. But—"

"Out with it!" Delhugh's interruption was an angry one. "What have you against the fellow?"

"Nothing, sir. I'm just worried about these Dokeby letters. With all those funds in Dokeby's safe—two hundred thousand—"

"I understand, Benzig. Well, I feel sure that Zurk was not here long enough to read the letters. I came in only a few minutes after him. I had a chat with him here and downstairs. You are too apprehensive, Benzig."

A trifle irritated, Delhugh took his place behind the desk. Harry and Benzig left the study. In the filing room, the secretary spoke to The Shadow's agent.

"The man who was here," explained Benzig, "was a former convict. I am a little worried about his visits. He comes three times a week. Steve Zurk is his name. Mr. Delhugh has been aiding him."

"Mr. Cranston mentioned it," observed Harry. "He said something, though, about two such men."

"Yes. There is another—Jack Targon. I keep an eye on him, too. But he has never arrived ahead of time, like Zurk. This is the second occasion when Zurk could have pried about Mr. Delhugh's study. But Targon never had the opportunity to do so—"

Benzig broke off. A bell was ringing from the hall, summoning him to the study. The secretary departed, leaving Harry alone in the filing room.

THE SHADOW'S agent set his lips and nodded slightly to himself. He was here on a definite task—

the very one that Benzig had taken on himself; namely, to watch Steve Zurk and Jack Targon.

Already, Harry had gained information. Not only had he seen Steve Zurk and learned of Benzig's suspicions of the fellow. He had also heard mention of a name and a statement regarding a fund in that person's possession.

Dokeby. The name was an unusual one. Moreover, the man must be connected with some philanthropic enterprise.

A small file stood on a table in the corner. Harry looked in it. He found the name Dokeby.

Richard Dokeby. A lawyer, listed in the file as custodian of a library fund that had been accumulated with interest for the past five years. The fund, Harry noted, was slated for delivery this present week.

Harry closed the file and went back to those that contained names of persons aided by charity. But the facts on Dokeby's card remained implanted in his mind. The lawyer's name and office address were points to be remembered.

Tonight, Harry intended to leave after brief preliminary work at Delhugh's. And immediately after his departure, he would put in a call to Burbank. Thus would The Shadow learn the facts that his agent had so promptly gleaned.

CHAPTER XV
THE MOB PREPARES

HARRY VINCENT was not the only agent who reported to The Shadow on that Wednesday night. Other word came through Burbank. Important news from Cliff Marsland. Results had been accomplished in the underworld.

The Shadow had foreseen that Beak Latzo, from his new hideout, would begin to replenish the thinned ranks of the mob that he had used for battle. As yet, The Shadow had not gained a key to the identity of Beak's chief lieutenant. Lucky Ortz had managed to keep his connection well covered.

But already, The Shadow's agents—Cliff and Hawkeye—had picked out the gathering places of Lucky's clan. The Shadow had ordered them to frequent those dives; and Cliff, now a habitué of the new hangout near Sooky's pawnshop, had gained an important contact.

Posing as a gorilla anxious to gain a berth, Cliff had received a tentative proposition from a tough-mugged slugger known as Mike Rungel. The cagey offer to join up with an unknown mob had come on Wednesday night, some time after Harry Vincent had reported to The Shadow.

Cliff had arranged a new meeting with Rungel for the next day. The Shadow, after receiving this report, had sent instructions back through Burbank. With Cliff moving to a definite goal, The Shadow had decided to bide his time until word came through again from Cliff.

Cliff had arranged his next meeting with Mike Rungel for four o'clock Thursday afternoon. He had learned one important fact: namely, that Mike was not in direct contact with the leader higher up. Mike, a second-rate gorilla, was working through some pal.

AT three o'clock Thursday afternoon, an event occurred that was to show the wisdom of The Shadow's waiting policy. Lucky Ortz, strolling from the neighborhood of Times Square, turned his paces in the direction of the building where Dangler's little office was located.

He was paying an early visit to the unwitting tool who served as post office for Beak Latzo. When he reached the building, Lucky went up past the Chinese restaurant and strolled into Dangler's office. The timid man blinked as he saw his visitor.

No customers were in the stamp dealer's shop. Lucky noted that fact and lost no time in questioning Dangler.

"Anything for Beak?" asked the lieutenant.

Dangler nodded. He produced a letter from the old stamp album beneath the counter. Lucky received it, noted Steve's scrawl on the envelope and uttered a gruff laugh as he pocketed the message.

Twenty minutes later, Lucky arrived at the door of Beak's well-secluded hideout. He rapped five times. Beak opened the door. Lucky entered and handed him the envelope.

Ripping the flap open, Beak snatched out the message and read it with eager eyes. A leer showed on his ugly lips.

"Looks good?" queried Lucky.

"Great!" returned Beak. "Here—read it."

"No use. I can't make out that writing."

"Well, I'll give you the lay. Steve's got hep to something. Big boodle. A lawyer named Dokeby has it. Richard Dokeby. In the Hanna Building."

"Where's that located?"

"Here's the address"—Beak pointed to a paragraph in Steve's letter—"and it's easy enough for you to read, being figures instead of words."

Lucky looked at the letter; then nodded. His tone was quizzical.

"Forty-eighth Street," he remarked. "I'm trying to figure out just where that street address is located. West of Sixth Avenue, it ought to be—maybe west of Seventh—"

"Steve says something here about an old garage. Place where they store cars from the Goliath Hotel."

"I got it now. Sure, I know the place. Say, that ought to be a cinch to get into. What's the system? Same as we used at the penthouse where we bumped Luftus?"

Beak nodded; then added a comment.

"The same, only easier," he stated. "Because there won't be anybody in this office of Dokeby's. Steve wants a lot of us on the job, though. Just in case there's trouble."

"From The Shadow?"

"You guessed it. We're going to hold off until nine bells, on account of there being a theater near Dokeby's building. You know the way those theater crowds go. All over the street until the show starts; then they're all stowed away until eleven."

"Inside, watching the show."

"Yeah. And no cops around bothering about traffic. Gives us a couple of hours in between. Listen now: here's the way Steve wants it worked."

"Spill away."

"WE don't move in a bunch. Instead, we tip the gorillas where to go. They slide around about the time people are getting into the theater across the street."

"Good stuff."

"It ought to be. It's Steve's idea. While the outfit's getting posted, you and I wait. Then we blow in from a taxi and walk into the building."

"It'll be open?"

"Sure. And it's an old dump with a stairway we can use to go up to the third floor. That's where we'll find Dokeby's office. Well, when we go in, we'll have a couple of good torpedoes waiting to follow us."

Lucky nodded his understanding.

"Sherry and Pete are the guys for that," he decided. "I'll wise them where to be. Say—Steve must have looked over this lay."

"He has." Beak gestured with the letter. "He walked around there last night, before he sent this message. Something else, too"—a glance at the scrawled sheet—"about a garage next door. There ought to be some guys up there."

"Up in the garage?"

"On the roof." Beak was applying a match to the letter as he spoke. "They can get there easy, just about the time we're going in. We want that lawyer's office covered right. Savvy?"

"Good idea. Do we snatch everything after we bust the safe?"

"No. Only the swag. It'll probably be bundled. It's some kind of a fund. Cash and securities."

"I get you. Suppose we have to blow the box, though?"

"That won't make no difference. It's just as easy to pick out what we want and carry a small load as it is to grab everything that's in the safe."

Lucky nodded. He agreed.

"We're set," decided Beak. "All except about the gang. Did you get that fixed up last night?"

"I got hold of some dock wallopers," said Lucky, slowly. "Three of 'em—and good ones—that Sherry picked for me. They'll do for the roof."

"What about the mugs that Pete was supposed to line up?"

"Well, he got a couple, Pete did. One of 'em was Mike Rungel."

"I know Mike. He's a good bet. Any others?"

"Yeah. Mike was to get one or two himself. I figured that was a good idea."

"Where's Mike now?"

"Waiting to hear from Pete."

"And Pete?"

"Waiting to hear from me."

Beak chuckled.

"Say," he approved. "you've got a system, Lucky. No wonder you get the breaks the way you do. Keep yourself covered up, don't you?"

"Why not? It pays, don't it?"

"Sure thing. Well, slide out and see those eggs of yours. Sherry and Pete. Tell Sherry to buzz the dock wallopers and have Pete talk to Mike. Then there's the gorillas down in that other hideout."

"I'll see 'em."

Lucky strolled. Beak scratched his big nose and chuckled in admiration of his lieutenant's methods. Alone in his hideout, Beak was congratulating himself on success that he could already see.

DOWN in the new dive near Sooky's pawnshop, Cliff Marsland was seated at a table in the corner of the smoke-filled room. Cliff's face, chiseled and expressionless, gave no indication of the impatience that he was feeling.

Four o'clock had passed; yet Mike Rungel had not arrived. Across the room at another isolated table sat a hunched-up little man who seemed concerned only with a bottle on the table before him.

It was Hawkeye. He, too, had a hopeful purpose here.

The outer door opened. A big, tough-looking rowdy entered and sauntered up to a dilapidated bar in the corner of the room. It was Mike Rungel.

Cliff glanced at the newcomer; then stared in another direction. This was in keeping with arrangements. Mike had arrived at last.

Rungel went out a side door—one that formed another exit through a passageway. A few minutes passed; then Cliff got up, strolled over to the bar, handed the proprietor a dollar bill and received some change. Cliff took the same exit that Mike had chosen.

Midway down the passage, Cliff stopped by a battered and obscure door. He rapped softly. The door opened. Cliff joined Mike in a gloomy storeroom, where empty bottles lay about in disarray.

"How about it?" was Cliff's question, as soon as he had closed the door.

"All set," returned Mike. "Usin' you tonight, Cliff."

"What's the dope?"

"You an' me's coverin' a job up on Forty-eighth Street. Office buildin' acrost from de Marcel T'eater. 'Longside of a garage."

Cliff grunted.

"What time?" he questioned.

"Nine bells," returned Mike. "But we get dere just when de crowd's goin' into de show. See? An' we ain't stickin' out of Forty-eight' Street, after it's clear. We're coverin' a couple of alleys dat go t'rough dere."

"Just the two of us?"

"Naw. I gotta get a couple more guys to help out. One to go along wid me—one to be wid you. I seen one bird I know. I gotta dig up annodder."

Cliff considered.

"Maybe there's somebody hanging around this joint," he remarked. "It ought to be easy to pick a guy here."

"Who's out dere?"

"One fellow I've seen around. A little squirt they call Hawkeye."

"Is Hawkeye out dere? Say—he's a foxy mug, dat boy. Dey say he can handle a gat, too."

"Know him, do you, Mike?"

"Sure. But you can go out an give him de high sign."

Cliff went back to the main room of the dive. Standing by the bar, he caught what seemed a chance stare from Hawkeye. Cliff gestured toward the exit; then went back to join Mike Rungel.

Three minutes later, Hawkeye joined them.

MIKE RUNGEL did the talking. He sounded out Hawkeye, found the little man interested, then began to loosen with the proposition.

Hawkeye grinned.

"If Cliff's in," he volunteered, "it's good enough for me. Who do I work with?"

"You stick wid Cliff," returned Mike. "Up by de t'eater. De alley on de left."

Hawkeye nodded. Mike dug in his pocket and produced a roll of bills. He peeled some off the wad and handed the cash to Cliff and Hawkeye.

"Dat's de start," mentioned Mike. "More comin' after de job. Meet you here, in dis joint, tomorrow. Four bells."

The group broke up. Cliff strolled out through the exit; Mike followed shortly.

Hawkeye went back into the dive. The little man had caught a secret signal from Cliff, meaning that Cliff, himself, would report the news.

Agents of The Shadow were ready for their later meeting. Details of coming crime were already on their way, to be passed, through Burbank, to The Shadow.

CHAPTER XVI
VANISHED SWAG

SHORTLY after eight o'clock that evening, a taxicab pulled up on Forty-ninth Street, just beyond the entrance to a garage. The driver of the cab chose a darkened spot to make his stop.

The door of the cab opened. A blackened figure edged forth. A shapeless phantom, that form glided across the sidewalk and merged with the front of a gloomy, four-story structure.

This was not the Hanna Building. Instead of going directly to the address on Forty-eighth Street, The Shadow had chosen another office building, even older and more dilapidated, that was at the rear of his objective.

The cab pulled away. Driven by Moe Shrevnitz, a reserve agent of The Shadow, the taxi had served its purpose for the night. From now on, The Shadow intended to move with swiftness.

The building which had been chosen was occupied by unimportant offices that were chiefly vacated for this structure was slated to be demolished. Ascending to the third floor, The Shadow found an office to his liking. The window was unlocked. The Shadow stepped out. He was on the roof of the garage that ran between Forty-eighth and Forty-ninth.

Manhattan's glow showed The Shadow as a dimly outlined form, close to the wall of the building that he had left. A modern structure, on the opposite side of the garage, blanked some of the city's illumination. Hence The Shadow was in semidarkness as he moved forward along the roof.

The front edge of the roof was well illuminated, because of an electric sign on the opposite side of Forty-eighth Street. This was the glittering sign of the Marcel Theater. Red, green and yellow lights, blinking in mechanical order threw an ever-changing glow across the front of the Hanna Building and the garage roof beside it.

The Shadow, however, found a perfect space of full invisibility when he reached the sheltering side of the Hanna Building. This structure was eight stories high. Windows of the third floor banked the garage roof.

There were shafts for light and air that led to the floors below; there were also bridgelike spots between these; and above the connecting braces were third-story windows. The Shadow chose the first crossing point.

WORKING in darkness, he used a thin instrument of steel between the portions of the window sash. The lock clicked. The lower sash came up. The Shadow entered a darkened office and closed the window behind him.

He next appeared in a gloomy hall. A dull grinding sound told that a night elevator was in operation. The Shadow lingered until he heard it pass above the third floor. Then he moved weirdly along the hall until he found an office numbered 318.

The name of Richard Dokeby was on the door.

The lock gave The Shadow no difficulty. He entered door 318 and found the outer room of a small suite. Opening a connecting door, he stepped into Dokeby's private office. He needed no flashlight to find his way about. The blinking glare from across the street furnished a dull but sufficient illumination.

Dokeby's offices were about midway in the building; their windows opened onto the garage roof. Below the windows, however, was one of the several air shafts. The Shadow could not have entered here from the roof, except by a leap across an open pit.

A study of Dokeby's offices told The Shadow much. It was plain that the attorney must have been a man long in practice. He had probably occupied these offices years ago and had persisted in retaining them, despite the decadence of the building.

Desks and tables were ancient, yet in perfect condition. The inner office was floored by an Oriental rug that Dokeby probably regarded as a prize possession. The Shadow's chief interest, however, lay in the safe that stood in the corner.

ALTHOUGH its paint was unscratched, this safe was of a vintage even older than the strongbox in the penthouse of Theobald Luftus. It was further proof that lawyer Dokeby was a fossilized individual whose ideas of modern mechanics had stagnated during the gay nineties.

The merest apprentice among modern cracksmen could have tapped that safe with ease. Beak Latzo and his henchmen were coming to find a setup. A made-to-order job that represented the utmost in simplicity.

It seemed plain to The Shadow, however, that Dokeby used this safe but little. It looked like a storage place for ordinary records that would be of no value to marauders. Probably the old attorney kept his funds and important documents in some safe-deposit vault.

Temporary circumstances alone had made the safe the repository for huge funds. Dokeby, unwitting that his safe was junk, but knowing that his possession of the funds was a matter unknown to the public, had probably decided that there would be no danger in keeping the wealth here for delivery to the library committee.

Men of crime were headed here tonight. The Shadow had learned that fact. He knew, through his agents, that henchmen would be posted on the front street. That was why he had chosen the rear entrance. The path along the roof would also offer a quick mode of departure.

Here in this office, The Shadow had found opportunity to trap Beak Latzo and whoever might come with the dangerous mobleader. The Shadow had left the details of action until his arrival on the scene. Hence his survey of Dokeby's inner office was sufficient cause for whispered mirth from The Shadow's hidden lips.

WHILE echoes of a soft, sibilant laugh still clung to the room, The Shadow approached Dokeby's safe and began to turn the dial. Head close to the steel door, he could hear the click of the dropping tumblers. Slowly, easily, The Shadow continued his manipulation.

The door of the safe swung open. Using a tiny flashlight, The Shadow probed the interior.

The stabbing glare showed neatly arranged stacks of letters and legal papers. One sheet alone was out of place. This was a dusty document that had drifted loose from a high stack at the right. The single sheet had dropped upright above smaller piles of letters.

Evidently someone—possibly Dokeby—had dropped the final pile of letters at the right and the top sheet had fluttered free.

That interested The Shadow. His gloved hands raised the stack at the right. The move resulted in a prompt discovery.

The stack was supported by half a dozen brick-shaped bundles. These were covered with heavy wrapping paper, and they were tied with heavy cord. The knots were gummed with thick chunks of sealing wax, which bore the impression of a metal stamp that The Shadow had noted on Dokeby's desk.

These bundles were the only objects other than letters and typewritten or printed documents. The bundles were alike, with one exception: The topmost package at the left displayed a tear in its paper wrapper.

Folding the torn paper back, The Shadow saw what he had expected. Through the opening in the paper he viewed the green-printed surface of an engraved bond; the top member of a thick packet.

These bundles contained the boodle. An easy grab for arriving crooks. It was plain that they could bag the swag and make a prompt getaway, leaving the useless documents that formed the remaining contents of the safe.

Two courses lay open to The Shadow. One was to leave the wealth here as bait and trap the crooks when they obtained it. The other was to remove the bundles and let the raiders find an empty nest.

Before deciding on either course, The Shadow found interest in that single sheet of paper that had fluttered from the stack of letters. The flashlight, guarded in front of The Shadow's stooped form, showed that sheet of paper as a printed document that was slightly soiled and dusty.

Plucking the sheet with gloved hand, The Shadow examined its printing. It was nothing more than an ordinary legal release, a printed form that resembled others in Dokeby's safe. It might have been dropped at random on the stack from which it had fallen.

Turning over the sheet, The Shadow made a discovery. On the back, at each side, were the impressions of fingertips, barely discernible to the keen eyes that studied them. Apparently, someone had picked up this sheet, glanced at it, then dropped it.

Carefully, The Shadow folded the printed paper and placed it beneath his cloak. A soft laugh sounded hollow, caught by the confining walls of the safe. The Shadow's gloved fingers picked up the bundle that had a tear in its upper side.

Extinguishing his flashlight, The Shadow arose. His gloved hands squeezed the bundle in viselike grip as he moved toward Dokeby's desk. Fingers managed to move the cord over one end of the bundle. Carefully, The Shadow opened the unsealed portion of the packet and drew its contents halfway from the sheathing wrapper.

Turning the bundle over, The Shadow saw another bond on the under surface. He riffled the ends of the papers in between, as one would do with a pack of playing cards. A soft, knowing laugh of discovery crept through the room.

A bond at the top. A bond at the bottom. Between the two lay a thick stack of blank paper!

SLOWLY, carefully, The Shadow pushed the worthless mass back into its sheath. Again a powerful grip enabled him to slide the stout cord back in place.

He carried the bundle to the safe and put it where he found it, the torn side of the wrapper still upward.

Again, The Shadow laughed. His keen brain was making a rapid deduction.

Fingerprints on the printed legal form indicated that someone had surreptitiously examined the contents of this safe. The torn wrapper of the uppermost bundle was proof that a person had removed the real swag and left wrapped packets of blank paper in its place.

That top bundle with its cunning tear was intended to deceive anyone who might pry into Dokeby's safe.

The lawyer himself had not done the deed. The committee that would receive the bundles could not be deceived, for the bundles would be opened by that same committee. Those faked packets were here to fool people who would not take time to examine them. Beak Latzo and his crew!

A double cross? The Shadow's laugh was negative. Chances were that Beak would forward the bundles unopened. Dokeby, whether he suspected crime or not, would have no need of bluffing crooks who would later find that they had been duped.

To The Shadow, the key lay in the important fact that Beak Latzo was working for another person, as evidenced by the letters that had come to Beak in Steve Zurk's scrawl. Another point was the trouble that Beak had encountered in his attack on Theobald Luftus.

Beak's mob had been ordered to come here tonight, to cover Beak when he grabbed the swag. Beak was an instrument, not the brain behind the game. Hence plans could have been changed without Beak's knowledge.

Someone had come here before The Shadow's arrival. That person had tapped Dokeby's safe. A simple job. The same intruder had taken the real swag. But he had left the dummy packages—obviously the boodle—so that Beak would go through with his job.

Had it been too late to inform Beak of the change in plans? Was the purpose to make the rifling of the safe look like a mob job? Another negative laugh from The Shadow. Beak, like the man ahead of him, would be able to tap this safe without leaving traces.

A momentary pause. Then came another whispered tone of mirth. It bore a strange touch. As The Shadow laughed, he swung up from the safe, pressed the big door shut and spun the dial with gloved fingers.

With a swift sweep, he headed toward the windows. Lights from the garage roof showed automatics looming in his hands.

Without loosing the weapons from his grasp, The Shadow clicked the catch and raised the sash. He peered out toward the roof. His keen eyes spied a lurking shape pressed close to the garage side of an air shaft.

Whirling about, The Shadow listened. His ears caught a creeping sound from somewhere in the hall. His fists tightened on the automatics. The Shadow had the answer that he wanted.

Beak Latzo had not been ordered here for r obbery. That had already been accomplished. The big-nosed mobleader was coming for another purpose: one that required a surrounding crew, larger than Cliff Marsland had supposed.

With crime completed, this secluded office had become a trap. Murder had been planned as a follow-up to coming theft. And death's victim—if the crooks prevailed—would be The Shadow!

CHAPTER XVII
GUNS IN THE DARK

UNTIL the moment of his final deduction, The Shadow had not foreseen the imminence of the danger that now threatened him. He had come to Dokeby's office knowing that he must beat Beak Latzo and a crew of mobsters to the swag. But he had expected to cope with a raid like that in the Luftus penthouse; not with a mass attack from every quarter.

The Shadow had realized suddenly that his agents had sent him incomplete information. He had learned that a trap was ready to be sprung. He had discovered the existence of unusual cunning in this plot that involved Steve Zurk.

Had The Shadow lingered longer at the door of Dokeby's safe, entering enemies would have surprised him. The only outlet—the way to the garage roof—would have proved itself a second snare.

But The Shadow, as quick in action as in thought, had gained a last-minute edge upon approaching enemies.

Dokeby's inner office was a veritable death trap. A spot in which the odds, as they now stood against The Shadow, would prove disastrous. One course alone was feasible: to meet advancing thugs before they could seal the exit to the hall.

Sweeping forward through the outer office, The Shadow gained the door to the hall. His move, though swift, was noiseless. The Shadow's left hand crept to the knob. Carefully, it avoided a click of the automatic against the metal of the knob.

Then with a suddenness that was astounding, The Shadow yanked the door open and whirled out into the hallway, his big guns coming up to aim. He was face to face with the approaching foe.

THE stairway, to both lower and upper floors, was less than a dozen paces away. It was from that spot that the enemy had advanced. One man had almost reached the door; another had sidled along the opposite wall, revolver drawn, ready to protect the entrant.

Others were at the head of the steps, waiting. For Beak Latzo and Lucky Ortz had sent their torpedo twins—Sherry and Pete—ahead to test the trap.

It was for Sherry, by the far wall, that The Shadow aimed his ready right-hand gun. He pressed the trigger of the automatic just as Sherry, recognizing the cloaked warrior, prepared to deliver a revolver bullet.

One gun roared alone. The Shadow's. A hot slug seared Sherry before the thug could press trigger. Sherry began to sag, snarling, unable to retain the gat that was slipping from his loosened fingers. The Shadow had delivered a mortal wound.

Pete hurled himself upon The Shadow. The space between this second gangster and The Shadow was but a half dozen paces. As he leaped, Pete came up with a revolver clenched tight in his right fist.

He wanted to burn The Shadow with a bullet—a shot that could not fail—at a target within a foot's range. Pete had a chance to gain that objective, for The Shadow's left hand, lowered to swing the door, had not yet come to aim.

But The Shadow's arm swung with Pete's; swiftly, with terrific upward drive. The Shadow did not try to beat the torpedo to the shot. That would have been impossible. His piston arm followed through with its upward drive; The Shadow's automatic cracked Pete's wrist just as the man fired.

Flame from Pete's gun burned The Shadow's hat brim. The bullet, speeding through, missed The Shadow's head by half an inch. The slug ricocheted from the ceiling. It was Pete's only shot.

For The Shadow's swing, carrying Pete's arm up with it, kept on to the springing mobster's jaw. Metal crashed bone. Pete's head bobbed back as if his neck had been made of rubber.

Sidestepping, The Shadow let the crook go sprawling forward on the floor.

Thus did The Shadow deal with the cream of Beak Latzo's outfit. One would-be killer lay dying; the other hopelessly unconscious.

And as The Shadow swung across the hall, he loosed new fire upon the stairway where Beak Latzo and Lucky Ortz was stationed.

DIVING for safety, the two returned fire. Beak leaped for the stairway to the upper floors; Lucky for the one that led below. Sherry and Pete had blocked them from immediate aim; the sight of the falling torpedoes had instilled the two leaders with desire for safety as well as fight.

Their shots were wild as they made their quick retreat. Each killer ducked again, as The Shadow, reaching the stairs, loosed shots along each flight of steps. Left hand pointing downward; right hand pointing up, the bullets from The Shadow's automatics came with the quick succession of a barrage.

Safe on their respective landings, Beak and Lucky kept undercover. Each was ready for The Shadow, whichever way he might come. Both had the same thing in mind: to block that terrible fighter until reinforcements came from the garage roof.

Rats had been driven to their holes. The Shadow's laugh rang out in mockery.

Automatics emptied, the cloaked fighter whirled and headed back toward Dokeby's offices. He dropped his bulletless guns beneath his cloak. A second brace of loaded automatics came forth in his gloved hands.

Beak and Lucky waited. They thought the game was theirs. They could picture The Shadow, scudding for the roof, going straight into the fire of the recruited dock wallopers. But neither Beak nor Lucky knew that The Shadow had detected the existence of an outside trap.

Well did The Shadow gauge the actions of the foe. Had the fight begun in Dokeby's office, the outside men might have kept undercover. But shots in the hall, muffled by intervening walls, would spell an indication that the fight was going inward, not outward. The Shadow knew that the men from the garage roof would be coming through.

They were. As The Shadow whirled through Dokeby's outer office, a window crashed as someone hurled a big gasoline can from the roof. The missile had been heaved at the center of the window. It carried the sash along with the glass.

A man, leaping across the air shaft, had caught the window ledge. Clinging there with his left hand, he was aiming a revolver with his right as he raised his knee to the sill, preparatory for entrance.

A weird laugh from the gloom. Straight ahead, the first of the dock wallopers saw the shrouded shape of The Shadow, sweeping from the dim light that pervaded the outer office. The fellow fired wildly at a fading target. As he did, the burst of an automatic answered.

The Shadow, dropping suddenly, had escaped the ruffian's fire. But The Shadow's own aim was true. The man on the ledge gave a gargling shriek. Backward, he plunged down into concrete-walled shaft.

NEW shots burst from those quick-pointed automatics. A second foe staggered upon the further brink of the shaft. Wounded, this enemy would have followed his companion into the pit but for the presence of the third dock walloper, who yanked his falling pal to the safety of the roof.

Leaving his wounded companion, the third fighter dived behind a stack of emptied gasoline cans and fired fast and furious at the shattered window.

His shots were futile. The Shadow, having repelled invasion from this quarter, had again reversed his tactics.

Hard on the echo of gunfire, he had swung out into the hallway. Beak and Lucky, peering from their landings, were startled by his unexpected arrival at the stairs. Almost before they knew it, The Shadow had leaped into view.

Nor did he stop. His spring, clear from the hall, carried headlong down the short steps to the lower landing, full upon Lucky, who was caught flat-footed.

As the lieutenant made frantic aim, The Shadow plunged upon him. Lucky collapsed. His head jolted the wall. His body rolled limp, while The Shadow, coming up against the wall, delivered a fierce taunting laugh and blasted bullets up the steps as a warning to Beak Latzo.

Then, as echoes still persisted, The Shadow took to the downward flight of steps. His cloak swept wide as he sprang toward the floor below, continuing on toward the ground floor of the building.

An elevator operator, peering from the lone car that was in use, ducked back as he saw a sweeping avalanche in black. Speeding ahead, The Shadow sprang out to the sidewalk of Forty-eighth Street.

THE thoroughfare was almost deserted—for the throngs had already entered the theater across the way. Cleared of the show-going crowd, the street had taken on that odd seclusion that grips so many byways close to more traveled avenues of Manhattan.

But there were eyes that saw The Shadow; and with them, ready hands. As the black-clad form zigzagged from the front of the old Hanna Building, mobsters leaped into view and opened fire from strategic points.

Again, there were more than Cliff had reported. Lucky Ortz had deployed a formidable array for emergency such as this.

The Shadow was equal to the battle. As the wild fray opened, he spun about straight for the front of the theater, then whirled again in a new direction.

The Shadow's automatic cracked Pete's wrist just as the man fired.

His automatics blazed like rifles in a revolving turret. A mobster hit the asphalt. Another sank wounded to the curb.

Mike Rungel had sprung from his alleyway, with another mobster. Cliff and Hawkeye had copied the move, coming from their own station.

The Shadow's agents were firing. But their shots were purposely wide. Backing to the wall as The Shadow swung toward them, they delivered a wild barrage that passed as an attack upon the cloaked fighter. But actually it stayed mobsters who would have otherwise closed in upon The Shadow.

Mobsters snarled as they saw The Shadow whirl clear of Cliff and Hawkeye. They might have suspected the ruse had Hawkeye not pulled a stagger. But the little agent, smart in the emergency, dropped his gun with a sharp cry and grabbed at his right shoulder.

Cliff, catching the cue, dived toward a doorway as he saw Hawkeye fake a collapse.

Timed to the second, The Shadow sprang into the deserted alleyway. Cliff, springing into view, headed after him, while Mike and other mobsters came dashing to the chase. Hawkeye, pulling himself together with a well-feigned effort, came up at the rear.

The Shadow was gone. With amazing swiftness, he had gained the Forty-seventh Street end of the alleyway. But the mobsters kept on their race. They had gained cause for flight.

Shouts were coming from along Forty-eighth Street. Men were piling out of the garage. The operator from the Hanna Building was bellowing for help.

Police whistles were blowing. Sirens followed; patrol cars were coming up. Along Forty-seventh Street, the fleeing mobsters were scattering. Cliff and Hawkeye were dashing in a direction opposite the others.

Sirens ahead, along Eighth Avenue. Cliff and Hawkeye stopped short. Their one course was to duck back, to mingle with crowds in the neighborhood of Broadway. Suddenly they spied a cab, cruising in the wake of other taxis that had passed through.

Cliff swung toward the curb and signaled. Moe Shrevnitz wheeled up, then increased speed as Cliff and Hawkeye came aboard. The Shadow's agents were clear for a getaway.

THE fray on Forty-eighth Street had caused arriving police to take up chase of fleeing mobsmen. Even the excited cries of the elevator operator had failed to bring an immediate search of the Hanna Building.

In Dokeby's inner office, Beak Latzo was working at the safe, mumbling low epithets while Lucky Ortz, dazed from his conflict with The Shadow, held a flashlight focused on the safe door.

The safe opened; Beak, though hasty, had managed the simple combination. The flashlight showed the bundles that looked like boodle. Green showing through the torn wrapping paper was sufficient. Beak bagged the swag.

Heading toward the shattered window, Beak hurled the bag to the roof beyond the air shaft. He made the leap to safety and whispered hoarsely for Lucky to follow. The lieutenant climbed the sill, steadied and made the jump.

The last of the dock wallopers had abandoned his wounded comrade. The man lay groaning near the edge of the air shaft. Beak and Lucky offered him no aid. Instead, they hurried along the roof, found a window in the rear building and climbed through.

Chaos had not reached Forty-ninth Street when the two crooks arrived there. Beak saw a cab by the curb; the driver was standing on the sidewalk, looking east toward Seventh Avenue, where cars had clustered to watch the passage of police cars.

Beak yanked open the door of the cab and thrust Lucky aboard. He tossed the bag in with the punch-drunk lieutenant. In casual fashion, Beak hailed the cab driver. The man trotted over and took the wheel.

As the taxi rolled from the curb, a figure emerged from a gloomy spot some thirty feet away. The Shadow had weaved a remarkable course back from two squares below. He had arrived just in time to witness the departure of the crooks.

A soft laugh hissed from The Shadow's lips. To deal with these killers at present might bring complications, now that police were flooding the neighborhood. Better that Beak and Lucky should getaway, believing themselves triumphant, though belated.

For The Shadow had bigger game. The recovery of the real swag. New evidence gained, he had won the conflict with guns in the dark. Through pretended flight, he had left the way open to a new thrust by men of crime.

And before that climax came, The Shadow's plans would be completed. Crooks, lulled by the fact that they had managed an escape, would be ready to strive again.

Then could The Shadow meet these ruffians and the remnants of their thwarted mob; and with new conflict, he might gain a triumph over the real leader who had issued commands to these fierce hordes of crime.

CHAPTER XVIII
FROM THE SANCTUM

BLUISH light flickered in a black-walled room. White hands lay beneath the downward focused glare. A glimmering stone, The Shadow's priceless girasol, sparkled from a moving finger. The Shadow was in his sanctum.

Clippings came between those deft fingers. These were newspaper accounts of the fray on Forty-eighth Street. For twenty hours had elapsed since The Shadow had fought his battle with Beak Latzo's underlings.

Lesser crooks, dead and living, had fallen into the hands of the police. Wounded mobsters had been unable to escape the advent of the law. Some—such as Mike Rungel—had managed a getaway. The Shadow's agents had ridden clear in Moe Shrevnitz's cab.

Beak Latzo and Lucky Ortz had eluded the law. The Shadow had known that Beak must be the man on the upper stairs; he had recognized Lucky when he had slugged the lieutenant. But The Shadow had gained no traces to the hideout where the pair had fled.

The police—according to the newspaper accounts—had learned nothing from the small fry whom they had captured. They had followed back to Dokeby's office; there they had discovered the opened safe. Dokeby had been informed and a search was on for traces of the missing funds.

The actual amount of the loss had been minimized—probably by Dokeby. For the stolen securities were negotiable, and certain facts had been soft-pedaled in the accounts that reached the press.

Clippings dropped from lithe fingers. Reports came under The Shadow's consideration. Word from Cliff Marsland, stating that he and Hawkeye were regaining contact with Mike Rungel. Details from Clyde Burke, adding points of inside information that had not appeared in newspaper accounts.

Each of these report sheets had been inscribed in code. Written characters vanished after The Shadow read the messages. Such was the way with secret communications between The Shadow and his agents. All were done in a special ink that disappeared after the messages had been opened.

A third report: From Harry Vincent. It stated that Jack Targon had paid a routine visit to Perry Delhugh, at dinner time last night. Delhugh had been in conference with the Talleyrand Hospital committee and had sent a message to Jack by Benzig, telling him to return later. Jack had come back sometime before eight o'clock, to spend an hour with the philanthropist.

In reporting these facts, Harry had been forced to rely upon remarks dropped by Benzig. For most of the time, the door of the filing room was kept closed. Footsteps and voices in the hallway were the only way by which Harry could guess at arrivals and departures when his door was closed.

Being Thursday night, Jack Targon's visit to the house was one that Harry had anticipated. There was no news at all regarding Steve Zurk. That also was natural, for Steve had come on Wednesday and was not due again until tonight—Friday.

A SLIGHT laugh shuddered through the sanctum. It carried a peculiar significance. It was The Shadow's own admission of neglected opportunities. For in this maze of combated crime, The Shadow had left one point uncovered.

Crime came at night. Through Cliff Marsland, The Shadow could keep tabs on gang movements. Through Harry Vincent, he could check on the visits of Steve Zurk and Jack Targon, at Delhugh's. But therein lay the weakness.

On nights when Jack Targon visited the philanthropist, Steve Zurk did not come there. Hence The Shadow had no watch upon Steve's actual activities except on those evenings when the ex-convict stopped in to see Delhugh.

Yet The Shadow's laugh was not an admission of failure. The mysterious investigator had deliberately allowed Steve Zurk to roam at large, despite the evidence which had been at Beak Latzo's first hideout, in the form of letters. For The Shadow had seen a definite system in the scheme of crime. The dirty work had been left to Beak Latzo, as a complete cover-up for the tip-offs.

The dope had been crossed last night. That sudden change of method was the one point that had upset The Shadow's scheme. Vanished swag had showed a double cunning in the routine of crime.

A crumpled paper came between The Shadow's hands. Long fingers smoothed the ruffled sheet. This was the letter that The Shadow had taken from Beak Latzo's; one of the two that Beak thought Goofy had burned.

Here, in Steve Zurk's ragged scrawl, was the order that had sent Beak and Lucky to rob and murder Theobald Luftus. This sheet of paper was a link for which the law had searched in vain.

The Shadow placed the sheet aside. In its place he brought forth a dusty printed form.

This was that chance paper that had been tossed aside in Richard Dokeby's safe. The Shadow placed the paper with the printed side downward. The bluish light from the shaded lamp showed the fingerprints with remarkable clarity.

A thick, glossy paper dropped upon The

Shadow's table. Upon it were photographic copies of thumb and finger impressions. This record, long in The Shadow's possession, was identified with a printed name: Steve Zurk.

The Shadow had already compared the finger-prints on the legal form with this photographic record. The impressions were identical. Thus had The Shadow gained an important link to the second crime. The paper from the lawyer's safe had been smudged by Steve Zurk.

The Shadow turned the paper, printed side up. This surface was less spoiled than the other. It was smudged, but no impressions had registered themselves. But what were two missing thumb prints, compared with eight finger impressions that stood out in detail?

The Shadow laughed. His whispered mirth was echoed as he placed the document and the records to one side.

Then came a *click.* The bluish light went out. Paper crinkled in total darkness. A final laugh throbbed from invisible lips. Amid the sibilant echoes came swishes of The Shadow's cloak.

Then silence.

IN contrast to the pitch darkness of The Shadow's sanctum, the outer world was illuminated by the light of day. Though the sun had set, dusk had not yet arrived. Evening was still an hour off.

Not long after The Shadow had departed from his secret abode, a tall, strolling figure appeared upon a secluded side street. This personage approached a parked limousine and stepped aboard the car. A uniformed chauffeur turned about.

"Club, Stanley," came the quiet order.

"Yes, Mr. Cranston," responded the chauffeur.

The Shadow had resumed the guise in which he so frequently traveled. As Lamont Cranston, quiet, leisurely millionaire, he was visiting the Cobalt Club.

The limousine required some twenty minutes to reach its destination. There the passenger alighted.

Dusk settled. Manhattan streets began to glow. Stanley was peering through the fading daylight when he saw his master reappear at the door of the club. Again The Shadow stepped aboard the limousine. He gave an order in Cranston's quiet tones.

The limousine rolled away. It followed a threaded course through varied streets until it pulled up in front of a secluded brownstone mansion. There The Shadow alighted and spoke a few words to Stanley. After that he went up the steps of the house.

This was the home of Perry Delhugh. Again, The Shadow—as Cranston—was calling on the philanthropist. He had chosen this hour for an early call, ahead of the time when Steve Zurk was due to arrive on an appointed visit.

CHAPTER XIX
THE SHADOW TALKS

"BENZIG told me that you had telephoned, Mr. Cranston."

Perry Delhugh, seated behind his mahogany desk, made this statement as he proffered a cigar to his calm-faced visitor. The remark brought a nod from The Shadow.

"Yes," he replied, in Cranston's tone. "I called from the Cobalt Club. I am going back there later."

"Will you wait until Vincent arrives? He usually comes early in the evening."

"No, that will not be necessary. Vincent is doing his work capably. There is no reason that I should see him until his job is completed."

"Indeed?" Delhugh's tone was quizzical. "This is surprising. I thought that you had come to talk about those lists that Vincent is making."

"No." A thin smile showed on the lips of Lamont Cranston. "I have come to discuss another matter."

"Another matter?"

"Yes. Crime."

Perry Delhugh looked puzzled. Then his strong face took on a sudden change. The philanthropist's eyebrows furrowed as an anxious look revealed itself.

PERRY DELHUGH

"Regarding those men whom I have aided?" he questioned. "Something to do with Zurk and Targon?"

"Yes," replied The Shadow.

Delhugh settled back in his chair. He puffed at his cigar and his face remained troubled. He seemed to be recalling hazy facts. His attitude, at the same time, was one of listener.

"YOU mentioned to me," began The Shadow, in a steady tone, "that Theobald Luftus had communicated with you not long before his death."

"He did," nodded Delhugh. His voice was grave. "In regard to a philanthropic contribution."

"Perhaps in writing to you"—The Shadow's voice was Cranston's, but it carried a steady monotone—"Luftus conveyed the impression that he had large funds available in his penthouse."

"I did receive that impression from his letter."

"And perhaps Steve Zurk or Jack Targon might have had opportunity to see that letter."

Delhugh did not reply at once. He tapped his desk with his fingers, again recalling past circumstances. Then he said, slowly:

"Steve Zurk could have read the letter from Luftus. Also my reply to that same letter."

A pause. Then came the quiet tone of Cranston.

"You receive a great deal of philanthropic correspondence," stated The Shadow. "Perhaps other letters concerned the library fund held by Richard Dokeby."

This time Delhugh made no delay in his reply. He leaned across the desk and spoke frankly.

"Dokeby wrote me a letter," he declared, "and stated that he had those funds available. What is more, Mr. Cranston, Steve Zurk could have read the letter. And my reply."

"Then you have probably come to some conclusion."

"I have. But it has left me bewildered. Often, Mr. Cranston, I have mistrusted certain persons. But Steve Zurk was not one of them. The man struck me as honest."

"And yet—"

"Yet circumstances are against him. My secretary, Benzig, made pointed remarks concerning Zurk. I chided Benzig for doing so. I have tried to maintain a faith in Zurk's integrity. I like the man."

Delhugh came upright and pounded the desk emphatically.

"I like the man!" he repeated. "That is enough to make me hold confidence in him. It takes more than idle rumor to shatter a well-formed belief.

"I hold no proof against Zurk. All that I know is that he did have opportunity to learn facts regarding both Luftus and Dokeby. Benzig was suspicious of him, yes; but one cannot take Benzig's opinion as a criterion."

A pause; then Delhugh added seriously:

"Targon and Zurk both started on a road to honesty. Targon had no opportunity to stray. But Zurk did have. Twice. And after each of those occasions, crime appeared on the horizon. Most damaging of all, it was crime of a type that Zurk could have aided."

Delhugh reached out and opened a desk drawer. He produced a stack of papers and spread them out upon the desk. He began to speak musingly.

"I HAVE hesitated to consider these documents," he admitted slowly. "They refer to Zurk's past; and, somehow, they link in with Benzig's suspicions. Had Benzig alone shown a suspicious trend, I would have remained firm in my trust of Zurk.

"But when a man like yourself, Mr. Cranston—one with philanthropic leanings—adds weight to suspicion, I am forced to listen. I am compelled to make a study of Zurk's past, as these papers record it.

"It happens that Zurk does not know how closely he was investigated. He does not know that he was linked with a vicious desperado called Beak Latzo, who is still at large. Even the police do not know that fact."

A pause. Cranston's tone came:

"Yet you have known it."

"Yes," admitted Delhugh. "And I know also that this man Latzo would be capable of perpetrating the two crimes that have occurred. I really believe"—he nodded seriously—"that if a new link showed between Zurk and Latzo, I could suspect Zurk of guilt.

"But as it stands"—again Delhugh pounded the desk—"I still swear by Steve Zurk! I like the man! I believe in him! Despite his past connections and all that the law once had against him."

DELHUGH leaned back and swept the papers half across the desk. Typewritten statements fluttered to the floor. A scrawled letter stopped short of the desk edge. Photographs slid apart. One was a rogues' gallery picture of Steve Zurk; the other a photostatic copy of fingerprint impressions.

"There's not an iota of evidence against Zurk," proclaimed Delhugh. "The man's new career shines blameless. This mass of data pertains to the past—not to the present."

"Sometimes the past links with the present," remarked The Shadow, quietly.

"Not in the case of Steve Zurk," decided Delhugh, with a shake of his head. "Suspicions—even from you, Mr. Cranston—are not sufficient to incriminate Zurk in my eyes."

A pause; then, as Delhugh, firm-jawed, maintained an emphatic attitude in defense of Steve Zurk, The Shadow reached leisurely into his pocket and produced a crumpled ball of paper that Delhugh eyed curiously.

"I should be interested," stated The Shadow, in the quiet fashion of Cranston, "to have your opinion regarding this paper, Mr. Delhugh. To learn whether or not it would injure your belief in Steve Zurk's integrity."

He passed the paper to Delhugh, who opened it. Delhugh's eyes registered genuine amazement. His mouth opened wide. He was reading the message that The Shadow had found in Beak Latzo's hideout.

Recovering suddenly from his astoundment, Delhugh snatched up a paper that lay on the desk. It was a specimen of Steve Zurk's handwriting. Delhugh compared the scrawls. He dropped both papers and sank his forehead to his upstretched hand.

"This is terrible," groaned Delhugh. "It shows Zurk's guilt, Cranston. It shows it beyond reclaim. The handwriting proves that Zurk wrote this message to Beak Latzo.

"How—when—where—" Delhugh paused speculatively as he raised his head. "Tell me, how in the world did you manage to find this damning document?"

"It came into my possession," replied The Shadow, quietly, "through an agency that I cannot name at present. It was brought from a house where Beak Latzo had been living."

"You have other evidence like this?" questioned Delhugh, indicating a briefcase that his visitor had brought. "Reports of investigators? Other facts against Zurk?"

"I have this." The Shadow produced the paper that he had found at Dokeby's. "A legal form, found in an incriminating spot. Note the finger impressions upon the underside, Mr. Delhugh. Tell me: Do they compare with Zurk's?"

DELHUGH made a study of the photostatic copy. He held it, with the legal form, close into the light. Then he nodded. With a look of puzzlement, he asked:

"You say this came from an incriminating spot? What place might that be?"

"From Richard Dokeby's safe," replied The Shadow.

Delhugh arose. He placed his finger upon the button that showed on his desk. Then he stopped and shook his head.

"I was going to summon Benzig," he declared. "I wanted you to hear his statements regarding the suspicions that he held of Zurk. But I have a better plan. Let us go downstairs."

He placed Zurk's papers in the desk drawer, added the documents that The Shadow had brought, then turned a key in the lock of the drawer.

"With your word for it, Cranston," remarked Delhugh, "the statement that the paper with the finger impressions came from Dokeby's is quite as damaging as the letter that speaks for itself. I suppose, of course, that you can reveal facts later. Regarding the investigation that you have apparently conducted privately."

He came from behind the desk and motioned toward the little anteroom. The Shadow picked up the briefcase and walked with Delhugh.

"Zurk is coming here tonight," informed the philanthropist. "It would be the logical time to confront him with these proofs. Are you agreed?"

They had reached the anteroom. The Shadow, with his briefcase, had stepped ahead at Delhugh's urge. He turned about as the philanthropist spoke.

"No," replied The Shadow, in the steady tone of Cranston. "We should not be too hasty, Mr. Delhugh. There are reasons why we should first watch Steve Zurk."

"Reasons?" quizzed Delhugh. He had stopped short at the entrance to the anteroom. "What sort of reasons?"

"Reasons that pertain to crime," replied The Shadow. "Ones that may prevent—"

ENDING his sentence, The Shadow stared sharply at Delhugh. From Cranston's immobile face gleamed burning eyes—a sudden revelation of The Shadow's true identity.

The briefcase left The Shadow's clutch; his hands shot forward with a sudden spring.

A change of Delhugh's expression had produced The Shadow's quick action. But, for once, The Shadow made a thrust too late. Delhugh's right hand had slid to the side of the doorway. The philanthropist pressed a hidden button.

The thick carpeting of the little anteroom split like a trap. The Shadow's leap ended almost as it began. As Delhugh dropped back, The Shadow's hands missed the philanthropist by an inch. Then the tall form of Lamont Cranston went plunging downward into a blackened pit.

Powerful fingers caught the edge of the study floor and clung there for an instant. Delhugh, gripping the side of the doorway, drove his foot toward The Shadow's hands. His brutal, grinding kick was calculated to loosen The Shadow's clutch.

But The Shadow, staring upward, defeated the fierce move by opening his fingers just before Delhugh's heel arrived. With that release, Delhugh saw his enemy go plunging down into the depth. A crash announced The Shadow's arrival at the bottom of the pit.

Delhugh pressed the switch again. The trap closed. The false philanthropist delivered an ugly, fiendish laugh. Himself a partner to crime, Delhugh had tricked The Shadow. The master foe of crime had dropped into a superplotter's snare!

CHAPTER XX
A HOUSE OF DOOM

"DID you ring, sir?"

Benzig, coming up the hallway, gave the question as he found Perry Delhugh stepping from the door of the anteroom. The secretary had been downstairs. He thought that he had heard the call of the bell.

"I rang," acknowledged Delhugh. His face wore a mild smile. "I wanted you to be about, Benzig, as I may need you later. Come along. Downstairs."

Benzig followed the philanthropist.

"Mr. Cranston is in my study," remarked Delhugh, as he and Benzig descended the long marble stairs. "He is not to be disturbed. Do you understand?"

"Yes, sir."

"Should any callers come, have them remain in the parlor. I am going down to the cellar; I shall return shortly."

They had reached the bottom of the stairs. Delhugh found himself confronted by Chilton. The servant's face was troubled.

"What is it, Chilton?" inquired Delhugh.

"Something odd, sir," replied the servant. "A great clatter from the cellar. The cook and I heard it, sir, from the kitchen. I was just on the point of descending, sir—"

"Some boxes may have fallen," interrupted Delhugh, in an annoyed tone. "The vibration of a truck passing in the street could have jarred them loose. It has happened before."

"I didn't know that, sir. This noise startled us—"

"Was it prolonged?"

"No, sir. It sounded like a crash. Nothing more."

"Boxes. Nevertheless, I shall look about. I am going down to the cellar to bring up some bottles of my special Tokay."

"Very well, sir."

To both Benzig and Chilton, Delhugh's explanation sounded logical. The reference to the Tokay was also understandable. Delhugh kept choice wines in a small storeroom to which he alone had the key. When entertaining special guests, he occasionally went down in person to obtain his treasured bottles.

The door to the cellar steps was a thin one. Delhugh opened it; then noted Chilton standing anxiously in the hall. Smilingly, he dismissed the servant, telling him that he would call if anything was wrong.

Delhugh descended.

Near the entrance of the cellar, Delhugh turned on a light. He opened the door of a coal bin. There, sprawled upon a heap of coal, was the figure of Lamont Cranston. The visitor's briefcase lay a few feet away.

DELHUGH noted that his victim was unconscious. The two-story drop had been a terrific one. The presence of the coal had evidently broken the fall, for The Shadow's legs were buried deep in the black lumps.

It was a backward snap that had stunned the victim. A gash across the side of the masklike forehead was testimony to the force of the blow.

Delhugh looked upward toward a solid ceiling. He smiled in satisfaction.

The Shadow had dropped straight through an unused closet on the first floor. Two traps had operated simultaneously at Delhugh's control: the one in the floor of the anteroom; another in the floor of the closet, directly beneath.

Two large boxes stood in a corner of the coal bin. Delhugh lifted the lid of one. He brought forth a coil of rope. Advancing to his victim, he yanked The Shadow from the heap of coal and began to truss him in expert fashion.

The limp form offering no resistance, Delhugh found no difficulty in binding The Shadow thoroughly. To make the job secure, Delhugh picked up a coil of wire and broke off lengths of it. He wound these sections into the knots of the rope, thus making possible escape doubly difficult.

As a final touch, Delhugh produced a thick handkerchief and used it to gag his victim. He wired the knot of the handkerchief, hoisted The Shadow's helpless form and flung it roughly into the big box. He closed the lid; turned around and picked up The Shadow's briefcase.

Opening this, Delhugh discovered a mass of folded black cloth. He began to poke into the cloak in search of guns, knowing that this was The Shadow's special garb. For Delhugh, from the moment that he had met The Shadow's blazing eyes, had had no doubt as to the identity of his victim.

Footsteps came from the stairs. Delhugh wheeled about, opened the lid of the box and dropped the briefcase in with The Shadow. He stepped from the coal bin just as Chilton arrived.

The servant's face was anxious.

"I didn't hear you call, sir," apologized Chilton, "but I did hear another clatter. I was afraid, sir, that someone might be down here. Some intruder—"

"I made the noise myself, Chilton," interposed Delhugh. "Look here, in the coal bin. See those boxes? One of them must have fallen from the other. Suppose we stack them as they were."

"Very well, sir."

Chilton started toward the box that contained The Shadow. Delhugh stopped him and motioned to the empty box. Together, the two men lifted it and placed it upon the other. The box was of heavy construction and made a sizeable burden.

"Now for the Tokay," remarked Delhugh. "I almost forgot it. Come with me, Chilton."

He led the way to the wine closet, unlocked the door and removed two bottles which he handed to the servant.

The Shadow's leap ended almost as it began.... Then the tall form of Lamont Cranston went plunging downward into a blackened pit.

Leading the way, Delhugh went upstairs, Chilton behind him. It was Delhugh who extinguished the lights, for Chilton was clutching the Tokay.

BENZIG was waiting in the upper hall. Delhugh beckoned to the secretary, then spoke to Chilton.

"Ice those bottles," he ordered. "I shall want them later, Chilton. And by the way, Benzig"—he turned to the secretary—"Mr. Cranston will be with me for some time. He wants his car to go back to the club. Give that instruction to the chauffeur."

"Yes, sir."

"And when Vincent comes," added Delhugh, "take him to the filing room as usual. Then knock on the door of the study to indicate that he is here."

"Very well, sir."

Benzig started away. He remembered something and turned about to Delhugh.

"What if Zurk arrives?" queried the secretary. "This is Friday night."

"Zurk called up some time ago," replied Delhugh. "He is going to Mr. Daykin's home tonight. A business matter."

"You have an appointment there also, sir."

"Yes, as a social call. You are going with us, Benzig. I shall ask Mr. Cranston if he wishes to accompany us."

Delhugh continued up the grand staircase. His face, usually benign, showed the traces of a fiendish nature. Unviewed by Benzig, the treacherous philanthropist was free to reveal his true feelings of evil.

For his wicked brain was formulating new plans to follow past success. Delhugh had used this mansion as a snare. He was planning to make it a house of doom. One which The Shadow, a helpless captive, would never leave alive.

CHAPTER XXI
STRATEGY BY NIGHT

PERRY DELHUGH had been crafty from the time when Lamont Cranston had been announced as a visitor. Adhering to an appearance of genuine honesty, he had let The Shadow bring up the subject of Steve Zurk.

In fact, Delhugh had definitely avoided mentioning that Steve had called up earlier to cancel his usual Friday evening appointment. In every way, the master crook had worked to retain The Shadow's confidence.

Delhugh had played a skillful game of crime. He was the sponsor, the actual author, of instructions that went to Beak Latzo. He was using Steve Zurk as an instrument to gain Beak's aid.

Posing as benefactor to two ex-crooks, Delhugh had pretended that he was setting them along an honest path. Actually, he had deliberately made a secret offer to one of the pardoned convicts, inducing him to return to secret crime.

Delhugh had gained a willing tool who had the ability to work with him. The Shadow, entering the game, had gained goods on Beak Latzo. The Shadow had also found facts regarding Steve Zurk. Then Delhugh had blocked The Shadow.

Delhugh, real brain behind crime—pretended philanthropist who had used benefactions merely as a buildup toward a career of master crookery—was a man who now enjoyed an evil triumph. Delhugh had bluffed The Shadow. He had caught the master investigator unawares.

But the very strategy that had enabled Delhugh to capture The Shadow also made it impossible for the crook to immediately eliminate his helpless foe. Delhugh, in his private life, kept clear of crooks. Benzig—Chilton—these servants of his were honest men.

Had they been crooks, The Shadow would have spotted it. He would then have been wary of Delhugh. He would not have met the treacherous philanthropist as man to man. The Shadow had walked into a snare only because Delhugh had refrained from keeping criminals as members of his household.

Thus the cleverness that had enabled Delhugh to trick The Shadow now forced the master crook to act with caution. Chilton had heard suspicious sounds from the cellar. Delhugh had lulled the servant with an explanation. But Delhugh, even had he been so inclined, could not have risked a revolver shot down in the cellar.

The Shadow still lived; and Delhugh, true to his policy of letting others do the dirty work, intended to have crooks dispose of their archfoe. He planned to keep Benzig and Chilton unalarmed, to make those honest servants serve him with alibis as he might need them.

REACHING the empty study, Delhugh closed the door behind him. He picked up the telephone on his desk. He dialed a number. He heard an answering response. Delhugh began to speak in a quick, cautious tone.

"I've bagged The Shadow," he informed. "No, not dead, but helpless... A prisoner. In a big box in the coal bin... Center of the cellar..."

A pause. Questions were coming over the wire. Delhugh answered.

"Get a note through at once... Yes, deliver it in person at Dangler's office... Yes, Lucky will be sure to go there before he and Beak start out...

"That's the idea. Have them split tonight...

Beak goes to Daykin's house, with a small crew... Yes, Lucky can come here... With the rest of the mob... Yes, they'll have to grab Vincent, too.

"Benzig is going out with me... Dinner downtown. I'm giving Chilton and the cook the night off... That's right... Right... Right... That's the way for Lucky to work it... He'll understand.

"Yes, Benzig and I shall come to Dangler's later. I shall look for you there... Good... Very good... You will be covered perfectly..."

Delhugh completed the telephone call. His square face was gleaming as he sat at the desk. Reaching into the drawer, the master crook removed certain papers and placed them in his pocket. Leering lips showed that Delhugh was formulating final schemes of new crime.

OUTSIDE the brownstone mansion, Benzig was speaking to the chauffeur in the limousine. The secretary was informing Stanley that Mr. Cranston intended to remain a while at Delhugh's. The car was to go to the club.

Stanley was not one of The Shadow's agents. The chauffeur merely regarded his master as an eccentric person who was likely to change plans at any time. Hence Stanley nodded in agreement with Benzig's order. He turned on the ignition and prepared to leave with the limousine.

As the big car started, Benzig turned back toward the house. At that moment, an approaching pedestrian stopped short some thirty yards away from the brownstone mansion.

The arrival was Harry Vincent, coming for his evening's work at Delhugh's.

In his contact with The Shadow, Harry knew that his chief was playing the part of Cranston. Hence the sight of the limousine told him that The Shadow was at Delhugh's. The fact that Benzig was dismissing the car without a passenger indicated that The Shadow had remained.

The situation struck Harry as unusual. Trained to use keen judgment in such cases, Harry decided that it would be a poor play to enter the house immediately. So he strolled back along the street, chose a good lingering spot and lighted a cigarette.

One smoke ended, Harry began another. At the end of a third cigarette, he glanced at his watch and decided that at least a quarter hour had elapsed. Turning forward, Harry approached the house and ascended the steps.

Chilton answered Harry's ring. Benzig appeared, nodded, and conducted the visitor up to the filing room. As soon as Harry was settled there, Benzig continued on and rapped at the door of Delhugh's study.

Inside, Delhugh glanced at the clock on his desk. He smiled. The time interval between Benzig's dismissal of the limousine and the signal of Harry's arrival seemed proof that Harry could not have seen the departing car. Delhugh arose and left the study.

Benzig had gone downstairs. Delhugh knocked at the door of the filing room. Harry opened it. Delhugh greeted him with a beaming smile.

"Ah, Vincent," greeted Delhugh. "Back at work again, I see. How long will you be here this evening?"

"Until midnight," replied Harry.

"Quite all right," decided Delhugh. "Benzig and I are going out to dinner, so I am giving the servants the evening off. However, we shall be back by eleven, before your time to leave. You do not mind working alone here?"

"Not at all, Mr. Delhugh."

"Good evening, then."

Delhugh went downstairs. He walked back to the kitchen, where he found Chilton and the cook. Benzig, seeing Delhugh's arrival, followed.

"Chilton," said Delhugh, "we shall not require those bottles of Tokay. Benzig and I are going out to dinner. You and the cook may have the evening off."

"Thank you, sir," returned Chilton.

"What about Mr. Cranston?" queried Benzig.

"He intends to work a while with Vincent," informed Delhugh, smoothly. "When he leaves, Vincent will show him out."

"And Vincent?"

"Expects to be here when we return at eleven. Come, Benzig. We must start at once. Call a taxicab."

FIVE minutes later, Delhugh and his secretary departed.

Twenty minutes after that, Harry, listening by the door of the filing room, heard Chilton and the cook make their departure. A deep silence pervaded the house.

Harry stole from the filing room. He approached the door of Delhugh's study. He rapped softly and received no response. He opened the door and entered. Harry looked about, puzzled. No one was in the room.

Had Harry not been convinced that The Shadow was still here, the finding of an empty study would not have troubled him. Delhugh, in leaving, did not care whether or not Harry chose to prowl about. For Delhugh was convinced that Harry thought the house was empty.

Harry, however, thought otherwise. His perplexity became anxiety. He went to Delhugh's desk, picked up the telephone and put in a call to Burbank. He made a brief report.

Burbank's quiet voice showed no alarm; yet it

was questioning. For Harry's report was not the first that Burbank had received. There had been another, previously, from Cliff Marsland.

Yet Burbank had tried both the sanctum and the Cobalt Club without response from The Shadow. Until now, that had not troubled Burbank. Sometimes The Shadow deliberately let reports rest until he needed them.

Harry's report, however, placed a most unusual angle to the situation. Burbank, like Harry, could not fully understand the reason for the dismissal of Lamont Cranston's limousine. Steady questions came across the wire. Harry answered them.

Burbank gave directions. This was within his province. There had been times when Burbank had directed the work of agents during The Shadow's absence. His present orders were ones that Harry could carry out without causing damage to any plans that The Shadow might have.

"Orders received," acknowledged Harry, when Burbank's voice had finished. "Will report back every fifteen minutes."

Hanging up the receiver, Harry went from the study. In the hallway, he drew a revolver from his pocket. He closed the door of the filing room; then stole to the head of the grand stairway.

The place was filled with oppressive silence. Not a living sound disturbed the massive residence. The home of Perry Delhugh seemed like a house of doom.

Tensely, Harry proceeded down the stairs, clutching his revolver as he went. Something was wrong within these sullen walls; and to Harry Vincent belonged the task of learning what it was.

CHAPTER XXII
SQUADS SET FORTH

A SINGLE light was burning in a stone-walled room. One dozen hard-boiled ruffians were seated about on battered chairs and benches. Facing them was an ugly-visaged rogue whose big, flattened nose marked his identity.

Beak Latzo was talking to his mob of gorillas.

"At last you mugs know who you're working for," announced Beak, in a growled tone. "Some of you thought you were in with Lucky Ortz. The rest of you didn't know who was paying you. You hadn't even met Lucky.

"Well, Lucky was handling things for me. While I kept undercover. Except when the jobs were on; then I was there. Two guys helped me and Lucky on the first job while some of you were guarding my old hideout. The whole bunch was in on the second. All except those of you who are new guys with the outfit."

Beak paused. He was bringing up ominous recollections. Only two of this mob were survivors of the original battle with The Shadow. Only three others—Rungel, Cliff and Hawkeye—were leftovers from the second fray.

"We ran into some tough breaks," stated Beak, "but tonight's a cinch. The job we're doing could be handled by me and a couple of torpedoes. But we're all going along, so's to take no chances.

"A house out on Long Island. Belongs to a guy named Joseph Daykin. An importer. He's got a storeroom loaded with a lot of fancy swag. Savvy?

"Well, this room of his is easy gotten into from outside. Down through the cellar. Daykin thinks nobody knows about it. That's why it's soft. A few of us are going in to bring out the swag.

"The rest of you will be around. Covering. Whoever we hand the swag to brings it here. Savvy? Because I'm going in with the torpedoes to see what else we can grab. Daykin's got a safe upstairs that we can hit after the big swag's gone.

"We'll have all the buggies we need for a getaway; but we want the heavy stuff riding clear before we start after the box upstairs. Lucky's coming here to join us—"

Beak broke off as five taps came from the only door of the room. Striding over, Beak opened the door and admitted Lucky. He started to speak to the lieutenant.

Lucky stopped him and motioned outside. They left together; while Beak closed the door, Lucky produced an open envelope.

"Lamp this!" he exclaimed, in an eager whisper. "I got it from Dangler, just now. From Steve. It was left in Dangler's office. I opened it riding in a cab. Steve's got The Shadow!"

BEAK grabbed the letter. He read the scrawl. He chuckled as he tore the paper to pieces and lighted the fragments with a match.

"Bagged The Shadow up at Delhugh's, eh?" chortled Beak. "Well, Steve's smart, however he managed to do it. Guess he must've nabbed him without anybody around there getting wise. Should have bumped him, though."

"Probably he couldn't," put in Lucky.

"Well, it fixes things the way we want 'em," decided Beak. "I'll only need three gorillas for that Daykin job. You take the rest and pull it the way Steve says. Get The Shadow and that other guy. Make it look like you were pulling a big job at Delhugh's."

"Leave that to me," grinned Lucky.

Mobleader and lieutenant went into the room where the gang was waiting. Beak looked about. Roughened faces were quizzical. Beak laughed.

"We're changing things," he stated. "Two jobs

instead of one. Both easy. I'm taking three guys with me. Stolly, Fresco and Marsland. No, not Marsland. I'll take you, Rungel, for the third. Lucky may need you, Marsland."

Beak did not specify why he made the change. The reason was that he remembered something he had heard about Cliff in the past. Once it had been noised about that Cliff Marsland was gunning for The Shadow. Cliff had not succeeded in that quest, for it had been a bluff, part of The Shadow's strategy to build up Cliff's reputation in the underworld.

But the fact that Cliff was still alive had always impressed Beak Latzo. Mugs who talked about getting The Shadow usually disappeared mysteriously from the badlands. Apparently, Cliff was too tough for The Shadow to get. Beak decided that it would be best to have him present at the kill.

"The rest of you go with Lucky," ordered Beak. "Split up now; then we'll start."

MOBSTERS arose and followed their respective leaders. The gangs went from the stone-walled room, followed a darkened flight of steps and came into the gloom of an abandoned East Side garage.

Here they entered touring cars and sedans, black vehicles that stood hazy in the darkness. Motors chugged. The cars rolled in procession from a curving outlet. Lights did not come on until they were clear upon a dismal, secluded street.

A few blocks on, cars separated. Cliff and Hawkeye, seated together in the rear of Lucky's sedan, kept silent. But both were thinking; and each was puzzled.

Cliff and Hawkeye had been tipped to the fact that a job was due tonight. Cliff had phoned that word to Burbank. Then Mike Rungel had met them and taken them directly to the rendezvous beneath the old garage. There had been no chance to get new word to The Shadow.

Cliff had been counting on some opportunity to call Burbank again. He had been working toward that end from the moment when Beak Latzo had announced that their objective would be the home of Joseph Daykin.

Then, out of a clear sky had come the changed plans. Cliff and Hawkeye were being whisked away to an unknown destination. There was nothing to do but play along and hope for luck. The fact that tonight's rendezvous would also be storeroom for the boodle was a piece of knowledge that could be used later.

Cars swung left from beneath an elevated structure. They rolled through secluded streets. At last they came to an isolated spot where they could park unnoticed.

Lucky stopped the sedan. The other cars pulled up. Climbing from behind the wheel, Lucky signaled. He started across the street. The others followed.

One block through another quiet street. Then Lucky picked a space between two buildings. Mobsters filed through. They came to the rear of a large house.

While mobsmen clustered, Lucky worked on a backdoor. It yielded.

With nine men at his heels, Lucky motioned forward through a darkened kitchen. They came to a huge, silent hallway. There, Lucky opened a door and revealed a flight of cellar stairs. He started men moving down—among them, Cliff and Hawkeye. Lucky stopped two gorillas at the rear of the mob.

"Listen," he whispered. "You birds slide upstairs. First door on the right is a filing room. A guy's in there we want to get. Plug him; then head down here."

The gorillas nodded. Lucky watched them steal toward the carpeted stairway. He followed down the cellar steps and joined the others. Using a flashlight, Lucky picked his way to the center of the cellar. There he found a light switch. He pressed it and pointed into a coal bin that was now illuminated by a single bulb.

Lucky noted two boxes stacked in the corner of the bin. He chuckled as he pointed them out to the mob. He saw ready revolvers in the hands of his underlings. The crew would do for a firing squad.

"See that lower box?" quizzed Lucky, in a snarled tone. "We're going to drill it—all together—because there's a mug inside it. We'll load it with lead before we drag it out of here.

"I'll tell you why. Because the guy that's in that box is tough, even if he is tied up and wired so he can't get out. The guy in that bottom box is The Shadow!"

GORILLAS stood astounded. Hawkeye shot a wild glance at Cliff. He caught a grim nod from his companion.

Cliff turned his automatic close against his hip, covering Lucky. Hawkeye was ready to open on the rest of the mob. Then came sounds from above that made Lucky hold up a restraining hand.

Shots from the second floor. Quick shots that came in muffled succession. Lucky chuckled at this message from the two torpedoes whom he had sent to the second floor.

"They've finished the mug upstairs," he announced. "That's all we've been waiting for. Open up. On the lower box. Drill it, everybody—"

Mobsters wheeled about. As they did, one gorilla leaped suddenly upon Cliff and sent

The Shadow's agent sprawling to the floor. The mobsman had spotted Cliff covering Lucky.

Hawkeye wheeled at the attack. Another gorilla piled upon him as he aimed for Lucky.

Shots roared through the coal bin. Lucky, not noting Cliff or Hawkeye, had opened fire on the

Wild-eyed mobsters looked up. The lid of the top box had swung open.

lower box. Other mobsters joined with him. Their bullets riddled the wooden-walled target.

Then, with the resounding echoes came a burst of terrific laughter. A wild, outlandish peal of mirth that challenged those who had dispatched the volley of their revolvers.

Down toward the would-be killers were peering eyes that burned like fire.

Wild-eyed mobsters looked up. The lid of the top box had swung open. Down toward the would-be killers were peering eyes that burned like fire.

Gloved hands were aiming mammoth automatics. A collared cloak, a shrouding hat brim covered the face of the mighty foe, save for the eyes that gleamed upon the startled mobsters.

The Shadow had given snarling killers a chance to loose their fire. Safe in the upper box, he had waited to deal death to those who had tried to murder him.

Unbound, no longer a prisoner, The Shadow had chosen an unexpected spot from which to answer the first barrage.

CHAPTER XXIII
LUCKY IS LUCKY

EVEN as The Shadow loomed vengeful from his improvised turret, the burst of an automatic came from the door of the coal bin. Cliff Marsland, rolling free from the mobster who had slugged him, had taken aim in return.

The mobster was leveling his revolver as Cliff fired. The Shadow's agent beat him to the shot. Then, coming up, Cliff aimed for Hawkeye's assailant. This fellow, swinging, was quicker than Cliff. The Shadow's agent would have lost this second combat but for an interruption.

Roars from The Shadow's automatics. The first bullets from those guns were aimed toward Cliff's new assailant. The gorilla sprawled, while others—Lucky among them—went diving through the entrance of the coal bin.

Mobsters, as they dived, sought spots from which to return The Shadow's fire. Booms from the automatics launched clipping bullets that sent two gorillas sprawling. Then, as The Shadow picked his targets, Cliff and Hawkeye threw him their aid.

With a quick swing of his arm, Cliff rammed his automatic down on the gun hand of an aiming crook. Hawkeye dived for Lucky Ortz and grappled with the leader of the band. The odds were ended.

Lucky and his mob totaled ten. The number had been reduced to eight when Lucky had sent two gorillas to get Harry Vincent. Cliff and Hawkeye, by their desertion, had dropped the total to six.

Cliff had spilled one; The Shadow had dropped one, then two. Four from six left only Lucky and a single gorilla. And Cliff, attacking the lone mobsman, had disarmed the fellow while The Shadow was aiming to meet the gorilla's revolver.

Only Lucky remained. He was struggling toward the stairway, while Hawkeye battled him savagely. A tough fighter, Lucky was dragging the little man along. Cliff aimed; but he hesitated, afraid of hitting Hawkeye.

Then The Shadow came vaulting from the upper box. He landed on the heap of coal and sprang to the door of the bin, to join with Cliff. The Shadow arrived just as Lucky and Hawkeye went struggling out of sight, up the stairs.

A figure came tumbling, crashing downward. At the same moment, footsteps pounded upward. The door slammed at the head of the stairs. Cliff leaped forward to find Hawkeye coming to his feet at the bottom of the steps. The little man grinned sourly.

Lucky had pitched him loose. Half groggy from his tumble, Hawkeye nearly collapsed as Cliff caught him.

Then came a hissed command as The Shadow swished by and took to the steps in pursuit of Lucky. Helping Hawkeye along with him, Cliff followed The Shadow up to the ground floor.

WHEN Cliff and Hawkeye arrived in the big hall, they found that Lucky had escaped. The Shadow was standing there; toward him was coming a man from the floor above. It was Harry Vincent, an automatic in his right hand.

"They started into the filing room," reported Harry. "Only two of them, so I opened fire from the anteroom of Delhugh's study. Both wounded. Here are their guns."

The Shadow's laugh whispered through the hall. Understanding came to Cliff Marsland. Somehow—Cliff was recalling Lucky's statements to the mob—The Shadow had been captured and stowed in that lower box.

Harry must have made a search. In so doing, he had found and released The Shadow. Knowing that mobsters would be coming for their kill, The Shadow had adopted the ruse of entering the upper box, garbed with cloak and hat from his briefcase, ready with the automatics that Delhugh had not removed.

Harry, in turn, had been waiting to turn the game on others. He had used a lurking spot upstairs to spring an ambush on crooks who might be dispatched to get him. The Shadow had planned well. He had counted on Cliff and Hawkeye being with the crew that came here.

Lucky had escaped through the rear of the mansion. Cliff wondered why The Shadow had not followed him. The explanation came. As Cliff and Harry watched, the cloaked form began to sway. Harry caught The Shadow and supported him.

Still jarred by his two-story fall from Delhugh's study anteroom, The Shadow had fought on nerve alone. The fray ended, his strength was slipping from the strain of combat.

Gloved fingers went beneath the cloak. The Shadow brought forth a vial that was half filled with a purplish liquid.

He raised the little bottle to the lips that were just above the cloak collar. He finished the draught; the effect was immediate. The Shadow had used half of this potent liquid before the fray. He was drinking the rest now that he might continue. His tall form steadied.

Whistles were sounding from the front street. Someone in the neighborhood must have reported the sounds of gun fray.

The Shadow motioned to his agents. They followed him out through the rear of the house.

The fresh air aided in reviving The Shadow. As for Hawkeye, he had already recovered from his tumble down the stairs. He was as quick as Cliff and Harry as they made their way toward the rear street.

The Shadow paused in darkness. Cliff came up beside him. He caught The Shadow's low-toned order. The Shadow wanted quick details regarding the moves of crooks.

More whistles from the street in front of the mansion. A siren whined from an avenue. Yet The Shadow waited while he heard Cliff's brief report. His laugh was sinister and whispered when he heard mention of Beak Latzo's destination.

Cliff spoke of the cars that the mobsters had left a block away. The Shadow turned and led a quick course in that direction. They found a sedan and a touring car.

The Shadow entered the first machine. Cliff, beside the wheel, responded to the instructions that he heard.

The sedan shot away. Harry and Hawkeye were in the touring car, Harry at the wheel. Cliff leaped aboard and repeated The Shadow's orders while Harry nodded. The second car moved off, following The Shadow's course away from the zone that would soon be in charge of the police.

IN another car—one that had pulled away before The Shadow had arrived—two men were growling in conversation, as they headed toward the East Side. The one at the wheel was Lucky Ortz; his companion was the mobster whom Cliff had disarmed in the cellar.

"So Marsland socked you, eh?" quizzed Lucky. "Cracked your wrist, eh, Pokey?"

"Yeah," returned the gorilla. "Just as I had a bead on The Shadow."

"Funny The Shadow didn't plug you."

"He didn't wait. He hopped from that big box when he saw me flop to the floor. He was after you."

"Why didn't you grab your gat and let him have it?"

"Huh! Why didn't you stick aroun' an' battle with him? Besides that, me fingers was all limp. I couldn't do nothin' the way I was. I scrammed for a window."

"And yanked it open."

"Yeah, with me left mitt. They was goin' upstairs then; The Shadow an' them other guys. I beat it for the buggies."

"You were lucky to get here before I started."

"Pokey" snorted.

"Me lucky?" he quizzed. "Say—you're the lucky gazebo. They don't call you 'Lucky' for nothin'. You was lucky tonight, Lucky."

Lucky laughed. His tone was ugly.

"Maybe I was," he declared. "And maybe it was The Shadow that was lucky. That's what we're going out to find."

"You're going to join up with Beak?"

Pokey's tone was incredulous. It brought a fierce growl from Lucky.

"That's where I'm going," returned the lieutenant. "I ain't calling no quits—and you ain't neither."

"I'm with you, Lucky. Seein' as me mitt is better. I can move these talons now. All I need's another rod. I didn't grab up that one I had—"

"You'll get another gat." Lucky was emphatic. "And you won't be the only torpedo that I'm taking with me. Beak's got the first bundle of swag by now. It ain't far in from where he went on Long Island."

"You mean there'll be guys back at the garage?" quizzed Pokey. "The ones Beak's sendin' in?"

"Yeah. They'll be there soon," returned Lucky. "And there'll be more with 'em. I'm going where I can get a crew in a hurry."

Lucky Ortz drove on in silence. His face was fierce and venomous. For Lucky, confident that his luck would hold, had concentrated his thoughts to a single goal. Vengeance against The Shadow.

CHAPTER XXIV
THE SHOWDOWN

"YOUR work has been commendable, Zurk."

Joseph Daykin made the statement. The portly importer was seated in his living room, talking to his new employee. Steve Zurk, puffing at a long cigar, was apparently enjoying this visit to Daykin's Long Island home.

"So commendable," added Daykin, "that I am going to send you on the road, visiting our customers throughout the country."

"Thanks, Mr. Daykin," returned Steve. "I may

find it tough sledding, though. Big orders may be hard to get unless you're going to push that line of Swiss cameras that just came in."

"That is exactly what we do intend to push," said Daykin, with a tired smile. "Galen Flix will be here shortly. I have arranged to place a huge advertising contract with his concern."

"To plug the Swiss cameras?"

"Yes. The Blorff camera will be known in every important city throughout America, before you start your trip, Zurk. But let us forget business until Flix arrives. I want to show you my storeroom."

"Isn't that it in there?" Steve nudged his thumb toward a door at the back of the living room. "Where you've got the big safe?"

"No, no," laughed Daykin. "That is my strong room. I told you about the storeroom that I have in the cellar. Surely you must remember that I spoke about those valuable curios from the Orient?"

"Jeweled idols," nodded Steve. "I remember. But I thought you had them in some warehouse. I must have misunderstood you."

"I mentioned that the items were very valuable," said Daykin. "Particularly the idols. I told you where I kept them; but you probably forgot. Particularly because it would seem strange to have such curios stored in a cellar. But no one—except myself and a few friends—has any idea of their worth. Come, Zurk—"

Daykin was rising when a servant entered the room to announce that Mr. Flix had arrived. The importer smiled and settled back in his chair.

"Tell him to come in, Rhodes," he told the servant. Then to Steve: "We can visit the storeroom later."

GALEN FLIX appeared. The advertising man shook hands with Daykin and Steve.

"A friend of yours was coming with me, Zurk," he said. "I refer to Jack Targon. I told him that you would be here."

"Why didn't Jack come?" asked Steve.

"He suddenly remembered an important appointment," replied Flix. "Some client he had promised to see."

"Too bad," rejoined Steve. "I'd like to have seen Jack."

"Well, gentlemen," began Flix, "this ad campaign looks like it should be a world-beater. If we don't sell half a million of those cameras, I'll—"

He stopped short. From the chair that he had taken, Flix was looking straight toward a pair of French windows that opened to a porch. The curtained portals were trembling. As Flix spoke in puzzlement, they swung open.

A rough-clad man sprang into view. His face was masked with a blue bandanna. His right hand held a gleaming revolver. As he covered the seated trio, this rowdy was followed by another masked ruffian who also flourished a gat.

"Stick 'em up!" came a growled command. It was Beak Latzo's voice. "Keep 'em up, you dubs! We're taking a look around here!"

HANDS raised promptly. Daykin's arms were trembling; Flix was by no means steady. Only Steve lacked fear. He held his arms poised and stared quietly at the bandits.

"We're looking for your safe, old bean," growled Beak, as he faced Daykin. "Guess it's past that door, huh?

"All right"—this to the other masked man—"you keep a bead on 'em while I go in. This guy in particular"—he motioned his gun at Steve—"because he looks tough."

Moving toward the door, Beak paused to deliver a contemptuous snort at Daykin.

"Don't feel happy, mug," he sneered. "That swag of yours downstairs has been loaded long ago. Sent it away where we can use it. We're just dropping in to see what else looks good."

Beak placed his hand upon the door and opened it. He looked into the room where the safe was located. His henchman was watchfully covering the seated men, ready to open up if anyone made trouble.

Steve, like Daykin and Flix, was watching Beak. None heard stealthy footsteps creeping in from the hallway.

A sudden exclamation came from the gorilla who was covering the seated men. The masked mobster had felt something cold press against his neck. He knew the sensation of a revolver muzzle. He loosened his fingers and let his own gun clatter to the floor.

Beak whirled about. He was too late. He was staring into the mouth of a gun held by a second arrival. Sullenly, Beak let his own gat drop. He knew the man who had him covered. It was Detective Joe Cardona.

DAYKIN and Flix turned. So did Steve. They recognized the man who had pressed a revolver to the neck of the second crook. Cardona's companion was Jack Targon.

The rescuers backed Beak and the gorilla into a corner. While Jack stood by with ready gun, Joe whisked the masks from the faces of the disarmed crooks. The detective uttered a grim comment.

"Beak Latzo," said Cardona, in recognition. "I thought so. All right, Targon"—Joe turned, keeping the crooks covered—"Have your gun ready and tell these gentlemen what you told me."

Jack hesitated. He looked squarely at Steve, who had let his hands fall to the arms of his chair. Then, with solemn lips, the ex-swindler spoke.

"I hated to do this, Steve," he said. "But you remember what I told you. I was with you while you played square."

Steve made no reply. He looked toward Beak. The mobleader's face was hard.

"I didn't like the looks of things," asserted Jack. "That murder of Luftus—the way you tried to pin it on some broker. After that the mess when the lawyer, Dokeby, lost a big bunch of dough."

"What is this, Targon?" questioned Flix, as Jack paused. "Are you accusing Zurk?"

"Yes," replied Jack. He faced the ad man. "I knew that Steve used to work with a crook named Beak Latzo. Those jobs looked like Beak's work. When you told me Steve was coming out here tonight, I had a hunch something was up.

"I wasn't sure. I went to headquarters and told Detective Cardona what I suspected. I asked him to come with me here, figuring that he could step out if things looked all right. But they didn't."

It was seldom that Steve Zurk smiled. On this occasion, however, his lips formed a definite grin.

"You're all right, Jack," he said, commendingly. "A swell fellow. And you've nabbed Beak Latzo. I'm glad of that. Used to work with me, Beak did; but that's all over. Long ago. Those jobs did look like Beak might have done them. But lots of other people might have pulled them, too.

"Think it over, Jack, and you'll see you shot too far. Just because it happened to be Beak doesn't mean that I'm in on it. Say"—he chuckled coldly—"wouldn't I be a dub to bring Beak to a place like this? Me, just out of the big house, pulling something as raw as all that. It don't fit, Jack."

"No?" The question came from Cardona. "Well, that's the smart part of it, Zurk. Crossing the dope. What better alibi would you want than to be with your boss when his place was robbed?"

Steve made no reply.

"Figuring we didn't have you hooked with Beak Latzo," added Cardona. "Well, we didn't—until this chap Targon put us wise. We'll dig up your record, Zurk, and put some frills on it."

"You'll prove nothing against me," remarked Steve. "The past doesn't make the present."

Beak Latzo, hard-faced and silent, looked ready to support Steve's statement. Cardona began a gruff growl. He paused as someone entered. It was Rhodes, Daykin's servant. The man quavered at the sight of guns. He did not know what had happened in here.

"There's a gentleman to see you, sir," stated Rhodes. "It—it's Mr. Delhugh, sir—"

"The man we want to see!" exclaimed Jack to Cardona. "The very man!"

"Have Mr. Delhugh come in," ordered Daykin.

Rhodes left. He returned with Delhugh and Benzig.

DELHUGH stopped short at the scene before him. He looked from person to person in apparent bewilderment.

"What's this?" he questioned.

"Attempted robbery," replied Cardona. "This man"—he motioned to the corner—"is known as Beak Latzo. Targon and I nabbed him. We think that Steve Zurk was working with him."

"Impossible!" exclaimed Delhugh. "This is a mistake. At least"—he paused, troubled—"at least, I hope it is a mistake."

"You have facts regarding Steve's record, Mr. Delhugh," put in Jack. "Don't any of them mention a hookup between him and Beak Latzo?"

Delhugh nodded slowly. He looked toward Steve and spoke in a quiet, reassuring tone.

"Zurk," he declared, "it is my painful duty to state facts that appear very much against you. Until I have finished, I shall ask you to remain silent. Is that understood?"

Steve nodded.

"Because," added Delhugh, "these facts are somewhat circumstantial. If you are innocent—as I hope and believe—they may not matter. I came here intending to discuss them with you privately. Since you are suspected of crime, it is better that I should reveal them. It is always a mistake to hold facts back."

Steve nodded in agreement.

"You are Detective Cardona?" asked Delhugh, turning to Joe. Receiving a nod, he added: "Since you and Targon are needed with your revolvers, I shall allow you to listen while I show this evidence to my friends Flix and Daykin. You can judge by their opinions."

"All right," agreed Cardona.

Turning to Flix and Daykin, Delhugh produced a bundle of papers from his pocket. As he handed documents to the two men, he described each paper.

"This," stated Delhugh, "is an investigator's report that connects Zurk with Latzo. Something that Zurk has apparently not denied as part of his past. Here is a specimen of Zurk's handwriting. This is a photograph of his finger prints."

Flix and Daykin nodded.

"Here"—Delhugh produced a crumpled sheet—"is a recent letter from Zurk to Latzo. I say recent, because it refers to a proposed robbery of Theobald Luftus."

Steve was staring hard at Delhugh. Beak's jaw had dropped. The production of The Shadow's evidence was something that no one had expected.

"And this paper," added Delhugh, "is a legal form that was found in Richard Dokeby's safe. Its reverse side bears impressions of Zurk's fingerprints."

"It's Zurk's writing," declared Daykin, studying the crumpled paper. "It compares with the specimen."

"And the finger impressions coincide with the photostatic copy," added Flix.

"And regarding those robberies," remarked Delhugh, "I shall call upon the testimony of my secretary. What have you to say, Benzig?"

"ONLY this, sir," stated Benzig. "Zurk was alone in your study twice. On each occasion he could have examined your correspondence. Some of it referred to Theobald Luftus; and some to Richard Dokeby. There are letters in your files, sir, which can be produced."

"I regret," declared Delhugh, turning toward Cardona, "that I did not inform the law earlier regarding these matters. You see, I had nothing but Benzig's suspicions to go on until tonight, when I obtained actual documents as evidence against Zurk. Then I decided to act promptly."

"This is a lie!" cried Steve, coming suddenly to his feet. "I never wrote a line to Beak since I came out of stir. I wasn't in Dokeby's safe—"

"Move over here," broke in Cardona, moving his gun. "Line up with the other crooks. And no more talk!"

Reluctantly, Steve backed along beside Beak and the mobsman. Beak growled in Steve's ear.

"Goofy was to have burned that letter," informed the mobleader. "That's what Goofy said he did; but he was croaking."

Steve stared blankly at Beak. A sudden look of puzzlement showed on the mobleader's ugly face.

"Someone phone headquarters," Cardona was saying. Then, to Delhugh: "You've given us the goods on Zurk. There is enough evidence here to convict him. Along with Latzo."

"Too bad," declared Delhugh, with a sad shake of his head. "You see, when I obtained this evidence—"

His voice broke. Delhugh saw heads turning. Papers in hand, he wheeled about, toward the doorway from the hall. As Delhugh swung, a burst of shivering mirth swept through the room. Delhugh quailed at the mocking tones.

Framed in the doorway, ready with steadied automatics, stood the enemy whom Delhugh believed dead. Again, the arch-crook faced his formidable antagonist; but this time the Nemesis of crime was garbed in his guise of black.

Papers crinkled between Delhugh's trembling hands as the false philanthropist stared at the tall, weird form of The Shadow.

CHAPTER XXV
THE SHADOW REVEALS

"EVIDENCE!"

The Shadow's tone was sibilant in its mockery. The black-cloaked visitant had picked up Delhugh's final word. Sinister in his contempt, The Shadow's blazing eyes were upon the papers that Delhugh held.

"False evidence against an innocent man," proclaimed The Shadow. "Papers brought back to their author. Testimony that proves Steve Zurk's innocence—not his guilt."

Joe Cardona had not made a move since The Shadow's entrance. The ace was standing with his revolver covering Steve, Beak and the mobster. Jack Targon, also armed, was rooted, his own gun pointing nowhere. He had swung; then stopped at sight of The Shadow's weapons.

"Contact between Zurk and Latzo," sneered The Shadow. "You needed it, Delhugh, that Beak might serve you in crime. So letters came to Latzo. You are holding one of them."

A pause. The Shadow's eyes were toward Steve Zurk. The ex-convict spoke boldly for himself.

"I did not write that letter," asserted Steve. "If Delhugh sent it, he fixed it up himself. Say"—Steve paused, his eyes on Targon—"did you forge that letter, Jack? That was a specialty of yours, wasn't it? Working for Delhugh—I get it—with him having samples of my bum scrawl—"

Jack Targon was rigid. He made a slight move with his gun hand; then stopped as he saw The Shadow's eyes upon him. Delhugh was chewing his lips. The Shadow had seen through the game. But it was Steve who continued talking.

"And Delhugh planting letters," declared Steve. "There in his study, where I could have found them and got wise to Luftus and Dokeby. Say, Benzig"—he swung toward the secretary—"were you in on this racket, too?"

"No, no," protested the bespectacled secretary. Honest Benzig was aghast. "I was duped! By Mr. Delhugh! I see now that he must have opened my portfolio and disturbed letters so that I would suspect you."

"Lies," snarled Delhugh, defiantly. "These fingerprints are Zurk's—on this legal form from Dokeby's safe—"

"Prove that it came from Dokeby's safe," ordered The Shadow in a sneering tone.

Delhugh stood bewildered. He had only The Shadow's own testimony to back his statement. Now The Shadow was challenging him to offer proof.

"State that it came from Dokeby's," hissed The Shadow, "because you had it placed there. By

Targon. When he entered Dokeby's office early Thursday evening. After he had received the paper from you. Before he came back to your home with the swag."

Delhugh's face was livid. Jack Targon's teeth were clenched. Beak Latzo, still covered by Cardona's gun, was glowering. Oddly, Benzig was the person who suddenly spoke.

"Targon did come twice that night," recalled the secretary, anxious to clear himself of suspicion. "The first time Mr. Delhugh gave him a note. The second time, Targon brought a package and left it downstairs. He—"

Benzig broke off as he caught a glare from Delhugh.

"A paper with fingerprints," sneered The Shadow. "But with no thumbprints on the other side—"

"I'VE got it!" exclaimed Steve, turning to Cardona. "Delhugh gave me a stack of letters. Told me to read the top one." He turned to Daykin. "A letter from you, sir, on top of a stack. That legal form must have been on the bottom. To get my fingerprints, so it could be planted in Dokeby's safe.

"And this job was to follow quick. Beak here grabbing the swag with me in the house. Jack coming in to snag him. They bluffed Beak and they framed me. Get that, Beak?" He swung to the mobleader. "They bluffed you."

"Yeah?" growled Beak. "Well, I'm all for 'em. There was dough in it. And I'd have worked for 'em anyway—and helped 'em to frame you. Going straight, all right, that's what you were. I'd have queered a yellow game like that myself."

Beak's ugly challenge was the final evidence of Steve Zurk's innocence. Crooks were at bay, their cause demolished. Perry Delhugh as the master criminal; Jack Targon, a corrupted tool who had double-crossed a pal; Beak Latzo, nothing but a crook—these formed a dejected trio.

For The Shadow held them at his mercy, and Joe Cardona, seeing truth, was ready to click the handcuffs on the cornered band. The detective motioned to Steve to relieve Jack Targon of the gun that the forger was holding. Steve stepped forward; then suddenly stopped.

French windows were swinging inward. Beyond them came the flash of revolvers; then upon the sill appeared Lucky Ortz, springing forward with a leveled gun. The gang lieutenant was aiming for The Shadow, while henchmen were following to cover others.

THE SHADOW wheeled as Lucky fired. With his swing, the cloaked warrior did a fading trick to the right. Had The Shadow possessed his normal quickness, he would have eluded Lucky's aim.

But The Shadow, wearied by his ordeal of this night, was lacking in the speed of his quick move. His cloaked form spun as it dropped. The red lining of the cloak swept wide as The Shadow sprawled upon the floor.

Lucky's shot had clipped The Shadow's left shoulder. Firing again, the lieutenant leaped forward, hoping to score another hit against his crippled foe. His second shot, hasty, sizzled wide. His third never came.

Flat from the floor, The Shadow loosed an answer. An automatic, swinging up in the gloved right fist, spoke forth with deadly aim.

Winged as he leaped, Lucky took a bound in the air. Then he flattened face foremost on the floor, writhing in death agony.

Even as Lucky fired his first shot, guns barked from the lawn outside of Daykin's home. The crash of the French windows had been seen by The Shadow's agents, stationed near the house. Cliff, Harry and Hawkeye had not spotted the stealthy arrival of Lucky's new mob until the leader had broken through the doors.

Gunmen, outlined against the light of the living room, were perfect targets for a rapid fire. Forgetting the prey in the living room, gorillas dived back to the porch. They fired wildly as they scattered under the withering fire of The Shadow's three reserves.

Jack Targon swung for Joe Cardona. But the detective, having the bulge, beat the forger to the shot. Joe's revolver barked; Jack's fell from his hand. Steve Zurk made a dive for it. So did Delhugh.

Cardona aimed for the arch-crook. Beak Latzo piled upon the ace detective and bore him to the floor. The odd gorilla hurled himself on Steve and sent the innocent man sprawling while Delhugh grabbed the gun.

Daykin and Flix grabbed the gorilla. Steve wrestled free and dived for Beak Latzo, just as the mobleader managed to get hold of Cardona's revolver. The three fought fiercely. As Cardona slipped, Steve twisted the weapon and pressed the trigger.

Beak Latzo slumped away. Cardona was half groggy on the floor; but he was safe from harm. Steve Zurk had settled scores with Beak; but right now, Steve was thinking of a bigger crook: Perry Delhugh.

BENZIG had wrestled with his former master. With one swing, Delhugh sent the secretary rolling across the floor. Delhugh swung toward the spot where The Shadow lay motionless after the effort that had enabled him to dispatch Lucky Ortz.

As Delhugh aimed for the foe he thought helpless, Steve Zurk swung about and leveled Cardona's revolver at Delhugh. Steve knew that he was too late; but he also knew that he could beat Delhugh before the man could fire a second shot.

From the floor, The Shadow's eyes looked up, straight toward Delhugh's down-swinging gun. The Shadow's gloved right hand was knuckled downward on the floor, an automatic limp within it. Fingers tightened. The forming of the fist snapped the gun muzzle upward; and with the same move, The Shadow pressed the trigger.

Finger motion was shorter than the swing of an arm. The Shadow's gun spat flame before Delhugh could fire.

The arch-crook swayed, wounded. He pressed the trigger of his wavering gun and sent a bullet ripping through the floor. He tried to steady as he saw The Shadow's fist repeat its tightening. Then came a roar from behind Delhugh.

Steve Zurk had fired. Delhugh slumped forward as The Shadow managed a final shot. The added bullet seemed to jolt the arch-crook backward. Delhugh twisted; then sidled to the floor and sprawled motionless.

The Shadow's right arm moved. Like a lever, it raised the weary body. The Shadow came to his feet, sagging to the left. Steve Zurk had joined Daykin and Flix; they added subduing touches to Beak Latzo's henchman.

Joe Cardona, half groggy and weaponless, stared toward the living room door. There he saw The Shadow moving slowly into the hall, two automatics dangling from his gloved right hand. Joe braced. He started after.

The front door was open when Cardona reached it. Joe managed to make out a wavering figure passing through a gate some thirty feet away. He heard a weary laugh. He saw the dim forms of three men springing up to aid The Shadow.

Lucky's gorillas had been winged and scattered. Lucky himself was dead, like Delhugh, Targon and Latzo, the three who had played major parts in the reign of crime. Steve Zurk, vindicated, had aided The Shadow in the fight for justice.

A motor chugged as Cardona, revived by clear air, stood staring through the darkness. Lights blinked; a car shot away from beyond the grounds. The Shadow's agents were traveling away with their wounded chief.

Only one thing more to be done: the notification of Murson, the broker hiding in the hotel at The Shadow's orders, that he need remain in hiding no longer. His evidence would not be needed, for the real killers of Luftus had been apprehended.

And as Cardona lingered, his ears caught a sound that boded well. The wild burst of weird mockery rang out through the night air. It shuddered to a fierce crescendo; then wavered into echoes.

A strong, amazing taunt. To Cardona, a proof that its author, though weary and wounded, would soon again be ready to war against hordes of crookdom.

The gibing, eerie triumph laugh of The Shadow.

THE END